What people are saying about Margaret

"Moving, thoughtful, and romantic in the classic sense, B... ....
brings to life the struggle of one young woman to change the course of history or go down
in glorious defeat, set against the backdrop of a rural America that would soon be
changed forever."
—Jacquelyn Mitchard, author *THE DEEP END OF THE OCEAN*

"Bill Stokes is a writer I have long admired. He has outdone himself with **Margaret's War.**
It's a tale that captures a time and place too often ignored; the American home front during
World War 2. Stokes delivers fear, longing, and suspense in equal measure. And some great
villains. This is a story that will linger with you long after the last page is turned."
—John Roach, *Madison Magazine* columnist, screenwriter

"Bill Stokes' wonderful way with words and his connection to nature make **Margaret's War**
a fascinating look at a mostly overlooked period in American history. It's a great read."
—Kathy O'Malley, former *Chicago Tribune* columnist/WGN radio host

"**Margaret's War** is a winner! It is a marvelous coming-of-age story about a young man
named Billy living in a small town in northern Wisconsin during World War II. He yearns
to get into the war; instead, the war comes to him in the form of a prisoner-of-war camp
for captured German soldiers. The pace never slackens. The writing is sparkling. And I will
never forget the ending...**Margaret's War** will go on the shelf where I keep my other 'holy
books'-- *To Kill a Mockingbird, Lonesome Dove, As I Lay Dying, The Old Man and the Sea,*
and a handful of others."
—Marshall J. Cook, Professor emeritus, Division of Continuing Studies,
University of Wisconsin-Madison

"**Margaret's War** is set in the rural village of Oxbow during the midst of World War II.
Everything changes when a German Prisoner of War camp is established on the outskirts
of town. The novel is filled with mystery, Intrigue, and wonderfully drawn characters. Nearly
every page had me wondering, what can possibly happen next to top what has already
happened? With his down-home, carefully crafted style of writing, Stokes grabbed me and
never let go."
—Jerry Apps, Author, Storyteller, and Historian

"I am not sure Wisconsin has ever produced a better storyteller than Bill Stokes. He proved
it for decades as a newspaper columnist with a marvelous affinity for rogues and rascals
-- anyone who wasn't boring. Now we learn that Bill saved his best story for last. **Margaret's
War** is a wonderful novel, over half a century in the making, and worth every day of the wait."
—Doug Moe, author of *The World of Mike Royko* and
Tommy: *My Journey of a Lifetime* (with Gov. Tommy G. Thompson)

MARGARET'S WAR

(A novel)

Other books by Bill Stokes:

Ship the Kids On Ahead
You Can Catch Fish
Slap Shot
Hi-Ho Silver Anyway
The River is Us
Trout Friends and Other Riff-Raff
Wisconsin's Rustic Roads

MARGARET'S WAR

(A novel)

Bill Stokes

Three Towers Press

Milwaukee, Wisconsin

Published by Three Towers Press
an imprint of HenschelHAUS Publishing, Inc.
www.henschelHAUSbooks.com

ISBN: 978159598-626-9
E-ISBN: 978159598-627-6
Audio ISBN: 978159598-644-3
LCCN: 2018947990

PREFACE

As World War II thundered to its bloody climax, there were almost half a million prisoners of war in the U.S. They were in 700 camps scattered across 46 states, and most of them were German. The government did not want this astounding fact known, and the media, necessarily focused on the shooting war, cooperated. But Gold Star mothers and thousands of war-traumatized citizens in isolated communities across the country found the sudden face-to-face encounters with the killers of their loved ones a jolting experience.

The collective history of those experiences has been largely forgotten. It was minimized as it occurred and, in the frenzy to recover from the ravages of the bloodiest war ever, there was neither time nor inclination to reflect on it or record it. As part of World War II history, the American POW story disappeared forever behind the horror stories of Auschwitz and Dachau.

CHAPTER ONE

One of those *I WANT YOU* recruiting posters hung over the ticket window at the depot and made me want to kick Uncle Sam's striped old ass because he sure didn't want me. I hoped what happened here on this day would change things; I was sick of doing the war-wimp shuffle just for being born too late. The war will end and then where will I be? Nowhere, that's where! Stuck in Oxbow—pumping gas down at Cliff's, mowing Deggerton's dumb lawn, yelling at Toby to get out of my mother's tomatoes—totally boring crap that nobody gives a rat's ass about.

And I'll still be doing those stupid things when the war heroes come home and the girls swoon over them like moon-struck pussy cats.

My chances are slipping away—not just for the girls but for me in general—left out of the one thing that matters enough to die for, and then having to live with that for the rest of my life. No wonder I stare at the ceiling all night like a damned Teddy bear, watching the day sneak in and knowing it's going to be another bummer.

This morning everybody was at the depot to see the Nazis come in. Margaret and Cy and I got there early to get a place to stand where we could see everything. Margaret hadn't been her old self since she got the telegram, but at least she was finally up and about. She wore a yellow dress that narrowed at the waist and flared out over her breasts and hips, so it was like a fragile vase for her pin-up-girl body and china-doll face. Her dazzling smile usually came and went like the sun on a pillow-cloud day and when it suddenly popped out full force, it could buckle your knees. But there was none of that this day, Margaret's expression was as flat as a frog's, and her big, dark eyes were one-way windows for her use only.

1

I glanced at her as she dipped her head and did that little curtsy-shrug of hers, like a bird crouching to take off. It always gave me a quick stab of sadness, like I was about to lose something I never had.

Margaret got curious looks—maybe envious ones—from some of the women on the platform. There were also quick glances and stares from most of the men; and there's never any doubt what the men were thinking. Margaret usually ignored it all, but I have seen her look back at a staring man in a way that made him jerk away like he'd been slapped.

Cy gazed out over the crowd like a bored tomcat. He had his bowler hat tipped forward and he stood leaning back with his hands deep in the pockets of his wrinkled khakis. Earlier he told me not to get too excited about prisoners coming to Oxbow because it didn't mean the war was coming, too. I didn't need to hear that kind of depressing crap from somebody who kicks my brain around the way he does. Half the time I thought he was smart and the other half I thought he was crazy. He got a law degree a long time ago, which doesn't make him smart or crazy, but I've heard him say it ruined him for straight talk and honest labor. Something had, that's for sure.

The crowd spilled out onto the side track where arm-waving kids balanced on the rails and high school girls huddled and giggled. People elbowed each other and made jokes and laughed as if a circus was coming and a calliope would start playing any second. The stink of cattle and coal smoke hung over the depot like the town's perfume, and the buzz of flies and machinery set summer's jumpy pace somewhere between rush and relax. Sparrows chirped and fluttered from every crack and cranny, pigeon wings clapped from a roof nearby, and in a backyard across the tracks, a dog barked until somebody opened a porch door and yelled at it to shut up. It was a lemonade day if there ever was one—sticky sweet and with parts flying around like butterflies.

The locomotive finally came lumbering and hissing slowly up the track like it was pulling the usual cattle cars full of bony old hamburger cows. When it got closer, though, you could see it was hauling passenger coaches, and prisoners and guards were peeking out through the windows like caged monkeys. A tiny shiver of something shook my bones and a flicker of dizziness was gone before it really took hold. The people around us stared at the train and pushed their faces forward like they were trying to figure out what they were seeing.

Once the train clunked and squealed to a stop, soldiers jumped off and shouted orders as the first Nazis stepped down onto the platform bricks. The Nazis were dressed in plain brown shirts and pants with big white POW letters on the back and front, which was a lot different than the fancy uniforms and boots and shiny gear you saw the German soldiers wearing in movie news reels. People whispered and mumbled and I heard someone say the Nazis looked like they'd been eating good. A few of them were big and tall, but most were just run-of-the-mill and some were even squat and dumpy. I looked for scowls or sneers but didn't see any. Some of the Nazis even seemed cheerful and I saw the glint of a gold tooth as one grinned. The Army guards shouted more orders and the prisoners lined up in formations and started marching off.

Then somewhere in the crowd a woman suddenly shrieked and wailed—a sound so mournful it seemed to blunt the sunshine. Everyone turned and watched as the man next to her put an arm around her shoulders and led her away. People looked at each other and shook their heads. I heard later it was Mrs. Borland, whose son Willard had been killed in Africa. Somebody whispered she probably shouldn't have come down to the depot, and others nodded. Maybe Mrs. Borland was the only one who really let on how she felt about the Nazis, while the rest of us were trying to figure it out, staring at the prisoners and sorting through years of hearing about Nazi brutality, or thinking of a neighbor's son or maybe an uncle dying on D-Day. Now Hitler's killer Nazis were suddenly here, close enough to touch…or to kill. How were you supposed to feel about that? Most people didn't seem to know.

Cy nudged me with an elbow and nodded toward the prisoners. "Those bozos don't look like Hitler stormtroopers to me," he said. "They look like farm boys from over by Almira."

"They are Nazi scum," Margaret hissed.

Then out of the blue, Cy shouted, "Hey, let's see some goose-steppin'!"

Several of the prisoners turned to look at Cy, and one of the Army guards moved toward us.

"Welcome to Oxbow, you super-race assholes," Cy shouted, and some of the people around us laughed. One of the Army guards motioned to Deputy Blasser on the edge of the depot platform, and Blasser came strolling over, scowling and resting his hand on his holster like he always does. He moved like a lumbering bear, his big head jutting out and his eyes squeezed to slits like someone looking for trouble.

"Butler," Blasser said, "Shut your mouth or you're going to jail!"

"Freedom of speech, officer," Cy said, "one of the things we're fighting for."

"One more word..."

Margaret tugged at Cy's arm and Blasser turned to her, "Bad company for you, Margaret," he said.

Margaret gave him a look. "My company is none of your stupid business," she snapped, and then she tossed her head in a way that erased Blasser from the face of the earth, or at least Margaret's part of it.

"You could do better than an old drunk and a dumb kid," Blasser said.

Margaret turned back to him and narrowed her eyes. "Oh, yeah?" she said. "Like you maybe—Oxbow's official draft-dodger." And then Margaret pointed at Blasser and laughed a loud, phony laugh that went on so long people turned to look.

Blasser jerked his head around and stared at Margaret, his eyes as steady as a snake's. Everything froze for a second, and the image of Blasser's cold stare smacked against my brain like a windshield bug. Margaret turned toward Blasser again and I thought she was going to spit in his face, but she didn't. She just shook her head and pulled again at Cy's arm and said we should leave.

She was right. All the Nazis had marched off toward the POW camp on the edge of town and the train was getting ready to pull out, so there wasn't any reason for us to hang around. The camp was just a few rows of big tents in an old hay field down between the cemetery and the county highway garage. It had a few strands of barbed wire around it, but not enough to keep anyone from getting in or out.

"Wouldn't stop a damned sheep," I heard a farmer say about the wire.

A story in the *Oxbow News-Banner* said everyone should stay away from the camp unless they had official business, which of course we didn't, so when we left the depot, we walked down toward River Park.

Margaret looked back in Blasser's direction and mumbled something about him being "a gutless wonder." Cy glanced at her but didn't say anything.

There are some old rumors about Blasser offering Margaret a ride home from work one rainy night and then pawing at her and ripping her dress and bruising her legs, and her scratching his face enough so blood dripped down onto the front of his shirt. There were whispers about the DA bringing charges but it all died down and nothing happened.

The river was running low, and from our picnic table, you could see rocks sticking up out of the rapids just below the swimming hole. Across the river, tamarack trees stood tall and straight along the edge of Windigo Swamp, and from somewhere back in the thick trees, a young crow was squawking. I hadn't been out in the swamp much lately. My mother was happy with that. She worried that something would happen to me out there, which was crazy. If you watched your step around the spring holes and took a compass along on cloudy days, nothing was going to happen, except maybe you might accidentally get a fishhook stuck in your arm or some weird thing like that.

My mother also worried about fire, especially if she caught me sneaking hotdogs out of the icebox. Then I had to lie and tell her that Toby and I ate them cold and didn't bother with a campfire. Once, when I was a little kid, I held my dad's hand as we stood on the Oxbow side of the river and watched a wildfire burn off a corner of the swamp. The clearest memory of that after all this time is of a doe and two fawns that came leaping out of the swamp just ahead of the galloping flames. The doe bounded out of sight down the river with the water splashing up around her legs like shattering glass, but the fawns turned back into the swamp just as tongues of yellow and red fire broke through the trees.

I remember glancing up at my dad's frowning face as he watched the fawns. His grip on my hand had tightened and I heard him whisper, "Son-of-a-bitch!" I had nightmares about the fire and my mother had been mad at my dad for letting me watch it. "He's too young to see such awful things," my mother said, and my dad had looked at her and then at me and nodded. That's all I remember because my dad had grabbed me up in a bear hug that almost crushed my ribs and squeezed out any further remembering.

The swamp was my all-time favorite place. For one thing, there were no adult know-it-alls out there and you could do anything you felt like doing—jump on old bear dens, swing like Tarzan from the tops of tall, willowy trees, stick your face down close to the cold spring water and breathe in the wild smells of things living and dying. There was just no end to it. Once out in the swamp, you shed your old self and turned into something new, like a shiny, green garter snake squirming out of its old skin. Toby and I were out there every chance we got.

It was the critters' place, of course, and if you remembered that and didn't go stomping around like you were more important than they were, they would put up with you. It took me a while to get that, and Toby, being a dog, still doesn't. He seemed to think that the swamp and everything in it was there for his exclusive investigation and entertainment, and mine, of course, but mostly his. Toby chased after everything, and sometimes I had to wait by the boat until he came panting back from his runs. I yelled at him for chasing things he had no chance of catching but it was like scolding a stump.

Cy sometimes kept a bottle stashed back in the cattails on the edge of the park, but when he went to look for it today, he couldn't find it. He came back grumbling and scowling.

"Just as well," Margaret said. "You need a clear head to help plan."

Cy looked at her.

"We're killing one of them, you know," Margaret said, and the memory of that day down at the station when she had grabbed that idea to mix in with her grieving came back like a rumble of old lightning.

Cy shook his head. "Can't do that, Margaret," he said.

It was like he had poked her with a sharp stick. Margaret jumped to her feet and shouted, "Don't say that! We're doing it!"

Cy shook his head again.

"We have to do it, for Jeff!" Margaret shouted and stomped in front of Cy. Her move scared a robin out of a nearby honeysuckle and Cy glanced at the bird as it landed over our heads and chirped loudly.

"It wouldn't help Jeff," Cy said.

"Yes, it would," Margaret shouted, and drew her fist back so it looked like she might smack Cy. It was a funny thing to see—a young woman in a yellow dress with her little fist clenched under a rumpled old guy's nose, threatening to punch him out, and him looking at her like she was a naughty puppy. But nobody smiled.

Cy reached out and put a hand on Margaret's shoulder. "I'm thinking about a plan that could totally change the war," he said.

Margaret ignored Cy's words and shoved her face close to his. "If you are too chicken to help, I'll kill one myself. Me and Billy will do it," she shouted. "Billy will help; I know he will. He cares about Jeff, and about me!"

Cy closed his eyes for a second, and then opened them to look at Margaret. "Killing a Kraut would just get everybody in trouble and wouldn't do your Jeff any good," he said.

"Cyrus Butler, you are a cowardly son-of-a-bitch!" Margaret shouted.

I have heard Margaret swear before, but not with such force. Her "son-of-a-bitch" was like a hornet buzzing around your ear.

Cy looked at her. "Margaret, we've got these damned Nazis right here under our nose and by God, we can do better than just kill one of them. Trust me."

"Nothing could be better," Margaret said, "except killing all of them."

Margaret slumped down onto the picnic table and covered her face with her hands. Cy glanced at her and then gazed off toward the swamp, shaking his head slowly back and forth and muttering to himself. It seemed crazy for Cy to ask Margaret to trust him, considering he has done so many goofy things around Oxbow that nobody trusts him. But that is the way it ended—with Cy saying he was working on a plan that Margaret would like, and Margaret looking up at him and shaking her head and saying we had to kill a Nazi, and then finally stalking off toward town with Cy and me following behind.

"I wonder if those Pickert rascals found my whiskey," Cy said, as we were leaving the park. They probably had. The Pickerts spend a lot of time hunting and fishing along the river and they don't pay any attention to fish and game laws. One summer afternoon I ran into them carrying a bunch of bloody mallards, and they said if I told anyone they would beat the shit out of me. Cy said they are little "dick heads" and need their asses kicked. He said that a day or so after the Pickert boys threw firecrackers under Mr. Hall's crippled old horse until it reared up and screamed like it was dying. It happened just down the street from the station and it all went so fast it was like a blur even though I was looking right at it.

Mr. Hall's horse is the last one in town and one of its front legs is pigeon-toed so it looks like it is going to fall on its long face with every step, but then it catches itself just in time to take the next step. It makes a clippety-clop sound that everyone in Oxbow knows, and likes, I guess, because when they hear it they always smile and say, "Here comes Clippety-Clop!"

When the firecrackers exploded and the old horse reared up, Mr. Hall flicked his whip out and caught Vernon Pickert across the forehead. There was a snap like one of the firecrackers and Vernon screamed louder than the horse. Chief Edwins showed up about then with his siren growling and red light blinking. The Pickert boys scattered like rabbits; Chief Edwins didn't chase them, which made sense because he weighed about four hundred pounds and was in no shape to be chasing anybody.

The blistering midday sun bore down like it might set Oxbow on fire. It seemed to squeeze everything out of the day until only the heat was left, bouncing up off the sidewalk and poking under your clothes to make you toad-clammy. Relief—even staying alive for some things—had to be in the nearest shade. But that seemed twisted on this day, and for reasons I could not understand, I had an odd feeling that in the hot summer days to come, shade might not be enough for relief—or staying alive. I don't know where that came from; maybe from Margaret's crazy ambition to kill a Nazi or maybe from worrying about what kind of goofy scheme Cy might come up with.

More likely it was from knowing that two hundred Nazis, fresh from bloody battlefields all over the world, were now camped right here in Oxbow, within shouting distance of our house. I got another one of those shivers, which was hard to figure on such a hot day.

The three of us went our separate ways at the edge of the park, me to work the afternoon shift at Cliff's, Cy to the pool hall, and the last I saw of Margaret was her walking toward her mother's house, head up and fists clenched. Her lips were moving and from a distance, you might have thought she was praying. She wasn't. She was swearing, muttering the same "son-of-a-bitch, son-of-a-bitch" over and over, like a chant. I had a strange urge to run after her and stand in front of her and tell her she should stop swearing and crying, that everything was going to be okay: Uncle Jeff was coming back to her, and in the meantime, she and Cy and I had the prisoners here to get us into the war by whatever plan Cy came up with. Maybe if I had done that, Margaret might have flashed one of her blazing smiles and touched my arm, or even given me one of her quick hugs. But I stood rock dumb and watched her disappear around the corner.

CHAPTER TWO

It was a hot, miserable afternoon at the station—fixing tires, climbing down into the pit to do grease jobs, struggling to get a stubborn fan belt on an old Chevy from Michigan, and pumping gas every few minutes. I was covered with grease and soaked with sweat and my fanny was dragging when it was finally over. But when I got home and cleaned up and took care of Toby and finally went up to bed, I couldn't sleep. No way. I'd been waiting so long to get into the war that now with the Nazis close enough to spit on, it was like trying to sleep on a keg of dynamite with the fuse hissing. It was coming up on midnight when I finally gave up and eased out of bed and pulled on my clothes. I didn't want to risk the stairs, so I crawled through the window, tiptoed across the porch roof, and swung down the branches of the maple.

I've been using this way out for a long time, at least since Wally Poole's birthday party last fall that didn't start until midnight and ended as the sun was coming up and the big "picnic" beer bottles were empty and the Pickert boys were passed out on the sand. Sometimes I wonder if my mother knows about the porch roof and the maple. One morning after I had sneaked down to the river, she looked at all my mosquito bites and said there must be a hole in my bedroom screen. She knows better.

Out on the sidewalk under the shadowy cover of the yellow streetlights, I headed toward the POW camp as natural as a buzzard gliding to stink. I didn't stop to think about what I was doing; I just did it. As I got closer to the back of the camp, I could see the dull glow of light bulbs hanging from poles just over the barbed-wire fence. I stopped behind the railroad tracks and dropped to my hands and knees and crawled up through the weeds and grass until I could peek over the rails. Sharp cinders jabbed into my elbows and knees, and the stench of train garbage started working up a sneeze.

Before my eyes had adjusted to the dim light, something suddenly moved in the weeds right next to me. I jumped about a foot and my heart did a back-flip. Then—I couldn't believe what I saw—Vernon Pickert's grinning face was sticking out of the long grass and weeds so close I could have pinched his nose, or better yet, punched it because he had scared the living crap out of me. In the pale light behind him, I saw his brother Chester. He was grinning, too.

"What the hell are you doing here?" Vernon whispered, poking a fist at my shoulder.

"Looking," I said. "Same as you."

"Yeah," Vernon said. "Well, we're doing business; made two bucks already getting beer for some guards."

Chester hissed then and whispered, "Somebody's coming."

Across the barbed wire, the big tents stood outlined by the suspended lights. Dark forms moved between them and there was the yellow flicker of a flashlight and a match flaring to light a cigarette. Then, off to the side of one of the tents, there was sudden shouting, some of it sounding German. It got louder and several men came running in our direction, their dark forms looming huge as they got closer.

I was about to dive for cover, but before I could move, there was more shouting and then a deafening blast of gunfire seemed to lift us up off the ground as a streak of red flame stabbed just over our heads. Before the echo of the blast died, a man's scream rose up and seemed to swallow the night. It went on in an agony of bellowing, and its power faded only because I was running away from it—running in a panic, falling over hedges, leaping across ditches, and straining to run faster.

Finally, I was back on a familiar sidewalk and out of sight of the prison camp. I gasped for air and shook and my legs were like spaghetti. I stood bent over with my hands on my knees until my chest stopped aching. Then I straightened up and shaded my eyes and tried to see into the darkness. There was no sign of the Pickerts. When I cupped my hands behind my ears to listen, there was only the soft buzz of insects and the distant hum of the power plant across town. The deafening muzzle blast and the awful scream were gone, but they seemed to have left a great yawning hole in the soft sounds of the night.

I walked home slowly. What had just happened was a little sliver of war and I had acted worse than a wimp. I had deserted, run off like a scared cat, like a coward. It didn't matter that there wasn't anything I could have done. What I had seen and heard was obviously what happened all the time in war—shooting and screaming that no one can do anything about, even a soldier right in the middle of it. The shot and the agonized bellowing had scared me down to my toes. I felt empty and sick—and embarrassed.

There was a lot of talk the next day, people guessing about the noise and claiming to have heard it when most of them obviously hadn't. The Pickert boys were behind some of the talk. They spread the story that there had been a big shootout between the guards and the Nazis, and the guards had killed six or seven prisoners. Early in the afternoon, Vernon rode past the station on his rusty bike and yelled, "We're going back tonight, Billy. You with us?" and then he laughed until he was out of sight.

The Army ordered the soldiers to keep their mouths shut about what had happened so nobody really knew anything for sure until a corporal from Illinois got drunk at the pool hall a day or so later and bragged to Cy and some others that he was the one who had "shot the Nazi bastard." He said one of the "hard-core Rommel tankers" went off the deep end when a guard ordered him to pick up a cigarette butt. The corporal said the Nazi tanker thought the guard was a Jew and he grabbed him and started choking him and yelling about dirty Jews and how he was going to help Hitler kill every one of them. Another guard clubbed the Nazi tanker over the head with a rifle butt, and that turned him into a raging maniac and he headed for the fence. That's when the corporal said he shot him. He said he aimed at the back of the Nazi's head but hit him in the ass, which he said was too bad for the Nazi because he would have been better off dead.

Who knew how much of that was true, but it does jibe with what the Pickert boys and I saw. There were other reports, rumors maybe, about a covered Army truck roaring out of town just before daylight, and soldiers pouring buckets of water on the camp grass early in the morning. Cy said that made sense because they know in the military that if civilians see too much blood, it can bog down whatever they are trying to do. "It's the same reason they never show dead GIs," Cy said, "like the ones on D-Day."

All we got were pictures of our boys jumping off those landing boats like they were going to a goddamn beach party."

Sometimes, no matter how much I don't want it to, an image of Uncle Jeff's face will suddenly pop up, all bloody and messed up, and I get a sick feeling. It started shortly after Margaret got that awful telegram several weeks ago. That changed everything, especially Margaret, of course, and it was why she was so fired up watching the prisoners come in. The telegram changed me, too, in ways I haven't figured out yet.

I'll never forget that day. It started when Mr. Dawkins stopped for his usual "dollar's worth of regular." While I was washing his windshield, he said he saw Buddy Dirks from the telegraph office stop at the house where Margaret and her mother lived. My guts dropped into my shoes!

"They're just across the street from me," Mr. Dawkins said, "and I tried to stop Buddy so I could talk to him. But he kept going and wouldn't even look at me."

It got worse after Mr. Dawkins' old green Dodge disappeared around the corner and I was alone. I tried to call my mother but the line was busy. I knew that Uncle Jeff was in the artillery, and I had read in one of Cy's newspapers how some of the artillery got overrun by the Germans, and lots of Americans were killed and captured. I tried not to think about it. When the phone finally rang, I almost jumped out of my skin. I wanted it to be my mother, but I didn't want it to be her, either.

"It's your Uncle Jeff," my mother said, "He's missing in action."

"That's wonderful," I said. "I mean, it's wonderful that he wasn't killed."

"The telegram only says he is missing."

What a foolish thing. Missing! Missing! It just means that some people don't know where a certain person is, but somebody knows. Uncle Jeff wasn't missing to everybody, just to us, and the Army, I guess. The Nazis probably knew where he was.

"This is very hard for everyone," my mother said, "especially Margaret. You must stop and see her."

Those words were like a punch in the guts. There was no way I could face Margaret in her misery. I have enough trouble being around her when everything is going good. To think of trying to help her deal with the shock of Uncle Jeff gone missing was too much.

"I don't think…"

"Billy, Jeff and Margaret are family," my mother interrupted. "Just go and be with her."

How was being with someone like me going to help Margaret? It was stupid! But there is no arguing with my mother. The rest of the day was one of the worst times in my life. A few customers stopped and I washed windshields and checked oil and pumped gas automatically, but mostly I watched the clock over the window. It didn't seem to move; then it would jump ahead like it had stripped its gears.

To take my mind off time not passing or passing too fast, I got out Uncle Jeff's V-mail letter and read it for about the two-hundredth time. I kept it in my wallet because it made me feel like I was with him in a way. Uncle Jeff wrote that he couldn't tell me where he was or what he was doing, and he asked me to watch over Margaret. He said he wanted me to be with her as much as possible to see where she went and who she was with. And he said not to say anything to Margaret because she might think he doesn't trust her, which he said he does, but he just liked to know what she was doing.

I have been writing V-mail reports to Uncle Jeff about once a week. I try to be as honest as possible and not report anything that might upset him. I didn't write about Margaret's riding past the station in the rumble seat of Benny Edwards' Ford roadster because there had been other people in the car so I don't think Uncle Jeff would care about that. Maybe if Margaret had been alone in the car and riding up in front with Benny that would have been different.

The afternoon dragged like the hours were sticking to each other, and I wished Cy would show up so I could talk to somebody. When he finally did and I told him about Uncle Jeff, he said, "Missing in action can mean anything."

"It could mean Uncle Jeff has been killed," I said.

Cy gave me a look and tipped his bowler back, "Yeah, but it could also mean he and some of his pals found a French wine cellar and decided to take a little break."

I doubted that; Uncle Jeff wasn't much of a drinker. But it was something to think about.

Cy said it probably wouldn't be much comfort to me, but he had been digging through his books and found a copy of Hitler's *Mein Kampf*. "He is one scary son of a bitch."

"He doesn't look scary to me," I said. "He looks funny, like Charlie Chaplin."

The news reels always showed Hitler swaggering around in front of goose-stepping soldiers, giving his dumb stiff-arm salute and acting like he had a bug up his ass. His Gestapo troops always looked big and mean, like they would stomp on anyone who got in their way. It was impossible to think that now they might have Uncle Jeff!

"Damn shame the young guys get the dirty work of stopping the bastard," Cy said. "They should be home drinking beer and making babies."

A crazy image of Margaret and Uncle Jeff making a baby popped in my head like a firecracker and then was gone.

"Hitler says in his book that it's criminal lunacy to drill a half-ape until people think they've made a lawyer out of him," Cy said. "He was writing about Negros, and whites who aren't part of his super-race and he said it's like training a poodle. So, am I a poodle or an ape?"

Cy hung his arms out and made grunting sounds and then yipped like a puppy. "What do you think, Billy?" he said, looking at me.

"Dumb," I said.

Cy paused and shook his head, "Yeah, sorry," he said.

A dog was barking somewhere over in the next block, and kids were yelling off in the distance. It all seemed so normal and peaceful with everything and everybody in the right place, everybody except Uncle Jeff—he was "missing."

"If it was me," Cy said, "I'd be in a wine cellar, and I'll bet that's where Jeff is." Then he slipped down off the pop cooler, gave me a Hitler salute, and headed off toward the pool hall.

"Poodle," I shouted at him when he was almost out of sight. He turned and did another Hitler salute and then walked on.

I couldn't picture Uncle Jeff in a wine cellar. All I could see were Nazis waving swastika flags and shouting *Heil Hitler*, and Uncle Jeff's smiling face mixed in with it all like a goddamn carnival. I try not to say "goddamn" too much. I know it's a sin, but sometimes it's the only thing that fits. I should have been a Catholic. Ronnie Swanson sat next to me in geography and he said all he has to do is confess his sins and he gets a clean slate. I really need something like that because sin just seems to follow me around like a damned swarm of flies.

* * * * *

At closing time, I carried in the oil racks and the tire displays, turned off the gas pumps and locked the door, and then headed off for Zanders' house. I dragged my feet because I didn't really want to get there; I still had no idea what to say to Margaret. I wouldn't mention any wine cellar, I knew that. Too dumb.

Light was showing through the front window when I stopped out on the sidewalk in front of the Zanders' house. Margaret's upstairs window was dark, and I thought maybe she was sleeping and it wouldn't be a good idea to wake her. I almost turned and left, but then there would be my mother to face. I stepped up onto the porch and stood in front of the mailbox and wished I could just drop a note in it and leave, maybe something like, "Don't worry, Uncle Jeff is okay."

I stood there so long that moths and mosquitoes found me, and I finally forced myself to knock on the door, softly at first and then, after a long pause, louder. A minute or so later, Margaret's mother opened the inside door and stood staring at me through the screen. She is like an older Margaret, with wrinkles around her eyes and gray hair pulled back behind her ears. I know her pretty good from her being my first-grade teacher. It doesn't seem like that long ago.

Once I waited too long to go to the bathroom and Mrs. Zanders had taken my hand and led me out of the classroom and told me to run home and get dry pants. I could never feel the same about her after that, and some of that came back as I stood there in front of her.

"Come in, Billy," she said. "I'm so glad you're here."

I stepped through the door and Mrs. Zanders touched my arm. "It's awful for her," she said. Her face looked old and like it might break into pieces. I had never seen it that way in the hundreds of times I had looked at it as a first-grader. Of course, then I had been looking up at her and now it was pretty much eye to eye.

"I am afraid for her," Mrs. Zanders said.

I was afraid, too. But I didn't know if it was for Margaret or for me.

"She's so fragile, Billy, so close to the edge sometimes."

I had never thought of Margaret as fragile; unpredictable maybe, because she has done some funny things, but not fragile. She always seemed full of energy and spirit and ready for anything. And that hadn't changed even after she and Uncle Jeff got married. She seemed even happier, except, of course, sometimes when she got to worrying. I thought about those times and then I knew I was more afraid for me than for her. There was no way I could help her in her suffering, and if I tried, I would dissolve into a puddle of stupidity. The shakiness in my legs was moving up and I didn't know what to say or do. I wanted desperately to be somewhere else, anywhere but there in the Zanders' living room, standing as clueless as a post and knowing it was going to get worse.

Finally, Mrs. Zanders pointed to the stairs, "Seeing you will be good for her," she said.

I don't remember climbing the steps, but somehow, I made it up to Margaret's bedroom. There were no lights on and the room was full of dark shadows. Then I saw Margaret. She was lying on a bed near the window, and she raised her head and looked at me.

"Oh, Billy," she said and held her arms out.

I stumbled across the room and Margaret clutched at me and dragged me down so I almost fell on top of her. I didn't know what she was wearing, maybe pajamas or maybe nothing, because I felt her against me like a soft, warm bath. She was saying Uncle Jeff's name over and over in a wailing voice, and she twisted toward me and wrapped her arms and legs around me. Her wailing got louder and she kept it up, squirming and pushing her body into me and then gasping for breath until I couldn't help what happened and I hoped to God she didn't know. But she had gone suddenly quiet and limp and didn't move when I got up and walked out of the room.

CHAPTER THREE

I didn't know how I'd ever get any sleep with the Nazis here. They could be plotting an escape at any minute, or planning to take hostages and hold them until they got what they wanted, or there might be another blow-up like the one the Pickert boys and I saw, and maybe it would spin out of control and Nazis would swarm all over Oxbow, to our house even—we're not that far from the camp. It was something I thought about when the house creaked at night or a raccoon tipped over somebody's garbage can out in the alley, or when I remembered that thunderous prison camp rifle blast and the horrendous scream that must still be echoing through the night somewhere. I'll never forget that sound, the way it seemed to come from somewhere way back in time, like a hairy ancestor screaming in agony through every last generation right down to Uncle Jeff and me. It may be the worst thing I ever heard and I just can't get it out of my head.

Then there's the worrying about what Cy might come up with. He said the other day he was working up something that would not only get all the soldiers home but might be the end of all world wars. Hearing that kind of ridiculous bull from him is scary and keeps me awake as much as worrying about Nazis creeping over the porch roof and in through my bedroom window. There are just too many things to think about. I may never sleep again. Maybe it's something I'll just have to get used to, lying awake hour after hour and listening, and trying to keep my brain from turning to mush.

It actually started even before the prisoners got here. I sure didn't get any sleep the night of that dumbness in Margaret's bedroom. As I walked home that night, my brain had jumped back and forth between Uncle Jeff and Margaret like a toad on a stove, and I remember thinking maybe it would be better if I turned up missing, too. It just seemed that with the telegram and Margaret's misery and my bedroom fumbling, it was all so mixed up, it could never be straightened out.

Maybe I slept that night. I don't know, but I know it was a long night, and I remember my mother had been on the telephone when I came down for breakfast the next morning. I could tell she was talking to Mrs. Zanders and it had to do with Margaret, but I couldn't really get the drift. After she hung up, my mother said Mrs. Zanders had said Margaret couldn't get out of bed and she doesn't want to live without Uncle Jeff. I thought about Margaret's bed, but only for a second.

"Margaret is in shock," my mother said, and I wondered what it meant to be in shock. Does it mean you don't know what you are doing, like Indian John maybe when he stops in the middle of the street and just stands there so cars have to drive around him, or like Margaret when she clamped onto me and wailed Uncle Jeff's name?

I got out of the house as soon as I could, before my mother had a chance to ask questions about Margaret or anything else. But I couldn't stop thinking about Margaret, and that's what I was doing when Doc Smith pulled up to the gas pumps in his big Buick coupe. Doc is short and pudgy and has a rim of gray hair, like a fuzzy carnival ring was tossed over his head, and when he looks at you, it's like he sees through to your bones. People talk about what a good doctor he is, and how he can fix anything that's wrong.

And if there isn't anything wrong, Doc can fix that, too, I guess, which people say he did when banker Torkelson went to him last Christmas with a sore back. Doc painted "Merry Christmas" with mercurochrome across Mr. Torkelson's back, which he didn't know about until he got undressed for bed and Mrs. Torkelson had a laughing fit. I once heard Cy say that some people thought Doc was a draft dodger, but he was really a "conscientious objector," which Cy explained was a person who thought that killing someone you didn't know was going too far just to make a point for the government.

Cy said Doc told the draft board that a lot of his work was patching people up when they did dumb things but he wasn't about to do it for something as dumb as a war. Cy said the draft board was still coming after Doc but things got complicated when they discovered Doc had flat feet which, Cy said, makes him unfit for military service. I don't understand that. It would seem that being flat-footed would give a soldier a steadier *shooting base. I've looked at Doc's feet and they don't look that flat to me, big, but not flat.*

Doc is one of the few customers who says, "Fill 'er up, Billy," and while I'm filling his tank, he always asks how I'm doing, and squeezes my arm like he's taking my blood pressure. He always asks if I'm catching any fish, because once when I was out in Windigo Swamp, I got a fishhook buried so deep in my arm I had to go to his office and have him cut it out. While he was going at me with the scalpel, he said that a worm would be better bait than my arm, and if I ever caught too many trout, I should bring him a couple. I hadn't done that, but I planned to.

"Billy," Doc said, "when do I get my trout?"

When I didn't say anything, he turned and looked at me. "Something wrong?" he said.

Before I had time to think about it, I blurted out that my Uncle Jeff was missing in action.

Doc looked at me for a few seconds. "Jeff Forrest, of course. I didn't think about his being your uncle." He shook his head. "I'm sorry, Billy."

I nodded and said my Aunt Margaret was in shock.

Doc stared at me. "I was just over to see her," he said.

"Is she in shock?"

"Well, her mother seems to think so, but I don't know. Nobody really knows what it is to be in shock. It's like breaking a bone that isn't there. But your aunt is hurting, that's for sure."

"Will she be okay?"

"Let's hope so. She is a very troubled young lady and these things are unpredictable."

"Can you help her?"

"Probably no more than you can. Be good to her. Get her out and try to take her mind off her misery."

Doc patted my arm and got into his car. "Be strong, Billy. Go catch some trout and bring me a couple."

He grinned, and I tried to smile.

"Take your Aunt Margaret trout fishing," he said as he drove off.

That sounded really dumb. How was fishing going to help somebody who is in shock, especially someone like Margaret, who isn't the fishing type in the first place? Margaret has been in my life forever, from way back to her pigtail days when my mom and dad would have her come over to keep me company while they went to a movie or a dance. We would sit on the couch, and Margaret would read magazines or story books, or we would play games until one of us or maybe both of us fell asleep or my parents came home.

Later, when we were older, but still separated by that little cluster of years that is like a mountain when you are on the down side of it, Margaret would sometimes stop by and we would sit out on the porch swing and talk. She would tell me about her boyfriends and I remember her once calling them "little puppies." One night, Margaret grabbed my hand and pressed it over the softness of her breast.

"You're my best boyfriend, Billy," she said, and kissed me on the forehead.

That moment might have been the start of the "Margaret dumbness," like the first germ of a disease sneaking in. Another evening when lightning bugs were blinking over the lawn, Margaret talked about running off to California with Benny Edwards. She said they got picked up by a deputy before she could even ask anybody where to get a screen test. The deputy told them they could either go back home or get locked up in a California jail full of cockroaches and spiders. Margaret had called home for bus money and a couple days later, she and Benny got off the Greyhound in front of the bank and went back to high school like nothing had happened.

Last spring, before she and Uncle Jeff started going together, Margaret and a few of her girlfriends put together a variety show to "improve the morale of servicemen home on leave," they said. They swept the dust out of an attic over Jensen's garage and set up a little stage where they planned to dance and perform for local sailors and soldiers when they were home on leave. It all ended when the first show—for Boyd Stewart—was interrupted by curious parents who were shocked to find their high-school daughters doing striptease dances to the sound of a scratchy old recording of Lili Marlene. Boyd, who was recovering from shrapnel wounds he got in the Philippines, said later that the show had certainly raised his morale and it was too bad it had to end.

Even as a little girl, Margaret seemed to have had a thing about doing show business kinds of stuff. I once heard her mother tell my mother that Margaret had a "worrisome talent for slipping away from reality" and when she was about ten years old, she had nailed the trap

21

door shut on the neighbor's tree house and said she wasn't coming out until her father came to get her. She doesn't even have a father, at least not one that anyone knows about. She had one, of course, but according to what everybody says, he hopped a freight train during the Depression and hadn't been seen since.

He was a strange man, I once heard my mother say, and she added that Margaret probably inherited some of her father's ways because you just never knew what she might do next. I've heard gossip down at the station that Mr. Zanders—everyone called him "Zany"—left Oxbow just ahead of two or three husbands who threatened to kill him. You never know about gossip, especially old gossip.

Not long after the variety show got cancelled, Margaret and Uncle Jeff started going together. If you saw one, you saw the other, walking with their arms around each other and stopping on the sidewalk to kiss and hug. Chief Edwins saw them doing that one day and honked his horn and shook his finger. Uncle Jeff got mad and yelled at the Chief that it wasn't against the law to kiss your girl. Margaret had been a big hit in the junior class play, which is maybe where she got her idea about being a movie star. But she didn't even try out for the senior class play and it had to be because of Uncle Jeff, my dad's younger brother. He had already enlisted and was leaving as soon as school was out. And that's what he did. So with him gone, I had Margaret times again, just the two of us, but it was never as simple as it had been back when she had pigtails or when we sat on the porch swing. The "dumbness" complicated it and sometimes when she was around, I felt that I had no more brains than a goat. "Take her trout fishing," Doc says. He's got to be kidding!

Of course, I would do anything if Margaret could be the way she was before she got the telegram; smiling and laughing and touching me like she enjoyed the way I felt. Back then, her visits to the station were like little parties and they left my brain bubbling and fizzing like a damned Coke. You never forget things like that, and I remember one of those pre-telegram visits like it just happened.

Doc Heifer had dropped his car off for a lube job, which is a pain because Doc, being a veterinarian, drives through a lot of mud and dirt and cow shit and the bottom of his Chevy coupe is always a stinking mess. Doc's real name is Hefner, but everyone calls him Doc Heifer, I guess because he works around cows and heifers a lot. Anyway, I was down in the grease pit poking at the caked-on gunk with a screwdriver to find the grease fittings when I heard Margaret before I saw her. She was singing, *"Oh, where have you been, Billy Boy, Billy Boy. Oh, where have you been, charming Billy?"* She knows I don't like that silly old song and so she sings it to tease me.

From under Doc Heifer's car, the only thing I could see was her legs going past along the running board. Her flowered skirt flipped back and forth against her knees and for some reason, it made me think about Uncle Jeff and the last time I had seen him and Margaret together. I climbed out of the pit and wiped my greasy hands on an oil rag and we went into the station. I opened Cokes, and Margaret hopped up to sit on the pop cooler like always. I perched on the station stool where I could keep an eye on the gas pumps and still see Margaret, mostly staring at her saddle shoes and trying not to look at her swinging legs. The sun was slanting in through the dirty side window and shining off Margaret's dark hair and it made shadows across her face so she looked like Judy Garland or Betty Grable, or maybe someone even more beautiful, if that is possible. The "Margaret dumbness" came on as usual, like a brain clog.

"I got a letter from him, Billy," Margaret said.

I almost blurted out that I got one, too, but I caught myself just in time.

"Oh, God, I miss him," Margaret said and put her head back and squeezed her eyes shut.

"Want to read it?" she said, opening her eyes suddenly and flashing that smile that makes my knees wobbly.

I didn't want to read her letter; it would be too private. But Margaret reached into the front of her blouse and took out a V-mail letter and handed it to me. It felt warm as I unfolded it, and I read it all, from, "My Dearest Darling," through the parts about "loving" and "being in your arms again," to the final "I love you forever."

"You're blushing," Margaret said, and she laughed as I felt my face get hot.

"Isn't it beautiful?" she said when I handed the letter back.

I nodded.

"I'll die if anything happens to him."

"Nothing will happen. He'll be back soon."

"Oh, Billy, I love you for that," Margaret said as she slid off the pop cooler and grabbed me in a hug so tight I couldn't breathe, and I knew I would feel her against me all the rest of the day. She closed her eyes again and held the letter to her puckered lips so her lipstick left a red circle. She looked at the lipstick mark and smiled and stuffed the letter back into her blouse. Her eyes were damp and I thought she might grab me again, but she didn't. She just touched my arm and said she had to go, and I had watched her walk off down the street toward her job at Harry Meyer's grocery store.

Uncle Jeff and Margaret got married when Uncle Jeff was home on his last furlough. They had borrowed my dad's '35 Chevy for a weekend honeymoon, and after they brought it back, I could smell Margaret's perfume in the upholstery. Their friends had a shivaree for Uncle Jeff and Margaret in the back yard of Margaret's mother's house. A big crowd gathered just at dusk and banged on dish pans and saws and rang cow bells until Uncle Jeff and Margaret came out and agreed to buy a keg of beer as the old custom requires. I sneaked down there when I heard the racket. I stayed on the edge of the crowd and drank a couple glasses of beer and it seemed like I started feeling more man than boy for a change, but it didn't last because my mother showed up and took my beer glass.

"Take good care of her, Billy," Uncle Jeff said the day we saw him off on the train. He stood there smiling and handsome with his arms around Margaret, and with everyone staring at him like he was a god. He had it all; the uniform, the glory of going off to war, the beautiful woman, everything. I still see every detail, down to the white steam hissing out from between the locomotive wheels; the sun bouncing yellow-gold off Uncle Jeff's uniform buttons; Margaret's eyes shiny with tears; the train pulling out, puffing and creaking and finally clanking off down the track and leaving us all waving at nothing and looking at each other like we didn't know where to go. Margaret was still standing by the tracks when I finally left, her head bowed and her arms hanging like they were broken.

Back then, before the prisoners got here and with the war being so far away, there wasn't much to keep my mind off all kinds of remembering like that, and that was the worst part of the station job—all the time to think about everything. That day, after Margaret's cheerful visit, I had watched Indian John shuffle past like he does every morning, his nose stuck in his book and his old Army jacket hanging like it's been through too many wars. Indian John is shell-shocked from the First World War and people say he could get an Army pension if he would just apply for it.

Once, when I was out sweeping the drive, he stopped and started telling me about a little rat terrier running around a French battlefield biting at puffs of dust where bullets were hitting. Then he had just stopped talking and stared at me like he didn't know who I was. Indian John is about the only person I ever see out in Windigo Swamp. Suddenly, he will just be there on the trail right in front of me. Then he fades into the brush and you can't believe he was ever there. I don't know why, but Toby never barks at him.

Whenever Cy sees Indian John. he shakes his head and says if Indian John's people had let the Pilgrims starve that first winter instead of sharing food with them, Indian John would be driving a Buick instead of stumbling around in worn-out moccasins. Cy obviously likes his Indian John view and he repeats it often. And he always laughs and ends up saying, "You have to be careful about sharing, Billy."

Watching Indian John that day had helped take my mind off Margaret; and then Vernon Pickert rode by the station on his bike with a string of fish hanging from the handlebars. He was standing up pedaling so the bike whipped from side to side and the fish swung back and forth like they might go flying. Vernon yelled something that sounded like "chicken plucker" but it might have been something else, and then he headed off down the street toward the Pickerts' house that squats in front of the junkyard like some of the junk.

The Pickert girls go to high school, but the boys don't, and the school doesn't chase after them. Vernon went for a while but then he lit up a Lucky Strike in Mr. Leon's algebra class and started blowing smoke rings, so he got kicked out. One Sunday morning when I was a little kid, my dad took me along to Pickerts' junkyard. Kids and dogs had been scrambling all over the front porch, and Mr. Pickert, wearing a dirty cowboy hat and greasy coveralls, was sitting by the end of a junky table drinking a bottle of beer. Mrs. Pickert was waving a spatula at the kids and kicking at the dogs, and with her wild hair and flowered robe, she looked like a big clump of ditch weeds blowing in the wind.

"What's for breakfast?" my dad yelled.

"Blueberry pie," Mrs. Pickert yelled back. "Want some?"

My dad laughed and told her we had just eaten, which disappointed me.

"How about a beer?" Mr. Pickert said. My dad laughed again and said no thanks, he was full of coffee.

Why that childhood morning hangs in my brain like an old spider web, I don't know. But it probably will always be there taking up space with a lot of other useless stuff. What's the sense of that, of using up brain space to store up images and experiences that will never do you any good, like the dark blotches of blood on the skating pond where Mr. Brindle and his son Louie had their fist fight one winter night? I know I'll never forget how that looked, like black ink spilled on glass, and the circle of us runny-nosed kids with our clamp-on skates staring down at it and thinking about what Mr. Brindle and Louie must have looked like after the fight.

Why get your head all wrapped up in such dumb things? My brain is like Pickerts' junkyard, full of trash and garbage with more coming in every day. I have no control over it. I know one thing: I should stop thinking about Margaret, and girls in general, because it just makes for more useless brain trash, some of it embarrassing if it stirs you up at the wrong time.

Then, of course, there's the sin of such thinking. "Lust," it's called. I looked it up once after Cy said love was nothing but "lust on a leash." The dictionary says lust is, "intense or unrestrained sexual craving." Jeez! That sounds worse than coveting, which I have a hard enough time with. Reverend Thorston says "To think is to do," which really complicates things and makes me wonder—if I did some things every time I thought about them, I'd be worn down to nothing. Something is not right about that.

I knew Margaret wasn't likely to visit twice in one day, but I remember looking for her that afternoon anyway. I could still feel her softness from when she had hugged me earlier. But the feeling was fading and I wanted more. It had dawned on me then that I was lusting and coveting at the same time. It came as such a shock that it made me dizzy and the shame of it went deep enough so I remember it to this day.

I also remember that I had been struggling with that shame when a farmer in a rattletrap Ford pickup had stopped in for chewing tobacco. I was counting out his change when he said he just got word his nephew had been killed on Okinawa. He said it like he was talking about one of his chickens getting run over. When I looked at him, he shook his head and said, "Goddamn kid hadn't lived long enough to poke the neighbor girls and now he's dead."

He shook his head again and curled a finger into his tobacco pouch and hooked out a big chaw. I said I was sorry, and he looked at me and said, "You're lucky you ain't older or you'd probably be dead, too."

I thought about telling him I wouldn't mind dying if the circumstances were right, but I didn't say anything.

"Too damn many Gold Stars around here," the farmer said, and he mumbled about "goddamn dead kids" and climbed into his pickup. At the end of the drive, he stuck his head out and spit a thick slug of tobacco juice that left a big, brown splotch that I would have to hose off later. I didn't know at the time how many Gold Stars there were in Oxbow, still don't, I guess. Three or four at least.

One night last summer, I walked past the one in Adelson's front porch window and I heard a sound like an animal choking on a bone. I finally figured out it was Mr. Adelson sobbing in the backyard. It was like he was trying to do something he didn't know how to do, like a cat trying to bark. It wasn't a thing you wanted to hear and I got out of there fast. The Adelsons moved away after that, to Kansas City, I think. Mr. Adelson went to work in a defense plant, and there was a rumor that Mrs. Adelson tried to kill herself with a steak knife, but I don't know if that is true. The Gold Star was for their son Bobby, who was a big football hero in high school. He liked to pick up girls and tear around town in his old car that didn't have any doors, and once he stopped and yelled at me, "Hey, Billy, jump in."

I hadn't jumped in because Toby was with me and I was afraid he might fall out and get hurt. The last time I saw Bobby Adelson, he had his old heap loaded with squealing girls and he was making it go around and around in a skidding circle down by the Legion Hall where the streets are gravel so rocks and dust were kicking up and flying off in all directions. There was word around town that Bobby fell off an aircraft carrier when he got in the way of a crippled torpedo bomber that was trying to land. When I think about him, I wonder if Bobby saw the bomber before it hit him, and if he did, what was going through his mind? Did he think, "Oh shit, I'm going to die?"

CHAPTER FOUR

Margaret's crazy idea to kill one of the Nazis didn't just come out of the blue. It came out of something that had happened down at the station right in front of my eyes. It was the damndest thing, sort of like watching a butterfly crawl out of a cocoon with a gun. It was before the prisoners came in, of course, and just a day or so after she got that awful telegram and there had been that stupid fumbling in her bedroom. I hadn't seen her since that humiliating mess-up, and the thought of ever facing her again had been like a dark cloud following me around. So, I was trying not to think about her, but that was impossible. And then suddenly, that morning, there she was standing in the station door!

"Hi, Billy, got a Coke for me?" she said.

It was like seeing a ghost, and I couldn't move. She looked different, but maybe it was the way I looked at her, not really straight on and somehow hoping she wasn't really seeing me straight on either. She stood in a little crouch, her face pale and blank, and the "Margaret dumbness" crept over me worse than ever. Most of the time, Margaret sang *Billy Boy* as she came through the door but she sure wasn't singing that day. When I finally handed her the Coke, she touched my arm and said, "I'm dying, Billy."

I didn't know what to say or do. Doc said I could help her, but this was sure not the time to talk about trout fishing, which still seemed like a really dumb thing for him to suggest. I didn't want to stare at Margaret, but I had to see if there were any signs of her being in shock, so I sneaked a little sideways look. I don't know what I was expecting to see, but whatever it was, I didn't see it. She just looked very sad.

"I feel Jeff reaching for me," Margaret said. She shut her eyes and made a sound in her throat, like a moan but not really a moan either, more like a soft little wail coming from deep down. It went on for a long time, mixing in with the buzzing of the flies up by the candy bar shelf, and it seemed like it might go on forever. I stood there feeling stupid and helpless. Then, finally, Gordon Keller drove up to the gas pumps in his rattling old pickup and that got things going again. I was washing Gordon's windshield when he stuck his head out and said. "Hey, Billy, you hear the Krauts are coming in?"

There had been rumors for weeks about prisoners coming to Oxbow to help with the pea harvest. But there had been rumors about lots of other things too—like the government buying live bats to make incendiary bombs and blonde women asked to donate their hair for bomb sights. So back then, I hadn't been counting on any prisoners being here.

"No kidding," Gordon said. "They're coming. I heard it from the bigwigs."

I've known Gordon forever. He works at the lumber yard and he's one of those guys who is always claiming to have the inside dope on everything. He's what people call a bullshitter because he's always saying he's going to do some heroic or dangerous thing, and nothing comes of it. I heard he never got drafted because there is some flaw in his private parts and he has to sit down like a girl to pee. Who knows if that is true?

I put the oil stick back in place and was dropping the hood down on his pickup when Gordon said, "I'm shooting a whole damned platoon of those Nazi bastards with my deer rifle."

Gordon bobbed his head up and down like a woodpecker and shoved his scowling face close to mine, "They say there are Geneva rules or some damned thing like that and we got to be nice to the goddamned prisoners. Well, screw that! It's war! A time for killing!"

I looked at Gordon's bugged-out eyes and stepped back to get out of range of the spray of spit that came flying out with his words. "I'm going up on Klondike Ridge with my thirty-o-six with the peep sights," he said, "and there's gonna be dead Nazis laying all over them hills!"

Gordon grinned at me as I collected the money for his gas and then he got into his pickup and drove off, yelling out the window that they could stick the Geneva rules up their ass. When I turned to go back into the station, I almost collided with Margaret. She had been standing straight and stiff in the middle of the doorway, and her eyes were so wide open it looked like they might roll out of her head.

"That's it, Billy!" she shouted. She grabbed my arms and put her face close to mine. "We will kill one of those Nazi bastards!"

Margaret stepped back and shook her clenched fists and actually laughed, a short laugh that didn't have anything to do with something being funny.

"We'll do it for Jeff," she said, and danced in a little circle, "You and me, Billy. We'll do it as soon as those murdering Nazis get here."

I stared at her and she grabbed me again and squeezed so hard I almost lost my breath. Her eyes were wide and wild and they seemed to be looking at something that only she could see.

So, that's how it had started. Hearing Gordon blow off steam had suddenly transformed Margaret from a grieving young war-wife into a fist-shaking Nazi killer. It was something to see, and I remembered what Cy says about war doing strange things to people. Margaret had paced about the station, raising her arms and shaking her clenched fists, and she said we had to start making plans right away. Then she left, saying she was going home to write a letter to Uncle Jeff telling him what we were planning.

It was all too crazy and when Cy stopped by later, I told him about it. He said Margaret had gone over the edge. "She's full of grief and hormones and she can't think straight," Cy said as he hoisted himself up onto the pop cooler and unfolded his *New York Times*. Cy had mentioned hormones once before when he had been talking about me, but I'm not sure I understand what they are. Cy said they had me by the balls and there wasn't anything I could do about it. I know hormones were mentioned in Mr. Custer's biology class, but I didn't remember what he said. I have this notion that they are like tiny bugs that get into your blood and stir up trouble.

But that doesn't seem to fit with Margaret. If she is full of hormones, I see them more as ant-like things scurrying around in her veins with important jobs to do. That sounds pretty childish and stupid and I need to listen up next time Mr. Custer talks about hormones. But I know Cy was right about Margaret not being able to think straight. She had grabbed onto her Nazi-killing idea like it was the greatest thought she had ever had, and anyone who didn't go along with it was in for trouble. She obviously couldn't think straight about such things, but I didn't think it was because she was grieving or she was having hormone trouble; I thought it was because she was in shock, like my mother said.

"Margaret can't be grieving because Uncle Jeff is not dead," I said to Cy.

"Well, we hope not," Cy said, "but he's gone from Margaret's life and she can grieve for him whether he's dead or gone."

I gave Cy a look.

"When you're dead, you're gone, and when you're gone, you might as well be dead," he said.

That didn't make sense to me. I said there's a big difference between being gone and being dead, and Cy said, dead is just being gone for good.

"Nobody knows what dead really is," he said. "There's all this religious bull about places where the dead go to enjoy themselves but there is no proof of that pudding."

Cy and I had talked about dying a month or so earlier after watching the Wagonback hearse lead Mr. Baldwin's fifteen-car funeral procession past the station. I don't know why but I always count the cars. The highest ever was thirty-six for Mrs. Guiliksen, who was an officer of the daughters of something or other. DAR, I think is what Cy called it, and he said the members tried to keep the Revolutionary War going for purposes of fund-raising, which he said is always an important part of any war. The lowest car count was two and was for Louie Lancaster, a hired man out on the Becker farm who hadn't been seen in town for twenty years.

Mr. Baldwin had been a cashier at the bank and he had a stroke and had been flat on his back in bed, not moving or talking or doing anything, for at least six years. People said they knew he had wanted to die for a long time, but he had no way of getting it done. I don't know how they knew that—that he wanted to die—but everybody seemed to be sure of it. I remember Cy saying that nothing like that would ever happen to him because he was going to be in charge of his own dying and it wasn't going to involve lying in bed for six years staring at the ceiling.

It was one of those times when he got really wound up and it seemed like he would never stop going on about how he was going to live the way he wanted and he was going to die the way he wanted and nobody was going to stop him.

"I might make it into an event," he said, "entertainment of some sort. And I'll want you there, Billy, because I plan to communicate with you from the grave and we will have to get that set up beforehand."

I had stopped listening to him then, after he said he might get reincarnated as a dog because he knew I could talk to dogs and if I could talk to a dead person through a dog, I could go into show business and end up rich and famous. I was about to stop listening on this day, too, but then we went on to argue about the difference between dead and gone as far as war was concerned, and Cy said it is probably okay to assume that most POWs are more gone than dead, which made me feel a little better. Cy said he had just read that some of the Nazi POWs were running some of the camps here in this country like Gestapo barracks.

"They celebrate Hitler's birthday and give the Nazi salute and even wear their goddamn Nazi medals and uniforms," Cy said.

"They have a birthday party for Hitler?" I said.

"Yeah, there are so damned many German prisoners in this country right now the Army can't handle them, so they let the prisoners control things inside the prison camps."

Cy shook his head. "They say Eleanor Roosevelt heard about some of it at a White House tea and she told FDR he had to put a stop to it. So the Army has been gathering up some of the worst Nazis and shipping them down to Oklahoma."

He looked up from his newspaper then and said, "Its a service to humanity to kill those Hitler-worshipping pricks," he said.

"Maybe some of the Krauts we get here in Oxbow will be Gestapo," I said.

"Maybe," Cy said and went back to his reading. When I looked at him again, the newspaper had dropped and he was staring off into space. "If they really do get here, we'll do something else," he said, "something really big."

"What?" I said.

"I'm not sure yet. Maybe get mothers into it," he said and then he had stuck his nose back in the newspaper and left me wondering what weird thoughts were going through his head. Mothers! It didn't sound like there was any hope that he would come up with something to get me into the war and I felt a jolt of anger toward him.

I knew Margaret's idea was too crazy to even think about, but I thought about it anyway, about actually killing a Nazi. Shooting would be easiest. Grandpa Forrest had given me a rifle for my twelfth birthday, a Winchester Model 69 bolt-action, .22 with a clip that holds five bullets so with one in the chamber, I can fire six shots before reloading. I can hit a squirrel almost every time and rabbits are as good as dead when they stop and sit like rocks. I could kill a Nazi as easy as shooting a pig.

Once, when I was seven or eight years old, I was at Grandpa's farm on butchering day and all the details of it stick in my head with the other brain trash. When Grandpa held the rifle close to the pig's forehead and it made its sharp little "crack," the pig flopped down onto the frozen ground as if to say, "Well, so much for that. What's next?" Most of the butchering was a steaming mass of blood and guts and cut-up meat and raw bones and generally a big mess. But the killing part of it—that had been neat and easy.

"Hey, Margaret should get Harry Meyers in on her Nazi killing," Cy said.

"Why would she do that?" I said.

"Harry is about the only Jew in town and I just read that the Nazis have killed millions of Jews in concentration camps."

People were just starting to talk about the concentration camps, and I heard someone say the news about them was so horrible it couldn't possibly be true. The talk seemed different, whispers of mass killings that were so far beyond understanding that you didn't want to really know about it.

"You know those Bund assholes over by Almira once tried to burn down Harry's store," Cy said. "They were just back from listening to one of Lindbergh's rants and they were full of America-first and Jew-hating bullshit, and probably rotgut whiskey."

Cy grinned and looked at me. "Wouldn't that be something, get a Nazi off somewhere and let Harry do whatever he wants with the son of a bitch!"

That didn't sound like such a good idea to me. Then I remembered that Cy once said to get the most out of a situation, you had to have a "sense of theatre." I didn't understand it, but maybe that's why he was thinking about Harry Meyers, and maybe that's why he does some of the really stupid things he does. Anyway, it sounded dumb to me.

When I was a little kid and went into Harry Meyers' store with my mother, Harry would pinch my cheeks and slip me a piece of candy. I remembered that and told Cy I didn't think Harry Meyers would want to kill a Nazi.

"This is all just bullshit anyway," Cy said. "Killing prisoners isn't something we can do."

He slipped down off the pop cooler then and said he had just had a brainstorm about what to do when the POWs got here and he was going up to the pool hall to do a Francis Bacon. Once, when he had been going on about all the philosophers, he said he had settled on Francis Bacon because Bacon said the best thing a philosopher can do is throw everything out and start over. Cy said he tries to do that on a daily basis, and he was half way out the door when he turned and looked at me. He raised one of his ragged eyebrows and said, "Billy, you weren't thinking of helping Margaret with her crazy plan, were you?"

"Are you nuts? I'm smarter than that."

"Yeah, but if Margaret told you to eat wood, you'd start gnawing on the door jamb."

I scowled at him.

"Mother Nature's fooling with you. You can't help it."

He left then, which was a good thing because I was tired of his dumb talk. Along with forgetting his newspaper, he also left a book, which he often does. I picked it up and read the title: *Under Cover* by Roy Carlson. Then I skimmed through it enough to figure out that it was about the secret Nazi organizations in this country. It told about Hitler Youth being the "future carrier of German radical ideals in America," and it listed a special prayer that had been written for them. I copied it down because it seemed like it just might help me figure out my praying problems.

"Adolph Hitler, we believe in Thee. Without Thee we would be alone. Through Thee we are a people. Thou hast given us the great experience of our youth, comradeship. Thou hast laid upon us the task, the duty, and the responsibility. Thou hast given us Thy name (Hitler Jugend), the most beloved Name that Germany has ever possessed. We speak it with reverence, we bear it with faith and loyalty.

34

Thou canst depend upon us. Adolf Hitler, Leader and Standard-Bearer. The Youth is Thy name. Thy name is the Youth. Thou and the young millions can never be sundered."

What it comes down to is—I don't understand prayer. And then something like this Hitler prayer comes along. People are praying to Hitler! How can that be? How do prayers get to where they are aimed? I thought only God could hear them. But maybe there are prayer waves like radio waves and if you have the right frequency you can hear them if you're somebody important like God or Hitler. I know from what Reverend Thorston told us in confirmation class that just asking these questions can get you into trouble. Faith! You have to have faith, and just believe, he said. Believe what? Whatever he says, I guess.

I remember him saying that all the answers to everything are in the Bible. But when I looked in there to try to figure out praying, there was just too much. I gave it up after reading that you should pray in a closet with the door shut so you are not praying just to show people that you are doing it, and you should not do a lot of repeating. It seems like a long time ago that I got too old for, "Now I lay me down to sleep..." and "God bless Mother and Father and everyone else..."

I never seemed able to go from that kid stuff to talking to God one on one. For one thing, wouldn't He be too busy with important things, like running Heaven and staying on top of the war to get involved with my little miseries? I thought of how Reverend Thorston said you should end your prayers with, "If it be the will of the Lord," and I'm thinking if it isn't God's will, it isn't going to happen no matter how I pray for it, so what's the sense of asking for something? It seemed it wasn't God's will that I get into the war, because that was the one thing I had been praying years for and it wasn't happening.

Or was it?

I remember thinking that day that if Gordon Keller was right and Nazi prisoners came to help with the pea harvest, that could be an answer to my prayers. People are always saying that God works in mysterious ways. Cy hasn't been much help in figuring out prayer. Once, when the subject came up, he said that praying to God makes no more sense than talking to a tree. Somehow, I expected that in the next instant a bolt of lightning would come ripping out of the sky and turn him into cinders. I might have some doubts about some things, but I would never go so far as to say something that just seems to challenge God to make a move.

Later, when I mentioned that people were praying to Hitler, Cy said Hitler seemed to have more power than God these days, so maybe it isn't so outrageous that people are praying to him. Then, there was that afternoon shortly after D-Day when Cy showed up waving his *New York Times* and grumbling that FDR had done something really stupid.

"You would think there might be somebody in the White House smart enough to stop him, but apparently not," Cy said.

I had no idea what he was talking about, but I knew he was going to explain it to me. He pointed to the front page of the *Times* and reached into his shirt pocket and took out a piece of folded paper. "I want you to read how these two prayers start and tell me if they aren't pretty much the same goddamn thing."

I looked at the prayer in the *Times* that President Roosevelt had read on the radio. *"Almighty God: Our sons, pride of our nation, this day have set upon a mighty endeavor, a struggle to preserve our Republic, our religion and our civilization, and to set free a suffering humanity…"*

"Now read this," Cy said, as he unfolded the paper from his shirt pocket and held it in front of me. "It's Mark Twain's War Prayer."

"O Lord Our Father, our young patriots, idols of our hearts, go forth to battle — be Thou near them! With them — in spirit — we also go forth from the sweet peace of our beloved firesides to smite the foe…"

"Same damn opening," Cy said, "and if you read them through, you see they both ask for the enemy to be smashed to smithereens with no mercy for anyone, including women and children and they use some of the same exact words and phrases. Twain was using satire, for God's sake, and FDR was serious. You'd think somebody at the White House would have caught that."

I said I didn't understand why Cy was so upset. He swore and said, "It's just such a goddamned joke to be praying about war. How the hell can anyone be stupid enough to pray to a god that lets a war get going, and then pray for your side to do more killing and maiming than the other side? Twain recognized that absurdity. FDR apparently doesn't and now he's pulling the whole country down into the great cesspool of religious ignorance and illusion."

Cy shook his head. "I shouldn't let it get to me, but sometimes all the spiritual flim-flam is just too much."

I looked at Cy and thought how there was no doubt he was going to hell. For some reason, I didn't feel sorry for him.

"You know what my favorite prayer is, Billy?" Cy said. "It's St. Augustine's, the one that goes, *'Lord, please grant me celibacy, but not yet'.*" Cy laughed and slapped his leg. "You know what celibacy is, right?"

I knew about celibacy from Ronnie Swanson in gym class saying he wouldn't want to be a Catholic priest because they had to be celibate. I hadn't known what it meant when Ronnie first said it, but I hadn't let on to him. I looked it up later, which was a good thing because the way "celibacy" sounded, I thought it had to do with celebrating, like having a party or something. So, I knew all about celibacy, but Cy didn't seem to care if I knew or not because he obviously wanted to give it his own take, for my entertainment, and his.

"Celibacy is when your wienie only comes out to pee," he said, and he laughed his jerky laugh and punched my arm. "It's when the great bird never flies up your spine. It's when the one-eyed snake doesn't poke into the phoebe nest. It's when..."

Cy was on one of his stupid rolls and it would probably go on until he came up with something that would send him into gasping fits of laughter. I had stopped listening.

CHAPTER FIVE

What good is it to have the enemy around if you can't get the war going? I woke up thinking that having the Nazis here in Oxbow might end up being just another tease, like when Percy Van Stout flew that B-24 so low over Oxbow it shook every dish in every cupboard and you could see one of the B-24 crewmen in an open side door looking like he was standing there smoking a cigarette. There was a big story about it in the *News-Banner* the next week, telling how Captain Van Stout was flying the bomber around the country on a war bond drive and thought it would be fun to buzz his home town. Of course, that had only lasted minutes, but the POW thing just keeps going on day after day and nothing happens. What is Cy waiting for?

I looked out my bedroom window in the direction of the POW camp but it was hidden by the other houses and all I saw was Mr. Deggerton standing on his back porch in his pajamas, scratching his butt and yawning. It reminded me I was overdue mowing Deggerton's lawn and I knew my mother would be on my tail about it. I waited until I saw her out in the garden, then I ran down the stairs and was headed out the front door when she caught me. If I kept track of the times I got away and the times I got caught, it would be like the worst batting average in history.

"William!" she said. "I want to talk to you!"

It is bad when she calls me William. But I had no choice, so I sat at the kitchen table and listened as she went on about how "irresponsible and slovenly" I was. Toby was in his usual spot under the table and I thought it was too bad he had to listen because he didn't have anything to do with what was going on. But then my mother said, "And I am sick of your dog getting into my tomatoes."

"It isn't him," I said.

"Yes, it is. You don't put him on his chain and he gets into the garden and digs holes."

"He's after gophers and he keeps the rabbits out."

"He does more damage than the gophers and rabbits."

It wasn't any use to argue, and I thought maybe I could still get away with not doing the lawn, but then my mother said, "And I am sick of listening to Olive Deggerton complain that you aren't mowing their lawn."

"It's so dry it isn't growing much," I said.

My mother looked at me over her glasses. "This morning, William, and I don't want to hear another word."

So, there it was! Unbelievable! I'm on the verge of mixing it up with the Nazis—actually getting into the war as soon as Cy comes up with a plan, and instead I've got to mow the neighbor's lawn just because my mother says so. I had a sudden urge to bang my spoon down into the Shredded Wheat and shout that I was no longer a baby she could order around. But I didn't. I just sat there and my face got hot, and I thought how my mother had been in a bad mood ever since my dad left for the defense plant in Kansas City.

When Dad is around, I can deal with him about things. If I explained that I had something important to do, he would let me do it and tell me to mow the lawn tomorrow. My mother doesn't make deals, and this keeps me forever on the edge of slipping into a childish tantrum. Why doesn't she see that?

Toby whined when I put him on his chain and I told him to shut up and not feel sorry for himself because I was on just as much of a chain as he was, maybe more of one. Then I dragged the lawnmower out and started pushing it around on Deggerton's stupid lawn. I tried to think of things to take my mind off the unfairness of it, but all I could think about was how my mother ran my life. She didn't tell me what to do out in the swamp and that was a big reason I liked it so much out there. If I ever have kids, I'll let them make their own decisions about everything, including whether or not they want to mow lawns or smoke cigarettes or read *Esquire* or whatever. Most Oxbow parents seem to be pretty much the same, all telling their kids how to live, and worrying about "putting food on the table," as they like to say. Cy says that everyone in Oxbow is still trying to recover from the Great Depression.

"You have no idea what it was like, Billy." I remember Cy saying. "When people have no house and damned little to eat, they start seeing wolves and catamounts coming for their little ones."

Cy says I am a "Depression baby," which means, according to him, I am "living proof that the sex drive is the only thing that trumps hunger and shivering."

I don't even try to fit my mom and dad into that. All I know is that they talk a lot about the days when they couldn't pay Harry Meyers for groceries and he carried them through the winter until my dad found work cleaning sewers. Yeah, I guess I've heard that story often enough. All of this brain trash rattled around in my head while I was pushing the dumb lawnmower, and then Mrs. Deggerton came out onto her front porch.

She is shaped like Humpty Dumpty with no neck and a little head, so you wonder if she tipped over if she could get back up on her feet. She smiled and asked me if I'd like some lemonade. I told her no thanks and she watched for a while and finally went back into the house. As I was finishing up around the lilac bushes, Mrs. Deggerton came back out and handed me fifty cents, which is what they've been paying me forever. I thanked her and she stood in front of me so I couldn't get around her.

"I pray for you, Billy," she said, and she reached out and rubbed my arm like she was petting a cat.

I stared at her, and she smiled. "Of course, I also pray for your Uncle Jeff and all the boys in service, but I say a special prayer for you, Billy."

So, why couldn't she just lump me in with Uncle Jeff and the rest? That would make me feel a lot better.

"Sometimes I see you with that awful Cyrus Butler and I just know it is the Devil's work, so I pray for you," Mrs. Deggerton said.

She and my mother had obviously been talking. My mother threatens to ask Cliff Huston to ban Cy from hanging around the filling station. Cliff told me she talked to him about it, but there isn't any way to ban someone from a filling station unless they are causing trouble. I told Cliff that Cy didn't make trouble, which was not totally true, and Cliff said I shouldn't let Cy hang around if he had been drinking. That's a laugh.

Mrs. Deggerton pointed a short, fat finger at me and said, "That man is just not good for you, Billy."

I nodded, and I guess she thought I was agreeing with her and would stay away from Cy because she said, "That's wonderful, Billy. But I will still pray for you."

I had this crazy thought then about what might happen if Mrs. Deggerton's prayers got on the wrong wavelength and ended up going to Hitler instead of to God. I mean, people are praying to both of them and who is to say it couldn't happen? Sometimes, I think weird thoughts like that keep me from going off the deep end.

When I was finally able to get away from Mrs. Deggerton and my mother, I took Toby off his chain and we walked over to Cy's house. Cy doesn't like it when I bring Toby because his cats start hissing and climbing up onto the tops of things. But I know Toby enjoys it. I found Cy out in his "Victory Garden," which is mostly tall weeds.

"Look at this wonderful garden," Cy said, swinging his arm out over the weeds. "It's very cleverly camouflaged so enemy bombers can't see it."

Cy has been talking about enemy bombers since Oxbow had its first blackouts several years ago, "Such bullshit," he said at the time. "Why the hell would an enemy bomb a place like Oxbow?"

Deputy Blasser once arrested Cy for violating blackout regulations when Cy used a flashlight to find his way home from the pool hall. Cy later sued Blasser for "unnecessary darkness." When the blackouts first started, Oscar Ronstead, who works at the pea vinery, was the Civil Defense Warden, and he walked around town yelling at people to pull their shades and turn out their lights. One night, according to the Pickert brothers, Mr. Ronstead was walking up the alley in back of the Johnson's house and saw some of the Johnson girls frolicking around in their underwear, which is something they had been doing for years to entertain anyone who wanted to watch.

Vernon Pickert said that instead of yelling at the Johnsons to turn off their light, Mr. Ronstead tried to move closer for a better look and fell over a garbage can and broke his arm. Of course, nobody knew that except the Pickerts and nobody would believe anything they said. Mr. Ronstead claimed he fell while running to turn off someone's porch light and he hinted there were some war-like heroics involved. Over time, more and more people bought into the Pickerts' version of the thing.

Toby was sniffing through the garden weeds, and Cy said I should tell him to sniff out an onion because that's what he came out to get. "I know I planted some," he said, "but I can't find them and I need one for a vodka soup recipe."

A dog, even one as smart as Toby, isn't going to be much help finding an onion and it seemed like we stomped around in the weeds forever. Finally, Cy said we might as well give up, and we should go into his house because he wanted to tell me about his big war plan. Finally! A little jolt of excitement zipped up my backbone and it was followed immediately by a shiver of doubt. Cy has done so many crazy things, how could he possibly come up with something meaningful to get me—us into the war? Toby slipped in through the back door ahead of us, and three or four cats went hissing and scurrying up the furniture and the walls.

"It's all right, ladies," Cy said. "It's just Billy and his wolf."

Cy's house hasn't been cleaned since his mother died years ago, and when you first come through the door, it is like sticking your head into a garbage can. I have told Cy I can't breathe in his house, and he says I must be allergic to cats. All of Cy's furniture, including a dusty old piano in the corner, is piled high with books and newspapers and magazines. There are dirty dishes and heaps of other junk on the table and the counter. Most of the time, Cy has jazz or Dixieland music playing on the radio or on his old phonograph. "The cats like it," he once said and then he gave me a long lecture about how jazz came from combining the music of highbrow educated Creoles with the music of poor working blacks in New Orleans and it was the freedom of expression in it that the cats liked.

"If I don't play them some Charlie Parker every day, they get cranky," he said. "And Poor Little Thing, that striped one over there, gets so upset she goes out and gets herself knocked up."

"Even Hitler has music in his life," Cy said, going from cats to Hitler without missing a beat. "Der Fuehrer likes the music of Richard Wagner, probably because he was another Jew-hater."

I hear more history from Cy than from old Mr. Russet at the high school, and usually it's more interesting than some dry account of some-body invading another country or some king being dethroned. Of course, I never know for sure if Cy's history is true or if he makes it up.

"Wagner wrote that Jews were repulsive, and of course Hitler loved that," Cy said. "Wagner's daughter-in-law Winifred brought Hitler the paper to write *Mein Kampf* when he was in prison and he wanted to marry her. Too bad, she wouldn't have the little prick. He might have ended up a harmless fiddler instead of the biggest murdering asshole the world has ever known."

That's obviously not the kind of historical speculation I would get from Mr. Russet and it clunked into place with the other brain trash I've gotten from Cy, which is a lot.

Ragged pieces of Cy's old musical rant came to mind as I tried not to breathe too deep until my lungs adjusted to the stink of his house. Cy's cats looked down at us from their perches and hissed at Toby, and Cy said I should get my dog under control. "Tell him cats were worshipped as gods by the Egyptians and he should show more respect."

Cy said we should sit down and he would tell me the plan, but all the chairs were piled high with all kinds of junk, so we stood leaning against the dirty kitchen counter. Cy gave me a long look, like he was trying to figure out if I was up to understanding what he was about to say. I looked back, and had the feeling you might get watching a summer boomer gather up muscle off in the distance; would the storm be useful and get the crops watered or turn into a dry bluster that knocked branches down and left a mess? I was leaning toward bluster.

"Billy," Cy said, "you know I've had some great ideas in my time, right?"

I nodded and waited, trying to recall some of his great ideas, or even one.

"We've got the Krauts here, right?"

I nodded.

"Margaret wants to kill one, and we know that is a bad idea."

I nodded again.

"Well, there's a great opportunity here and we can't let it go to waste. First thing we've got to do is capture one of those goddamn Krauts."

I stared at him and had a feeling the bluster was coming. "They're already captured," I said.

"I mean you and Margaret and I have to capture one."

"What for?"

"To set up a trade."

"Trade? Trade for what?"

"Think about it."

I tried but the only thing I could think of was Uncle Jeff.

"You mean trade a Kraut for Uncle Jeff?"

Cy nodded and grinned. "That's it, Billy! You got it!"

I tried to picture how such a trading thing might work, but sometimes if your brain gets a sudden jolt of unexpected stuff, it slips out of gear, and that's what seemed to happen to mine. Pieces of ideas and images came flying in, but nothing held together. How could we—a wierdo lawyer, a grieving war bride, and a too-young war reject possibly bring off such a thing in the middle of a world war? Thoughts kept flying like zigzag bats.

At some point, no matter how such a thing might go down, we would probably have an actual German soldier in our control, at least briefly. I liked that. The war wouldn't last forever, and if I was going to get into it, something unusual would have to happen soon. I liked that, too. Also, since this would be aimed at helping Uncle Jeff, Margaret would love it. I liked that a lot.

Then I guess my head got back in gear again and it dawned on me how outrageous and impossible the whole thing was. I opened my mouth to tell Cy how I felt but he held his hand up and stopped me.

"I'm writing a letter to Mrs. Roosevelt," he said, and he reached into the clutter on the table and handed me a sheet of paper.

"You're writing to the President's wife?" I said.

"That's right. She's the only one who could help us pull this off."

I stared at him and maybe my head went out of gear again.

"Read it." Cy said.

It was getting crazier by the minute. I looked down at the letter.

Dear Mrs. Roosevelt:

We are asking your help in establishing an official Mothers Of Prisoners (MOP) Exchange in the War Department. As you know, in all wars, the mothers' real and only concern is getting their sons home safe and sound. I'm sure you feel that way about your sons. That is the only purpose of the MOP Exchange, and it must therefore be independent of the military where sons are as expendable as mess kits. As a start-up case, we will be holding a German prisoner isolated from military custody and ready to be exchanged for one of our servicemen. In this test case, that would be PFC Jeffrey Forrest, who is thought to have been captured recently in France. Your earliest response would be much appreciated.

*Signed*_____

It was the craziest idea Cy had ever come up with. I stared at him and my mouth must have been hanging open because Cy reached over and pushed up on my chin.

"You're catching flies, Billy."

I shut my mouth, and stared at him.

"We've got to involve mothers," Cy said. "Mothers pretty much run their sons' lives until they get old enough for the tribal warriors to send them off to war. Then, the mothers are told to sit home and worry and grieve and keep out of the important business of killing and maiming. This results in a hell of a lot of pent-up power and that is what we are tapping into."

He paused and looked at me.

"I've given this a lot of thought, Billy, and it's pretty simple. You get the mothers involved in a war and it is damn sure going to be different. It is going to be over, in fact, because mothers will demand that their sons come home right now, and the generals are going to be left standing out in their underwear."

Maybe it was the image of the generals in their underwear, or maybe it was thinking about how my mother runs my life, or maybe the thought of Cy writing to Mrs. Roosevelt, but anyway, I laughed. Cy ignored me and went on.

"First thing we've got to do is get your Uncle Jeff's mother to sign the letter. Mrs. Roosevelt has to know this is all being done by mothers."

Uncle Jeff's mother? Grandma Forrest? Maybe I should have laughed at that, but I didn't. It was just too crazy.

"This will take a little organizing," Cy said, "but once MOP gets rolling, there will be no stopping it. We'll get us a prisoner with a mother in Germany and put her in contact with Jeff's mother, and bingo!"

45

CHAPTER SIX

It was what I had been dreading. Cy had come up with something too crazy to even think about. It was a total let-down. All the time I've known him, his crazy schemes have been interesting to watch, from a distance, if you were lucky enough to have that choice. And sometimes, of course, you couldn't help but get involved, like when he "borrowed" all those chickens at the county fair and turned them loose in the Odd Fellows meeting hall and I had to help him catch them and take them back to the fairgrounds.

But this was too much. This was something I had a personal stake in. It involved practically my whole family, and it could come crashing down on all of us, especially Margaret and Grandma Forrest. I didn't have to think about it. It was so crazy that putting it down didn't call for just saying no, or even "Hell, no!" It needed some way of showing that your whole being was in on it.

I felt sad and angry. I had been counting on Cy to come up with a way to use the Nazi prisoners to get us into the war in a real way. And now this, this outrageous, totally unworkable bunch of bullshit! I shook my head and stared at Cy. He grinned back. He was crazier than I had ever imagined, and I needed to get away from him before I got mad enough to do something dumb, like pop him on the nose. I shook my head and turned to walk out the back door. I had only taken a step or two when Cy clamped his hand down hard on my shoulder and spun me around.

"Where the hell do you think you're going?" he said, and there was something in his voice that I had never heard before. It was beyond being annoyed or irritated; it was anger, sudden and intense, and it was aimed at me. Cy's grin was gone and his eyes were narrowed and had a flinty look that didn't fit with anything I knew or had ever heard about him.

"Goddamnit, Billy, sit down and listen," he said, and swung his arm so it sent a jumble of trash flying across the room and cleared off one of the chairs. Cy pointed at the chair and said, "Park your ass and let's see if we can get you to grow up just a goddamn fraction."

I was the one who had a right to be mad, but Cy's anger had come so suddenly and with such force that anything I was feeling was cancelled out, or at least delayed. Cy jerked my arm and pushed on my chest, so I either had to sit down or fall over the chair.

"I'm going to tell you some things you may not want to hear," he said, "but I really don't give a shit. I think you're old enough to handle it. If not, well then I've been wrong about you all along."

All I could do was sit and stare at him.

"First off, Billy," Cy said, "you've been acting like this war is some kind of a goddamn sporting event and the only thing that matters is that you get into it. Well, your self-centered attitude is understandable in someone your age, but it's time for you to grow up. It's time for you to look beyond the end of your nose and your pecker and realize that you can either plod through life like the rest of the herd or you can grab onto some things once in a while and twist the hell out of them in the off chance you might make a little difference."

Cy paused and looked at me. The anger had gone out of his eyes some, but there was a glint that signaled he wasn't through talking.

"People think I do crazy things, and you've been around for some of them. Well, what I'm doing, Billy, is rattling cages, rusty goddamned old cages that have had people locked up for centuries."

Cy paused and fished a cigarette out of his shirt pocket. He raked a kitchen match across the edge of the table and looked at me over its flame.

"I usually end up taking a fall of some kind, but you know what, Billy, I always feel better when it's over. Maybe I've made somebody look at something a little differently or at least have sense enough to ask a question next time ingrained ignorance carries the day."

Either Cy was going too fast for me or I was too slow to catch the drift of what he was saying. He blew out a big cloud of smoke and glanced at me.

"I've had hope for you, Billy, but you've got some growing up to do. This thing with the mothers, you think it is total bullshit and has about as much chance as a fart in a whirlwind. Well, hell, of course it's outrageous and if it ever came to anything, it would be the biggest goddamned miracle in the history of warfare. But that's no reason not to try it. It's something different, and that's its virtue. It's shaking a cage, and, from my personal point of view, that kind of thing is damned entertaining!"

I was trying to listen and not be all wrapped up in what Cy had said about me having to grow up, but it was heavy going.

"I've been watching you, Billy, since you started getting pimples and hard-ons, and for some reason, I thought you might be worth separating out from the riff-raff. At least, I figured it might be worth my time to get you to look at things with your own eyes instead of running with the herd."

I was hanging on by my fingernails. What the hell was he talking about?

"When people think about war, they think about guns and bombs and blood and guts, but they never think about mothers. Well, that's where original thinking comes in."

Cy shot me a look, and I couldn't tell if he was just disgusted or if he was still mad. Trying to see into his mind was like trying to look into an egg.

"Next to survival, motherhood is the most powerful thing biology has come up with," Cy said, "and there is no reason why it shouldn't be used as a tool for human welfare beyond suckling and nurturing. It's the most logical force that could ever be introduced into the insanity of war, which is when we really treat mothers like shit. Planter tells me that Mrs. Borland went out to the cemetery one night last week and tried to dig down to her son's coffin with her bare hands. That's the kind of horrible thing war does to mothers."

I thought about Mrs. Borland and Mrs. Adelson and Grandma. I wondered how my mother would handle it if I was killed in the war, but then I realized I was being what Cy had called self-centered.

"What I'm trying to do here, Billy," Cy said, "is steal some of the absurdity of a world war from the smug structure that men have built up to conduct it. I'm trying to pull off a heist here, an out-and-out robbery of some of the rotten underpinnings of meaningless, wholesale organized slaughter that has been going on for thousands of years. I'm trying to use MOP to get people to see the big picture."

He was using too many big words and going too fast. I tried to keep up and I was catching enough to know that some of the things he was saying made sense. But they were complicated, and I needed some time. I got it when Cy stopped talking and stood puffing on his cigarette and stared out the window.

"Wherever this goes," Cy said, "if it stops at the Oxbow Post Office or gets as far as Washington or ends up with us playing *Ring Around the Rosy* with a damned Kraut, it will be worth it. At some point, people will find out about it and a few of them might even think it wasn't so dumb. Most, of course, will say MOP is too crazy to be a part of organized war. And if we go ahead with it, that line of thinking will prevail and we'll probably end up in trouble. But until that happens, I'm going for this whole hog, and, goddamnit, I hope you are with me."

It was quiet then. Cy crushed his cigarette out in a dirty saucer and used his foot to kick a milk bottle under the table where he wouldn't trip on it. I watched him and slowly realized I was looking at a different person than the one I thought I knew. I flipped back through the brain trash and found some places where things didn't add up unless you came at them from a different direction. It wasn't all thoughtless trouble-making with him. He did some of his crazy things to make points, to others, he hoped, but maybe it was mainly to himself, which didn't make them worth any less.

I stared at Cy, and he finally looked back at me.

"You want out?" Cy said. "There's the door," and he nodded toward the back porch.

I watched as Cy bent and picked up some of the things he had knocked off the chair. My thoughts were tumbling over each other again, and they stalled at what Cy's plan might mean to Margaret and Grandma. It could turn on them and leave them even more war-damaged than they already were. I tried to think about how they would react to a plan that offered them a chance at the only thing they wanted out of the war—Uncle Jeff safe and sound back home.

I looked at Cy and noticed for the first time the gray hair around his ears and the deep grooves in his forehead. He seemed to have aged years since the last time I looked at him.

"Does it have any chance of working?" I said, and Cy jerked his head around and stared at me.

"Same chance as a snowball in Hell, which is damned slim, but not one hundred percent zero," he said. "Crazy things happen in a war. Soldiers stop shooting and sing Christmas carols together and then go back to shooting each other. Things happen that nobody would ever believe. Hell, yes, the MOP Exchange could become as much a part of war as the Red Cross. Like I said, it isn't likely but I'm going to believe in it until it either works or the roof falls in."

That slim chance would be enough for Margaret and Grandma. It would give them something beyond grieving and waiting, and the magic of it for them would be thinking of Uncle Jeff coming in through the door, and they probably wouldn't dwell much on the details of how it happened. It would give them a kind of hope they didn't have now. I sat for a long time and watched as Cy lit another cigarette and stared out the window through a cloud of smoke. I thought of how he was always blowing smoke in his own way, and how people reacted to it. I thought of how I had reacted to it. I had a funny feeling and got slowly to my feet. It felt like I was someone else, someone a hair taller than the one who had sat down. That's goofy, I know, and it can't be true, but what the hell!

"I'm with you, Cy," I said.

Cy turned and we stood looking at each other, for a long time it seemed. Finally, Cy reached a hand out. "I knew it," he said.

We shook hands and Cy stepped over and put an arm around my shoulders for a just a second. It felt strange, a lot different than a hug from Margaret. There was more bone and muscle to it and other things came with it that I might figure out down the road, or maybe not.

I can't explain why I felt good about what happened. Teaming up with Cy in the MOP Exchange was different than it was with most of his schemes. Usually he came up with them and I stood off to the side and watched, or sometimes joined in at his direction. But this time, I would be a part of the action from start to finish, whatever that might be. It wasn't raising your right hand and getting sworn into the Army or the Navy, but it was putting yourself on the line for something that promised to be exciting and even dangerous—and was part of the war. As soon as those thinking-about-myself things popped up, I forced them down and tried to see "the big picture." I'm not sure I saw it, but I had the feeling Cy had me looking in the right direction.

"I don't know if Grandma will sign the letter," I said.

"She will sign it," Cy said. "There isn't a mother in the country who wouldn't. And your grandmother has been active with that Mothers First outfit that has been giving FDR fits about making cannon fodder out of their sons. She'll sign it in the blink of an eye."

CHAPTER SEVEN

I t turned out Cy was right about Grandma in a way, but it took longer than the blink of an eye. When Cy and I took the letter out to her, she stared at us standing on her back porch like she didn't want to see what she was seeing. Looking back at her, I had the feeling that we might be in for some tough going. Maybe I hadn't taken a good look at Grandma for a while, but she seemed to have suddenly gotten really old. Her face sagged and the bags under her eyes were as big as golf balls. She finally reached out and grabbed me in a grandma hug, and the kitchen smells of her fluttered up my nose like powdered sugar. When she dropped her skinny arms and stepped back, she looked at Cy and said, "Billy, your mother does not want you in the company of this man."

Cy didn't say anything, and the two of them stared at each other. It reminded me of sometimes when Toby and one of Cy's cats get into a staredown. Usually, something has to happen to break it up or it will build until there's an explosion and fur goes flying. I could feel that maybe that was coming with Grandma and Cy, so I said, "Grandma, Cy has a plan to help Uncle Jeff."

That was obviously not something she expected to hear. She sucked in her breath and jerked her head back like she had been hit by a spitball. Nothing happened for a long time, and I know if Grandma's brain had been a machine, we would have heard it clanking and grinding and maybe squeaking. Grandma knew all about Cy. In Oxbow, everyone knows about everyone else, and what they don't know they make up. In Cy's case, it wasn't necessary to make stuff up. Grandma knew it all, and she glared at Cy until he finally shrugged and said, "We're here to help your son, Mrs. Forrest."

"You?" Grandma said. "You and Billy?"

"Yes," Cy said.

It's hard to figure how older people will react to things sometimes. Once Mr. Ruder, the quiet old guy who used to take naps in the station restroom, slapped Orion Homer's face for saying Chief Edwins was a dumb fat ass. Nobody expected Mr. Ruder's slap, especially Orion, who was teed off at the chief over a speeding ticket. So there was no way of knowing what to expect from Grandma, whether she might invite us in and listen to what we had to say or if she might grab a broom and whack Cy over the head and lock me in her pantry and call my mother.

"You need to listen to Cy's plan," I said, and Grandma turned and looked at me.

"What kind of awful trouble are you getting my grandson into?" she said, turning back to Cy.

"It's okay, Grandma," I said. "It might get Uncle Jeff home."

That must have been the right thing to say, because Grandma stared at us some more and finally stepped aside and motioned for us to come into the house. Once we sat down at the kitchen table, Cy put his hat on his knee and started talking, looking Grandma in the eye so she had to look back at him.

"This is about mothers," Cy said. Then he explained the whole MOP Exchange thing, especially how if Mrs. Roosevelt got involved, there was a chance it would work. Grandma listened with her wrinkled face in a tight scowl and her shoulders slumped over. But the longer Cy talked, the straighter her back got and by the time he stopped, she was sitting up like she was posing for a portrait. I imagine she was thinking about Uncle Jeff walking in through the kitchen door and giving her a big hug. She blinked and stared at Cy.

"Mrs. Roosevelt has sons in the war," she said.

Cy nodded.

"I have no time for her husband—that damned FDR—but Eleanor is different."

I had never heard Grandma swear before and it surprised me.

Cy nodded at her again.

"Eleanor gets things done. I like that," Grandma said.

"If she will help us, this has a chance," Cy said.

"It's just so crazy," Grandma said. "Even what you are calling it— MOP Exchange!"

"It's a symbol of power, don't you think—mothers with mops?" Cy said. "I don't think anyone is going to laugh at Mothers Of Prisoners."

Grandma gave Cy a doubtful look. "It is still crazy," she said.

"War is crazy," Cy said.

Grandma's head machine went into its grinding and clunking again and she stared at Cy so hard and for so long that he squirmed in his chair and shot me a glance. I shrugged and looked back at Grandma as a tiny smile turned up the corners of her mouth.

"Mothers," she said. "I am a Christian lady who does not question the Lord. But I have never understood how mothers must send their sons to die in the name of God, or what our leaders, like FDR, tell us is in the name of God."

Cy looked at her, and it was like some little thing flashed between them, a tiny spark that wasn't going to do any harm but wasn't going anywhere either.

"If God were a woman, war wouldn't be happening," Cy said, and he gave Grandma a weak smile.

I have seen a thousand expressions on Grandma's face, but I had never seen the one that came up then. I don't know how you could possibly combine outrage and delight on the same face, but Grandma did it, and she turned so Cy could see it, and maybe try to figure out what it meant.

Grandma ended up signing the letter, and she even warmed up to Cy a little more when she found out he liked cats. Grandma always had lots of cats around and the only time I ever heard Grandpa say "goddamn" was when he tripped over a cat in the milk house and spilled a full pail of milk.

Cy told Grandma that while we were waiting for an answer from Mrs. Roosevelt, we would be "separating" a German soldier from the Army's custody and holding him in readiness for the exchange.

"Timing will be important," Cy said. "We've got to get the trade going before the Army gets all bothered about a missing prisoner."

Grandma's doubts seemed to grow as Cy talked and by the time we left, she was shaking her head and rolling her eyes some. But it was obvious she wanted the MOP Exchange to work.

"It's so outrageous, it just might succeed," she said. "Mothers could do it."

"We'll never know unless we try," Cy said, and he stuck out his hand. Grandma hesitated and looked at him. Then, she slowly reached out and they shook hands. I thought about doing the same, but it didn't seem right to be shaking hands with your grandmother. I gave her a little peck on her wrinkled cheek and she grabbed me in a hug that was pretty strong for an old lady. Cy said it was very important that Grandma not tell anyone about our plan. "Not even your family," he said, and I wondered about Grandma not telling my mother because they seem to talk about everything. Grandma looked at Cy and nodded, and then she stood on the porch and watched as we left and headed toward the post office.

"Interesting old dame," Cy said.

CHAPTER EIGHT

As we waited to hear from Mrs. Roosevelt, a routine was settling in with the prisoners. The Army brought some of them over to work at the pea factory every day, but what was more interesting was that farmers were going to the camp and picking up a prisoner or two to help put up hay, or harvest peas or do other farm stuff. That meant that most days there were Nazi prisoners scattered all over the county, like a shadowy occupation force with no force.

Most of the time, this worked pretty well, according to the farmers who stopped at the station. They say the prisoners were mostly cheerful and polite and did what they were told, though telling them can be a problem if they don't understand English, and most of them didn't. One farmer said it's a funny feeling to pass the pot roast to someone at your dinner table and realize just weeks ago, he was killing your relatives and friends.

Then there were some prisoners who are real Nazis, like the dead one under the rock pile out on the Borowski farm. Nobody is supposed to know about it, of course, but everyone does. Dustin Kolb was the first one to tell me about it, and he said he was right there to see it, so I believe him. I hadn't seen much of Dustin this summer. I knew he had been helping out at his Uncle Manny Borowski's farm and I saw him ride by one day in his uncle's pickup. Then, shortly after the prisoners got here, he suddenly showed up at the station one afternoon and stood around drinking a Coke, not saying much and acting strange, like he had a problem.

Dustin and I have known each other for a long time, in school and sometimes down at the river, but we're not what you would call "bosom buddies," where we tell each other everything and do a lot of things together. I would never talk to him about Margaret or Uncle Jeff, for example, and he never said anything about anyone in his family. We can talk about the river or fishing or maybe something about school, but that was it. As he fidgeted around the pop cooler, it didn't seem like Dustin wanted to talk about anything, so I just sat on the station stool and watched the pumps and waited. Then, Dustin suddenly made a noise in his throat and looked at me with an odd expression.

"Billy, I've got to tell you something," he said, working his mouth like he needed to spit out a plum pit. I had no idea what was coming, but he had this desperate look, like he might either explode or bust out crying, so I just looked at him and didn't say anything.

"They killed a prisoner and buried him under rocks at my uncle's farm," Dustin said in a rush of words with no spaces between them.

I stared at him and Dustin stared back. Then, he started talking like a knot in his vocal chords had suddenly come untied. He said when the farmers first picked up prisoners to help with field work, his uncle and some neighbors went to the camp and got a prisoner to help put up hay and castrate a bunch of pigs. When they got the prisoner out to the farm, Dustin said, he strutted around like a rooster and acted like he was too good to do farm work and even gave the Hitler salute to Mrs. Borowski hanging up her washing in the back yard.

"The farmers, especially one whose brother was killed at Normandy, started getting mad. Then, when they were castrating the pigs, someone saw a swastika tattooed on the prisoner's leg, and without even talking about it, they nodded to each other and grabbed the prisoner and started trying to castrate him. They'd been drinking beer all day, and they had a bottle of whiskey for disinfecting the cut pigs and they'd been drinking that, too. When they were struggling to hold the prisoner down and he was fighting like a crazy man, the castrating knife slipped and cut a big artery high up on the prisoner's leg. In just a minute or so, all his blood was in a pool on the barn floor."

Dustin stopped talking like he'd hit a wall. He was breathing hard and shaking his head.

"Sorry, Billy," he said between gasps. "I had to tell somebody."

And I guess he had to tell more, because after he caught his breath, he went on talking, slower and stopping between words. He said his uncle and the others dragged the dead prisoner out of the barn, loaded him onto a lumber wagon, and hauled him to the end of a pasture where they buried him and piled big rocks on top of the grave.

"I didn't want to be there," Dustin said, "but once it got going, it was just too late for me to run off."

I stared at him in disbelief. I didn't want to hear any more, but Dustin wasn't done.

"The whole thing sobered them up some and they swore everyone to secrecy, including me," Dustin said. "But it's like having a rat in your chest. I couldn't tell my mother or anyone else. But I had to tell someone or go crazy."

Dustin was rubbing his arms and rocking back and forth. "You won't tell anybody, will you, Billy?" he said, looking at me like I could either save his life or ruin it forever. I couldn't stop staring at Dustin. He looked like somebody who had just kicked a cat and was sorry about it and needed to be told it was okay. I tried to sort through the images of the Nazi's blood running out on the barn floor, and then of his bloodless body under the rocks.

"Uncle Manny told the Army the prisoner ran off toward the swamp," Dustin said, "and they said for everyone to keep their mouths shut because they didn't want to scare people, and the prisoner would probably come back to the camp in a day or so and if he didn't they would find him."

Dustin seemed like a different person after he unloaded his story, relieved and grateful to me for listening. He offered to buy me a Coke and was smiling when he left. I felt dumped on, and then I thought how Dustin had been in a bloody part of the war in a way I hadn't and I felt a pang of jealousy. He had even been in on killing a Nazi, and when I thought about how that would make him a hero in Margaret's eyes, the jealousy bumped up a notch. Dustin hadn't sworn me to secrecy, so later, I guess for some of the same reasons Dustin had to tell someone, I told Cy. He listened and nodded like he already knew some of what I was telling him.

"The Borowskis have some Jewish stuff in their background," he said. "They don't talk about it, but they brought some papers to me once that showed they left Germany ahead of some nastiness about hidden money. I helped them straighten it out with the tax guys."

"Money and blood," Cy said, "It's the great recipe for war, but who would ever think of it playing out in Borowski's barn?" He shook his head. "I've got a feeling we might be in for more of that craziness."

I looked at him and waited because I can tell when there is more to come.

"We're sitting on a powder keg, Billy," Cy said. "People think they can handle having their sons' killers at their dinner tables, but they can't, really. It's asking too much, like trying to get a bitch dog to give up her pups. It just goes against nature."

There was a lot of whispering about what went on out at the Borowski farm. Then it got to be more than whispering. Within days, everyone knew about the dead Nazi, even Margaret, it turned out. She probably heard talk up at Harry Meyer's store. Cy said there is a path worn into the grass along the edge of Borowski's hay field where people have been going out to look at the pile of rocks over the Nazi's grave. Margaret must have walked the path one afternoon because Mr. Borowski found her sitting on the rocks. When he brought her home, he told Mrs. Zanders he had a hard time convincing Margaret she couldn't stay out there. Mrs. Zanders told my mother that Margaret was getting more confused by the day, mumbling one minute about killing a Nazi and saying in the next minute that she was leaving for Minneapolis to help with the war.

The Army had to know all about the dead Nazi but nothing official was ever said. There was only a little story in the *News-Banner*, obviously from an Army press release, saying a prisoner thought to be missing had actually been transferred to a different POW camp and all prisoners were accounted for.

I have been waiting for Dustin to show up so I can ask him what's going on, but I had a feeling he was staying away from me. Maybe he feels guilty about telling me or maybe he blames me for everyone knowing. If he does show up, I hope Margaret is not around because it could come out that he was in on killing a Nazi and I could imagine Margaret grabbing Dustin in one of her powerful hugs and that just wasn't something I wanted to see.

Andy Stevenson, a farmer out on the rocky hills north of town, said he had to take a prisoner back to the camp in the middle of the day or he would have killed him with a post-hole digger. They were building a fence across the end of his pasture, Mr. Stevenson said, and when he told the prisoner to dig a hole, the prisoner threw the post-hole digger down and said something in German that Mr. Stevenson understood to mean he should screw himself.

Another farmer listening in nodded and said, "I heard one of them went after Delbert Ruepel's wife. Had her cornered in the silo when Dell heard her yelling."

"Ain't no corners in a silo," another farmer said.

The farmers had all laughed, and Mr. Stevenson said, "Some of the Krauts are okay, but that son-of-a-bitch I had was as Nazi as a goddamn swastika and he thought he was really hot shit."

"Yeah, there's a big difference in them," a farmer said. "Some got that 'super-race' thing and others don't."

"I took that Nazi back and told the guards he screwed one of my sheep," Mr. Stevenson said, "the homeliest one in the flock."

The farmers laughed again.

When you think about that kind of thing happening right here in the middle of Oxbow—Nazis acting up and POWs all over the place—it stirs your blood and makes it hard to remember how dull the war was around here before the prisoners came in. No wonder I had felt so left out.

I look back on that long, miserable stretch before the prisoners got here as almost a prison sentence. In a way, that's what it was, a punishment for being too young. All the older guys like Uncle Jeff had long since gone off to the Army or Navy, and everyone talked about what heroes they were. I would have signed up in a minute, but I know they would have laughed my skinny ass out of the recruiting office. Why couldn't I have been born a few years earlier, and not in boring old Oxbow?

It hasn't always been so dead around here. The old gummers up on the courthouse bench are forever yakking about how it was once a logging town with whores and drunks and fistfights and even shootings. They say lumberjacks drowned trying to break up logjams and got crushed by falling trees, and sometimes just wandered off into the deep snow and never came back. The geezers say some of their ghosts are still moaning around out in Windigo Swamp, and then they peek out from under their shaggy eyebrows to see if anyone is listening. I don't hang around up there anymore. Kid stuff.

After the Japs bombed Pearl Harbor, I thought there might finally be some excitement around here. The way people huddled over their radios, shaking their heads and talking about the World War, you'd think bullets would be flying everywhere, even in Oxbow—it may be out in the sticks, but it is part of the world. But all the fighting and killing was way off in places nobody ever heard of, and there might as well not have been a war, for all the good it was doing around this hick town.

The one time it looked like I might get into something related to the war, it turned into a big embarrassment and I've been trying to forget it ever since. It was supposed to have been a big deal, me flying as an Air Cadet in Huskie Olson's little yellow Piper Cub to drop flour sack bombs on Oxbow in a mock bombing raid. I got pretty excited about it and couldn't think of much else in the days before it happened. I had never been up in an airplane and just the thought of it and then doing something war-related was enough to even take my mind off Margaret for a time.

But almost from the minute I climbed into the cockpit and Huskie gunned the motor and we bounced up off the hayfield airport, things began to turn bad. When we started diving and climbing so I could toss the flour sacks out over town, my guts suddenly went out of control. I tried to use the puke bag Huskie handed me, but the wind whipped it away and the inside of Huskie's airplane turned into something I don't even want to think about. I helped Huskie wash it out about fifteen times after we landed but it was like trying to clean Toby up after he tangles with a skunk. Huskie tried to make me feel better by saying it was just something that happened and next time I shouldn't eat a big breakfast before a mission.

Some of the older Boy Scouts found out about it and spread the word so everybody knew. I'm glad I never joined the Boy Scouts. I almost did once. I went to one of their meetings at the library and Randy Kerstin, the troop leader, followed me into the boys' room and said I had to pull down my pants and show him I had what it took to be a Boy Scout. I had been so shocked that the only thing I could think to do was turn and run. Later, I told Cy what had happened and he said Randy was a "homo." I knew what that meant, of course, though I didn't really understand much about it. I was shook up and Cy knew it and said I should calm down because homosexuality was a common thing and had been around forever and is just something folks had to deal with in their own way. "It's one of those weird facts of life," he said, "and it probably never will get totally figured out."

I'll never figure it out, I know that. I tried, and I think that is about the last time I went to the Bible looking for answers. I found a story in Genesis about Lot offering his virgin daughters to a bunch of ruffians so they would leave some visiting homosexuals alone, and that just left me more confused than ever. When you start going backwards with what little you know about something, you might as well give it up.

CHAPTER NINE

There has been no word from Mrs. Roosevelt yet, but Cy says she's obviously got a lot of things going on and we could hear from her most any time. I thought maybe we should get our trade prisoner ready, but Cy said there was no hurry. It would just be a problem to take care of him, Cy said, and added that he hadn't figured out all the prisoner trade details yet. Waiting is tough. Every day, I think we'll hear from Mrs. Roosevelt, but there is nothing.

After one of those downer days, Cy showed up at the station late in the afternoon and said we should go to the Bund meeting over in Almira because it was a war-related thing I could get into, and he could get some free rotgut whiskey. I had heard about the Almira Bund, mostly that it was a bunch of German farmers who thought Hitler was the cat's ass when he first got going. I hadn't heard anything about it lately, but, like Cy said, going to one of their meetings would be more or less war-related so it sounded interesting.

Augie Kunzie agreed to drive us after Cy told him the Bund showed stag movies with the real thing. Cy said he would pay for the gas, which Augie said was no more than right, considering Cy was a millionaire. Cy isn't a millionaire, but everyone says his father had a lot of money and before he died, he put it in trust or something to keep Cy from getting at it. Cy talked about it one day at the station when some radio news guy said the stock market took a big jump.

"I made thousands today, but I have to die to get it," Cy had said. I didn't understand it, but Cy said his old man wanted to control his money even after he died. "I'm going to be the richest guy in the cemetery."

Everyone in Oxbow pretty much knows about the Butler money and how Cy can't get at it except for some kind of a monthly allowance, so there is a lot of talk about what will be in Cy's will. I once heard him say

63

he might fix it as a joke, so his family money goes to the women who ran around smashing up saloons during Prohibition. The "booze busters," he called them, and then he said that once he died, he wouldn't be drinking so saloons would not be important.

Cy said the German Bund had been a really big deal in places like Minneapolis and Milwaukee and Chicago before the war and that was when it got going in little hick places like Almira. "Lots of kraut heads around," Cy said, "and they thought their fatherland was hot shit, even after that mustachioed dingbat took it over."

He says most of the Bund yahoos shut their mouths and crawled into their holes after Pearl Harbor, and even their hero Charles Lindbergh changed his tune. All I know about Lindbergh is he flew across the ocean in that little tin airplane and that made him a big hero, and then his baby son got kidnapped and killed. Cy said Lindbergh got a medal from Hitler and after that, he went around giving speeches that the Germans were on the right track and we should stay out of it and let them go ahead with what they were doing, including slaughtering Jews, I guess.

It's mostly Germans living around Almira, and Cy says a few of them have kept the Bund going long after it died out everywhere else. They still have meetings and show dirty movies to raise money, he said, and they still think Hitler is going to win. "Shit for brains," he said.

The hot night air blowing in through the windows of Augie's car smelled of hayfields and cow yards, and now and then, you could see a yellow light from a farmhouse slipping past. The farmers were probably sitting around in their undershirts listening to the radio or reading Western pulps, and their wives were maybe darning up socks or writing letters to someone in the Army. Cy says farmers are dumb but harmless. He said somebody named Mencken wrote that farmers were so dumb they should only be fed one meal a day, and Cy says he agrees with that. I don't think farmers are dumb—some maybe, but not all. Grandpa wasn't dumb.

Cy was slumped down in the passenger seat taking slugs out of his bottle so his bowler hat went up and down like a big, black fishing bobber, and Augie was hunched over, doing the war-time speed limit of thirty-five and gripping the steering wheel like we were going about a hundred. I could see their side profiles against the yellow glow of the headlights—

Cy's face angling back from his pointed nose, and Augie's round mug bulging like a jack-o-lantern. In the dark cocoon of the car, we could have been a bomber crew on a night raid over Germany. But the cow yard smells and the lighted farmhouse windows would have shucked that out of your imagination in a hurry.

The Schmidt farm is a mile or so out of Almira, down a gravel road so rough it made Augie's car rattle like a bucket of rocks. Dust came boiling up from the floorboards and rolling in through the windows until it was like we were swimming in dirt. Cy got into a coughing fit that turned into a cussing fit. Cough. Goddamn! Cough. Goddamn! It went on and on until Cy finally got it drowned with gulps of whiskey. When we got to the farm, a fat guy in bib overalls and a black shirt waved a pitchfork and stopped us at the end of the driveway. He stuck his head in the window and shined a flashlight in my face. "No damned kids," he said.

Cy leaned across Augie's big belly and said, "He's here to visit the Schmidt girls."

It beats me how Cy came up with that one. I knew the Schmidt girls from high school. They ride in on the Almira bus that hauls about a hundred kids and they are as fat and homely as bulldogs. I wouldn't visit them in a million years. The guy with the pitchfork poked his flashlight into my face again and muttered something and then waved us on.

"Dumb bastard," Cy said.

"Well, it ain't any place for a kid," Augie said.

I looked at the back of Augie's fat neck and wanted to smack one of his big ears.

"Oh, hell," Cy said. "Billy never makes trouble. Right, Billy?"

I wanted to bop Cy, too.

Cy tipped his bottle up again and offered it to Augie. Augie shook his head and told Cy not to get drunk and pass out somewhere. "You ain't around when I'm ready to go, I'm leaving you," he said.

"Got to be drunk to mix with these assholes," Cy said.

Cy wasn't as drunk as he is sometimes, but he was on the way. He once told me he drank so he wouldn't get a tapeworm. He said tapeworms can't live in whiskey, and I wondered at the time if maybe I should be drinking whiskey occasionally for the same reason.

The driveway was like a black tunnel under thick arching tree branches with cars parked along both sides. Augie stopped and switched off the headlights and it was suddenly pitch black as we climbed out of the car. I heard Cy grumble that he had gone blind as we felt our way with our feet toward a sliver of yellow light coming through a shed door. Cy stumbled and swore and I heard Augie mumble that he should have stayed home. There was the strong smell of pig shit, and Cy snorted and said, "Some of these guys need a bath."

At the shed door, a big, heavy guy with sagging eyelids and ragged whiskers stopped us. He wore a swastika arm band and a revolver around his thick waist and big boots that would be just right for stomping someone into the pig shit. I don't know why that thought about stomping came popping up, but it did, and I suddenly started feeling that maybe Augie was right and we never should have come to the Bund meeting. The guy at the door scowled and said we were too early for the movies and we would have to wait outside until the official Bund meeting was over.

Cy stepped up to the guard until their faces were only inches apart. "We've got to get in now," Cy said. "We are on the program."

The guard frowned and said, "Who the hell are you?"

Cy pushed his face even closer to the guard's. "Cyrus M. Butler, attorney at law. I'm here to give legal advice on taking over the POW camp in Oxbow. Now goddamnit, get out of the way."

The man with the revolver took a quick step back and stared at Cy. His eyes narrowed and then slowly got owl big. "What? When?" he stammered.

"Soon," Cy said "These guys are in on it," and he waved his hand at Augie and me.

The guy at the door did more of his big-eyed staring and finally focused on me.

"Hitler Youth," Cy said and then he pointed at Augie and said, "Undercover Gestapo."

The guard took another step back and stared some more. Then as a corner of his mouth twitched up, he nodded and raised his arm in a Hitler salute. Cy grinned and returned the "*Heil!*" as we walked in through the door.

Inside it was nothing but dark shadows and flickering lantern light and the stink of pigs and burning kerosene. It was like being in a den of loud, shuffling creatures that you couldn't really see, and I felt a sudden urge to turn and run. Then, over the shouting and cackling laughter, a loud voice blared from up in the front near a big, red swastika flag. Next to it, flames from torches flicked out and made weird shadows dance along the dark walls. The flaming hell that Reverend Thorston is always preaching about flashed into my brain and the urge to run got stronger. Then Cy jostled my arm and pointed at the man up in front. "He's reading from Hitler's book," he shouted in my ear.

I tried to listen: "... *the will of the Almighty ... defending myself against the Jew ... work of the Lord.*"

There was a shout of *"Sieg heil!"* from somewhere, and the man up on the haybales talked louder; "... our *Fuehrer* has written of the Jew ... satanic joy in his face ... black-haired Jewish youth lurks in wait for the unsuspecting girl ... defiles with his blood ... stealing her from her people."

The rumble of voices got louder and I could pick up bits and pieces of the shouting. "Enough goddamn talk, let's get..."

"Roosevelt, phony bast..."

"Jew parasites!"

"It's all lost unless we..."

"The money! They got the..."

"America first, goddammit!"

It seemed like everyone was shouting or talking and nobody was listening. I lost track of Cy, and then mixed in with the other loud voices, I heard his. It was coming from near the back of the shed and he was shouting something over and over. Then finally I could make out the words: "Lindbergh is an asshole! Lindbergh is an asshole!"

I could just barely see Cy in the smoky shadows. He was standing on a stack of haybales, waving his arms and holding a whiskey bottle in one hand and a cigarette in the other. In the flickering torch light, he was like a crazy, dangling Halloween figure, and I knew that if he didn't get down and shut up, there would be trouble. Some of the men turned to look at Cy and a few edged closer to where he stood. Cy's voice got louder, and someone nearby shouted, "Get that son-of-a-bitch!" There was more shouting as Cy kept up his chant, and suddenly arms reached up and jerked him down. His bowler went flying and I heard him whoop and cackle his crazy laugh. Then there was grunting and swearing and thuds, and I couldn't hear or see anything more of him. When I looked around, some of the men looked back at me and one of them grinned and said, "Your old pal has a big mouth."

"Maybe the kid needs a dose of that," someone said.

"He's harmless," another voice said, and I recognized Mr. Schmidt, who stops at the station to gas up his Chevy flatbed with the pig crates on the back. His black eyebrows were pulled together over the top of his big nose and he held a thick, wooden cattle prod, like a baseball bat, in his hands. He glared at me and said, "Bad place for you, boy." He pointed the prod at the door and his gravel voice got louder. "You get the hell out of here and don't come back!"

I wanted to run, but that was impossible in the cluttered darkness and the jostling of the crowd. I turned and moved toward the door, and some of the other faces fading in and out of the shadowy light seemed familiar. Maybe I had also seen them at the station. Then I saw one I knew for sure. It was Deputy Blasser, his big head sticking out like a dog sniffing the air and his hand resting on his holster like always. I ducked behind some haybales, so he wouldn't see me and was just past him when the voice up in front started again, shouting about blowing up a Jew store.

The men around me turned to listen and I eased toward the back of the shed. In the darkness, I saw someone or something crawling toward the door and I finally figured out it was Cy. I walked toward him and then followed as he struggled along the dirt floor on his hands and knees. He was lurching against the shed wall and falling on his face and then crawling on until finally we were outside in the tall grass off to the side of the door. He was spitting blood and gagging, and in the shadows, he looked like a strange wounded critter that had come up out of the weeds. He shook his head, and I felt him looking at me even though I couldn't see his eyes.

"War's a bitch, Billy," he said, and he groaned and choked and it sounded like he tried to laugh. I didn't know what to do, so I just stood there looking down at him in the dim light from the shed door. He moaned and swore and I reached down to help him as he tried to get up.

"My hat!" he said suddenly. "The bastards got my hat!"

He spit more blood and fell back into the grass.

"Billy, you got to get my hat."

I didn't want to go back into the shed. I might end up as bloody as Cy. But I did it. Don't ask me why, except I felt sorry for Cy and I knew that getting his hat back would make him feel better. I stumbled along the back wall, trying to stay in the deepest shadows, and then groped around until I finally found Cy's battered bowler under a piece of rusty machinery. On the way back to the door, someone suddenly stepped in front of me. I looked up to see Deputy Blasser's scowling puss.

"Billy," he said, "what the hell are you doing here?"

I stared at him.

"That goddamned Butler brought you, didn't he?" Blasser said, glancing down at Cy's hat. "Hang with that crazy old soak and you're in for big trouble," Blasser said, and he reached out and shoved me toward the door. "Get home to your hot-pants aunt," he said. "She needs a little pimp like you."

Blasser's shove at least got me away from him, which was a relief. I didn't even have time to think about how someday I would smash his stupid face. It was more of a relief to get out of the stinking shed and find Cy and get him loaded into Augie's car so we could leave. Augie wanted to stay for the stag movies, but Cy told him he thought he had a broken rib and had to get home to put ice on it.

He also said there had been a mix-up with the Bund movies and Snow White was not going to "take on the seven dwarfs"—she was just going to "wait around for the prince." I don't think Augie believed him, but we left anyway. On the way home, Augie said if Cy puked in the car, he would stop and throw him out.

Cy groaned. "No danger, Augie," he said, "I don't want to lose any Bund whiskey, as bad as it is."

"That was really a stupid thing you did," Augie said.

"Think so?"

"Totally dumb."

"Just having a little fun," Cy said and then he laughed his weird barking laugh that makes his cats stare at him.

"Lindbergh?" Augie said, "Why him?"

"Because he's an asshole."

"He's a national hero."

"He's a Nazi-loving, Jew-hating jerk."

Then Augie said that Cy wasn't as goddamned smart as he thought he was, no matter how much schooling he had; Cy said there wasn't enough schooling to help Augie and Augie said Cy was nothing but a drunken bum staggering around town carrying books and newspapers and thinking he was smarter than everyone else.

"Hell, I *am* smarter," Cy said.

"Yeah, you're smart all right. Twenty years at the university and all you learned was how to be a drunk.

"That's no way to speak to an honorable attorney."

Cy told Augie to just drive the car and keep his stupid mouth shut, and they went on like that most of the way back to Oxbow.

And that's the way the night ended—with Cy punching his bowler back into shape and feeling around inside his mouth to count his teeth; Augie hunched over the steering wheel and yelling at Cy not to get blood on the upholstery; and me in the back seat thinking that if the Bund meeting was part of the war, it was a pretty stupid part. Maybe if I'd been beat up like Cy, I would have felt better about it.

It was after midnight when Augie finally dropped me off at the station. I walked home and just made it over that creaky fifth stair step when my mother nailed me. I should have used the porch roof.

"Billy, where in the world have you been?" she asked.

I knew she wouldn't believe anything I said but I had to say something. "Fishing," I finally said, which wasn't a totally stupid answer because sometimes I go to the river at night and fish for the big brown trout that come out from under the banks after dark to slurp mayflies and June bugs. I've brought home some big ones and my mother has made some really good baked trout dinners, so she was probably running some of that through her head and wondering if there was a slim chance I could be telling the truth. Dealing with my mother since my dad left has been like trying to get along with an owl, and this was just another dumb part of that, me standing in the dark stairway like a cornered rat and her at the bottom trying to keep her baby on the straight and narrow. I'm taller than she is and she still treats me like I'm sucking my thumb and grabbing at her skirt.

"I didn't catch any fish," I said, but she didn't answer.

I could hear the clock in the hall and I swear the ticks were getting farther apart and louder.

"What is that awful smell?" my mother finally said.

My clothes stank from being in Mr. Schmidt's pig shed, and for a second, I didn't know what to say.

"I had a campfire," I said.

More time went by and I wondered if we would stand there in the dark all night. Finally, my mother said we would talk in the morning, and I staggered up the stairs and fell asleep before my head hit the pillow.

CHAPTER TEN

The morning after the Bund meeting, I snuck out of the house early, before my mother was up—I didn't need any more of her third degree. It was going to be a long day: Cliff was off visiting his wife's relatives, so I had to work both shifts and wouldn't get back home until late. By then, my mother might have forgotten some of what she wanted to rag on me about. That happens, but not often.

Down at the station, the trash barrel had been tipped over and a ratty-looking dog was sniffing through the garbage. It ran off when I yelled at it, and I got the shovel and picked up all the spilled stuff. I had seen the dog before, all bones and matted hair and eyes that are always looking for a way out. I think it's a stray from the pack that hangs around the back of Pickert's junkyard. The Pickert boys throw rocks at the mutts and chase them through the weeds and junked cars.

Once when I was over there, they invited me to join in a game of "rock-a-dog." Vernon Pickert said that if you hit a dog with a rock so it yipped, you got one point and if it howled, you got two points. It sounded mean to me, even if the dogs were strays. I hadn't joined in, but I had watched. Most of the time the dogs stayed out of sight and nothing much happened except for the Pickerts arguing over the difference between a yip and a howl. I told Cy about it once and he said if the Pickerts' meanness had been stronger down through the ages, wolves never would have hung around campfires until they got tame and turned into dogs. I remember that bouncing around in the brain trash for three or four days and making me think of Toby in a different way.

I could do the station routine with my eyes closed—unlock the door; turn on the pumps; set out the oil racks and tire displays; sweep out the station and the restroom; fill the pop cooler; wash out the chamois skin and run it through the wringer; and get out a clean windshield rag. Then maybe hose off the drive or sweep around the grease pit. Usually, I get interrupted by somebody coming in for cigarettes or chewing tobacco, or to use the restroom.

For a long time, Old Man Ruder would shuffle across the back lot every morning and go into the restroom to take a nap. I know that's what he was doing because one day I forgot he was in there and opened the door. He was sitting on the toilet with his eyes shut and his head hanging and he didn't even have his pants down. But Mrs. Ruder came looking for him one morning and when she asked if I had seen him, I pointed at the restroom door. I've thought since that maybe for Mr. Ruder's sake, I should not have done that, but what could I do? I haven't seen anything of Mr. Ruder since, so either he's staying home or has found a new place to nap. I miss him. He was always smiling and he tried to tell me a joke every morning, the same one, about two dogs hooked up in front of a hotel and a drunk pointing at them and saying the hotel's sign had fallen down.

Trucks rumbled past on their way to the creamery and the pea factory, and three or four cars turned the corner toward downtown. A few customers stopped in for gas and somebody dropped off a tire repair and the day just started taking over, so I didn't have time to think about last night's Bund meeting. It was afternoon when I finally saw Cy coming down the sidewalk. He was walking slowly and limping, and when he got closer, I could see dark bruises on his face and black circles around his eyes. He was wearing his usual khaki pants and frayed dress shirt with the cuffs turned up, and his bowler hat, of course.

"Billy," he said, "You got my Purple Heart ready?"

Cy hobbled into the station and unfolded his newspaper. He groaned and swore as he hoisted himself up onto the pop cooler. His bowler was tipped back, to keep it off his bruised forehead, I suppose, and there was a cut on his mouth that made his face lopsided.

"Why did you do it?" I said.

"I presume you are inquiring about my scintillating performance of last evening?"

I nodded.

"Damn, you're worse than that stupid Augie."

I didn't like being compared to Augie, but I let it go.

"They might have killed you," I said.

Cy looked at me. "Yeah, I can see the headline: 'Local Attorney Stomped to Death in Almira Pig Shit.' Oh, they wouldn't say shit, would they, Billy. They'd say 'Pig Shed'." He shook his head and sighed. "War makes us all goofy!"

That obviously didn't explain why Cy had acted so stupid last night, but it was apparently all he was going to say. I thought of some of the things he had said when he got mad at me just before we set up the MOP Exchange—about rattling cages and getting people to maybe think a little different about some things. But it didn't seem that any of that fit into what he had done at the Bund meeting. It just seemed like he had opened his big mouth and said, "Come and beat me up." It was one of those times when I wondered just how smart Cy really was and if the MOP scheme might be some totally dumb thing that was going to blow up in our faces.

"Listen to this," Cy said, rattling his newspaper. "Churchill says there could be a victory this summer."

I should have been happy to hear that, but I wasn't. Cy knew that.

"Don't worry, Billy, if this war ends before you get into it, there'll be another. There always is."

Maybe, but it wouldn't be as good as this war with all the chances to get out of Oxbow and get medals and all of that. Cy must have known that because right after Pearl Harbor, he had enlisted in the Navy, even though he was too old. But he was home after a month or so. He said the Navy kicked him out because he got caught in a whorehouse. "The shore patrol didn't bother you if you went into a white whorehouse," Cy said, "but they caught me in a Colored one."

Another time, he said he was afraid of heights and couldn't climb high enough to "trim sails," so you don't know what to believe. Later, I overheard at Stubben's Drug Store that Cy had gotten a "Section Eight" discharge which I know means you're too nutty for the military. I know from listening to people that Cy went to the university when he was young and stayed there on an allowance from his parents' estate until he finally had a law degree. He once told me the university really had kicked him out because he had more credits than the dean. Another time, he said he quit because they took away his canteen of cough medicine.

"Listen to this," Cy said, nodding at his newspaper, "Adolf Hitler's newest terrifying weapon is a jet-propelled bomb larger and faster than anything heretofore revealed that makes pursuing Spitfires appear as gliders'."

Cy shook his head. "Jesus, they'll have rocket bombs landing on little dumps like Oxbow if we don't put an end to this damn soon."

I thought about a rocket bomb landing on Oxbow and wondered how many people it would kill and what would happen if it hit the pea factory and scattered the stack of stinking pea vines all over town.

"The war news is nothing but damn numbers," Cy said. "Here's a story about 1,800 German prisoners taken from the Island of Elba, and another about 300 Jap airplanes shot down off Saipan. They make it sound like it's some kind of a goddamn game."

I remembered back when Cy had said I needed to grow up and stop thinking of war as a sporting event that I was too young to get into. Now he was calling it a game.

"If it isn't a game," he said, "why the hell does everyone keep score? Every damned day, they tell us the number of bombers that drop so many tons of bombs, and in the trenches, they count up the dead so the poor bastards who die or get captured are just numbers."

"Uncle Jeff is more than a number," I said.

"Well, hell yes, to you and Margaret," Cy said, "but to the Army, he is just a number and that's the way it has to be so when the generals light up their cigars and toast each other with cognac back at headquarters, they don't have hundreds of dead young men on their consciences, just the goddamned numbers."

Cy shook his head and I thought maybe he was through ranting, but he wasn't.

"Look at this story," he said, "it's full of numbers: 800 bombers drop 2,000 tons of bombs on Berlin. Berlin, for god's sake! We're talking civilians—women and children, babies. They say there was a funeral plume four miles high. That's what they call it, Billy, a goddamn funeral plume! Jesus H. Christ!"

Cy shook his head and seemed to simmer down some and then he slid down off the pop cooler and said he was going to the pool hall to get treatment for his war wounds.

"When do you think we'll hear from Mrs. Roosevelt?" I asked.

Cy paused and looked at me. "I don't know, but we've got to get this thing going while the mothers are still pissed off enough to take on the generals."

"Maybe we should think about getting a Kraut prisoner lined up and ready."

"Not until we've got a plan in place. It would just be a big problem."

Cy touched the bruise on his forehead and winced. "Keep a sharp eye out for spies," he said, and limped off down the street. I was thinking about how long we might have to wait to hear from Mrs. Roosevelt when an old Chevy drove up to the pumps. I had just turned the drive lights on because it was starting to get dark, and I could see two women sitting in the front seat. They didn't look like women from around Oxbow—all made up and wearing sleek clothes, and I glanced down to see the car had Minnesota plates so they were probably from Minneapolis. The woman in the driver's seat looked at me through the open window and smiled a smile that seemed all teeth.

"We're here!" she said. "Whoopee!" and she pumped her fist in the air.

I stood in the station door staring at them until the driver said, "Come on, Handsome, do us up." There was a burst of laughter from the car and I stepped over to the Chevy and wiped at the bugs on the windshield. The women watched and I tried not to look at them or at their clothes, which draped over their bodies in a way that seemed to show more than was covered.

"Check the oil," the driver said. "My boyfriend says always check the oil, and the battery, check that too. Check everything."

"Yeah," a voice from inside the car said. "Check this," and then there was more laughing.

I filled the gas tank and put in a quart of oil, and the women sat in the car and watched. They lit cigarettes, which is not a good idea when you are having your gas tank filled but I didn't say anything, and then the driver said, "The battery, Handsome. Did you check that?"

The battery on old Chevys is under the floorboards just in front of the driver's seat and you have to lift up the floor mat and pry out a wooden cover to get at it. I told the driver that the battery was under her feet and she would have to get out for me to check it. She gave me a look, and then her toothy smile. Then she flung the door open and let one of her legs flop out onto the running board.

"Check this, Handsome," she said and stuck her leg out even farther. The women looked at each other and laughed loudly enough to be heard across town. I got the battery kit from where it sits by the pumps and bent down by the driver's door, trying not to touch the woman's legs or even look at them as I crouched between them. Her silky blue skirt was up over her knees and she jerked it even higher. "Is this in your way, Handsome?" she said and then they were back laughing again.

By the time I got the lid off the battery case and unscrewed the caps to fill the cells with water, I was soaked with sweat and could feel that my face was as red as the Standard Oil gas pumps.

"Oh, look," the driver said, "Handsome is blushing like a virgin. Hey, Handsome, are you a virgin?"

I turned away and didn't look at them.

"We could fix that," one of the women said and there was more of their dumb laughter. The driver fished around in a big purse and paid me for the gas and oil and then she handed me a dollar bill and said it was for "services rendered." I stared at the dollar like it might burn my hand. "It's a tip, Handsome," the driver said, "They're big in our business." Then she laughed and asked, "Where's the POW camp?"

I pointed in the direction of the camp and then it dawned on me that the women must be prostitutes. I looked down at the dollar bill again and thought how I would enjoy telling Cy that two Minneapolis whores had paid me a dollar and called me "Handsome." Later, when I actually did tell him, he laughed his jerky laugh and said I should keep the dollar as a souvenir of being ahead of the oldest game in the world. To me, it had just been a couple of women making fun of me, and I tried to forget it but kept remembering the white legs spread wide, so I could get at the battery.

At closing time, I locked up and walked down to the river. It had been a long, hot day at the station, and that thing with the prostitutes had left me even hotter and sweatier than usual. I needed to cool off. Some of the Pickert boys were at the swimming hole, hanging on the tire swing and making lots of noise like they always do.

"Hey, Billy," one shouted, "You bring any beer?"

"Billy, look at this boner," another yelled.

They're always talking about boners, and I know sometimes the Pickert boys and some of the other guys get together in a circle to see who can get off first. They have yelled at me to join them, but I haven't and I never will. I tried to figure out some of this once by looking in the Bible like Reverend Thorston said to do when you are looking for answers. I found a really strange story about a guy named Onan who was supposed to impregnate his dead brother's wife but "spilled his seed on the ground," which made God so mad He killed Onan. I did not know where to go with that at the time, and still don't.

Bats were zigzagging over the water, and from way back in the woods, a barred owl hooted. Sometimes if you imitate their call, they will come and perch over your head and peer down like stern teachers, and other times they will argue with each other like crabby drunks. Toby usually puts an end to it by barking.

Over across the river, the whip-poor-wills were having at it and night was easing up out of the swamp and creeping toward the yellow street lights of Oxbow. Sometimes in the middle of this, it's almost like you can hear the shuffling of day and night creatures coming and going, and your backbone does a little shiver-dance, like it doesn't know whether to join the ones coming or the ones going.

There was no sign of the Johnson girls, so I shucked off my clothes and waded out into the river. The water was cold and smooth and I let the current carry me through the swimming hole and down over the gravel bar. I floated on my back with my face half-covered with water so the stars looked like they were swimming, and I could feel the river holding me up and pulling me down at the same time. Maybe that's what it's like when you drown—the thing that's holding you up slacks off and the thing that's pulling you down takes over and that's it.

The stars seemed to get dimmer as I floated along, and when I took a breath, I got more water than air, and suddenly, I had to flail my arms and kick my legs to get my head up! I felt stupid, standing there gasping in waist-deep water that was no more dangerous than a mud puddle. I almost had to laugh.

I was pulling my clothes on when Deputy Blasser's squad car coasted down the grassy slope with the motor and the headlights off. He always sneaks in that way, quiet as a damned coyote. We never know he's there, right on top of us, until suddenly the whole river is flooded bright yellow when he clicks on his headlights. As usual, there was a lot of yelling and splashing as the Pickert boys dove into the water. Sometimes Blasser's headlights catch the Johnson girls and there is even more yelling and screaming and diving. Blasser shouts pretty much the same thing every time he shows up: "You juvenile assholes can't swim here!"

There's been a "No Swimming" sign at the river since Barbara Wallace drowned last summer. At least, they said she drowned. Most of us couldn't figure that out because she spent most of her time back in the willows rolling in the sand with anyone who wanted to roll with her. The older boys pass around a story about the time Whitey Johnsrude got a new pocket watch with a big second hand, and he and some of the guys used it to each take sixty seconds with Barbara. I wasn't there, but I remember Whitey showing me his new watch later and saying that sixty seconds was a long time under certain circumstances.

Nobody really knows what finally happened to Barbara and there was a lot of gossip. Some of it about Doc Becker fixing Barbara's teeth up in his office late at night and taking her for rides in the country. But once you're dead, you're dead, and it doesn't make much difference how you get that way, unless there is a war going on and you can take advantage of the heroic dying opportunities that come with that. Barbara's body was never found. Everybody just figured the river had done its natural disposal job and her bones were buried in the sand somewhere between Oxbow and New Orleans.

Walking home along the quiet streets made me think about Uncle Jeff, halfway around the world and in the middle of thundering artillery and bombs. As usual, I wished I could be with him, whereever he was, even if he was a prisoner of the Nazis. Maybe I could help him get to a place where it would be easier for the MOP Exchange to find him. Such dreaming runs the risk of turning into a nightmare and I tried not to go too far with it. Of course, it would be better if Uncle Jeff were here with me, which would really mean he would be with Margaret, and I would still be walking down the street alone, so the best thing would be for me to be with him in the war.

When I walked past Margaret's house, her upstairs bedroom light was on and the shade was half up so there was a pretty clear view into parts of her room. I stopped out on the dark sidewalk for just a second, never considering that what I was doing was casual window-peeping. Then suddenly, Margaret walked across the room as naked as a puppy, her breasts jutting out and her little black triangle showing like a pennant. The split-second glimpse more or less knocked the wind out of me and I turned away as fast as I could. When I looked back, the shade was down and the room was dark.

CHAPTER ELEVEN

The hot summer days had been coming with no let-up and this one was going to be another scorcher. All the farmers who stopped at the station complained about the heat and about not getting enough rain. There was a story in the *News-Banner* that the pea crop wasn't going to be as good as usual because of the dry weather. I didn't know about that, but I did know that the creeks out in the swamp were running low and that had forced the brook trout to school up in the deep pools, which made them easier to catch. Sometimes, if you sneak up real quiet, you can look down into a trout hole and see the fish silhouetted against the sand like delicate little speckled torpedoes. Usually, trout stay hidden under the stream banks and you never see them, but when the alder and the dogwood grow thick overhead so the herons can't sail down for easy lunches, the trout loll around out in the middle of the sheltered pools as bold as pickerel.

It was a dull afternoon shift and I was sitting with my elbows on the counter, half asleep, listening to the Andrews sisters sing *Rum and Coca Cola,* and wondering if we were ever going to hear from Mrs. Roosevelt, when—like a bolt of lightning out of a clear blue sky—there was a tremendous explosion. I almost fell off the station stool. Crazy war thoughts charged through my head like swarming bees: the Luftwaffe is bombing us, a rocket-bomb missed London and crossed the ocean to Oxbow; Nazi prisoners got loose and blew up the courthouse!

The explosion rattled the windows and rumbled up and down the street like a tumble of giant boulders. I ran outside and didn't see anything at first, but then black smoke rolled out of the pea factory across the street and workers ran out of the factory doors waving their arms and yelling at each other. The fire whistle up at the city hall wailed, and in a minute or two, the old Ford V-8 fire engine came skidding around the corner. The volunteer firemen jumped off and ran into the pea factory, except for Eddie Stensen, who unrolled one of the hoses and hooked it up to the hydrant on the corner. The firemen—I knew them all from seeing them around town—carried two people out on stretchers and loaded them into the Wagonback ambulance, which is also the Wagonback hearse, depending on which sign is in the windshield.

The smoke slowly died away and then was gone, and the firemen drifted out of the factory door and stood around talking to the crowd of people who had gathered. Eddie rolled up the hose and the firemen climbed back on the fire engine, and as it disappeared around the corner, a truck full of MPs and two car loads of Army officers came roaring up to the pea factory. The soldiers jumped out and ran in through the doors and around the back toward the pea vine stack. I could hear the soldiers shouting orders as prisoners filed out of the pea factory doors with their hands in the air.

The whole thing didn't last all that long, but it was long enough to get my heart pumping, and my brain thinking that maybe this was the start of the real war in Oxbow. But there was no such luck. Everything quieted down after an hour or so. The prisoners went back into the factory and most of the soldiers left, and it looked like they took one of the Nazis with them. I found out later that one of the pea cookers had blown up due to a jammed valve. A couple of people got burned pretty badly and had to be taken to the hospital, but it could have been a lot worse, according to Emil Pederson, one of the foremen.

"Five minutes before it happened, nine or ten people were standing around that boiler," Emil said later when he stopped at the station for cigarettes. "They all would have been scalded to death." He shook his head and added, "There's a few of those Kraut bastards I wouldn't trust with a bucket of spit. We watch them like hawks, but you can't cover every move they make."

Last week at the pea factory, there had been a shutdown when the prisoners buried all the pitchforks in the vine stack. "It took a while to get that straightened out," Emil said. "The Krauts did it very gradually, just buried a fork or two at a time until there wasn't a damn one to be found anywhere in the whole factory."

Emil said that suddenly pea vines stopped coming in and they had to shut the factory down. "That pissed us off," he said, "so we took a couple Krauts into the hose room for a little interrogation and they finally told us about the forks and even agreed to dig them out—with their bare hands. The Army wasn't happy with us because some of the Krauts got what you might call interrogation bruises."

Emil stops at the station often to pick up cigarettes and to tell me about his son Emil Junior, who is somewhere in Europe and just got promoted to corporal.

"Sometimes when I think of my boy over there dodging bullets from those Nazi bastards, I feel like smashing heads," Emil said. "Some of the Krauts still think they're going to win it for Hitler, and we've got a couple of guys over at the factory that are real good at adjusting that attitude."

Not long after the boiler blew, some of the pea haulers started having lots of flat tires on their trucks. Some of them said the tires looked like they had been deliberately punctured. One of the pea haulers—Gary Winthrop, who has a little farm on the edge of town—had three flats in one day. There was a rumor that one of the Nazis helping Gary at the time ended up with puncture wounds to his butt. Gary later told someone there had been a "pitchfork accident."

The next thing that happened was that the prisoners went on strike. Nobody could believe it, but the prisoners said they weren't getting paid and so they weren't going to work. There was a big uproar for a while, but it didn't last long. The Army told the prisoners if they didn't work, they wouldn't get fed. Within a day or two, the prisoners were back pitching peas and helping the farmers. The Army tried to keep the strike quiet, but everyone knew about it and a lot of people were pretty mad.

"Who the hell do those assholes think they are?" Lenny Stalker said one morning when he stopped to gas up his cattle truck. "We need to start kicking some ass!"

Lenny drives into the Minneapolis stockyards every week with a load of cattle from farms around Oxbow and so he is viewed with some respect because of his big-city connection. The farmers also listen to him because he is the one who decides whether or not a cow is healthy enough for hamburger or if she goes to the glue factory. The word is that even if a cow has to be dragged into Lenny's truck with block and tackle, he will get it sold for hamburger which, of course, pays a lot more than if she had gone to the rendering works for glue. This gives Lenny more authority than God, according to Cy, who once looked through the slats and saw downed cows in Lenny's truck and said he would never eat another hamburger.

It's hard to imagine what Lenny and everyone else talked about before the Nazi prisoners got here, but that's all everyone seems to talk about now. I woke up early the other morning and was tiptoeing out of the house when I ran into Dooby Lemke just as he was setting milk bottles on the back porch, and we barely said hello before we were talking about the prisoners. I told Dooby I couldn't sleep for worrying about Uncle Jeff, and Dooby nodded and said, "If he's a prisoner, I'm sure he's not being treated as good as the ones we got here."

"There's no way to know what's happening with Uncle Jeff."

"That's the tough part, not knowing."

I nodded, and Dooby said, "You wouldn't believe what's going on in the camp here." He shook his head and scowled. "Every morning, just as it's getting light, I see girls sneaking off around the back of the prison camp and I'll bet you silver dollars to sour cream, they've been entertaining Krauts and not our boys."

That shocked me, and I didn't even want to think of such a thing. "They must be meeting soldiers," I said.

"Not a chance," Dooby said. "The gals don't have to sneak around the prison camp to get laid by our guys. They are all over the place."

I still didn't want to believe it. Dooby gave me a look and shook his head again. "It's the adventure of the thing that gets them, sneaking through the weeds and laying up with a Kraut, maybe even a Nazi!"

I didn't ask Dooby who the girls were, but I knew which ones would be suspected if anything ever came out about it—the Pickert girls and maybe Delbert Hackle's sister Mavis, who had quit school when she was fifteen and gone off to live with relatives in Minneapolis. Delbert said Mavis came down with polio and had to go to the Sister Kenny Institute for treatment. But most people thought she got knocked up and went off to have a baby. And that didn't change even when Mavis came back with a crippled spine and bad limp that made her rock back and forth when she walked. People still thought she went off to have a kid. Cy says in places like Oxbow you are forever what people decide you are and they decide that "while you are still tangled up in the umbilical cord."

When I talked to Cy about what Dooby said, Cy laughed. "We might see some little goose-steppers around here in about nine months," he said. "Hitler's children, you might say, right here in good old Oxbow."

That reminded me of the big hassle with my mother when the *Hitler's Children* movie came to the Majestic. I'm not sure how she found out that I went to it—one of her busy-body friends probably saw me and blabbed, but anyway, she yelled at me for about an hour and said I was not to go to any more movies without her permission. Can you believe that? At my age, I need my mother's permission to go to a movie!

Cy had told me to go see *Hitler's Children* because the young Nazi in it reminded him of me. The Nazi in the movie was a member of Hitler Youth and had a girlfriend who was going to be sterilized because she was part Jew. I didn't see any resemblance between him and me except that we were both young. The part of the movie I remember best was the big blonde soldiers gathered at the top of a stairs eyeballing the beautiful German women giggling down below, and that's probably the part my mother blew a fuse about, which is a little hard to figure. There sure wasn't anything very sexy about that movie scene—everybody had their clothes on and the soldiers and women weren't even touching each other. But you had to know, of course, that things were going to happen and you could imagine what they would be.

As far as my mother is concerned, I should stick to movies like *Bambi*, which is a bunch of childish trash that makes deer hunters look like evil killers. In fact, when it was first shown down at the Majestic, some of the Oxbow deer hunters got together at the pool hall and after they beered up their courage, they marched down to the theater and threatened to shoot out the light bulbs in the marquee. Sheriff Curtis showed up and told them if they didn't leave immediately, he would confiscate their rifles. After some shouting about constitutional rights and freedom of speech, the deer hunters went back to the pool hall and took up their beer drinking where they had left off.

The *Bambi* movie set off the Lutheran Ladies Aid too, where my mother is a member. I heard her say later that Mrs.Thorston, the preacher's wife, asked that they vote to oppose all deer hunting. Most of the members were married to deer hunters, but the vote against it was unanimous. Even my mother voted against deer hunting and she, of all people, should have known better. The *News-Banner* carries a weekly story about the Ladies Aid—who read the Bible verses, and which members made the lunch, and usually nobody reads it except the members looking for their names. But when it carried the news about the "no deer hunting" vote, everybody in town read it and talked about it.

Cy said he would really like to join the Ladies Aid, but they probably wouldn't have him. He said the pool hall gossip was that Wilbur Bender, the blacksmith who shoots the biggest buck every fall and spends a lot of time showing it off, had plans to bake up a venison casserole for the next Ladies Aid meeting. Wilbur told everybody he would be using a fawn's head as the centerpiece, with its big brown eyes propped open with toothpicks and its little pencil legs smothered in blood-red gravy.

But it was all just pool-hall bullshit and the *Bambi* movie didn't change anything, Cy said, except to put a lot of money in Walt Disney's pocket. Everyone went to see it. A lot of people went to see *Hitler's Children*, too, and that must have put a lot of money in someone's pocket. I wonder who got my fifteen cents.

When you think of how some simple thing like a movie about deer hunting can cause so much trouble in a hick place like Oxbow, it is no wonder that dropping a couple hundred enemy soldiers on it might really rile things up. One of the more unusual things the POW camp was blamed for was causing a ruckus with the Lutheran Ladies Aid, which was even harder to believe than the anti-deer-hunting fiasco.

My mother had been there, and I asked her about it, but she just shook her head and said it was nothing. But I overheard her talking to someone on the phone about it, maybe my dad. She said it was very embarrassing and was due to so many Ladies Aid members being nervous wrecks from worrying about somebody in the war, a son or a brother or a nephew. My mother doesn't ever swear, but I heard her say to whomever she was talking to, that it was "the damned German POWs being here and reminding everyone that our boys are still dying in the war."

It is still not clear exactly what went on. None of the members wanted to talk about it, but of course they all did—to husbands and close relatives—until enough information got out for people to piece it together. As near as it can be figured out, one of the members—it might have been Mrs. Holloway—suggested the ladies sew up little American flags for the Kraut prisoners to wear as arm bands. She said the prisoners need something to remind them who is winning the war. Another member—some think it was Mrs. Martin—said that was a bad idea because it would insult our flag to have Nazis wearing it and the Army would never allow such a thing anyway. That apparently offended Mrs. Holloway, who was said to be "high-strung," and she said Mrs. Martin was a negative person and unpatriotic to boot.

Nobody will ever know just how the conversation went from there, but it was obviously downhill because, according to very iffy information, none of it directly from any of the members, Mrs. Martin picked up one of Mrs. Bledsoe's cherry-filled cupcakes and threw it at Mrs. Holloway, missing her and hitting Mrs. Potter, who is the oldest member and always seems so dignified you could never imagine her doing something as natural and common as going to the bathroom. The best of the sketchy information has it that after the first flying cupcake, there were others, along with a couple of small ham sandwiches and a dill pickle. It is pretty unbelievable, these gentle Lutheran ladies suddenly losing it and throwing food at each other. It obviously only lasted for seconds, until their better natures and steadiness got control, and then they were so embarrassed, they couldn't look at each other.

The incident was something men seemed to love to talk about whenever two or three of them got together at the station or elsewhere. Cy said up at the Pool Hall, it was known as the "cupcake skirmish" and it kept growing in the telling and retelling until it became an all-out free-for-all with flying potato salad and gobs of hurtling Jello, none of which was true.

CHAPTER TWELVE

I would like to blame it on tossing and turning and a wild dream about an army of screaming women coming at me waving mops with Cy behind them cracking a whip and Toby barking alongside, but I can't. I woke up damp and clammy and it took me a minute or two to realize that I was safe in my bed and no closer to the war than I had ever been. I tried to think of the good parts of Cy's—our—prisoner exchange plan, like Uncle Jeff coming down the street with his duffle bag and Margaret running out to meet him, which I'm sure was the way she and Grandma were seeing things.

But there were complications. How were we ever going to actually get control of a prisoner for trading purposes? And what if Mrs. Roosevelt turned our letter over to the FBI or the Army? And what if...? The doubts and questions popped up like backwater swamp bubbles and grew bigger with time. So I would like to blame what happened on being distracted by all of that, but the fact was it was an ambush pure and simple and I should have seen it coming. I was about to dive into a big plate of pancakes at the breakfast table when my mother said, "You are going to church with me."

What a rotten way to start the day! If my brain had been working at all, I would have been up early and long gone out into the swamp with Toby. I thought about saying I had to work, or there was an Air Cadets meeting out at the airport, but it would be no use. When my mother gets a certain look, that's it! My dad calls it her dead-end look and he says when it comes on, "...you might as well put the ball away because the game is over." I slipped Toby a piece of bacon and thought how lucky dogs are, not having to go to church.

Then it got worse. My mother said we would be visiting Grandma after church. Damn! There goes most of the day. And visiting Grandma is a pain, though I feel a little different about her since she signed onto our MOP Exchange. But the truth is she turned into a bitter old lady after

Grandpa died. Visiting her has been pretty much listening to rants about FDR screwing up or the Jews killing Jesus. And she doesn't make sugar doughnuts as often as she used to.

When I was a little kid, going out to Grandma and Grandpa Forrest's farm was the most exciting thing in my life. There had been long, happy days of following Grandpa around while he tended animals or fixed machinery—me handing him tools and running to pump Mason jars full of cold drinking water, and him talking to me in a way that made childhood slip away like itchy underwear. Sometimes he would tell me about something my dad or Uncle Jeff had done when they were boys, and I would think about those two brothers in the places where I now played or puttered with Grandpa. I remember wishing I could have been there when they were around; it sounded like they had a lot of fun together and I thought it was too bad there is no way for sons and fathers and uncles to be boys together.

Back then in the evenings at Grandma's, we would gather under the yellow lamp light in the living room, rich with the smell of fresh popcorn, and moths fluttering at the windows, or maybe snowflakes if it was winter. Grandma sat in her rocker and read from *Huckleberry Finn* or *Black Beauty* and I listened as contented as a puppy full of warm milk. Grandma was a good reader and it helped to sit where you could stare into the deep shadows of her big, old geranium plants and inhale their earthy aroma as her voice built word pictures of endless abuse to Black Beauty or the mischief of Huck. It never occurred to me to wonder how a horse could not only talk but get a book published, or how Huck, considering his age, was smart enough to arrange to attend his own funeral.

Grandma's expressive reading answered such questions before they came up and transported my spongy brain to the cruel streets of London or the swirling eddies of the muddy Mississippi as easily as she might slip me one of her date-filled cookies. Off to the side, Aunt Sylvia, with her crooked smile and twisted arm, would page through her scrapbooks full of photos of the Dionne quintuplets and obituaries of the neighbors and lots of clippings about guys in the service.

Early in the war, Aunt Sylvia started writing to a long list of men in the Army and Navy. She got the addresses from church bulletins and the *News-Banner*, and she was a very prompt and faithful writer, answering letters the same day they came to her. I can't imagine that her letters were very exciting because Aunt Sylvia's life was pretty dull. She had been born with one side of her body crippled so she had to drag her left foot like it was an anchor, and her left arm made a right angle at the wrist so when she used it to grip something, it looked like a cat trying to pick up a marble. She never left Grandma's side, except to do a few simple chores like collecting eggs and limping after chickens when they sneaked into the garden.

Grandpa always sat in his old stuffed chair with his feet up on his footstool and his pipe sending up curls of blue smoke that smelled like burning chocolate cake. Sometimes, he would look up from his reading and smile at me and I would feel something powerful, like a smile from God himself. I don't know how those evenings ended because I always fell asleep and I guess Grandpa carried me upstairs to bed because that's where I would wake up the next morning.

Then one day, Grandpa didn't come in for his mid-morning crackers and coffee and when Grandma went looking, she found him lying in a heap under the horses with the harness piled on top of him. She told my mother the horses didn't move a muscle even when she screamed and collapsed down next to Grandpa.

Grandpa's funeral is the only one I've been to and I'm never going to another, except my own, I suppose. Grandpa was in his Sunday suit and his hair was combed and I heard somebody say he looked "so natural." How dumb—flat on his back in a big, shiny box, not moving a muscle, his eyes closed while his friends and family are gathered all around him. The only thing natural about that is that it's natural for every living thing to die and Grandpa was definitely dead. But that's not what people meant when they said he "looked natural." They meant he looked like he could jump up and dance a jig or pitch grain bundles.

I guess people say things like that so they don't have to face up to anybody really dying. If they looked at somebody lying in a coffin and said, "Well, he looks dead; we might as well bury him," that would make more sense, but that isn't going to happen as long as there are undertakers to phony things up.

I think I get some of this from Cy, who says dying is big business for coffin-makers and undertakers and churches, especially churches, and it provides jobs for guys like Mr. Reed, the gravedigger. Everyone calls Mr. Reed "Planter" and when you see him walking out Third Street, you know that somebody died. He usually stops at the station and buys a Baby Ruth candy bar to take with him out to the cemetery. Mr. Reed is always complaining about Oxbow's "hard pan," which I guess is a mixture of gravel and clay that is very hard to dig through. I heard Mr. Reed once say gravediggers should be paid according to soil conditions and since he was dealing with hardpan, he should get twice as much as the guy digging over at the Almira cemetery where it is all sand. "Digging graves in sand would be downright fun," Mr. Reed said, and I remember thinking that was an odd thing for somebody to say.

At Grandpa's funeral, Reverend Thorston had talked some about Grandpa, but he talked more about Hell, as if he thought that was where Grandpa was going. Cy says there's a contest between preachers and tavern keepers to see who goes to Hell and who doesn't, and preachers are losing because they don't sell booze. But Grandpa never even went into taverns.

Grandma quit smiling after Grandpa died. When we had talked after Grandpa's funeral, my mother said Grandma likes to control things and she was losing all the men in her life and couldn't do anything about it. She blamed President Roosevelt and the Jews, my mother said, especially after she started listening to Father Coughlin and somebody named Smith spout pro-German and anti-American stuff on the radio. Grandma had joined the "Mothers' Movement" that tried to keep the US out of the war and then tried to keep their sons out of combat.

"It almost killed her when Jeff enlisted," my mother said, and she had touched my shoulder. "You just have to love your grandmother and not try to figure her out."

There was no way I could figure her out, that's for sure. How could she blame the Jews and Roosevelt for Uncle Jeff's being in the war? Some of this old stuff was mixing in with other brain trash as we left the house and headed for the church. It didn't help put me in a good mood, but I don't know of anything that would have—maybe seeing Uncle Jeff coming down the street, but that wasn't going to happen and just thinking about it was dumb.

Indian John was sitting in his usual place on the stone steps outside the church when my mother and I got there. He's there almost every Sunday, year 'round, no matter what the weather. He never comes inside, just sits out there in his ragged Army jacket reading his book. He moves his lips and he never looks at anybody or anything. Indian John's book, the same one he's been reading for years, is *All Quiet on the Western Front*. Once, a long time ago, Cy handed me a copy of it and said, "You might read this when you get to lusting for war."

I read all of it and even copied some of it down because it seemed to tell what war was probably like for Uncle Jeff, even though it was a different war and the soldier in the book was a Kraut. There were some pretty tough things in it, about guys with no faces and walking on bone splinters and holding their intestines in with their hands, and how finger-nails keep growing after you die. When we talked about it later, Cy said the author was Erich Maria Remarque and he made war sound so revolting that people thought there could never be another one. Cy also said Remarque left Germany a long time ago and was living in California, dating movie stars and making lots of money writing movies.

"If you had any sense, Billy," Cy said, "you'd stop trying to go to war and head for Hollywood."

Reading *All Quiet on the Western Front* didn't change the way I felt about war. It just made me all the more anxious about missing out, and when I mentioned this to Cy, he said that is the problem, people thinking war is noble and honorable. He said he tried to change that ignorance once and got kicked out of the American Legion, for life. He said he told the veterans they were goats and not heroes, and when they marched in parades, they should wear dunce caps.

As we walked up the church steps, my mother reached into her purse and fished out a dollar bill and dropped it into Indian John's lap. He grabbed it and stuffed it into his pocket so fast it was hard to believe it had happened. I glanced at my mother, but she didn't look at me. I was think-ing how Reverend Thorston said just a couple Sundays ago that people shouldn't give money to Indian John until he comes inside and "accepts the Lord."

We sat in our usual spot under the big, purple, stained-glass window that shows Jesus crouched over a rock with His hands folded. It reminds me that I don't pray enough so I try not to look at it. Grandma was in her regular place in the second row, and Aunt Sylvia was next to her, lean-ing her head on Grandma's shoulder like she always does. Grandma was wearing her shiny blue hat that's shaped like a guard helmet and has a veil that hangs down over her eyes so from the side it looks like her head is in a cage.

Margaret and Mrs. Zanders were over across the aisle. Margaret sat with her head bowed and her eyes closed. I didn't look at her because when I do, I am back in her bedroom and all the dumbness comes rolling back. I also try not to look at the Johnson girls, because I get a strange feeling my mother somehow knows what sometimes goes through my head. She will give me a sideways glance and I swear she's reading my mind, except she can't be or she would whack me with a hymnal. I don't understand it, but the Johnson girls—the one they call Tulip, especially—gets my blood churning more in their frilly Sunday get-up than they do down at the swimming hole. Sometimes there are stirrings that could be embarrassing and I look up at the purple Jesus window to quiet things down. It works every time.

Telly Swensen, the mechanic at the Ford garage, is one of the ushers and he stands near the back door in a baggy gray suit that makes him look like a scarecrow—a smiling scarecrow because Telly smiles through everything: hymn singing, praying and even things like Mr. Slatter's heart attack last year, which people didn't think was serious at first because of Telly's smile. But it was serious. Mr. Slatter died right there in the church aisle, with Telly down on his knees beside him, smiling and trying to get Mr. Slatter to stand up even though he was dead.

I tried to listen to Reverend Thorston, but he was going on and on about how there wasn't much chance for any of us to make it to Heaven, but we should keep trying anyway because Hell is so bad. How does he know? Finally, he wrapped up his preaching and started praying. He asked the Lord to watch out for all the men in service, like Bert Osterhaus in the Pacific, and Kenny Wiggins in Normandy, and then he said that everyone should pray for Jeff Forrest, who was missing in action in France. When he said Uncle Jeff's name, Margaret made an awful sound—half sob and half scream—that was like nothing anybody had ever heard in church. Reverend Thorston stopped praying and looked down at Margaret, and people in the church turned their heads and stretched their necks to try to see her. Margaret put her hands to her face, and in the next pew, Grandma lifted her veil and wiped at her eyes.

After the last hymn and the benediction, it was finally over, and Reverend Thorston stood out by the front door shaking hands and smiling at people as they filed out. When we walked past he stuck out his hand and said, "Billy, I'm so happy to see you."

I nodded and relaxed my hand, but he held on.

"Your mother worries about you, Billy," Reverend Thorston said. "I want to come and talk to you."

My heart dropped about a foot and I gave my mother a look, which she ignored.

"Yes, please do that, Reverend," she said.

Great! I had heard everything Reverend Thorston had to say during two years of forced Catechism lessons—two years of ruined Saturday mornings when I could have been out in the swamp with Toby. Now I had to hear it again? But there was nothing I could do, considering my mother's determination and Reverend Thorston's mission in life.

After church, my mother said she needed a day off from cooking and wanted to go to the Pal Café. I was in no mood for sitting with her after what she had pulled on me at the church, but of course, we went to the café. We sat at a table by the window where you can see Main Street and the Courthouse and the Majestic Theatre. A few people were strolling up and down the sidewalks, stopping to look in store windows and keeping a close watch on little kids scurrying around like kittens. Sparrows fluttered over a tangle of dried pea vines that had fallen onto the street from somebody's truck, and down toward the grist mill, a dog loped across the street in the direction of the alley garbage cans.

It was a sunny, peaceful Sunday morning scene, about as far from anything war-like as a morning could get. Cy calls Sunday "hangover day" and says it goes back to wine drinking in biblical times. I remember his rant about it one Sunday morning when I was working the station and he came stumbling in, banged up and hung over. Creating heaven and earth in six days was a lot of work, he said, and so obviously everybody got drunk on Saturday night and the Lord, seeing this, told them to take a day off to sober up and come in Monday. That morning had been yet one more time when I knew Cy was going to Hell.

There were other churchgoers in the restaurant and everyone was in a cheerful mood, talking and laughing at jokes that weren't funny and patting each other's backs. I was still steamed about Reverend Thorston's plan to come and hassle me and I felt like standing up in the middle of everyone and shouting, "Oh, shit!" but of course, I didn't.

My mother ordered fried chicken and I had a hamburger and we didn't talk, except when people stopped by the table. Several of them said they were sorry to hear about Uncle Jeff and felt bad for Margaret and the rest of the family.

Mrs. Spence from the beauty parlor leaned over and whispered in my mother's ear that she had some silk stockings if my mother was interested. "I can't tell you where I got them, but they're real," she said.

Half the people in town, maybe more than half, were into black marketing. But they don't call it black marketing. People seem to figure it's just fighting over scarce stuff and if you don't get it, someone else will. I hear Deputy Blasser's name whispered around a lot of the black-market talk.

"Business as usual," Cy says. "No way to control it; like trying to keep people from drinking booze."

Cy is always ranting about that, about Prohibition and how it was so dumb. Last year, he wrote a poem about it for the *News-Banner* but Delbert Clinton, the editor, wouldn't print it. Not in good taste, he told Cy, which made Cy mad as a wet cat. He printed some copies and tacked them up on telephone poles around town. He said Delbert Clinton was too dumb to recognize great poetry. "My God, it's an updated version of some of Keats' best stuff," Cy said.

He gave me a copy and someday I plan to see if it really is Keats, whoever he is.

Ode on a Grecian Urn Full of Whiskey

Thou still unravished bride of revelry
Thou foster-child of din and fast time.
Fair Youth, beneath the trees thou cans't lie
Thy song, to get the maiden bare,
Ah, happy, happy booze that can be had
More happy love! More happy, happy love!
Forever panting, and forever young;
A friend to man, to whom thou say'st,
"Booze is truth, truth is booze." That is all
Ye know on earth, and all ye need to know."

Cy recites his ode whenever he can find anybody to listen, and also sometimes when there is nobody around to listen.

My mother and I were just leaving the restaurant when Sheriff Curtis drove up in his blue '39 Ford with the big sheriff badges painted on the doors and the spotlights on the side and the big chrome siren on the front fender. He and my mother had gone to school together about a hundred years ago—she calls him Rollie—and I know from past experience that whenever they run into each other, they talk for hours. Sheriff Curtis is built like a badger—wide and low to the ground, and he laughs a lot, which seems strange for someone who's always dealing with people doing bad or dumb things.

Cy says Sheriff Curtis does a good job, and Cy should know, because he ends up in the county jail a lot, and sometimes even goes up to the sheriff's office and just hangs around. "Good place to take the pulse of the community," Cy says, "and you never know when some dunderhead might need a lawyer."

Sheriff Curtis got out of his car and he and my mother started talking, while I stood on one leg and then the other and they paid no attention to me whatsoever. My mother told him about Uncle Jeff and he said he'd already heard. "I'm so sorry, Eleanor," he said. "Let's hope he's a prisoner and is being well-treated."

My mother nodded. Sheriff Curtis said some of the prisoners here in Oxbow were from Rommel's tank outfit in Africa and they required special treatment. "Some real high-steppers," he said. "They still think Hitler is going to win."

Several people stopped and were listening to the sheriff. "Except for those troublemakers, the prisoners are pretty much like our boys," he said.

"How do we get boys to kill each other?" my mother asked.

Sheriff Curtis and the others looked at her.

"I don't know, Eleanor," the Sheriff said.

There was more talk, but I didn't hear it because I was trying to figure out how to duck Reverend Thorston when he came to talk to me. And he will come. I know that; I am like a minnow in his big fish net and if I try to jump out, my mother will throw me back in. I don't have a chance.

CHAPTER THIRTEEN

The sun was slanting in through the windows when I woke up, and I could hear birds twittering so I knew it was time to crawl out. But I didn't feel right. I felt as if I had been sleeping in those filthy, bloody trenches on the "Western Front." I looked at my fingernails and thought how they would grow after I died, and I wondered how long Grandpa's fingernails were by now. I put my hands over my stomach and doubted I'd be able to hold my intestines in if an artillery shell blew my guts open.

When I finally got up and looked in the mirror, it was the same dumb story—skinny, freckles, no chest hair, and damn little down there. How long, oh God? I should quit looking because nothing ever seems to change.

Down at the station, it was just another day. I watched traffic to see if there was anything going on with the prisoners but didn't see much—a milk truck and a car or two going through town with people I didn't know. Then Old Man Rockford pulled up to the gas pumps in his beat-up International pickup that leaks oil all over the drive and smokes like it is burning pine knots. Mr. Rockford has a farm out on the edge of town and has his nose in everything he thinks he can make a buck at—trading cattle and cars and selling pumpkins in the fall and doing maple syrup in the spring. He always demands that I check all his tires, wash his windows and headlights, check his oil and battery and radiator and grease his water pump. And if I don't do it the way he wants, he orders me to do it all again.

Once when he stopped and Cy was there to see it all, Cy said I was lucky Mr. Rockford hadn't used the restroom or he'd demand that I wipe his ass. Cy doesn't like Mr. Rockford any better than I do. He claims Mr. Rockford owes him money for representing him when Mr. Rockford got sued for selling an old car with sawdust in the tires. Cy's defense had been that carpenter ants put the sawdust in the tires unbeknownst to

Mr. Rockford. Judge Proctor didn't buy it, and Mr. Rockford had to pay for tires that held air instead of sawdust. Mr. Rockford has refused to pay Cy's legal fee and they yell at each other about it whenever they meet.

"Give 'er the works, Billy," Mr. Rockford said as his pickup creaked to a stop in a cloud of blue smoke, and he squeezed his big belly out from behind the steering wheel. I leaned over the hood to wash the windshield, and suddenly, there within inches of my face, was a Nazi! I saw the POW markings on his shirt and the strange face close enough to touch. I jumped back like I'd seen a snake, and I heard Mr. Rockford laugh.

"What's the matter, Billy," he said, "Ain't you ever seen a Kraut up close?"

I hadn't, of course. I'd seen lots of them at long range, riding by in trucks or sometimes walking around over at the pea factory, but I'd never been really close to one. I was suddenly hot and sweaty.

"He's my new hired man," Mr. Rockford said. "Got him cheap and don't even have to give him a place to sleep. Just take him back at night like a rented horse."

I stood in a trance, I guess, as it dawned on me that I was in reach of a Nazi for the first time—a genuine GI Joe-killing, Uncle Jeff-capturing, goose-stepping Nazi—and all I'm armed with is a windshield rag.

"He won't hurt you, Billy," Mr. Rockford said, and laughed again.

I stared at the Nazi and he turned the edges of his mouth up in a little smile. His eyes were blue and so close to me I could see the little red veins around his eyeballs. He blinked and dipped his head in my direction and I felt my guts doing a shuffle.

"He's Otto," Mr. Rockford said, "He talks American."

I nodded before I realized what I was doing, and then jumped to finish pumping Mr. Rockford's gas. I could feel the Nazi watching me.

"He's cutting thistles in my pasture," Mr. Rockford said, "Doing a good job too, and I don't even have to be out there watching him."

When Mr. Rockford drove off, the Nazi lifted his hand toward me and I thought if he lifted it any higher it would be like a *"Heil Hitler"* salute. Then they were gone. I was weak in the knees and short on air. I guess I'm not adjusting to the Nazis like everyone else. People seem to get more comfortable every day with having them around. One of the Army officers gave a talk at the City Hall and he said the prisoners were common

German citizens and not Nazis, except for a very few. Cy had listened to the talk and he said later that he wasn't convinced.

"Any one of them could be a murdering, evil, brainwashed, Hitler-loving, son-of-a-bitch," Cy said, "and just because he says he isn't, doesn't make it so."

I heard from someone that Cy had been kicked out of the City Hall meeting when he wouldn't shut up and kept insisting the Army officer was covering up the truth about Nazis in the camp. When I asked Cy about it later, he said the Army was trying to get us to forget what the hell was happening in Germany, especially in the concentration camps.

"It is beyond belief," Cy said. "It's just starting to come out, but the goddamned Germans are gassing millions, even women and children, for Christ's sake. It's the worst slaughter in human history! Think of it, Billy! People put into ovens by the hundreds of thousands!"

I tried to think about it, but it was too much. It couldn't be happening. It is probably something our government was making up to sell more war bonds.

"The farmers around here don't know a goddamned thing about these Krauts," Cy said, "and yet they invite them to their tables as if they were family. The rules of war say that POWs have a right to try to escape, but the Krauts here have it so good they don't even think about it."

"There are rules for war?" I said.

"Yeah, from the Geneva Convention," Cy said.

I had heard about the Geneva Convention and I remembered Gordon Keller yelling about Geneva rules, but I didn't know what it was really about. It doesn't seem possible there could be rules for war. For deer hunting, okay, but for war!

"The Nazis don't obey any rules," I said.

"They sure as hell don't," Cy said. "Hitler has turned his whole goddamned country into a gas chamber for everyone who isn't blond and blue-eyed."

"Uncle Jeff has blue eyes."

Cy looked at me from under his eyebrows. "The reason we pussy-foot around our Kraut prisoners is so we don't give Germany an excuse to abuse our boys," he said. "It says in the Geneva Convention articles that prisoners aren't to be exposed to unpleasantness. Can you believe that,

Billy? They use the word 'unpleasantness.' and 'salubrious,' they use that too. Good God almighty!"

I didn't know what salubrious meant, but I didn't say anything.

"We need more guys like Archie Skogstad," Cy said.

The Archie Skogstad thing had happened a couple days ago, but people are still talking about it. Archie was a gunner on a B-24 when his arm got blown off by anti-aircraft over Germany. He's been home on leave for a week or so, his left sleeve pinned up over where his elbow used to be and a big red scar on his forehead. He happened to go into the Pal Café one morning and saw prisoners and guards sitting around a table eating hamburgers and drinking coffee and having a good old time. Archie went home and got his deer rifle and came back to the Pal and fired one round into the floor close to the prisoners' feet and another just over their heads. Then he marched the prisoners and guards down the middle of Main Street and back to the prison camp. He told the camp commander that if he saw any more prisoners out having fun, he would blow their heads off.

"A deer rifle finally went to war, Billy," Cy said later. "That should make you happy."

Cy was remembering what happened a year or so ago when the State Legion Commander tried to organize deer hunters into a civil defense force. I got excited about it until they said you had to be eighteen. There was a lot of talk for a while, but the only thing that came of it around Oxbow was one meeting at the pool hall. Cy had been there and he said when they tried to call the thing to order, they couldn't find anyone sober enough to stand and lead the Pledge of Allegiance.

"I volunteered to be Commander in Chief," Cy said, "but they told me I wasn't a deer hunter, and they were pissed when I said they were all sissy-assed Bambi shooters."

It's pretty easy for Cy to get off on a deer-hunting rant. On one of them, he said around most the world, deer are farmed like goats and that could happen here if people put down their rifles and built a few fences.

"Then you'd be milking them instead of shooting them, Billy," he said.

Cy also likes to go on and on about what he calls "the phallic twaddle of big antlers," which I couldn't figure out when he first said it, but it was the kind of thing I knew he would talk about again, so I just waited.

"The bucks with the biggest antlers do most of the doe screwing," Cy said, "and somehow deer hunters have latched onto this biological verity and they see antlers symbolizing the size of their peckers."

I was learning how to deal with his goofy talk, so I didn't say anything.

"You know how long Wilbur Bender drove around last fall with that big buck on the fender of his pickup? Must have been damned near a month. He wasn't just showing off deer antlers; he was saying 'Look over here, ladies, I've got a big one!'"

Cy had inherited an old deer rifle from his father and he once told me that when he can't find his BB gun, he uses it to shoot mice. He said when the rifle goes off, it makes him deaf for an hour or so and his cats all disappear for the rest of the day, but he always gets the mouse. His neighbors have reported some of the shots because they are really loud when they echo around between the houses. Chief Edwins has talked to Cy but Cy tells him, "What shots? I didn't hear anything."

When Cy says the week of deer hunting is nothing but a big drunk, I remember what Augie—our driver to the Bund meeting—said about Cy not being as smart as he thinks he is. Cy has no idea what it is like to be alone on a cold, snowy poplar ridge on the edge of a swamp and you see a little movement in the first light of dawn. Something pokes deep down inside and you get shaky and hot and can't get enough air. It's what they call buck fever, and it seems pretty silly unless you have had it. I once tried to talk to Cy about it, and he laughed his cackle-laugh and said that buck fever was just predatory genes kicking in.

"Same thing a cat feels when a mouse peeks out of its hole," he said.

I didn't think so. A cat having buck fever! But I didn't argue with Cy because it isn't any use to argue with him about anything, and certainly not about deer hunting. Of course, I haven't had buck fever all that much, though there were a couple times last year when Uncle Earl took me along with his old hunting gang when buck fever hit me hard. It was the great adventure of my life, borrowed deer rifle and all, but the more I yearned to be part of the gang, the more I seemed to be "the kid."

I remember lying awake in the middle of the night with the old deer hunters snoring in the dark all around me. It felt like I was in a den of hibernating bears and I couldn't sleep. Maybe not getting enough sleep has something to do with buck fever because I got it bad the next day when I missed a shot at a deer the old hunters chased past me. I can still see the end of the rifle barrel wavering around like a tree branch in the wind, and the huge buck staring at me for what should have been the last second of its life, but wasn't, because when I pulled the trigger, the barrel kicked up even higher.

The deer bounded off into the thick spruce, its Christmas-tree antlers knocking showers of snow off branches and breaking dry underbrush until it sounded like an elephant crashing through the swamp. Some of the old hunters came out of the woods to stand and look at the buck's tracks in the snow and to see how close to it I had been when I shot, and I saw one of them give a little smile and turn away to spare me looking him in the eye. I think I even got buck fever once when Toby chased a rabbit straight at me. My arms shook until I couldn't hold the rifle steady. I haven't told anyone about that—buck fever from a rabbit! Come on.

Sometimes I wonder where hunting leaves off and killing starts. Hunting is for eating, I guess, and you can think of it that way, not all that different than shooting a pig on butchering day, except what you kill is wild and there is a thrill in bringing it down and standing over it like a hawk over a fresh-caught squirrel. Being a successful hunter or predator depends on pretty much the same thing. You have to act immediately— right now—or your chance to kill will be gone.

When something pops up in front of you, there is no time to think and I have wondered if that is why I have killed things for no good reason, like owls, and once an American bittern that leaped out of the tall grass in front of me. The rifle came up like a reflex to a mosquito bite and the bullet shattered one of the bittern's wings so it tumbled down like a broken kite and when I ran to it, its snake eyes were indignant with the burning question: *Why did you do that to me?* I had no good answer, not even the old country thing about shooting owls because they nab farmers' chickens.

And even that bit of foggy thinking went down the drain one winter morning when I came over a ridge and there perched on a fence post was a magnificent snowy owl, a creature of such mystery and beauty that it stopped my breath. And in that split second of not breathing, I killed the owl with a bullet to its breast. The snowy owl had obviously never tasted chicken in its life, and its big yellow eyes followed me around for most of the rest of that winter.

The bittern thing was even worse; there is not even a moldy old rumor about them ever doing harm to anything except the frogs and minnows they spear to eat. I hung the bittern's limp carcass on a barbed-wire fence and had no idea I was also hanging it in with the brain trash, where it would rot and stink things up forever.

I have never talked about this with Cy, I think because I'm ashamed of whatever it is that has me killing inedible things so thoughtlessly and I have a feeling he would not let me excuse it simply as predatory instinct or youthful dumbness. The old brain trash thing gets out of hand sometimes.

All the wartime meat rationing and high prices have made people more interested in shooting deer. It's mostly at night when car headlights make a deer's eyes glow like emeralds and they are as easy to shoot as pigs. Sometimes I hear the shots when I'm lying in bed and can't sleep. I've tried to turn it into gunfire from the war, a Gestapo patrol sneaking along the river toward Oxbow maybe. But it doesn't sell. I'm too old for such fantasy stuff, and anyway, I know exactly what is actually happening.

Somebody is pointing a rifle out of a pickup window and aiming between the emeralds and pulling the trigger and then running out to drag the dead deer to the road and tossing it into the back of the pickup before tearing off for home. Game warden Louie Robbins stops at the station sometimes and he says deer poachers keep him up almost every night.

"I haven't had a good night's sleep since that big blizzard last spring," I heard him tell somebody.

Mr. Bennings from the Chevy garage once offered me five dollars to shoot a deer for him. He said I would just have to ride with him and shoot the deer when he got it in his headlights. I thought about it, but finally told Mr. Bennings that Warden Robbins would take my rifle if we got caught.

"Oh, hell," he said. "Louie Robbins couldn't catch a wood tick."

Mr. Bennings got Vernon Pickert to go out with him and they almost shot one of Harry Moen's Jersey heifers, according to the way Vernon told it later. He said the heifer was big and brown and behind some brush and he thought it was a deer until it opened its mouth and let out a loud cow bellow.

"Scared the bejesus out of Old Man Bennings and he drove straight back to town," Vernon said. "He told me to keep my mouth shut and the cheap bastard never paid me a nickel."

CHAPTER FOURTEEN

There was simply no excuse for Mrs. Roosevelt not getting back to us by now. I don't care if she gets ten thousand letters a day—and maybe she does—but when something as important as the MOP Exchange hits her desk, you would think a secretary would pluck it out and tell her it needs immediate attention.

I haven't even had a chance to talk to Cy about it because he hasn't been around for a day or so. I thought about checking to see if he was in jail but didn't. Once when he'd been locked up for getting drunk and opening the gates at the Oxbow power dam so the millpond drained, he had sent word for me to go to his house and feed his cats. He said later I had probably saved their lives, which I don't think is true because Cy's house is full of mice and the cats have plenty to eat if they just get up and do a little hunting.

Sometimes Cy disappears for a few days. I think he might go to Minneapolis, maybe for some lawyer thing, though he has mentioned going to shows at the Alvin, a Minneapolis burlesque theater. I've never been to it, of course, but I've heard a lot of talk about the jazz music and the strip shows. Maybe he goes there.

He once said he had a girlfriend at the Alvin who was a great singer. He said her name was Lobelia Cardinalis and she is named after a red swamp flower that is pollinated by ruby-throated hummingbirds. She's a red-headed Negro, Cy said, and he claimed he has proposed marriage to her at least fifty times. You never know what to believe with him, especially when he comes up with that kind of wild stuff. It wears on you, sorting for facts and truth and thinking after a time that maybe it's not worth the effort so you just listen for the entertainment of it.

The last time he stopped at the station, he had a book about Oliver Wendell Holmes and he went on a rant about how stupid it was for everyone to believe that Holmes was such a great thinker.

"He was nothing but a goddamned warmonger," Cy said. "He loved war. The dumb bastard almost died of war wounds three different times, and you'd think he might learn something from that, but listen to what he wrote about the glory of war."

Cy picked up his book and read, *"I do not know the meaning of the universe. But in the midst of doubt, in the collapse of creeds, there is one thing I do not doubt, that no man who lives in the same world with most of us can doubt, and that is that the faith is true and adorable which leads a soldier to throw away his life in obedience to a blindly accepted duty, in a cause which he little understands, in a plan of campaign of which he has little notion, under tactics of which he does not see the use."*

Cy slammed the book shut and shouted, "Adorable! Good Christ Almighty! Have you ever heard such shit, Billy?"

I remember thinking that Cy was getting more emotional than usual, and so when he said I should remember Holmes' words, I just nodded. I don't know if any of what Cy said about Holmes is true or not, except for what he read out of the book. But it was entertaining to hear about somebody who loved war.

Shortly after that, Cy got into trouble again with the veterans down at the Legion hall. He said they should not only wear dunce caps, they should also apologize for their medals. Bert Kirkwood, the janitor at the school, was there that night and said some of the veterans got so mad they kicked Cy out and started a petition to have him committed as a "patriotic deviant." When Cy heard about it later, he said he would have signed the petition himself. He ended up getting drunk and was arrested for disturbing the peace when he tried to force his way into the next Legion meeting. Cy claimed he wasn't disturbing the peace, he was disturbing the war, and he sued the county for false arrest. But nothing ever came of it, which is what happens with most of his lawsuits.

* * * * *

My mother says Margaret is back in bed and can't get up. I didn't want to think about that because then I would wonder if I should do like Doc said and take Margaret trout fishing, or at least talk to her about it. But I still can't buy it, that something like that would help somebody who is in shock. Doc must have grabbed that one out of thin air because it couldn't have come from any medical school. Trout fishing cures shock? I don't think so, especially when Doc says people don't even know what shock is.

So, everything is pretty much on hold as people get more and more used to having the prisoners around helping with the pea harvest. The stack of vines behind the cannery is getting high enough to see from the street and it's starting to give off its fermenting stink. It's a smell that seems to fit the situation around here, like there's some strange thing starting to rot but nobody knows what it is. It's all starting to get to me, especially not hearing from Mrs. Roosevelt.

I worked the morning shift and so the afternoon stretched out there like an invitation to get away from everything for a while. When Cliff showed up to take over, I went home and got Toby and my rifle, grabbed some pictures of Hitler for target practice, and we headed for the swamp. Toby was excited to be going anywhere and he ran in circles all the way down to the river. We crossed in my old boat, and Toby barked at the ducks that flew up out of the cattails, quacking like they were mad at something and looking like they were scrambling up invisible ladders.

Usually, the swamp is a thick, green jungle, but there hasn't been much rain this summer and things are different. Walking into the thick tamaracks on the edge of the swamp was like stepping through a ragged old curtain and into a moldy attic with cobwebs and dusty stuff hanging all over. There were brown edges on everything, even the ferns and the skunk cabbage. Dried moss crunched underfoot and much of the mud had dried up and was as hard as concrete.

I stopped next to one of the massive old stumps from the first-cut pine and watched a line of ants snake across one of the ancient gray roots. The stumps are so huge and so solid, even after so many years of being dead, that it's hard to think of them as once being alive and growing. Sometimes when I stand with one of them, I hear voices. Not like the geezers' voices up by the courthouse, but like people talking from the deepest grave ever dug, except the grave is not down in the ground, it's towering high up in the air where the giant tree once stood.

If I stand there long enough, I can see into it, a great, ghostly, white tree skeleton. Toby will tolerate only so much of that and then he barks me out of my trance and we go back to wandering the trails. That's how it happened today. We went deep into the swamp. It felt good to be out there on our own with just the summer breeze stirring things and nobody telling us where we should or couldn't go. You could sense the wild creatures all around, never showing themselves, at least to me, but you knew they were there, watching and sniffing and waiting for us to be gone.

The swamp was very dry, dryer than I had ever seen it, and the mud holes had shrunk to hard-edged hollows with just small centers of stale green water. There is always talk about what a threat the swamp is when it doesn't rain for a few weeks. The dead vegetation builds up season after season until the whole thing becomes a big tinderbox and people in Oxbow look out at it and shake their heads. They talk of cancelling the deer season when the autumn rains don't come, but it hasn't happened yet. It was close last year, but a late October shower eased things temporarily and hunters roamed the dry swamp without incident.

But then there was a snowless winter and a dry spring and summer. The swamp always gives you the feeling it is waiting for something—a new season or a change in the weather, and that seemed stronger now as it shriveled under the hot sun. It was waiting for rain, of course, and so were all the people in Oxbow who looked across the river and remembered their grandpas and grandmas talking about the hellish night right after the lumberjacks left when the swamp caught fire and burned and took Oxbow with it. There was a cluster of old graves out in the cemetery of a family that hadn't made it to the river.

Toby and I crossed several of the little trout streams and there was barely enough water to keep them running. One, in fact, had shrunk to a tiny trickle and left a series of rocky pools where trout were trapped. I could see their black backs and white fins under the shaded banks. It would be a snap to catch them and if taking Margaret trout fishing ever does happen, this would be a good place to bring her.

Toby doesn't understand target practice and when I shot at the Hitler pictures, he ran back and forth like he was going crazy. On the last shot, I put a bullet in the middle of Hitler's forehead, which made me feel good, and then we headed back toward the river. I thought about going out to the old logging camp where Toby and I like to hang out, but it was too late in the day. A corner of one of the old log buildings at the camp still stands and it holds up enough rusty roofing to make a good place to ride out thunderstorms or build a little campfire and roast up a few hotdogs.

Toby and I have spent a lot of time there, and we consider it our place. It's one of the few spots where a cluster of the original giant white pine still stands. People say they are virgin pine, which seems like an odd name for something so old, considering what I think of as virgins. The trees are like pillars holding up the sky and their branches don't even start for fifty feet or so up the huge trunks. They reach out so far and are so dense with needles that just one branch could shade a whole house.

One evening a long time ago, I heard Grandpa Forrest tell of seeing a panther stretched along the high branch of a towering white pine. He said its tail hung down like a big fishhook, and the image of that is something Grandpa handed off to me like a brain trash treasure. I see it as if I had been there, and maybe in a way I was. There is a thick carpet of brown needles under the big pine and it makes a great place to lie on your back and listen to the sighing and whispering high up in the dark treetops. It's like hearing the hissing birth of secrets and gossip, and it soothes your curiosity and loads you up with questions all at the same time.

There are only a few of the virgin pines left out in the swamp, a half dozen here and a cluster there where rock outcrops or impassable sink-holes kept the loggers from getting to them. I heard all about that back when I hung around the courthouse geezers and listened to them pick through their lives and argue about facts and dates like old monkeys grooming each other's history.

Night comes into the swamp as sneaky as a bull snake and it was almost dark by the time we got back to the river. Usually, I like to get out of the swamp while there is still some daylight but sometimes I don't make it. It isn't that I'm afraid of the dark, but if you spook a deer that goes crashing and snorting away through the brush, or a rooster pheasant explodes under your nose and cackles off into the darkness, the shock of that makes your rear end clench up like a fist and you'd rather be home.

Toby and I were about to climb into the boat when I heard voices drifting down from upstream. I figured it must be somebody fishing, and I stood in the shadows as the voices got louder. Then, in the dim light,

I could see the outline of a rowboat floating downstream. I couldn't see who was in the boat, and as it got closer and the voices got louder, Toby suddenly started barking. The oars thumped and the boat turned sharply and headed straight toward me and Toby.

"Who's there?" someone yelled.

There was no way to make Toby shut up so it wasn't any use to try to hide. When the boat got closer, I stepped out from behind the willows and said, "It's me, Billy Forrest."

Somebody in the boat swore, and another voice that sounded familiar said, "What the hell are you doing out here?"

When the boat bumped against mine, I realized that one of the men was Deputy Blasser. Even in the dim light, I saw the glint of his badge and recognized the bullet shape of his big head.

"You're a dumb little shit," Blasser said.

I didn't know what to say and so I just tried to make Toby stop barking, which was impossible.

"Shut that goddamn dog up before I shoot him," Blasser said.

I grabbed for Toby's collar but missed and finally got him by the neck and tried to calm him.

"Just what the hell are you doing out here?" Blasser said.

"Target practicing," I said.

It was quiet then, just the gurgle of the river mixing with the night sounds of the swamp.

"Maybe he saw something," the man with Blasser said, and I realized it was Mr. Schmidt.

'What the hell's he gonna see?" Blasser said, and it got quiet again.

"Billy," Blasser finally said, "We're patrolling the river for the Army. It's secret military stuff. Nobody can know."

I didn't say anything, but it flashed through my mind that I might spend the rest of the war in jail to protect military secrets.

"So what the hell do we do with you and your goddamn dog?" Blasser said.

"We can't take any chances," Mr. Schmidt said.

Toby had finally stopped barking and was standing on the front seat of the boat growling at Blasser and Mr. Schmidt. They talked in low voices and I couldn't make out what they said.

"We're going to let you go, Billy," Blasser said finally, "but if you say one word about seeing us, or if I catch you out here again, you're going to be in bigger trouble than you ever thought possible."

It was quiet again, except for the gurgle of the river and Toby's growling, and I could feel the two men looking at me and expecting something.

"I won't say anything," I said.

For a few long minutes, there was just the sound of the river and Toby's growls.

"You get the hell out of here before I haul you in for hunting at night," Blasser finally said, and he pushed against the river bank with an oar. The current caught their boat and it drifted slowly away.

"Keep your mouth shut, kid," Mr. Schmidt said, and then they were gone into the darkness down the river.

I couldn't figure it out. Maybe it was about black marketing. There were rumors about Blasser having special connections. All I know is that I didn't feel good about running into Blasser and Mr. Schmidt, but I sure wasn't going to say anything to anybody. A whip-poor-will called as I crossed the river, its monotonous song sounding like an odd warning from way back in the swamp: "Watch-out-will, watch-out-will, watch-out-will." Watch out for what?

When I finally got home, my mother jawed at me for missing supper, but she put out a plate of food anyway. While I ate, she went on about not listening to Cy, and staying out of the swamp and not smoking or doing anything stupid and staying right with God. She must have had all this stored up and I thought it was never going to end. Toby went to sleep under the table and I wished I could join him.

When I finally got up to my room I was too tired to even think of reading a magazine, which I usually do because it puts me to sleep almost immediately. Cy gives me his *Esquires* when he's done with them, even though he says they are unfit for my eyes because the post office said the magazine is "lewd and lascivious." When he gives me an *Esquire*, Cy makes me raise my right hand and swear I won't look at the Vargas paintings or pictures of women unless they have clothes on. Then he laughs and smacks me on the back. Cy says the postmaster general doesn't have enough to do and instead of bothering perfectly good magazines, he should be on a rural delivery route somewhere out in the sticks. He told me about some newspaper guy named Mencken he has mentioned before being called into court to explain that the words "behind" and "fanny" and "backside" were not lewd and obscene.

"Mencken wouldn't even let *Esquire* pay his carfare from Baltimore because he said he enjoyed himself so much in the hearing room," Cy said. Some of this goes past me but it sure entertains Cy. He shakes his head and laughs until he chokes.

Cy also gave me his old 1943 Vargas calendar and told me not to look at Miss April because that was one of the paintings objected to by the postmaster general. "He's an important government official and knows about the dangers of looking at things that stir you up," Cy said. "You could go blind, Billy!"

CHAPTER FIFTEEN

Margaret showed up at the station just before noon. She stood so close I could feel her warm breath on my face. It didn't take a doctor or a mother to tell there was something seriously wrong with her. You could see it in her eyes; they were as blank and hopeless as windows in a burning house and I had to look away. A sudden feeling of dread—that something bad was going to happen to Margaret, and maybe to me—crept over me for no good reason.

"Today, Billy. Today!" Margaret said and then she just burst out crying, little choking sobs, like hiccups. They hurt my ears and I wanted them to go away. I thought about reaching out for her, but all I could do was stand and stare out the window and hope that no customers came in. It took a long time for her to pull herself together, and when I finally looked at her, she seemed different. She wiped at her eyes and stared at me and there was something in her expression that I couldn't figure out, some wild glint I had never seen. It made me want to fix her, go at her with the right tools as if she were a car engine with bad timing that backfired and had lost its power. I thought about Doc saying nobody knew how to deal with shock and I wondered if he ever wished he was a mechanic instead of a doctor.

"Get your rifle, Billy," Margaret said suddenly. "Now!"

Of course, I couldn't do that, but that didn't seem to register with Margaret.

"We've got to kill a Nazi now!" she said, her voice rising to a shout. She grabbed my arm and pinched so hard it hurt. I put my hand on her shoulder and we stood like that until finally she jerked me to her and wrapped her arms around me. She squeezed so hard I could feel the heat from the length of her body and I wondered if she would ever let go. She did, finally, but not before her closeness had turned me hot and sweaty and stirred up.

"Today," Margaret said.

We stood looking at each other, and Margaret said, "Today! Today, Billy. I'll die if we don't do it today. I can't sleep. I can't think. I have nightmares about Jeff. I'm begging you."

She was about to start crying again and I couldn't bear to stand next to her for anymore of that.

"We've got a plan," I said, and was immediately sorry.

"For killing a Nazi?" Margaret asked.

I knew there was no going back.

"Better," I said.

"Nothing could be better."

"It's about trading prisoners."

Margaret opened her mouth and then shut it. There was just the noise of the flies and the traffic passing by outside. She gasped and said, "How in the world could...?"

"One for one."

Margaret stared at me for a long time. "You mean trade a Nazi for Jeff?"

"Yes."

Margaret stared some more. "Oh, my God!" she whispered and her eyes seemed too big to ever close again.

"Cy said not to tell you yet."

"It's crazy."

"Cy thinks it might work. It uses mothers to trade their sons."

It was like Margaret was suddenly a statue. No part of her moved. She didn't even blink. She stayed that way so long it was eerie, and I had a crazy thought about Lot's wife getting turned into a pillar of salt. I remember when we read Genesis in a catechism class how Reverend Thorston had seemed to be in a hurry to get past some of that story, especially the part where Lot's daughters got him drunk and had sex with him. That was certainly an unusual way to use family ties to accomplish something, and remembering the story made me think that our trying to use family ties in the MOP Exchange was maybe not that unreasonable.

"Cy calls it the Mothers Of Prisoners Exchange, or MOP," I said.

Margaret gave a little gasp and turned toward me and I swear I could feel the heat from her eyes. She stood very still again and then suddenly squealed and grabbed me in a bear hug, even tighter than the last one. "Oh, Billy, we have to start now. Now!"

She finally relaxed her hold and stepped back. I told her we had to wait to hear from Mrs. Roosevelt, and that the MOP Exchange would be done by American and German mothers. But she didn't seem to listen. She wasn't interested in details. In her wanting it to be so, she figured it was a done deal and it was just a matter of time before the trade went through and Uncle Jeff walked in through the door and into her arms.

Margaret gave me a quick kiss on the cheek and said she was going home to get some of Jeff's clothes ready. I wanted to tell her she was jumping way ahead of things, but she wouldn't have listened. Instead, I just told her not to tell anyone. She smiled and put a finger to her lips and walked out the door, her step suddenly brisk and sure.

Later, after Cliff showed up to take over at the station, I walked over to Cy's. I wasn't looking forward to telling him what had happened, but I knew I had to. I found him sleeping on his dirty sofa, one cat curled near his feet and another draped over the sofa back. He and the cats blended in with all the junk like hairy bags of rags. In the total disarray, there was an odd harmony, like it all might have been dumped out of an artist's trash can and was waiting to be painted or photographed.

I jerked on Cy's arm and he rolled over and started a groaning trip to consciousness, which seemed like as good a time as any to tell him what I had done. Maybe his grogginess would make it easier for both of us. I don't know if it did or not, but he suddenly pulled himself up and shouted, "Goddamn you, Billy, I told you not to tell her. We're not ready!"

One of the cats came over to rub against my leg, and I watched Cy as he reached down beside the sofa and grabbed a whiskey bottle. He tipped it up, shook himself, and rubbed at his eyes. He took another slug and looked at me.

"You've got a big mouth," he said.

I said I had told Margaret to make her feel better. Cy shook his head.

"Yeah, you're a sad case," he said. Then he swore and kicked at an empty soup can on the floor. "This isn't going to work if you can't keep your damned mouth shut."

I said I wouldn't tell anyone else, but Margaret was part of the plan, so she had to know about it sooner or later.

"Later would have been better," Cy said, and swore again. Finally, he shrugged. "What the hell! We should hear from Mrs. Roosevelt any time, so we might as well get the thing going before you blab to the wrong person and it all goes down the drain."

Cy scratched his head hard with the tips of his fingers like he was trying to rub something into his skull that would clear his thinking and then he blinked and scowled at me. "So, Mr. Big Mouth, do you have any ideas what we do next?"

I had been thinking about it since we sent the letter to Mrs. Roosevelt, and then after Mr. Rockford had stopped at the station with the Nazi prisoner, it had all seemed to fall into place, at least in my head. Cy looked at me with his ragged eyebrows raised and I knew he was waiting for me to say something dumb that he could pounce on. But I had more or less rehearsed it, and I dove in, telling Cy about the Nazi cutting thistles in Mr. Rockford's pasture and how we could use Margaret as bait to help capture him and then how we could keep him at my camp out in the swamp until we got a trade worked out.

Cy stared at me with a scowl that started out bone-deep. Then as I talked through some of the details, the wrinkles in his forehead smoothed out some and when I finally stopped talking, he was looking at me like maybe there might be somebody dumber than me. He didn't say anything for a long time and I kept my mouth shut and waited.

"That's not bad," he finally said. "I like it, but that goddamned swamp is about as unpleasant a place as there is, bugs and snakes and every other damned thing."

The swamp was the perfect place to hide a Nazi, and Cy knew it. It seemed dumb for him to be talking about how bad it was out there. It's a wonderful place. It's just downright strange that someone as smart as Cy didn't recognize that, and at the very least see how perfectly it fit into the MOP trade plan.

Cy's expression had gone back to the deep scowl and something about it got under my skin. I guess I got a little mad at him because I said maybe Margaret and I should go ahead with the MOP Exchange without him. I knew as the words came out of my mouth that it wasn't a very smart thing to say.

Cy snorted and said, "Billy, you are still just a dumb kid and there isn't enough blood in your system for both your balls and your brain."

I had been thinking that since Cy and I were working together on the MOP Exchange, he might treat me with a little more respect. But nothing had really changed since he told me I needed to grow up and stop thinking of the war as a sporting event that I wasn't old enough to get into. I felt like telling him he could go to Hell; it is one thing to be called a dumb kid by some jerk like Deputy Blasser, but when it comes from Cy, it was just too much.

Cy must have known that because he said he didn't mean anything personal and that all kids are dumb, and as a matter of fact, I wasn't as dumb as some, which I guess was supposed to be a compliment or an apology, but I didn't take it that way. Once before, when we got into an argument, Cy said it is important to recognize your own dumbness or you will never learn anything. That time, we had argued about Laura Ingalls. I don't remember how her name came up, but I said she wrote books that Grandma Forrest read to me when I was a little kid, and Cy said no, she was a famous woman pilot who was in prison for being a German spy.

I knew he was wrong. There is no way that Laura Ingalls could be a spy.

"I'll bet you a dollar she's a spy," Cy said, and I jumped at the offer.

"Well, Billy," Cy said, "the one you are talking about, the one who wrote *Little Outhouse on the Prairie*, or whatever it is, was named Laura Ingalls until she married a guy named Wilder and added his name to hers. The one I'm talking about is just Laura Ingalls. She holds more flying records than Lindbergh, and a couple of years ago, she ended up in prison for taking money from the German government for spy work."

I didn't believe him and told him he was just making up a story to get a dollar out of me.

"It's true," he said. "It must be the long, solitary flights that warps their brains, but both Laura Ingalls and Lindbergh ended up being Nazi sympathizers. I think she's still in prison to this day."

And later, after he had gone to the library and returned with a magazine story about Laura Ingalls being a pilot, he said, "Never take another man's bet, Billy."

It was hard for me to believe there had been two Laura Ingalls, even after I read it with my own eyes and saw it was true. I think he tricked me with a technicality. When I gave him my dollar, he said he was going to keep it until I learned never to argue with him and then he would give it back. He never has, of course, and I don't mention it, but sometimes I think about it, like when he said I wasn't as dumb as some kids.

Maybe Augie is right, and Cy is not as smart as he thinks he is. Maybe nobody is as smart as they think they are. Maybe it's even simpler than that and nobody knows whether another person is dumb or smart, like Aunt Sylvia, for example. Everyone thinks she is just this simple, homely crippled girl who lives like she is physically attached to Grandma, and who writes all those nice letters to the poor, lonesome guys in service, which is all true, but it turns out there is more.

I wouldn't have known anything about it if I hadn't heard my mother and Grandma Forrest talking on the back porch one day. I hadn't intended to eavesdrop, but I came into the kitchen for a drink of water and the window to the porch was open and they were sitting out there drinking coffee and talking. I couldn't hear all the words, but I got enough to figure out that Grandma Forrest saw one of the letters that Aunt Sylvia got from a soldier and it was full of stuff about having sex. Grandma said she was shocked and had looked in Aunt Sylvia's writing desk and found a cigar box full of those little, novelty comic books that show people like Maggie and Jiggs going at each other when you let the pages flip past real fast.

There was also what Grandma Forrest called filthy postcards and "erotica" in the cigar box. Aunt Sylvia told Grandma she found the cigar box behind some junk in the chicken coop and she thought the soldiers and sailors would enjoy some of the illustrations, so she had been including a few in her letters, except when she used V-mail. Then she had drawn little sketches of her own showing some of the same stuff. As I listened through the porch window, I thought my mother was starting to cry, but it turned out she was giggling.

Then both of them were laughing, and then even more after Grandma Forrest told my mother she thought at first the cigar box must have been stashed by Uncle Jeff or my dad or one of the hired men. But then she recognized items in it from when she and Grandpa had gone on their honeymoon to the World's Fair in Chicago. It had been Grandpa's cigar box! They had been quiet then and I was about to tiptoe out of the kitchen when my mother said, "It's so funny. Poor Sylvia is about as sexless as a dishrag and now she has a world-wide reputation as a hot mama."

"And she's not as innocent about it all as she'd like me to think," Grandma said.

They were quiet again. Grandma Forrest sighed. "Men!" she said. "They're all alike."

I remember thinking that was a dumb thing for her to say. Men are no more all alike than women are. But it wasn't worth thinking about then and it wasn't worth thinking about now. I do remember that I got something out of the accidental eavesdropping: I had gone to the dictionary and learned I was confused about the difference between "erotica" and "exotic."

CHAPTER SIXTEEN

After Cy said I wasn't as dumb as some kids, we stood there nose to nose like two dogs trying to decide if they want to go back to growling at each other. You can't call somebody dumb and then think you can smooth it over by pointing out that there are people who are dumber. But that's what Cy was trying to do, and I wasn't ready to buy it. I wanted to talk about how dumb he was for thinking the swamp was a bad place and maybe for some other things, too.

The thing is, Cy and I were both probably a little wound up about not hearing from Mrs. Roosevelt, and nervous about how the MOP Exchange might go awry, and maybe that is why we had our little blow-up. Neither of us moved for a while and then Cy finally shook his head and said, "Aw, hell, Billy, we've got to hang together to give this thing any chance at all."

I looked at him and nodded, slow enough to let him know I understood what he was saying, but I was still mad at him. Cy came up with a little weasel smile and stuck out his hand and I grabbed it and we shook. I felt a sense of relief that seemed bigger than it needed to be.

"There are parts of your swamp plan I don't like," Cy said, "but, in general, it is pretty damned good."

I looked at him and nodded.

"The goddamned muck!" Cy said. "It's nothing but muck out there."

"Most of it has dried up," I said.

Cy gazed out the window and then turned to look at me. "Let's give it a try," he said. "Go get your rifle and I'll meet you and Margaret down at the park. And keep your goddamned mouth shut."

He said that last part like he might be talking to a "dumb kid," and I felt my face start to heat up again, but I let it pass. What it comes down to is we simply have to work together, or the MOP Exchange will be done before it ever starts.

My mother wasn't around when I got home, which was lucky. I called Margaret and told her to meet Cy and me, and then I gathered up my rifle and some bullets. Toby had a fit when he figured out I might be going somewhere without him. I thought about taking him along, but that would not have been smart. I snitched a hotdog out of the ice box and sneaked away from Toby in the seconds it took him to wolf it down. So long as I can distract him with hotdogs, I have the upper hand, but only for those few seconds.

I walked the back alleys down to the park, carrying the rifle next to my leg to hide it, and ducking behind garages if I heard a car pass by out on the street. Cy and Margaret were already at the picnic table, and as I walked up to them, I felt a sudden nervousness, like the early stages of buck fever. I knew I had to control it or it could ruin everything. I tried to think about Uncle Jeff and that seemed to help.

"Oh, Billy," Margaret said. "Cy told me all about it and I think the MOP plan is wonderful!"

I looked from her smiling face to Cy's scowl. He shook his head. "It's all up to Mrs. Roosevelt," he said.

"She'll help," Margaret said. "I know she will." And she reached out and squeezed Cy's arm. He ignored her and glanced at my rifle.

"Damn, let's get out of sight with that thing," he said.

There was nobody at the park, but Cy was right—we didn't want anyone seeing us, especially with a rifle. We went over the plan again and then I led the way through the tall cattails to the trail that twists through the thick willows and alder along the river. Behind me I could hear Cy swearing at the mosquitoes. We followed the trail for a mile or so, then climbed the steep river bank and came out on the edge of Mr. Rockford's pasture.

Patches of thistles and hazelnut bushes were scattered across the grassy slopes and a few tall pine trees stood over it all like giant lookout towers. Under one of the pines, half a dozen black-and-white cows stood chewing their cuds and switching their tails, and in a distant corner, grazing sheep clung to a green hillside like giant grubs. But there was no sign of the Nazi.

"Maybe Rockford didn't get him today," Cy said, but he no more than got the words out when Margaret said, "Look!" She pointed across a wide gully and there was the Nazi swinging a scythe back and forth through a patch of thistles. He looked like any regular farm hand, but then he turned, and the white POW letters showed on the back of his shirt. My heart jumped. It was like the first time a big buck came trotting toward me during the deer hunt, only this was more powerful. I hadn't gotten so hot and sweaty over the buck as I did now over the Nazi, but the weather had been a lot colder then, so maybe that was part of it.

What happened next was just like we planned. Cy and I ducked behind some hazelnut bushes, and Margaret stood and waved at the Nazi until he finally saw her. He looked for a long time, and then walked slowly toward Margaret as she smiled and waved at him. My hands started to shake, and it dawned on me that I hadn't loaded my rifle. I was fumbling for bullets when I looked out from behind the bushes and saw Margaret. I will remember forever the way the wind blew her hair and tugged at her clothes and the red scarf around her neck and the way she held her chin up and shaded her eyes with her hand. Then suddenly the Nazi was in front of her, grinning and nodding. It was, of course, the same one I had seen in Rockford's truck, and I remembered how I had been all nervous and sweaty then too.

"Nothing to it, Billy," Cy whispered.

The Nazi was standing close to Margaret, and she turned suddenly toward us and shouted, "Now!"

I didn't move, and Cy jabbed me and stumbled to his feet. I scrambled after him with the rifle pointed at the Nazi.

"Kill him! Kill him!" Margaret shouted, and I stepped around her and aimed my rifle at the Nazi. His eyes widened and his square chin dipped as he looked at me.

"Stop! Stop! For Christ's sake, stop!" Cy shouted as he jumped in front of me and pushed the rifle barrel down. I wasn't going to shoot. I don't think so, anyway. It was just that Margaret's unexpected shout had hit me like a club and for just a second, common sense and planning and everything else had gone out the window and I had almost acted as thoughtlessly as that day with the snowy owl.

Then the whole scene seemed to freeze and Margaret started to cry. Cy glanced at her and said, "Damn, Margaret, we can't trade a dead prisoner!"

Margaret wiped at her eyes with a handkerchief and stared at the Kraut.

"I forgot," she said.

Cy kept looking at her and then he turned to me. "Goddamnit, Billy, we're not playing cowboys here."

I didn't like what he was saying, but I knew he was right. I had lost it—just for a second when Margaret had shouted. I felt stupid about it. It was a "dumb kid" thing to do. "Sorry," I said.

Cy shook his head and looked back at Margaret. Her shout to kill the Nazi was another sign that her grip on things was not as tight as it should be, in particular her understanding of the MOP Exchange. As much as she wanted Uncle Jeff back and obviously was in favor of the Exchange, she had slipped back to her original urge to kill a Nazi like a hound snapping at red meat. Maybe I should have seen that as a sign of things to come, but I didn't. And I don't think Cy did either.

"You've got to be with us here, Margaret," Cy said and Margaret looked at him and nodded.

Cy gave me another frowning look and turned to the Nazi. "You speak English?"

The Nazi stared at him.

"You are our prisoner," Cy said.

The Nazi still stared, mostly at Cy, but at Margaret, too.

"Try anything and Billy will shoot you in the head," Cy said, jerking his thumb in my direction. The Nazi turned to look at me again and I raised the rifle barrel and tightened my finger on the trigger, forgetting that the safety was on and it wouldn't fire no matter how hard I pulled, and also thinking about how Cy had said we couldn't trade a dead prisoner.

So that's how we captured him. Pretty easy, actually. And once it was done, we just stood there looking at each other. For a long time, it seemed.

Finally, Cy said, "English? You understand English?"

The Nazi looked at Cy and after a long pause, nodded his head slowly.

"We need to know about your mother," Cy said.

It was a pretty strange thing to say under the circumstances, and the Nazi jerked his head and looked at Margaret, then back at Cy.

"We're organizing war mothers," Cy said.

The Nazi looked at Cy and tilted his head like he couldn't understand or believe what he was hearing.

"Well?"

The Nazi didn't move.

"Come on, do you have a mother?"

Finally, the Nazi nodded slowly.

"Good, we'll tell you about it later, but that's all we need to know for now. Let's go."

We marched the prisoner down to the river and along the trail to my boat. Then we all climbed in and I started rowing us across. Cy held my rifle on the Nazi, and Margaret sat with her head down and muttered "Jeff, Jeff, Jeff," in a monotone that went on like the endless chirping of a cricket.

The Nazi sat on the front seat of the boat and I couldn't see much of him because I was sitting backwards so I could row, but when I twisted around to keep us headed in the right direction, I got glimpses. He sat stiff and straight and there was a deep frown on his Nazi face, which, it seemed to me, still didn't look as stern as most of the German soldier faces I had seen in newsreels. I tried to look for meanness, but he just seemed like an average guy worrying about something, a toothache maybe.

Once across the river, we climbed out of the boat and up the bank and I led the way along a deer trail into the thick grass and trees. It was at least a half mile to the old logging camp and even though there was a rough trail, it was tough going. I went first, pushing dead branches and clumps of weeds out of the way as much as I could. Margaret was next, and sometimes I had to stop and help her over a deadfall or across ditches of black muck. Then came the Nazi, who never seemed to take his eyes off Margaret, except to turn back occasionally to look at Cy.

Last was Cy, holding my rifle more or less pointed at the Nazi. Cy stumbled often, and once a branch knocked his hat off and he swore and jerked the rifle toward the Nazi. I don't think Cy even knew how to take the safety off and I wondered what he would do if the Nazi made a break for it. I remembered the feeling I had when we had climbed out of the boat and Cy said he would keep the rifle because I couldn't lead the way and guard the Nazi at the same time. It was both relief and regret, I guess. In a way I wanted to be the one to shoot the Nazi if he tried anything, yet in another way, I thought it would be better if Cy shot him.

It was very hot down in the thick brush, and clouds of mosquitoes came streaming up out of the weeds and swarmed around us. Margaret was moaning and half crying, and Cy suddenly shouted, "Damn it, are we lost?"

I had been down this trail so many times that I knew every bush and tree, and I didn't bother to answer. Then, finally, we were at the camp. I stopped under the big pine trees, and the others came up to stand beside me. They looked at the shelter of rusty roofing and rotting wood and at the river gurgling and glittering behind a screen of fluttering leaves. Always when Toby and I came here, it all seemed so inviting and right and simple, like it was our special place where we could do just as we pleased. Now it was suddenly very different: complicated, invaded, crowded. Nobody moved for a minute or so, then finally Cy said, "Well, Billy, we'll make it work."

Waist-tall bracken fern covered the ground like a shaggy green-brown carpet, and dogwood clumps and wild cucumber vines wove everything into a great tangle. I turned to see the Nazi staring at the river as Margaret suddenly shouted, "Jeff! I want Jeff!"

Cy looked at her. "In due time, Margaret," he said.

"Now!" Margaret shouted and looked at the Nazi.

"Jeff," she muttered.

Maybe there should have been some tip-off in the way Margaret said Jeff's name but if there was, I sure missed it. Looking back, it would be reasonable to think that somewhere in Margaret's wiring, there was a short circuit that allowed her to size up the prisoner trade in her own way. It was as if she was beginning to see the Nazi as Jeff, or at least a strong symbol of Jeff, one so real to her that she had to grab for it, maybe as she had grabbed for me in her bed the night of the telegram. There wasn't time to give it a lot of thought.

Cy took a flask out of his pocket and offered it to Margaret. "It's the only medicine we've got, and you need something," he said.

Margaret pushed his arm away and looked past him to where the Nazi stood next to a clump of ferns. "Jeff," she moaned again.

Cy took a swig from his flask, shoved it back into his pocket and then turned to the Nazi.

"What's your name?" he said.

The Nazi hesitated.

"Well?" Cy said.

"Otto," the Nazi finally said, and I remembered Mr. Rockford telling me his name down at the station.

"Well, Otto," Cy said, "What did you do back in Hitler heaven?"

The Nazi gave Cy a long look and finally said he was a language teacher and had been teaching English to German soldiers.

"Getting them ready to occupy the good old USA, I suppose," Cy said.

The Nazi looked at Cy and nodded slowly.

"How do you say *bullshit* in German?" Cy said, and he and the Nazi stared at each other until the Nazi looked down at his shoes.

"It is done," the Nazi said.

"Done!" Cy said. "It's done, all right! How the hell did you Kraut-heads let that demented mustachioed misfit turn you all into murdering Jew haters?"

"Not all," the Kraut said. "Not my family. Not lots of people."

Cy shot him a dirty look and shook his head. "No point in getting into it now. You're here and we're here, and Jeff is in Germany, and we're going to try to do some creative rearranging."

Cy stood in front of the Nazi like he was making a case before a jury. He waved his arms and pointed at the Nazi as he explained how the MOP Exchange would work. When he said Mrs. Roosevelt would be involved, the Nazi straightened his spine with a jerk. "Your president's *Frau*?" he said.

"We call her Eleanor," Cy said, "and she's one hell of a *Frau*."

The Nazi stared as Cy talked. Then he began to nod slowly. Cy finally shut up and the Nazi looked at Margaret and me, and then back at Cy. "It is too crazy," he said.

Nobody said anything for a long time.

"Of course, it's crazy," Cy said finally. "That's why it has a chance."

There were more long moments with just the noises of the swamp.

"It is impossible," the Nazi said, "like trading fleas in the middle of a dog fight."

"Say, I like that, Mr. English teacher," Cy said. "Damned near poetic. Truth is the chances for the MOP Exchange to work are pretty slim. But we're going to try it, and if you are not with us, we'll get another Kraut."

That left a lot of things unsaid and raised a bunch of questions, and there's no way to know how deep the Nazi got into any of it. He looked around at us again, his eyes lingering longest on Margaret as she sat with her hands folded on her knees, her face as blank as a board.

"It is so impossible, we must try it," the Kraut said finally.

Margaret gave him a thin smile as he stared at her.

"I will help," the Nazi said, and Cy looked at him for a long time. Finally, Cy told him we would bring food out tomorrow, and paper and pen so he could write to his mother and explain her role.

"She will do what you want," the Kraut said. "I know it."

The mosquito clouds got thicker, and Cy said we had to get the hell out of the swamp before we lost all our blood. He told the Nazi to rub mud on himself for mosquito protection, and we chained him up and got ready to head out. I had to hand it to Cy for thinking through the chaining details. When we were making plans, he said we would have to chain the Nazi to a tree so I volunteered Toby's garden chain. Cy came up with a couple of padlocks, one to keep the chain around the Nazi's neck and the other for looping around a tree. It worked great. The Nazi was chained up solid and he'd be staying that way until the trade went through. Lucky for him, Toby's chain was long enough so he could step through the brush and reach a back eddy of the river.

Margaret had been muttering Uncle Jeff's name, and as we got ready to leave, she suddenly said she wanted to stay with the Nazi so he wouldn't get away. Cy shook his head and told her she had to help set up the MOP Exchange. She scowled at the prisoner, and finally agreed to go with us. She stopped and looked back as we stepped onto the trail, and she stood that way until I touched her arm and we headed out.

127

CHAPTER SEVENTEEN

It was my day to work the afternoon shift, so I had the morning free to go with Cy to get food out to the Nazi. Cy had it ready when I got to his house: canned beans, a ring of baloney, some cheese, a loaf of bread, and several bottles of beer.

"Krauts love beer," Cy said. "They like the way it makes them belch and fart and piss like stallions."

I was stuffing everything into an old backpack when Cy said, "I'm not going with you, Billy. I can't take any more of that goddamned swamp."

That surprised me and a pang of anxiety poked up. I would be out in the swamp alone with the Nazi and I wasn't sure I was ready for that.

"There's no point in my going out there," Cy said. "I've got to clean house and scrub floors and hoe the garden."

He glanced at me to make sure I got the joke. I shrugged like I didn't care one way or another, which wasn't one hundred percent true. The MOP Exchange was his plan, after all, even though I had signed on and considered myself in as deep as he was. It just seemed like he should be on top of whatever was happening. But then he said he wanted to be around in case there was word from Mrs. Roosevelt, and that made some sense. And I would have Toby along, so I wouldn't be totally alone.

"If the mosquitoes haven't eaten him," Cy said, "tell that dunderhead Kraut not to get any ideas about crossing us." Then he handed me a blanket and some writing paper and a pencil.

"And tell him he could become famous as the first soldier in all of military history to go through the MOP Exchange. He might get the Iron Cross with mother clusters."

"Be careful," Cy said as I got ready to leave. "Otto the Kraut seems okay, but you never know about those bastards."

I settled the backpack straps on my shoulders and Toby and I headed for the swamp. I had my rifle along because it just doesn't make sense to go out into the swamp without either a rifle or a trout rod. And even though we had left the Nazi chained up like a circus elephant, he was still one of Hitler's soldiers and, like Cy said, there is no telling what one of them might do. I wondered what I would find as I headed back out there. I hoped it would all be just the way we had left it yesterday, with the Nazi—I can't think of him as Otto yet—sitting under the tree he was chained to, probably swatting at mosquitoes and looking forward to the food I was bringing. One thing is sure; I would make better time without Cy stumbling along behind me. That should get me back home earlier.

It was a quiet, dewy morning and I felt the dampness of it as I got close to the river. The moisture would burn off early and I knew that by mid-morning, the swamp would be as crisp as toast. I was thinking about that when I stepped around the stump where my boat is tied up. What I saw stopped me dead in my tracks: Margaret was sitting in the bow holding an old wicker suitcase and squinting at the sun! She wore slacks and a blouse and a hat with a wide brim that drooped down over her ears. She smiled and raised her hand. "I'm going with you, Billy," she said.

I'm not sure how long I stood there with my mouth open, but it was long enough for mosquitoes to home in on me as an easy target. I waved a hand in front of my face and tried to make sense of what I was seeing.

"I want to help," Margaret said.

"Help?" is all I could think to say.

"Help with Jeff. I have his clothes."

"But Jeff isn't..." I said, and stopped. It has been more obvious by the day that Margaret was losing it. To her, the prisoner trade meant only that Uncle Jeff was coming back to her. Maybe, in a way that only she can imagine, he already has, and that was all that mattered. The details had slipped away from her and now here she was like a roadblock, keeping the real thing from happening.

Possibilities went through my mind. I could take Margaret back to her home and to her mother, or maybe to Cy's house, or to my house, where my mother could deal with her. But none of it made any sense. Someone was sure to see us, and first, I would have to convince Margaret that it would better if she didn't go with me. One look at her and I knew that wasn't going to happen.

"Come on, Billy, let's go," Margaret said in a cheerful voice.

Toby knew the river-crossing routine and as I stood there wondering what to do, he jumped into the boat. He gave Margaret a sniff greeting and sat on the floor and looked back at me.

"Toby's ready," Margaret said and smiled as she reached out and patted Toby's head.

Where was that damned Cy? He needed to be here to decide what to do. Finally, I told myself maybe something would come up later to give me some options. So, I untied the boat and climbed in and started rowing as Margaret watched and smiled.

The dew and the morning sun had turned the swamp into a great tangle of bejeweled branches and vines and shaggy bogs.

As we got closer to it, the musky smell of damp decay was like the breath of wild things long dead. It would all turn dry and brittle as the sun moved higher, and even this early, I could feel the beginning of the day's heat. I glanced up to see a trio of turkey vultures circling high overhead, their black forms outlined against the white of a summer cloud like bat shadows.

Once across the river, I dragged the boat up onto the sand, and Margaret stepped through the weeds and climbed up onto the river bank. She carried the wicker suitcase as if it were full of breakable things, and she turned and smiled at me as we headed down the trail. Toby, as always, romped off in all directions and stuck his nose into everything. He seemed even more rambunctious than usual, like he was behind in his work, which I guess he was because he hadn't been with me last time I was in the swamp.

As we got closer to the camp, Toby stopped, sniffed the air, growled a couple of times and then started barking, which is bad because it's like blowing a horn to tell everyone and everything just where you are.

But it didn't matter on this morning because when we got to the camp, Otto the Kraut was sitting quietly under the rusty metal roof, Toby's chain and the padlock hanging down from his neck like awkward jewelry. He had smeared his arms and face with mud for mosquito protection, so he looked pretty strange, like something that had crawled up out of the river muck. He smiled and nodded when he saw me, and I noticed that he glanced at my rifle. Then Margaret stepped into view and he suddenly stood and stared at her. Margaret gazed back, her forehead pulled into deep creases. "Jeff?" she said.

The Nazi looked at me, and I shrugged and handed him the food. Margaret whispered Uncle Jeff's name again and sat on a log beside me as we watched the Nazi eat the baloney and beans and drink a bottle of beer. At one point, he raised the bottle and said, "Good! Thank you."

I tried to figure him out. Was he putting on a good Nazi act to back up his story of being drafted into Hitler's madness, or was he a clever believer just waiting for a chance to do his Nazi bit? I made sure my rifle stayed out of his reach, and I sat far enough away so the chain would keep him from grabbing me. When he finished eating, he glanced at me and looked at Margaret.

"Is Jeff your husband?" he said to her.

Margaret stared back at him. "Jeff," she said.

"They were married just before he left for Germany," I said.

The Nazi nodded and we sat there in the middle of the swamp noises and stared at each other. Then I remembered to give him the paper and pencil so he could write the letter to his mother. He scribbled for a long time, then folded the paper and stuffed it into an envelope that he addressed. He handed it to me and said, "My mother will like your friend's plan." He looked at Margaret and turned back to me, "Where was her Jeff captured?"

I didn't know how many Nazi questions I wanted to answer. Like Cy said, we didn't know much about our prisoner except that he had a mother in Germany, if we can believe what he says, which is a very big if. It was time for me to be more in charge instead of letting him question me like he was the one who had the upper hand.

"We should hear from Mrs. Roosevelt soon," I said and stood up.

The Nazi looked at me "It's a crazy thing we're doing," he said.

I nodded and turned to Margaret. "Let's go."

Margaret looked at me and shook her head.

"Come on," I said. "I've got to work the station this afternoon."

Margaret was sitting on the log, holding the suitcase handle in one hand and waving at mosquitoes with the other. She smiled at me and said, "I will wait here."

I got a sinking feeling. It had been a mistake to let Margaret come out to the camp. Now what was I supposed to do? Why hadn't I taken her back to her mother when I first saw her? And why wasn't Cy here to help me deal with her?

"You can't wait out here," I said.

Margaret shook her head up and down. "Soon," she said. "Jeff will come soon."

"It could be weeks, even months, before there's a trade," I said.

Margaret smiled and looked from me to the prisoner. "I'll wait," she said.

"I can't leave you out here alone with this Nazi," I said, and a feeling of exasperation boiled up like a spicy belch.

"Not a Nazi," the Kraut said suddenly. He shook his head and scowled, "Never a Nazi."

I turned back to Margaret and reached down to help her up. "Come on, Margaret," I said and realized I was begging.

She didn't budge. "Jeff is coming. I have to be here for him," she said.

I tugged at her arm, but she sat tight and smiled up at me. I looked from her to the Kraut.

He stared at Margaret with curiosity, as if he were trying to guess what she would do next.

"You can't carry her out," he said.

He was right, of course, and the upshot was that I left her there with him because I had no choice. A mix of anger and frustration roiled my insides. That damned Cy! I needed him to be there.

"She will be safe," the Kraut said.

There was no way for me to know that, but there was nothing I could do. I told Margaret to stay far enough away so the Kraut couldn't reach her, and she looked at me and nodded as if she understood. I thought fleetingly about leaving my rifle with her, but she didn't know how to use it and there was the danger that the Kraut would somehow end up with it.

I gave her the blanket and watched as she spread it over the log where she sat. Then I called Toby and we headed back down the trail. I took one last look at Margaret and the Kraut. Margaret smiled and waved as the Kraut looked at her. I had to force myself to turn and leave them. I thought back to the Kraut saying he wasn't a Nazi, and if there was any comfort in that, it wasn't much. I had the feeling I was betraying Uncle Jeff and everyone else. This was not the way I wanted to get into the war.

Toby ran ahead, obviously happy to be back on his swamp snoop. He was out of sight most of the time, and then I heard him barking off in the distance. It was the kind of barking that tells me he has chased something into a hole or up a tree and wants me to come and check it out. His barking got more intense and I stopped to listen. He was definitely onto something that had him getting more wound up by the second.

I was about to step off in Toby's direction when there was a single sharp pop, like a fire cracker…or a gun shot. Toby's barking stopped abruptly. My heart skipped a beat and I got a cold shiver that did not go away. I stood and listened but there were only the swamp sounds—insects and birds and the whisper of the wind. I finally called to him, tentatively at first, but then as loud as I could shout. There was no response, not even a distant yip or faint bark.

I walked and then ran the trails and river bank, calling his name and feeling more desperate each minute. A couple of times, I thought I heard Toby running through the brush and grass, but it had to be something else, probably a deer. Finally, I had to give up or be late for work. Crossing back over the river without Toby was like rowing through mud. It seemed to take forever and when I looked back at the swamp I felt things about it I had never felt before: dread, even fear.

My hands fumbled as I tied up the boat and looked back across the river for one last glimpse of the swamp. I wanted to see Toby come bounding out of the weeds and plunge into the river to catch up with me. There was nothing.

I hurried to Cy's house to tell him what had happened with Margaret and Toby. But he wasn't home, and it looked as if he had not been there all day. His morning newspaper was still out by the door and his cats whined at me as if they needed attention. One of them, the one he calls Poor Little Thing, was curled around a new litter of kittens on an old blanket behind the couch, and another had dragged in a dead gopher and was gnawing on it in a corner. I turned and walked out the door, feeling let down and abandoned. It was as if Cy and I had been carrying something heavy and important and he had suddenly dropped his end.

Damn him! Where was he? We needed to talk. Anger and doubt came boiling up. Why had I let him get me into something that was turning into so much trouble? The anger set in more as I headed for home to wash off the swamp grime and get down to the station. I tried not to think about Margaret, or Toby, but that was impossible. I needed to grab Cy around the neck and shout into his face that the MOP plan was falling apart, and my dog was gone and it was his damned fault.

CHAPTER EIGHTEEN

The house was quiet and empty when I went in through the back-door, eerie without Toby expressing his opinion about being either chained up outside or allowed to come in with me, which was always his preference. My mother had left a note on the kitchen table. It said Margaret had disappeared earlier in the day and she and Mrs. Zanders were looking for her. "She took her suitcase and she may have gone to Minneapolis," the note said, but it didn't say if my mother and Mrs. Zanders were going there to look for her.

I felt like somebody had poked me with a stiff finger to get me to do something. I didn't know what. For now, I only knew I had to hurry and get down to my job. Cliff is a pretty easy-going boss but he likes me to be on time, especially if he has plans to go bluegill fishing, and he goes almost every day. I smeared peanut butter on some bread and was running around the corner of the garage on my way to the station when I literally ran into Mrs. Deggerton.

"Billy," she said, "I need to pray with you."

We had almost collided and we were standing so close together I could see little white hairs growing out of the tops of Mrs. Deggerton's ears and I could smell the cooking smells of her. Her sudden presence had surprised me and for a minute I didn't know what to do or what to say. I stood there for a second like a dummy and then when I was about to step around her, Mrs.Deggerton reached out and wrapped her short, fat fingers around my wrist in a grip tight enough to cut off blood flow.

"I'm late for work," I said but she ignored me.

"We will talk to the Lord," she said in a bossy tone I've heard her use with Mr. Deggerton. I kept my mouth shut and looked for a way out. Short of jerking myself out of Mrs. Deggerton's clutches and running off like a spooked rabbit, there wasn't one. Looking back, that's what I should have done.

"We have to pray for you, Billy," Mrs. Deggerton said, "right here and now. Get down on your knees."

I thought she was joking, but she tightened her grip on my wrist and more or less leaned on me as she knelt in the grass. Her weight pulled down on my arm and put me off balance so the next thing I knew, I was on my knees too, which made it too late to even think about making a run for it. I dropped my head down in frustration and Mrs. Deggerton apparently took that as a signal that I was ready to get on with praying because she shut her eyes and pulled my hands in against the fat ridges around her stomach.

Then she started talking in a monotone and I didn't listen to the words until I heard her say something about Cy. Then I paid enough attention to realize she was asking God to more or less do away with Cy. She said if God would immediately send Cy to Hell, it would be in everyone's best interests, especially mine. I remember some of her exact words: "Please, God, let Satan take Cyrus Butler as soon as possible. He is an evil heathen and he is leading Billy astray."

I opened my mouth to object but thought better of it. When someone is into prayer as much as Mrs. Deggerton seemed to be, it's probably best to let them finish up. I don't know if there is such a thing as a prayer cramp, but there might be. So I didn't try to stop her, even though she was out of line. Or was she out of line? The President himself had prayed to God for help in killing and maiming, so for Mrs. Deggerton to ask that someone like Cy be whisked off the face of the earth and sent to Hell was probably not that big of a deal when compared to other war-time praying.

My knees were starting to cramp up and I'm sure Mrs. Deggerton's were too and that is likely the reason she finally pulled my hands tighter against her fat stomach and said *Amen*. I got to my feet easily, but Mrs. Deggerton lurched and swayed and I thought she was going to fall over, so I had to grab her arm and help her up.

"Oh, Billy," she said. "Can't you just feel the love of the Lord?"

I couldn't. What I felt was worry about being late for work and guilt for being involved in praying for Cy to be sent to Hell. I remember thinking that I would not tell him about it, though I'm sure he would have hooted with laughter and probably thanked me for praying that he would end up in a place where he had friends. I told Mrs. Deggerton I had to hurry or I would be late for work and I turned and ran toward the station.

I looked over my shoulder once to see Mrs. Deggerton standing by the corner of the garage with her arm up like she was either bestowing a blessing on me or giving me the Hitler salute. Some of the left-over anger at Cy bubbled up in Mrs. Deggerton's direction and I felt like returning her salute and shouting, "*Heil*, Satan!" or something like that. I didn't, of course. It would have just meant more trouble, and I already had enough of that.

Cliff looked at his watch as I came puffing in through the door. I told him I was sorry about being late, but I had been looking for my lost dog. If I had told him the truth—that I had been waylaid by a neighbor lady to pray with her in her backyard, he probably wouldn't have believed me. Cliff shrugged and said my dog would probably show up and then he got his worm bucket out of the pop cooler where he keeps it and left to go fishing.

I slumped down on the station stool and thought about what a rotten day it had been: Toby lost and Margaret lost in a different way, and my mother and Mrs. Zanders off on a wild goose chase to try to find her; Cy gone and still no word from Mrs. Roosevelt, even though we've got the MOP Exchange started and are obviously going to need her help very soon. I felt hollow and helpless.

Maybe I should have told Mrs. Deggerton about Toby and asked her to pray for him, or maybe I should have gone directly to God about Toby. But then I remembered Cy saying you might as well talk to a tree, and with that kind of a godless stuff percolating in my head, it would be no use for me to ask for any favors, even one as simple as finding a lost dog.

Cy would not have been surprised to hear that Mrs. Deggerton prayed for him to be sent to Hell. I heard him say in one of his rants that the most unreasonable and dangerous person on earth is one who demands that you believe in their god because if you don't, that person will feel totally justified in tearing you to pieces and burning the pieces in a ceremonial fire. He said it is worse if you don't have a god of your own—which he says he doesn't, because then the people with all the different gods hate your guts. This had been part of one of his longer rants—one that was sure to shore up his place in Hell, and he had gone on to describe how the godly gather in their tax-free edifices every Sunday to participate in symbolic, cannibalistic rituals centered around an autocratic spook nobody has ever seen or heard, and they come out of this absurdity and look down on the folks who don't buy into it.

It was miserable sitting there on the station stool staring out at the gas pumps and running countless scenarios through my mind of what might have happened to Toby and I would have bought into anything if I had felt it might bring him back. I felt a fresh stab of resentment at Cy for kicking dents in the "faith" that Reverend Thorston said was necessary for effective communication with the Almighty.

I tried anyway, getting as far as "Please, God," and then it dissolved and I went back to the scenarios. They kept getting worse, even to the point of Toby being attacked by a sow bear protecting her cubs. There are bears out in the swamp. I have not seen one, but I have seen their brush-pile dens and their tracks, and once on a sandbar near where my boat was tied up, I followed what I thought were bear tracks but they turned out to be made by one of the barefoot Pickert boys. I never told anyone about that.

There wasn't much business at the station, just an occasional farmer stopping to buy gas or a kid coming in for a candy bar, so there wasn't anything to stop me from worrying about Toby. Then suddenly, Reverend Thorston was standing in the door. He was wearing a long-sleeved white shirt with his clerical collar tight around his neck, and black pants, and a yellow straw hat that sat square on his head. Sweat trickled down his forehead and he fanned at himself with one hand and wiped a handkerchief at his face with the other.

"Billy," he said, "I have come to pray with you."

More praying! I should have told him I had already done my praying for the day with Mrs. Deggerton, but I kept my trap shut.

"Sometimes it's hard to accept the Lord's way," Reverend Thorston said as he put his hand on my shoulder and squeezed. "If God takes your Uncle Jeff, He must have an important job for him."

I was staring down at Reverend Thorston's shiny black shoes and thinking to myself that so far, God had arranged for Uncle Jeff to only be captured and it seemed pointless and even out of line for someone to suggest something worse, especially someone like Reverend Thorston, who claimed to have higher power connections. A job for Uncle Jeff! That just didn't make any sense, a job where? Obviously, Reverend Thorston was thinking of Heaven. He has been very good at creating a vision of Hell in my mind with raging fires and half-burned Toby screaming and howling in agony, endless stretches of misery and pain, paths of red-hot coals leading to boiling cauldrons, and bottomless fire pits.

Yeah, I know about Hell—but Heaven? I'm not so clear on that. Clouds and harps and angels is about as far as I get, and quite frankly, I'm not that impressed. There's got to be more than that. Apparently, there are "jobs." Maybe God is remodeling and needs carpenters and masons and all kinds of workers. That kind of speculating could probably be seen as disrespectful, so it was a good thing Reverend Thorston couldn't read my mind as he reached down and took my hands in his.

"Let us pray," he said.

His hands were soft and damp, and you could tell he didn't do much work with them. He closed his eyes and so I closed mine, but opened them again so I could watch the gas pumps in case somebody drove up. Reverend Thorston's praying was different than Mrs. Deggerton's, more reasoned, I guess, as if he were making a case for improved conditions but if they didn't happen that would be okay, and we would accept whatever God handed out.

Mrs. Deggerton's praying had been more demanding, as if God were a butcher and she was ordering up a soup bone and it had better be a good one. She had been particularly direct when she had said she wanted Satan to get Cy. Reverend Thorston, being a professional, obviously knew more about what he was doing, and instead of coming right out and requesting that someone be sent to Hell, he would likely just make a suggestion. I thought fleetingly about asking him to suggest that I'd find Toby, but that would mean involving him in my problems and might encourage him to go on longer than he otherwise would, so I let it pass. Then he might come up with some odd thing that would really bug me, like Toby dying and making friends with all the creatures in Heaven. Toby would never do that: if there are deer and rabbits in Heaven and Toby gets there, he is going to be chasing them. And nobody is thinking he is dead anyway. It just seems that Reverend Thorston has a tendency to favor the worst possible outcome of a situation and I didn't want him doing that with Toby.

A car drove up to the pumps just as Reverend Thorston seemed to be warming up and he was right in the middle of asking God to give me the strength to bear up when a voice shouted, "Billy, get your goddamned ass out here, I ain't got all goddamned day!"

Reverend Thorston opened his eyes and stopped praying. He glanced out toward the gas pumps and shook his head. "You better take care of your customer," he said, and there was a heavy sadness in his voice.

The customer was Danny Flaherty, a farmer from west of Oxbow who stops in often, sometimes before a prolonged visit to the pool hall and sometimes after, which was the case on this day. As I stepped out of the station, Mr. Flaherty opened the door of his pickup truck and hung onto it as he pulled himself out. "Jesus Christ, Billy," he shouted, "You in there playing with yourself?"

It was embarrassing that Reverend Thorston had to hear Mr. Flaherty's dirty mouth, but there wasn't anything I could do about it. I glanced through the station window and couldn't see Reverend Thorston, so maybe he had gone into the restroom and shut the door. I washed Mr. Flaherty's windshield and was just putting the gas cap back on his banged-up old Dodge pickup when Wilber Bender came walking up. He and Mr. Flaherty were obviously old friends who spent a lot of time drinking together, and they immediately went into a loud routine of greeting each other with insults.

"You had any good sheep lately?" Wilber asked.

"No, but I rented one to a blacksmith," Mr. Flaherty said.

They both whooped with laughter, and Wilber said, "Flaherty, you'd better have something to dilute that load of whiskey you're carrying. Come on, I'll buy you a pop."

Wilber walked into the station and Mr. Flaherty staggered after him, and when I went in after them, there was no sign of Reverend Thorston. The door to the restroom was shut so that had to be where he was.

"I shouldn't rust my guts with this horse piss," Mr. Flaherty said, "But if you're buying, I'll do it because you are the cheapest son-of-a-bitch on God's green earth."

"Shit," Wilber said, "If I was as cheap as you, I'd still be sucking my mama's tit."

They went on and on like that as they drank a couple of sodas, their jokes and insults getting dumber by the minute, and I was getting more and more concerned about Reverend Thorston. Why didn't he come out? I didn't feel it was my duty to inform Mr. Flaherty and Wilber about his presence, but it was an odd situation and I didn't know what to do. It more or less got resolved when Mr. Flaherty suddenly said, "Jesus, I have to piss really bad!" and lurched over to grab the restroom doorknob. When the door wouldn't open, he shouted, "What the goddamn hell?" and he pounded on it and turned to me. "Some asshole in there, Billy?" he said.

I nodded, and Mr. Flaherty said, "Well, Jesus Christ, he's been in there a long, goddamned time." He turned back to the door and pounded on it so hard I thought his fist was going to go through the wood panels.

"Hey, you son of a bitch," he shouted. "Pull your goddamned pants up and come out of there. I gotta piss."

Nothing happened, and Mr. Flaherty danced around on one leg and yelled, "Hey, asshole, we got an emergency out here, goddamnit!"

Still nothing happened, and it was looking more and more like Mr. Flaherty was either going to piss in his pants or somewhere on the station floor. His voice went up about two octaves until he was almost squealing. "You goddamn son-of-a-bitch, bastard jerk-off, come out right now or I'm breaking the goddamn door down."

There was a click and the door opened slowly and there stood Reverend Thorston. Mr. Flaherty stared at him for a split second and then reached in and grabbed Reverend Thorston by the front of his shirt and jerked him out of the restroom and flung him aside as if he were a bundle of rags.

For just a few seconds, all you could hear was Mr. Flaherty's forceful stream of piss going into the toilet, the sound coming through the door as loud as a waterfall. Wilber let out a whoop and said, "By God, Reverend, that was a close one," and went into a laughing fit that ended up with him coughing and choking and wiping at the tears running down his face.

Reverend Thorston stared at Wilber.

"What were you doing hiding in Billy's restroom?" Wilber said, and started laughing and choking again.

"Yeah, Reverend," Mr. Flaherty said from the restroom doorway, "and for such a long time?"

He and Wilber laughed and whooped and slapped at their legs.

"Begging your pardon, Reverend," Wilber said finally, "but it's a little odd."

"Billy and I were praying," Reverend Thorston said.

"In the damned shit house?" Mr. Flaherty asked.

Then he and Wilber were off again.

Reverend Thorston glanced at me and walked out the door. He had forgotten his hat on the counter and so I grabbed it and ran outside to give it to him. He stopped and looked at me. "They're going to Hell, Billy," he said. "Don't let them take you with them." Then he turned and walked off down the street.

Back inside the station, Wilber and Mr. Flaherty were whooping and laughing. They finally went out and got into Mr. Flaherty's pickup and said they were going back up to the pool hall because drinking pop had made them thirsty. Mr. Flaherty's pickup almost hit the fire hydrant as it swerved out onto the street.

CHAPTER NINETEEN

It was quiet after Wilber and Mr. Flaherty left and there wasn't anything to keep me from thinking about Toby. I came up with a new scenario where he got onto the trail of something that really interested him and he decided to follow it no matter what. I was trying to fit the little popping sound into it when Mr. Rockford pulled up to the pumps.

"My man ran off on me," he said as he hauled himself out of his pickup.

I stepped toward his windshield, but he waved me off. "Never mind that," he said. "I'm in a hurry. Gotta go talk to the Army. Just give me a dollar's worth."

Mr. Rockford watched impatiently as I pumped his gas, rocking back and forth on his heels and rubbing his hands together. "Best damned hired man I ever had, and I was getting him so cheap," he said. He was talking about Otto, of course, and I felt a strange little surge of power from knowing more about it than Mr. Rockford did.

"He just disappeared," Mr. Rockford said, "Went out to cut thistles and never came back."

Mr. Rockford plucked a dollar out of his wallet and handed it to me. Then he climbed into his truck and drove off without another word, which was good because I didn't want to be talking about Otto the Kraut. I wanted to be back out in the swamp looking for Toby. He had to be out there, maybe caught in a raccoon trap or stuck down in a hole. I will find him! He's all I can think about, except for Margaret, of course.

If I hadn't been so preoccupied with all of that, I might have noticed that there was more military activity around town as the day wore on. It probably had to do with Otto missing from the prison camp, and once I started watching it, I got an uneasy feeling. It would be totally dumb to think they wouldn't be looking for him by now and that they wouldn't be asking around to find out what people might have seen. Maybe somebody had spotted Margaret and Cy and me with him.

I started watching the traffic more carefully, and then a car I didn't recognize pulled up to the pumps and two men got out. They wore slacks and short-sleeved shirts and it was plain to see they weren't workers from the pea factory. They watched me as I washed their windshield, and one of them said, "Lots of bugs out last night." He was tall and slim and had a crewcut that was so flat his head looked like a block of wood. The other man was too bald to wear a crewcut, and the rim of hair around his head was mostly gray. He was short and muscular, like a badger.

"You're Billy," the crewcut man said suddenly.

It was more a statement than a question, but I nodded and looked at him.

"We're from the FBI," the bald one said, showing a badge in the palm of his hand.

My heart dropped.

"Nothing for you to be concerned about," Flat-top said. "We just want to have a little chat."

I felt something bad closing in on me. They must know everything. I'll be in prison until I'm an old man, or maybe shot as a traitor. Little sweat creeks trickled down my ribs and my knees felt wobbly.

"Sheriff Curtis says you know the Windigo Swamp pretty good," Flat-top said.

"Yeah, he says you spend a lot of time out there," Baldy said.

I could feel my face turning red and I gripped the windshield rag tight to keep my hands from shaking.

"We were wondering if you've ever seen anything unusual going on out there?" Flat-top said.

I stared at him and he smiled, "Have you seen anyone along the river or out in the swamp who wasn't fishing or hunting?"

My mind was going a mile a minute. It didn't sound as if they knew we had Otto, or maybe they were just playing dumb.

"There's some black market stuff going on around here and if you know anything that might help us put a stop to it, we'd really appreciate it," Baldy said.

"Yes," Flat-top said, "it could be important to the war effort."

They were smiling and looking at me like we were all in the same game, which was ridiculous; they were cats and I was a damned mouse, and they were playing with me.

"You were out at the Bund meeting in Almira," Baldy said.

It was like before when the other one had said my name—not as if he was asking a question but stating a fact and letting it hang out there as if it meant something.

"We're not accusing you of anything, Billy," Baldy said, "But there are some people in the Bund we worry about. Maybe you can you tell us who was there and why you were there?"

"I was visiting the Schmidt girls," I said before I really thought about it. It just seemed that if I didn't say something soon I might lose it and blab everything, and that old lie about the Schmidt girls that Cy had come up with out at the Bund meeting was the first thing that popped into my mind.

"Well, I can certainly understand a handsome young fellow like you visiting girls," Flat-top said.

"We're not going to bother you anymore," Baldy said, "but maybe you can help us."

"Yeah," Flat-top said, "we're asking you to be our agent in the swamp."

"Just tell us what you see out there."

"It could be a big help, Billy."

"Really."

They weren't being straight with me. They were treating me like I was a dumb kid and that's what I was feeling like.

"We'll be back," Baldy said.

"You're with us, now," Flat-top said as they drove off.

It's a good thing no customers came in right then because I don't think my legs would have held me up to pump gas. I collapsed onto the station stool inside and stared out at the pumps as Frank Sinatra sang *All or Nothing at All* on the radio. A news guy came on and said Tojo had resigned as prime minister of Japan. Well, who gives a rat's ass? The FBI is on my case and J. Edgar Hoover is probably looking at my file this very minute—and my dog is missing. I've got troubles bigger than Tojo's.

I was trying to get myself collected when Vernon Pickert came skidding across the driveway on his rusty old bicycle. "Billy, ain't you heard?" he shouted.

"Heard what?" I said, knowing I had to play Vernon's little game of being dumb about something he knew.

"A Kraut got loose," Vernon shouted. "There's all hell to pay at the camp."

Vernon made a circle around the pumps and slid to a stop so his back wheel tipped over a Quaker State oil display.

"There's MPs all over town," Vernon said. "Even came to our place and looked through the sheds and the junkyard. Pissed off the old man. He told them he wouldn't hide no goddamn Nazi unless it was Hitler himself, and then he'd get a good ransom for the bastard."

Vernon circled the drive again and headed off down the street. "Better get your gun, Billy," he shouted.

I had an odd feeling that things might be slipping even more out of control. It had been one calamity after another: Margaret stuck out in the swamp with the Kraut, Toby disappearing, Cy gone. And then I got trapped into that stupid praying with Mrs. Deggerton, and the embarrassing thing with Reverend Thorston happened, and finally the two FBI guys showed up and treated me like I was a dumb kid.

My brain hurt and I felt weak as I carried in the oil and tire displays at closing time, locked up, and finally headed for home. Thoughts tumbled over each other until none of them made any sense and then the final blow came like the whack of a two-by-four over the head. As I stepped into the kitchen, my mother said, "Your grandmother is in jail."

I looked to see if she was joking. She wasn't. Her eyes were wide and her face was white, and she stared at me like she couldn't believe what she was saying.

"The FBI made Sheriff Curtis lock her up," my mother said. "They said she was a threat to the White House and had to be jailed until she confessed."

The sinking feeling got worse.

"I have no idea what she might have done," my mother said. "Maybe wrote a threatening letter to the President. She won't say a word to anyone, even to me."

Fireworks exploded in my brain, half-formed thoughts shot off in all directions, questions sparked more questions, and finally I felt something like panic creeping in. The two FBI guys had obviously known all about the MOP Exchange and must have suspected that I was part of it. They had played me for a total fool.

There had been too much to handle in the last few days, too much to sort through and figure out. Now as my mother said this unbelievable thing about Grandma Forrest, I felt a fresh burst of anger at Cy for what he had gotten me into: my dog was gone and I was sick from worrying about him; my Aunt Margaret—my lovely, suffering Aunt Margaret— was stuck out in the damned swamp, far from the help she desperately needed; and now my grandmother was in jail—my grandmother, for God's sake! And in the middle of it, with FBI agents circling like vultures, Cy had abandoned me.

It all suddenly became clear: Cy might have convinced me there was reason to try the MOP Exchange, but I could no longer go along with it. I couldn't let these things happen to the people around me just to prop up a scheme that Cy himself said had the same chance as a snowball in Hell. And now even that slim chance was apparently gone. The letter to Mrs. Roosevelt had obviously been turned over to the FBI, and probably the one we had mailed to Otto's mother in Germany as well.

It was all going to end and it was going to end badly, and the longer it went on, the worse it was going to be. Certain things had to happen: Otto the Kraut had to go back to the POW camp; Margaret had to come home from the swamp so her mother and Doc could take care of her; Grandma had to get out of jail immediately; and somehow Toby had to come back home. Yeah, that definitely had to happen. Toby had to come home.

I thought about talking to my mother about all of it, even the part about Margaret, but that wouldn't make sense. There wasn't anything she could do. It would just be more reason for her to get on me for doing stupid things. I didn't need that now. I had to lay it all out for Sheriff Curtis, everything, every last detail. I had no idea what that might lead to— certainly exposure as the dumbest of "dumb kids" and maybe even prison for being a threat to the war effort. It didn't matter, I had to do it, as beat and worn down as I was, I had to do it, now!

The night still had baby softness about it as I stepped out into it. Its growing darkness softened the shapes of buildings and garbage cans and utility poles, and it made shafts and random pools of yellow light along the street. I had a weird thought that it would be nice to dissolve into it and come back with the fresh dew in the morning.

The shortest route to the Sheriff's office is the back alley that runs the length of Oxbow. It's where kids snoop for trash treasures and dogs sniff for pork chop bones, and I know it much better than the sidewalk out in front of the houses and business places. The alley runs along the backs of the stores all the way through town, and certain spots have little personal histories: the burning barrel in back of Harry Meyers' grocery store where Jerry Curren caught his shirt on fire trying to fish out a broken box of cookies; the pile of greasy car parts behind the Chevy garage where one of the younger Pickert boys got a smashed toe from a dropped manifold; and the piss corner inside the grist mill that is just a funnel and a piece of hose going down through the floor so the pee runs out onto the ground under the mill. It is handy for the farmers who get full of beer while they are waiting in the pool hall for their grain to get ground up. It smells bad and there is a risk in using it because Sherm Morgan who runs the feed mill sometimes whacks on the tin partition and yells, "Quit playing with yourself in there," which scares you so bad you can't pee for hours even though you needed to really bad.

Some of this brain trash sifted through my mind as I walked the alley. Maybe it was just a way to keep from thinking about the mess I had gotten myself into, or that Cy had gotten us into. I felt the anger rise up again. As if that surge of emotion had been a summons, I suddenly spotted Cy. He was standing on the sagging back steps of the pool hall smoking a cigar and talking to someone I couldn't see clearly. I stopped and stared at him, and he looked up and saw me.

"Billy," he shouted, and waved his arm. "Come on over here."

I felt like marching up to him and punching his old pointed nose, but I just stood and glared at him.

"Come on," Cy shouted. "I want you to meet someone."

When I didn't move, Cy stepped down off the porch and walked over. He stopped with his face close to mine and I could see the little red blood vessels on his nose and smell a faint soap aroma, which was odd because Cy always smells like booze, never like soap.

"Jesus, Billy, you look terrible," Cy said. "What the hell you been doing?"

I couldn't talk, partly because I didn't know where to start, and I was mad at Cy and also because I wasn't sure I could keep myself together to get through it all, especially the part about Toby. Cy suddenly grabbed my arm and pulled me along behind as he walked back to the pool hall steps.

"Give me your drink," he said and an arm reached out and handed him a glass. "Here," he said. "It's whiskey and Coke, just what you need."

The glass felt cold and solid in my hand and I tried to see where it had come from, but the back steps were in deep shadow and all I saw was somebody standing just outside the door.

"Drink it," Cy said.

I looked at him, at the familiar jut of his jaw and the wrinkles across his forehead, and the look in his eyes, and for reasons that made no sense then or haven't since, I tipped the glass up and drank until it was empty. The mixture of sweet and bitter went down easy and pooled in my guts as soothing as malted milk, and then there was a sudden little electrical thing in my head that made my eyes blink.

I looked at Cy and he took my glass and handed me another.

"Here," he said. "I don't know what you've been doing but I can see you need to back off and take a fresh run at it."

None of this was making any sense, and as I stood there in the fading twilight, I suddenly didn't care. I gulped down the second drink, and heard Cy say to somebody they'd better slow me down. I had this crazy feeling that I didn't want to slow down. I blinked some more and looked toward the back corner of the steps, and it flashed through my head that I must be suddenly drunk and seeing things.

Back in the shadows was a woman, a colored woman. She was looking at me and smiling and I saw a row of white teeth with gaps. She wore a bright red turban and a flowered dress that squeezed her sturdy body. A glittering necklace hung down over her jutting breasts and her black skin blended into the shadows like she wasn't really there. That must be it—she wasn't really there. The whiskey and Coke was having its way with me already. There are no colored people in Oxbow, never have been, except maybe once briefly when that patched-up circus came through with its one limping elephant and "genuine African savages," who were former head hunters, according to the circus advertising.

On top of that, women aren't allowed in the pool hall, although strictly speaking, the colored woman I thought I was seeing wasn't really in the pool hall, just on the back steps. I had never seen a colored woman before and I blinked and stared to see if she would go away. She didn't and I felt Cy nudge me and hand me another drink. He pointed at the woman and said, "Billy, meet my new wife, Lobelia Cardinalis. Her mama named her after a swamp flower. Ain't she pretty?"

CHAPTER TWENTY

Maybe I had died and gone to Hell. If so, it was nothing like Reverend Thorston described. There was no fire, at least none that I could feel, and there was no moaning and wailing and screeching. But there was music, like something I might have heard at Cy's, a raunchy saxophone blistering the paint off the walls and a trumpet poking at cracks in the ceiling, and somebody was singing. The singing was low and soft, with a strange attraction that made you want to inhale it, draw it in until it was vibrating in your bones like a cat's purr. The sax and the trumpet stopped then, but the singing went on.

Wherever I was, it smelled like lye soap, strong lye soap, like the whole place had been scrubbed clean, which didn't make sense if I was in Hell. There was an odd comfort in not seeing what I was hearing and smelling and an ominous feeling about waking up to unpleasantness. I did not want to open my eyes, but curiosity took over and I blinked them open and shut quickly.

In the middle of what I saw was the colored woman from the back steps of the pool hall, her black face shiny with sweat and her spaced white teeth showing a smile. But now her jewelry and red turban were gone and a white scarf was tied around her head and a few strands of red hair were sticking out from under it. And in that first one-blink look she was carrying a spear. I blinked again. It wasn't a spear, it was a mop.

Then I heard Cy's voice. "Billy, a guy who blinks ain't dead."

Where was I? Certainly not at Cy's. It couldn't be his place. It didn't stink. But then I opened my eyes and saw Cy sitting in a chair off to the side, his bowler tipped back and a grin making his cheeks stick out.

"Wake up," Cy said. "We've got a war to win."

Some of it started to come back when I heard "war" and I shut my eyes to turn it off.

151

"It's no use," Cy said. "You've got to face up. I've been through it too many times. Open your eyes, get up, empty your bladder, and drink a big glass of buttermilk."

Buttermilk! The thought of it made my stomach heave and that forced me do some of what Cy suggested: I opened my eyes, struggled to my feet and lurched into the bathroom. In the confusion of answering to multiple body demands, I realized again that I couldn't be at Cy's house. His bathroom was always a filthy stink hole. This one was clean and smelled of that lye soap. When I finally got myself together as much as I could, I eased the bathroom door open and peeked out.

"Come on out," Cy said. "I'll pour you some buttermilk."

I slammed the door shut and turned back to more retching. When I did finally step out of the bathroom, I couldn't believe it. It was Cy's house, all right, but it was like I had never seen it. The clutter and the garbage were gone, at least in the room I could see, and the top of the table, which I had never seen before, was cleared and it even looked as if someone might have tried to polish it. Even the old piano in the corner had been cleared off and dusted.

"Isn't it something?" I heard Cy say. He was sitting in a chair near the door and he made a sweeping gesture with his arm. "She's a cleaning fool, did all this since yesterday. Can you believe it?"

What I saw was truly amazing and it helped take my mind off my miseries. I looked around for the "cleaning fool," and Cy said, "Oh, she's moved on to more challenges. She saw you were going to be okay and she headed for the kitchen with a mop. That's her singing to the cats."

I listened for a few seconds to the sound of a woman's singing sifting through the open door, and then I stumbled across the room and collapsed into one of the chairs. My head felt as if it might fall off.

"You're doing pretty good," Cy said, "all things considered."

I didn't think I was doing pretty good. I felt terrible.

"You got a little drunk last night. Came on kind of sudden-like, and before we realized what was happening, we were hauling you home in Harry Meyers' grocery cart."

I didn't want to think about any of it, but the first crazy thing that came to mind was how I would ever explain things to my mother. I would have to tell her I had camped down by the river and hope she believed me. But then it began to dawn on me that I had bigger troubles than trying to sell a dumb lie. Slowly, it started coming back. I'd been on my way to the sheriff's office, to tell truth about the MOP Exchange so Grandma Forrest could get out of jail when suddenly Cy had come out of nowhere to jerk me back like he had me on a leash.

I looked at him and felt a surge of anger. "Grandma Forrest is in jail," I said.

It made my head hurt to talk but it had nothing to do with the words. They were true. It was the effort of putting them together that hurt.

"I know about your grandmother, heard about it at the pool hall yesterday," Cy said. "Everybody was talking about it. It is unfortunate, but it is not a disaster."

"How can you say such a dumb thing?" I asked and scowled at him.

"Well, as you know, I've been in jail, quite often actually, and it isn't all that bad. The experience might even be good for your grandmother."

"She's in there because of your...our plan," I said.

"No doubt about that. So, I guess you and I and Margaret will have to go explain to the sheriff and get her out."

"Margaret's in trouble. She's out in the swamp with the Kraut."

Cy jerked his head back and looked at me. "Well, I didn't know that," he said, "but it doesn't surprise me. We've been losing Margaret since she first got word about your uncle."

"She needs help, but she won't come back to town with me."

"We've got to fix that."

"And Toby is lost in the swamp."

Cy stared at me for a second or two. "How the hell could your dog get lost in the swamp?" he said.

"I think something happened to him, maybe something bad."

Cy wrinkled his brow and wiped a hand through what little hair he has left. "Sorry to hear that, Billy," he said, "but Toby's a smart dog, he'll show up. He's probably chasing a coyote in heat."

Thinking about Toby made all the worst woozy feelings come crashing back and I thought I might have to head for the bathroom again. Then I looked up to see the colored woman standing at the kitchen door. She smiled at me and nodded. "Welcome to the world," she said, and laughed a lilting sound that went up and down the scale and settled in a low chuckle. Her sudden appearance startled me, and I must have jumped because Cy snorted and said, "Don't be afraid, Billy. She won't hurt you."

They both laughed. To be honest about it, I was afraid of the colored woman, not afraid in the sense that she would do me harm with a spear or anything like that, but in the sense that I had never even seen a colored woman and here was one coming into my life like she was just another human being, which I guess she was.

"Billy," Cy said. "I can see you are struggling. You've never seen a colored person before, have you? Sure never been in the same room with one."

The colored woman laughed and said, "Go gently, Cyrus."

"Only one thing to do," Cy said. "Just like with a hangover, face up to the situation." As he spoke, Cy walked across the room, grabbed the colored woman by the hand and pulled her over to where I sat. "Easy, Cyrus," I heard her say as she stopped in front of me.

"First, you shake hands," Cy said, and he pulled the woman's hand out toward me and grabbed at my arm. The palm of her hand was different than the rest of her skin, lighter colored, like it had been used so much the black was starting to wear off. I couldn't help staring at it.

"Come on, take her hand," Cy said.

I got to my feet and was suddenly shaking the woman's hand and looking into her eyes. They were brown and shiny and framed in the corners by V-shaped wrinkles. It seemed like you could see a long way into them.

"Hot damn, Billy," Cy said. "You are touching a genuine Negro. How does it feel?"

It didn't feel any different than shaking anybody's hand, except maybe her hand was cleaner than a lot of them I shake down at the station.

"Don't let go," Cy said and stepped back. "Lobelia, I know you and Billy met last night, but there were some complications, so I want to introduce you again. Billy, meet Miss Lobelia Cardinalis, the best damned jazz and blues singer to ever grace the stage of the Alvin."

I looked at the colored woman, and her smile widened.

"Everybody in the jazz world knows her as 'Red Honey' and she can sing the birds out of the trees. Wait until you hear her!"

The woman and I were still holding hands and looking at each other.

"We got married two days ago," Cy said, "so she's still a bride, Billy, and if you want to kiss…"

"Cyrus!" the colored woman said in a sharp voice.

"Well, yeah, I guess we'll leave things at hand-shaking," Cy said.

"I'm proud to know you, Billy, and I hope we can be friends," the woman said. Her voice was soft and soothing, and I felt the pressure of her hand tighten on mine. I looked at her and nodded. "I've heard a lot about you," she said. "Cyrus says he's trying to save you from Oxbow, whatever that means."

"Just like I'm trying to save you from the decadence of show business," Cy said, and reached out to put an arm around the woman's shoulders. She looked at him and laughed.

"Mr. Cyrus Butler," she said, "I'm loving you to death, but we'll see who saves who from what."

CHAPTER TWENTY-ONE

I don't feel like the same person. I am, of course, Billy Forrest, too young for war and too old for motherly molly-coddling. But there have been changes. I can feel them, some good, some bad, though my judging them has no more significance than a dog figuring out where to scratch first. Looking back, I'd have to say that Cy marrying Lobelia was probably the big turning point. So, I'll go back to when I found out about that, to me standing there holding her hand and her telling me she hoped we could be friends.

I now see that from the very second Lobelia came into my life, everything seemed to be different. We stood there looking at each other and she said, "We're just people, Billy." She gave my hand a squeeze and let go and we sat down at the table with Cy.

"Yeah," Cy said. "That's the first thing you've got to get. Coloreds are people just like you and me, not animals, not savages, just goddamned people with different skin."

I tried not to stare at Lobelia.

"It's okay," she said. "Look as much as you want."

"Yeah, she's used to being looked at," Cy said. "Show business, you know."

Lobelia looked at Cy, then at me. "Cyrus," she said, "it might help if I told Billy a little about myself."

"Good idea," Cy said, "and don't be leaving out the bad parts."

"Bad?" Lobelia said. "I don't know what you mean, Mr. Cyrus Butler. What happens happens. It's life, not good or bad, just life."

Then I listened as she told about being born on a Mississippi farm and of a joyous childhood of running through the woods and fields with her brothers and sisters as free as wild animals. She told of her sharecropper father, who was always singing, and her "Queen" mother, who loved wild flowers and had an old book with the pages falling out that had a picture of a beautiful red swamp flower called a *Lobelia cardinalis*, and that's where her name came from because she was born with red hair. She told of being so poor they lived on turnips and wild rabbits and how when she was thirteen, she went singing with a banjo player from Jackson, Mississippi. She got dumped off somewhere in Alabama, she said, and sang in a bunch of different places in Kansas City and New York, and got her show business name—Red Honey—and made lots of money.

Lobelia stopped talking and looked at Cy.

"She was big time," Cy said, "Even made some recordings."

Lobelia shook her head. "From Harlem to the Alvin in Minneapolis wasn't a pleasant trip, Billy, and let's just say we all have our vulnerabilities."

"Except me, of course," Cy said.

"You, Mr. Butler," Lobelia said, "have more vulnerabilities than a fresh-hatched duck."

They laughed, and Cy turned to me, "I've been proposing to her for years and she finally gave in."

"I didn't give in," Lobelia said, "I just decided this last caper of yours was probably going to get you into serious trouble and you'd get locked up and I'd miss your sorry company."

"You have to understand," Cy said, "that Lobelia is the smartest person I have ever met. It pains me to say it, but she may even be smarter than me."

"There are times when that's not a high bar," Lobelia said.

The two of them looked at each other, and Cy turned to me. "Billy, you know once I make up my mind to do something, I do it, right?"

I nodded.

"And I guess you could say there have been times when I haven't thought things through to the end."

"You could say that," Lobelia said, and laughed.

"What I'm getting at," Cy said, "is that after long consultation with this woman, I have been convinced that we've got to back off our MOP Exchange plan and we've got to do it right away."

I couldn't believe what I was hearing. Cy looked at me with a vague expression of amazement and doubt. It was something I don't remember seeing in him before.

"You can't fool around with a government at war," Lobelia said. "It's too nervous and out of control and it'll throw you in prison or shoot you just to get you out of the way, like sweeping bugs off a gun deck."

"My compliments on that analogy, Miss Lobelia," Cy said, "and I don't take the bug part personally."

"Nothing personal intended, but you go fooling with the Army's POWs and writing to the President's wife in war time, you are asking for big trouble."

"I still think MOP has possibilities," Cy said, "but there are some indications things aren't going the way we planned."

"Your heart may have been in the right place," Lobelia said, "but I do believe you overlooked a few details."

"The lady is right, Billy,' Cy said. "We've got to back off. If it were just me, that would be one thing, but there's you and Margaret to think about, and, of course, your grandma."

I thought about Margaret and Grandma with their focus on Uncle Jeff walking in through the door and their not worrying much about the incredibly slim chance of that happening, but just wanting it so much they didn't care about anything else. Now that unrealistic hope would be jerked away from them like a bone from starving dogs. But it was all collapsing; the MOP plan was coming apart before it even got off the ground.

Lobelia was right. We had to end it before bad things started to happen. I remembered how I had concluded on my own that once the FBI got involved and the prisoner scheme got Grandma Forrest in jail, MOP had pretty much run out of bounds and had to be stopped. That's what I had been on my way to do when Cy had detoured me onto the back steps of the pool hall.

"I'm not looking forward to this," Cy said. "It feels a little like pissing on your own campfire before it has a chance to get going."

"You were going to get your privates burned," Lobelia said.

Cy looked at her and nodded. "See what I mean about her being so smart."

Lobelia shook her head and patted Cy's arm. "It just comes from living with trouble," she said. "You see it coming and try to figure a way out."

"First," Cy said, turning to me, "we'll tell the whole story to Sheriff Curtis so your grandma can get out of jail. Then we'll see to getting the Kraut and Margaret out of that goddamned swamp."

"Margaret!" Lobelia said, and she turned quickly to face Cy. "Margaret is out in the swamp?"

Cy nodded and then told her how Margaret had refused to leave my swamp camp after she had gone with me to take food out to Otto.

"Oh, that poor woman," Lobelia said. "From what you say, she's losing her mind with grief and now she's marooned out in the wilderness with a German prisoner."

"We didn't plan it that way," Cy said.

"Well, we've got to get her out of there, right away. She's got to be where people can take care of her."

"We'll get her," Cy said, "before anyone even knows she was out there."

"You'll need my help," Lobelia said.

Cy jerked his head around and looked at Lobelia. "Lobelia, you don't want to go out into that goddamned place. It's nothing but bogs and bugs and muck and spring holes and…"

"I've been in swamps before, grew up on the edge of one."

Cy shook his head. "We will have to see how things go at the sheriff's office."

"There is one thing I need to attend to," Lobelia said, "I need some boots and long pants for swamping. Billy, how about doing a little shopping with me? You can show me where the stores are and help me carry stuff."

I was starting to feel better—not so tired and woozy—and moving would probably be better than sitting around Cy's house wondering how long a hangover lasted. And there wasn't time to go looking for Toby, which is what I really wanted to be doing. It was mid-morning, and I had to work the afternoon shift at the station. I thought about Cy saying that Toby might be chasing a coyote in heat, and I remembered how dogs get stuck together after they get through humping, and just for a minute, I thought maybe, just maybe that might be it. I've heard Cy say a dozen times that strange things happen in sex and war, but that would just be too strange.

It's a lot different, I know, but who would think in a million years that Cy would bring a Negro woman to Oxbow, which probably has a little to do with both sex and war if somebody ever tried to figure it out.

"Get your shopping done this morning," Cy said. "I called Sheriff Curtis and he said to come down to his office early this afternoon."

I told Cy it would have to be early because I had to work in the afternoon.

"We'll be out of there in plenty of time," he said, "unless they decide to lock us up, which is a definite possibility."

Cy looked at Lobelia. "You'll be the first of your kind to grace the Farmers' Store," he said. "I hope nobody has a heart attack."

CHAPTER TWENTY-TWO

There are always the sparrows, thicker than blackbirds, in the swamp. They seem to own Oxbow. They flutter around the stores and the houses like flying mice, building ragged nests on the awnings and ledges and crapping all over everything. And they chirp, loud and long, not singing like other birds, but just chirping endlessly so it sounds like constant commenting and complaining. They were going at it as Lobelia and I walked down Main Street, and just as we stepped off the curb in front of the Majestic Theater, Lobelia suddenly stopped and said, "Listen, Billy, isn't that beautiful?"

I didn't know what she was talking about and I looked at her.

"The sparrows. I haven't heard them singing like that for years."

I looked up at the theater awning where a few strands of grass and a short length of twine dangled from a hole in the faded canvas. Five or six sparrows fluttered around it and they were all chirping.

"They're my kind of bird," Lobelia said. "Just listen to them, so beautiful."

I listened for something beautiful, but all I heard was dumb sparrow chirping.

"Oh, God, "Lobelia said. "Sights and smells bring things back, but sound does it better."

I tried to figure where she was going with her sparrow-chirp talk, but I didn't get anywhere.

"Jazz birds, Billy," she said. "They sing like they're on a chain gang. I love them."

I stopped trying to make sense of it. Walking through the middle of Oxbow with Lobelia was strange in itself, like leading an invisible parade through an empty town. But it wasn't empty: people were watching from behind doors and through narrow little slits in drawn curtains. I wasn't

161

really aware of it until Lobelia stopped suddenly and said, "Billy, this may be the strangest stage I've ever been on."

We were in front of the First National Bank and across from Yereko's Shoe Shop at the time. Lobelia made a sweeping gesture with her arm and bowed low. I didn't figure it out right away, but then out of the corner of my eye, I saw faces duck out of sight in the bank window and there was movement behind the shoe shop door.

"I love it," Lobelia said. "They're taking nervous peeks like I might be the Pied Piper come to steal their little ones."

Gone with the Wind lettering was back on the marquee at the Majestic, and Lobelia paused and looked up at it. "Supposed to be about the Civil War, but it's mostly about a spoiled white woman," she said. "Have you seen it?"

I said I had, a couple times, and Lobelia said maybe someday they would make a movie about a spoiled colored woman, but she herself would be too old to be the star. "Servants and porters and field hands is the only way we get into movies," she said. "A big-shot white man once promised to put me in a movie as a blues singer, but he made demands and I ended up throwing his boney ass down a metal stairway."

Lobelia looked at me and laughed, and I tried to generate up an image of her throwing somebody down a stairway. I wished I had seen it. In front of the Farmers' Store, Lobelia stopped before the big window and pointed at the display of drab women's clothing and patriotic war posters.

One of the posters said, "Dress for Victory." Lobelia looked at it and smiled. "That needs some editing, don't you think, Billy? 'Undress for Victory' would do a lot more for the war effort."

That sounded like something Cy would say and I looked at her. The way she said it seemed to imply that we were on equal-adult footing, and except for some of the rough-talking farmers down at the station, that hadn't happened to me all that much, certainly not with adult women. I looked at her again and she winked and smiled and I had a sudden weird regret that I hadn't been able to take Cy up on his offer to kiss the bride. It would have been an adult thing to do.

We went in through the Farmers' Store front entrance and as the big glass door swung open, Lobelia said, "Everybody uses the same door. I never get over thinking how nice that is."

She rubbed her hand along the side of the door and smiled.

"Where I grew up, there are separate entrances for whites and coloreds, separate drinking fountains, separate restrooms, separate park benches, separate everything," she said.

I had seen pictures of that in a magazine story about a southern bus depot.

"The reason you don't have separate things for coloreds is you don't have any colored people," Lobelia said.

Indian John came to mind. He's colored, I guess. He isn't white, anyway. I wondered how many Indians there would have to be before they got their own entrances, and would the sign say red or colored?

Usually the Farmers' Store is pretty noisy, people jabbering all over and moving stuff around, and the zip and clank of the change system that is a series of little cup-like carriages traveling back and forth on cord tracks between various places in the store and up to Irene Kreuger in the second-story cashier's cage. Every kid in Oxbow goes through a stage of high fascination with the system, starting back when he's holding his mother's hand and watching slack-jawed as a clerk crams cash and a sales slip into a carriage and yanks on a dangling handle to send everything zipping over everybody and everything to clang to a stop in front of Irene, who matter-of-factly deals with the business at hand and sends the carriage back where it came from.

As Lobelia and I stepped through the door, one of the carriages went sailing over our heads. It startled Lobelia and she jumped, "Oh, my God, Billy, flying money."

That struck me funny and I laughed, and then realized that my laughter was the only sound in the store. It was like the Farmers' Store's heart had stopped beating, or at the very least, it was holding its breath. It had to be Lobelia's presence. It was eerie. Obviously, she had to be aware of it but she didn't let on.

"Where's shoes, Billy?" she said. "We've got to find me some swamp boots."

I led the way through the silent store to the shoe department under the ladieswear balcony, and I could feel eyes looking at us from behind clothing racks and display cases.

"Mighty quiet store," Lobelia said. "Think there's anybody around to wait on us?"

As if it were his cue, Boob Wanner stepped out from behind a stack of shoe boxes, his bald head suddenly rising up like a moon with big ears. "Can I help you, Billy?" he asked, but he was staring at Lobelia when he said it.

"Boots," she said, "I need some boots."

It was like Boob didn't hear her. He stood as still as one of the plaster mannequins over in dress shirts and he stared at Lobelia until she turned and looked back at him. "I think I've had about enough of being a zoo specimen. Can we please get on with things here?"

I reached out and touched Boob's arm and it was like I had stabbed him with a hot poker. He jumped about a foot and jerked his head around. "Yes, sir, I mean, yes, ma'am. What size?"

"Long," Lobelia said. "I have very long feet."

I glanced down and saw that she wasn't exaggerating: her feet were the longest woman's feet I had ever seen, and her toes were as long as fingers. Boob had looked down, too, and then as we both looked up, our eyes met briefly. In that instant, Lobelia said, "Nigger toes! Right, Billy."

I had no idea what to do or say. *Nigger toes* is what everyone calls the Brazil nuts in the Christmas nut mix and so the term is only around once a year, with no real racial or social meaning. I certainly hadn't been thinking *nigger toes*, not until Lobelia brought them up the way she did. I looked at her and saw that she was smiling.

"I've been north long enough to know about some of these things," she said, "so I'm just having a little fun with you."

I don't know about Boob, but I felt like my brain was a tin can that Lobelia had just kicked down the street. Then, she seemed to dismiss the whole thing as she sat down in one of the shoe-fitting chairs. Boob scrambled around and came up with a wooden foot measurer. He put it down in front of Lobelia and tried not to react when her foot wouldn't fit into the longest setting.

"I don't want lady go-to-church boots," Lobelia said. "I want something for muck and mire."

"Shit boots," Boob said, as if the words had popped out of his mouth without going through his brain. "I mean," he stammered, "that's what

164

we call barn boots in the men's department. That might be what you're looking for."

Boob's hands were shaking as he held the shoe-size measurer and there were beads of sweat on his red face.

Lobelia looked at him and said, "Billy, I think we're working this man too hard. Let's give him a chance to rest up."

Boob mopped at his face with a handkerchief and smiled as he pointed toward the men's department across the store. Once we got over there, Lobelia more or less waited on herself while manager Ralph Pitzer lurked in the background. She looked at the box labels until she found a pair of extra-large men's knee boots, then she pointed at a mannequin wearing a pair of striped bib overalls and said, "Those, I want a pair of those."

I couldn't believe it. Women didn't wear bib overalls, especially the striped ones that make even some men look clownish, but that's what Lobelia bought. Then she tried to pay Ralph with a $100 bill. Ralph looked at it like he'd never seen one, and maybe he hadn't, at least not very often. Nobody in Oxbow ever used hundred-dollar bills.

"I don't know," Ralph said, "We don't see many of these, but I'll try it."

He stuffed the hundred and the sales slip into one of the little carriages and jerked it up to Irene. There was a long wait, long enough for Irene to stretch her neck and peer down at us and then send Toad Jensen, the store flunky, over to the bank with the hundred to make sure it was good. Toad went slinking out the side door and I pretended not to see him.

While we were waiting, Lobelia sorted through a stack of men's work shirts and picked out a blue one to go with her striped overalls. Finally, the change carriage came clanking down into place over Ralph's head and he took it down and counted out Lobelia's change, mostly in fives, so there was a sizable stack of bills.

As we turned to leave, Mrs. Arlene Erickson and her three little kids came in through the front door. They all stopped dead in their tracks when they saw us. The littlest kid, a girl, probably six or seven, pointed at Lobelia and in a screechy little voice you could hear all over the store, said, "Mama, there's a nigger!" Then the kid darted over to grab at her mother's skirt and sent a fearful look back over her shoulder at Lobelia.

Mrs. Erickson had been staring at Lobelia and without moving her eyes, she reached down and patted her daughter's head. "It's okay," she said. "She won't hurt you."

Lobelia looked at the little family group more or less cowering in front of her. It didn't take a mind-reader to guess she was thinking over just how to proceed. Finally, she smiled and said, "That's right, Honey, a nigger. But, like your momma says, I won't hurt you."

By this time, Mrs. Erickson had collected herself some and she looked at Lobelia and opened her mouth. Before she could say anything, Lobelia said, "No harm, ma'am. That's what I've been called all my life. I do prefer Colored or Negro, however, if you don't mind."

Mrs. Erickson was obviously too flustered to go on with it, and she suddenly turned and herded her brood off toward the grocery department, the kids stretching their necks to look back at us.

Lobelia watched them go and sighed. "I think that we have just become part of their family lore, Billy. It will come down through the years: 'Remember the day we ran into Billy and that nigger mammy.'"

By the time we finally left the Farmers' Store, there was the feeling that it was starting to breathe again, not in its steady old-dog way, but as if it was gasping to catch up and get back to where it had been before Lobelia's visit.

Out on the street, Lobelia spied the Pal Café sign and said, "Billy, how about a malt and a hamburger? All this cultural pioneering has made me hungry."

That sounded good to me and so we went into the Pal and sat at the table by the window where my mother and I usually sit. The only person on duty was Phyllis McPhee, who is older and lived in Chicago until her husband got shot in a moonshine raid, according to local gossip, after which Phyllis moved back to Oxbow with four kids and three dogs. I knew them all from seeing them around town, both the dogs and the kids. They are all kind of wild. Phyllis looked at Lobelia as we sat down and then she walked over to the table and said, "I'm Phyllis. Welcome to Oxbow."

"Why, thank you," Lobelia said.

"You're in good hands with Billy, here," Phyllis said.

"Yes, he's a very good guide," Lobelia said.

Sometimes you can see curiosity on somebody's face as plain as freckles and so it was no surprise when Phyllis said, "What brings you to our little backwater, if I might ask?"

Lobelia looked at Phyllis standing next to us with her order pad and pencil poised. She paused and finally said, "That is definitely a legitimate question for someone in Oxbow to ask." Then she paused again and smiled at Phyllis and said, "I recently became the wife of one of your illustrious citizens, Mr. Cyrus Marian Butler. That makes me Mrs. Lobelia Butler, and I am happy to make your acquaintance."

It must have been her big-city experience that conditioned Phyllis to hear this from Lobelia and barely blink an eye, though I did see her pencil give a little jerk when Lobelia said she was married to Cy. Phyllis stared at Lobelia for a couple seconds, smiled and said, "Well, congratulations. I hope you and Cyrus will be very happy together."

"We're not exactly Romeo and Juliet," Lobelia said. "More like a couple of old dogs looking to relax in a spot of warm sunshine."

"I love it," Phyllis said, and went to get our malts and hamburgers. Lobelia had ordered hers with fried onions and as we ate, she remarked about how good it was. Mine was too, without onions. When we were about half way through eating our hamburgers, Lobelia looked at me and said, "Cyrus tells me your mother runs a pretty tight ship with you."

It surprised me to think of her and Cy talking about me, especially about something so personal as my relationship with my mother.

"It just means she loves you; it's the way of mothers."

I looked at her and didn't say anything because I had a feeling she wasn't done talking, "The way Cyrus is in your life is the kind of thing that gives mothers fits. Cy is like an old tomcat dragging dead mice to a nursing kitten, if you will pardon an over-reaching simile. Your mama sees him as a big threat to her baby."

I had figured that out a long time ago, but I didn't say anything.

"Cyrus knows all this, of course," Lobelia said, "and it bothers him some. But for whatever reason, he feels a need to somehow impact your life. I think the truth is, Billy, you are the son he never had, though he would consider that to be utter nonsense."

I didn't say anything, but I thought that I would also consider it utter nonsense.

"The thing that gets me about Cyrus," Lobelia said, "is that he is one of those rare color-blind white men. It may be something in the genes, like being double-jointed, but in any case, the first time I met him, he told me I was beautiful and that he wanted to marry me."

Lobelia laughed and was quiet for a minute or so. "I thought he was just another old drunk white guy who considered me a novelty, but he kept coming back. I was fighting drugs, for about the hundredth time, and he kept talking to me about Oxbow and it started to sound like the ideal drying-out place."

As she talked, Lobelia pulled her sleeve up and pointed to marks on her arm. I'd seen something like it in a movie about a drug addicts and I tried not to stare. She tugged her sleeve back into place and sighed.

"Then Cy came up with that crazy prisoner-of-war scheme," she said, "and I saw a chance to maybe do a little trade-off. He was going to end up in prison if he didn't back off, and I was probably going back on the needle if something didn't change."

Lobelia laughed and said, "So here I am, Billy, and I'm going to bust my fanny to make this thing work because the alternative could be very bad for both Cy and me."

I felt sudden warmth toward her and wondered if I were somehow betraying my mother. I thought about what Lobelia said, and some of it seemed to clunk into brain trash empty spaces. I thought about telling her what Cy said about why he does some crazy things, including setting up the MOP Exchange. But I didn't. She probably knew already.

"I'm sure by now you've learned how to balance your mother and Cy in your life," Lobelia said. I looked at her and nodded, and I suddenly saw myself as a skinny kid bending in the wind and trying not to tip over. It wasn't a flattering image, but it wasn't all that unpleasant either. I'm not sure why Lobelia's comments brought it into such sharp focus, but they did, and I was grateful to her for it. I was also grateful that the image was there only briefly and then it dissolved like smoke.

When she had finished her hamburger and malt, Lobelia ordered a cup of coffee and as she drank it, she talked about Cy's cats. "It's the one area where Cyrus and I may have a little problem," she said. "Cyrus likes cats because they are smart, and they don't take crap. Well, that's fine and good, but they're also uppity, and I have problems with uppity. There is way too much of it in the world and we don't need it in our damned pets."

Lobelia sipped at her coffee and smiled. "I know that's crazy, but that's just me. Now dogs! I love dogs. You can have a relationship with a dog. You treat one right and it will treat you right. It never thinks it's better than you are, and it will do anything for you."

Lobelia must have seen something in the way I reacted because she stopped and looked at me. "You're a dog person, too, huh? You've got a dog, I know it. Tell me about him."

It was like she had lifted the top off my head and looked in to see that my brain was so full of Toby that there was hardly room for anything else.

"My dog is lost in the swamp," I said, and saying the words was painful, like clawing off a fresh scab.

"Oh, no," Lobelia said, and she put her coffee cup down and looked hard at me. "What's his name?"

"Toby. I got him as a puppy."

Lobelia reached out and touched my arm. "Tell me about him."

And so I did, probably in more detail than she had bargained for but she listened through it all as if it was the most fascinating thing she'd ever heard. I went way back with it to bringing Toby home as a bright-eyed, sharp-toothed pup and both of us more or less growing up together. At times, it seemed I was talking more for my own benefit than for Lobelia's. I talked about how Toby and I got into trouble; and how we learned about the swamp, and how we spent days and days out there until it was where we wanted to be all the time. Lobelia looked at me in a way that made it seem as if she had been with Toby and me on some of our adventures.

"From the time I was a little girl, I went out into the swamp with my daddy," she said. "He taught me to shoot and I got to be damned good, could hit a squirrel in the eye every time. We didn't have a dog. My daddy was the dog, chasing rabbits in a circle so I could shoot them."

I tried to imagine it—a skinny girl and her father roaming around out in a swamp like Toby and me.

"Tell me how your dog got lost," she said.

I looked at her. "I don't know if I can," I said. But I went at it, telling how Margaret insisted on going with Toby and me to take food out to Otto and how she wouldn't come back to town with me. When I came to the part about Toby running off to chase something and the little popping sound I heard and Toby not barking any more, I suddenly had to stop. I blinked to clear my vision, and was surprised when Lobelia reached out with a napkin and dabbed at my cheek. I was embarrassed, especially when Phyllis came over with the coffeepot. She pretended not to notice anything, which was nice of her.

"We will find your dog," Lobelia said. "We will find Toby."

The way she said it made me believe it.

"When we go out to get Margaret and the prisoner we'll find him. I'm sure of it."

I looked at her and nodded, and we sat there in cluttered silence.

"We should be getting back to Cyrus," Lobelia said. She looked at the check Phyllis had left and counted out the money for it. Then she put a fiver next to her coffee cup.

Phyllis looked at the money, then at Lobelia. "Don't ever get tips like that," she said. "Thank you very much, Mrs. Butler."

Lobelia looked at Phyllis. "Mrs. Butler?" she said. "You're the first one to call me that, and I thank you very much."

"Well, damn," Phyllis said, "I guess that's who you are, so that's what I'll call you."

"Oh, just call me Lobelia," Lobelia said. "I like that Mrs. Butler, but you're Phyllis and I'm Lobelia, okay? You too, Billy, call me Lobelia."

I hadn't had occasion to call her anything and if I had it would have been total confusion. I don't think I could bring myself to call her by her first name, and "Mrs. Butler" didn't seem to fit, considering that Cy was Mr. Butler. She might have thought that her comment straightened it all out, and maybe it did for Phyllis, but not for me.

CHAPTER TWENTY-THREE

When we got back to Cy's house, he was sitting at the table drinking coffee. He raised the cup as we came in. "Thought I might have to send a search party," he said.

"Oh, Cyrus, Billy and I had a wonderful time," Lobelia said. "We met some interesting people and I found just what I wanted at the Farmers' Store."

As she talked, Lobelia lifted the lid off a box and held up her boots. "Look here, Cyrus, shit boots. I've got me some genuine shit boots."

"Well, damn," Cy said. "They are just plain beautiful."

"And feast your eyes on these," Lobelia said as she held the bib overalls so they draped down her front.

Cy slapped the table and whooped with laughter. "Oh, baby, you're adjusting to Oxbow like a pig to mud."

"Beg your pardon, Counselor," Lobelia said. "I don't approve of your analogy. How about, like a butterfly to a garden?"

"That'll do. Are you planning to wear your new duds to see the sheriff?"

"I'm not going with you," Lobelia said. "I would just be a distraction. You and Billy go see if you can extract yourself from your tangled web enough to get that poor grandma out of jail. She must be a psychological mess by now."

I thought about Grandma Forrest being a psychological mess and wondered just what that meant. The mention of her gave me a pang of anxiety and guilt. I had called my mother earlier and while she was upset that I had "camped out," she was obviously relieved that I was okay. She was even more relieved when I told her Grandma would soon be out of jail. She had pleaded for an explanation, but I told her there wasn't time and I would tell her all about it later.

I thought about telling her that Margaret was okay, but that would have taken too long to explain: it made more sense just to wait until it all worked out and we brought Margaret home. Cy heard what I said to my mother and when I hung up, he said, "I'm afraid, Billy, you and I are going to be a long time explaining all of this." He shook his head and sighed. "But we've got to do it." He sighed again. "I just can't believe one of my brilliant ideas is falling apart this way, but I will yield to a superior thinker—the lady here with the shit boots."

"Cyrus Butler," Lobelia said, "You know that once you got cold-stone sober, you yourself saw your scheme was going to be trouble."

"Yeah, but I still think it has possibilities and a man doesn't enjoy 'fessing up."

"All men make mistakes, but big men own up to them," Lobelia said.

"Well, Billy," Cy said, "let's go over to the sheriff's office and be big men."

"Yes, go," Lobelia said. "I've got cleaning to do and I plan to have a little meeting with the cats about who is boss in this house."

"Be gentle with Poor Little Thing," Cy said. "She's easily offended."

"And easily knocked up, judging by the cats around here that look like her," Lobelia said.

Cy laughed, "Sing to her. She loves jazz, and, like I've told Billy, if she doesn't hear it enough, she goes out and finds a tom."

We left then, heading down the alley toward the sheriff's office. I noticed immediately there was something different about Cy. His stride seemed steadier and he had straightened up some form his usual slouch. I realized that he was as sober as I had ever seen him. Back at his house, he had been drinking coffee instead of whiskey, and I remembered that even last night before my brain went dumb, I hadn't seen a drink in his hand, other than the ones he had handed me. To think of him not drinking or not hungover was impossible. I looked at him more closely and he seemed like the same old Cy, even down to wearing the same old derby hat. The hat, however, was cleaner than usual, like somebody might have been brushing at it.

As we walked past the back door of the pool hall, Cy paused. "That wasn't very smart of me to get you drunk last night, Billy," he said. "Just when I'm trying to swear off, I go and get you messed up."

172

I didn't say anything and we walked along in silence for a while.

"Reflex dumbness, I guess," Cy said. "You just looked like hell, and I thought booze was what you needed."

"Maybe I did. It made me forget things for a while," I said.

"I've been living that way forever. It works, but you pay a price," Cy said.

A cat ran across the alley ahead of us and I wondered if Lobelia was singing to Poor Little Thing by now. We were getting close to the sheriff's office, and Cy slowed and turned toward me. "Billy," he said, "I have no idea what's going to happen when we lay this thing out, but whatever it is ,we can't let the bastards get us down."

I looked at him and nodded.

"I don't mean Sheriff Curtis," Cy said. "He's okay, but as Lobelia says, we have poked a sharp stick in the government's eye, which in this case is the Army with its stupid war-time rules, and the FBI with more authority than God Almighty. We may both end up in jail with your grandma."

An image of the three of us locked in a cell together flashed through my mind. Then it was gone, like a weird offshoot in a bad dream.

"You would think somebody might have had enough sense to let her go," Cy said. "I now see it was a mistake to have involved the poor old lady in the first place. And Margaret, we've got to get her the hell out of this thing before anyone knows she is in it. She's more of an innocent than your grandmother."

We stopped at the bottom of the stone steps leading up to the court-house door. Cy turned to face me and stuck out his hand. "Well, Billy, I don't feel like a big man; I feel like an asshole."

"Me, too," I said, and we shook hands and headed up the steps.

CHAPTER TWENTY-FOUR

I've been in the sheriff's office and jail many times, starting way back when my dad visited his friend Monty Roberts, the dispatcher, and then later with my mother when she stopped to gossip with her old classmate, Sheriff Curtis. I know its shadowy looks and sour smells and the sense it gives you of being in back rooms where bad things are stored and sorted through and there are cages for people and guns on the walls and pictures of wanted men and stolen things.

If stepping into a church can give you a certain feeling—of people trying to live a clean life, or at least pretending to—then walking into the sheriff's office can make you feel that slipping off the straight and narrow is bigger business and done in grittier quarters. I've heard Cy say that the phonies go to church and the fools go to jail, which may have something to do with how mixed up I sometimes get trying to figure things out.

Monty's hobby is taxidermy and sometimes my dad would bring him a dead squirrel or a road-killed snake. Monty would take it home and skin it and a month or so later he would bring it back to the sheriff's office looking like it wasn't quite as dead as when we had given it to him. Then it would go up on the wall with all the rest of the stuffed animals and fish. In the shadowy room where Monty sits at an old wooden desk with a telephone and a typewriter and wire baskets full of papers, the walls are covered with examples of his taxidermy: a cross-eyed deer, a grinning muskrat, a lumpy fish, a horned owl that does not look wise like an owl should, and lots of other strange things.

I remember my dad once saying to my mother that if Monty were Oxbow's undertaker, there could never be an open-casket funeral. Sometimes, when my mother came to visit Sheriff Curtis, I would wait in a chair out by Monty's desk and gaze up at the critters until they came to life and leaped down to attack Monty and me.

The remnants of such childish fantasizing can linger and it was just one more reason to feel apprehension as Cy and I stepped up onto the courthouse porch. Cy swung his arm to shoo flies off the screen door and we opened it and went in. Monty looked up and scowled. "Damn," he said, "Now, we've got trouble."

"Without trouble, you don't have a job," Cy said.

"Well, you're my job insurance," Monty said.

"You sure as hell couldn't get work as a chef," Cy said.

Cy is forever complaining about the jail food, especially the bean soup. Monty keeps a huge kettle of it brewing on the back of the big, black jail stove and Cy says it is cruel and inhuman punishment to eat that soup with three or four other guys when you are all crammed into the same cell.

"We need to talk to the sheriff," Cy said.

"I know," Monty said. "He told me you were coming in. He got called to a barn fire over by Almira. Nineteen cows and seven sheep, and the insurance guy is saying it's arson."

"Hey, that sounds like a money-maker," Cy said. "Who's the agent?"

"He's got a Minneapolis lawyer, so you're out of luck," Monty said.

"Not necessarily," Cy said. "Some of those big city dudes are afraid they might get cow shit on their wingtips and they'll split a fee quicker than you can say fifty-fifty."

Monty turned from Cy and looked at me. "Billy," he said, "I'm sure you know your grandma is back there in one of our cells?"

I nodded.

"I can't believe it," Monty said. "Nice old lady like that locked up like a common drunk."

"What's she charged with?" Cy said.

"Nothing," Monty said. "Goddamn FBI came marching in here one day and said go arrest her and hold her as an enemy of the people or some such bullshit. The sheriff raised Hell, but they said he had to do it or they would lock him in one of his own jail cells."

"Well, damn," Cy said, "they can't do that."

"They did it," Monty said. "They say they have special war-time authority and they can do any goddamned thing they want to. They tell us we have to hold Mrs. Forrest until she talks and she ain't saying anything to anybody. Won't even speak to the sheriff or me and we've known her all our lives."

Cy and I looked at each other as Monty put his pencil down and scowled at Cy. "You wouldn't know anything about any of this, would you, Cyrus?"

"It's possible," Cy said. "We…, I may have done something without thinking it all the way through."

"Something dumb, you mean. You did something dumb."

Cy shrugged.

"Well, that wouldn't be a first," Monty said, "but admitting it would be."

"This one's a little different," Cy said. "It involves the US government."

Monty stared at Cy. "Why am I not surprised?"

"Ah, Monty, you're a wise old fart and you've known me too damned long."

"That last part's right."

"Promise me one thing."

"What?"

"When they take my head off, you'll stuff it and hang it on your wall."

The front door slammed open and Sheriff Curtis stood in the doorway, his squat build and wide shoulders and scowling face making him look like an unhappy woodchuck. He paused and looked at Cy and me and motioned for us to follow as he headed for his office.

"Get that Army captain and those FBI assholes down here, Monty," Sheriff Curtis yelled over his shoulder.

Cy and I followed Sheriff Curtis into his cluttered office and sat in chairs next to his desk

"Nice to see you, Billy," Sheriff Curtis said. "Your mom's been worried about you."

"I've been looking for my dog," I said.

"So she tells me." Sheriff Curtis said.

"Something might have happened to him," I said.

"What?" Sheriff Curtis said.

"I heard something, maybe a shot," I said.

Sheriff Curtis tossed a folder down on his desk and looked at me. "Who the hell would shoot a dog?"

I shrugged and Sheriff Curtis sat down and turned to Cy. He stared for a minute and then said, "Did I hear right that you have taken a bride?"

"That's right, Sheriff," Cy said. "I am now a happily married man."

"Jesus, Cy," Sheriff Curtis said, "Of all the things you've done to stir things up around here, this takes the cake."

"Getting' married?" Cy said.

"Oh, goddamnit, you know what I mean," Sheriff Curtis said.

"That she's colored?" Cy said.

"Well, no shit, Cy, you think I might wonder how such a thing might go down around here."

"She's smart enough to handle this town with one hand behind her back," Cy said.

"The question is, can the town handle her? We've got a couple hundred German prisoners making people crazy, and then you bring in somebody who'll give them an excuse to be even crazier."

"People seem to be fine with her. Billy took her to the Farmers' Store this morning and there was no trouble."

"I hope it stays that way, but everybody's talking, and one of my deputies asked me if he should run her out of town."

"Don't tell me which one or I'll have to kill him."

"I'm sure you know which one."

Cy nodded. "Yeah, I'll make a point of introducing him to Mrs. Butler at the earliest opportunity."

Sheriff Curtis shook his head. "He's the kind I worry about. He's never seen a colored person in his life and he's immediately a racist asshole. And he isn't the only one around here with that potential."

"My wife is nobody's goddamned business, Sheriff, not yours or anyone's, and it's not what we're here to talk about."

"Not much goes on around here that isn't my business sooner or later, but you're right. Let's get on with it here. You said you wanted the Army and the FBI here and I assume they're on the way."

"Good, I don't want to go over this more than once and I don't think Billy does, either."

I didn't, of course. I didn't even want to go over it once. Except for getting Grandma out of jail, there didn't seem to be any point to it. It wasn't going to help find Toby and it was going to finally end any hope, however far-fetched, of helping Uncle Jeff. I wished it was over.

Then it was, just like that: twenty minutes, a half hour, maybe an hour. I don't know because once Flat-top and Baldy came in through the door and nodded at me, and the Army captain showed up and the yelling and arm-waving started, I didn't pay any attention to time. It started quiet enough. Everyone got introduced and sat down, and Monty came in with a notebook and pencil. Sheriff Curtis turned to Cy and said, "Let's have it."

Cy looked around at everyone and ended up staring at the Army captain. He wiped a hand over the top of his head and said, "Your prisoner is out in the swamp. If you leave us alone, Billy and I will see that you get him back."

That's when it started going crazy, Flat-top and Baldy jumping up and shouting questions and the captain joining in like an irate coach and Sheriff Curtis pounding on his desk and demanding that everyone sit down and shut up, and Monty scribbling like mad until he finally gave it up and slammed his notebook shut.

Finally, after several outbursts like that, with Cy alternately laughing and shouting back at whoever was shouting at him, Sheriff Curtis got it quieted down enough so Cy could tell how the MOP Exchange plan had made it necessary for us to capture a prisoner and why the letter to Mrs. Roosevelt had been signed by Grandma Forrest. Everyone stared at him as he talked and periodically someone would shake his head or suck in his breath or mutter something to express disbelief.

Cy wound up saying he regretted involving me and Grandma, and said he still thought the plan had merit. He didn't say anything about Margaret. Sheriff Curtis leaned back in his chair through it all, occasionally nodding, and at one point, it looked as if he might have smiled briefly. But if he was amused, however slightly, the FBI and the Army were not. Flat-top and Baldy and the captain demanded that Cy be locked up immediately and the whereabouts of the prisoner disclosed so he could be returned to the POW camp.

Sheriff Curtis tried to reason with them, but they told him they were getting so much high-level heat that it had to be done their way. At one point, Baldy put his face close to Sheriff Curtis's and shouted, "The White House, for Christ's sake. You have any idea how they can come down on us?"

The Army captain, whose face had turned from white to red and back to white during some of the shouting, said his general told him there might be a court martial if he didn't get the prisoner back, and the captain wasn't sure if it would be the general or him who got hauled up on charges. He said the situation was even worse because there were now two prisoners missing, one from Mr. Rockford's pasture and another one who walked away from the prison camp yesterday.

"The first one, apparently the one you took," he said, gesturing at Cy, "isn't dangerous, but this last one is a hard-headed Nazi and we were about to ship him down to Oklahoma with the rest of his kind."

"Damn," Baldy said, "If they hear this in Washington, we'll have J. Edgar out here in person."

"It's all been reported," the captain said, and Baldy swore.

It wasn't pleasant to see how the FBI and the Army bullied Sheriff Curtis, but he obviously recognized their authority and handled the situation as well as he could. When they demanded that a search of the swamp be done as soon as possible, Sheriff Curtis talked them into letting him conduct it, and he set it up for tomorrow morning as a civilian posse.

When they wanted me locked up, Sheriff Curtis said absolutely not, and added that he was releasing Grandma Forrest, and if they didn't like it, they could kiss his ass, which I suppose is a hard thing to translate for purposes of an official response. It was enough, Sheriff Curtis said, that they would have Cy in custody, and when he tried to object to that, they pounced on him like he was off his rocker.

"I'd like my usual room," Cy said to Monty as the meeting was breaking up, "the one with the veranda and the view."

Then he turned to me. "Billy, tell my dear wife I might be late for supper." Then he whispered that I should talk to Lobelia about helping get Margaret out of the swamp first thing in the morning before the posse headed out.

I hurried out the door then, partly because I didn't want to run into Grandma anywhere near the jail and partly because I had to hurry, or I'd be late for the afternoon shift at the station. As I walked out of the sheriff's office door, Flat-top grabbed my arm. "Your FBI credentials have been cancelled, Billy," he said.

CHAPTER TWENTY-FIVE

From somewhere, something or somebody was looking at me. I had felt it off and on since earlier in the afternoon when I took over the station from Cliff. After everything that had gone on at the sheriff's office, and thinking about what might happen tomorrow, I probably wasn't as tuned into things as I should have been, but the feeling of being watched finally got through to me. And then I saw Indian John.

He was standing very still in the deep shade of the big lilac bush on the lawn next door and he was looking at me, not really staring but looking steadily like somebody maybe watching a fishing bobber. I stepped out onto the drive and motioned for Indian John to join me. He hesitated, and finally walked slowly out of the shade and over to where I stood. He stopped several feet away and lifted his face slightly and looked at me.

Indian John's eyes are like holes drilled into coal and the lines around them splinter off and run so deep they look like cracks in his skull. I tried to read his expression but all I could see were the deep wrinkles and the stray, black whiskers growing out of his chin. We stood that way for what seemed like a long time, and then Indian John raised his right arm very slowly until his hand was only a foot or so from my face. It held something and when I focused on it, I almost passed out. It was Toby's collar!

Maybe it was a good thing that my brain had been kicked around by so many things in the past twenty-four hours. Maybe that had made it mushy enough to handle what Indian John was holding without it exploding into a million pieces. Neither of us moved. Indian John stood with his arm out like he was offering me a gift and I stared at what he held, a hideous thing I could never touch.

But I touched it, finally. I reached out to take it from Indian John and turned it over to look at the tag with Toby's name and our address. The worn leather was swollen and soft, like it had been soaking in water. I looked at it for a long time and then looked back at Indian John.

"In the river," he said.

I looked at him and waited.

"Down two miles," he said, and I waited again.

"Shot," Indian John said and he pointed a finger at his temple.

I looked down at the collar and remembered when I had last fastened on a new name tag because Toby was forever losing it.

"Good dog," Indian John said. Then he paused and slowly turned and walked away. I watched him in a daze, and for some reason, I remembered the time he had told me about the little rat terrier biting at the bullets kicking up dust on the French battlefield.

When you don't know something bad for sure, you can assume it isn't true, and, of course, that had been the way I had been thinking about Toby. But all of a sudden, I couldn't go that way anymore. Indian John had handed me the brutal truth as gently as he knew how, but it was like being conked over the head with a baseball bat. My knees were so weak I didn't know how I made it back into the station.

But I did and found myself sitting on the stool and staring down at Toby's collar on the counter in front of me. A fly landed on it and I flicked my hand at it. Fortunately, no customers came in because I don't think I could have handled a "dollar's worth of regular" or even a "pack of Luckies." I just sat there like something full of poison waiting to die so the pain would stop.

"Who the hell would shoot a dog?" Sheriff Curtis had said. Out of my smothering grief, I slowly began to focus on that. And I immediately thought of Blasser, and remembered how he had once pointed his gun at Toby and made a threat. But there was no way to know. Mr. Schmidt? Maybe Toby had found something and he had been shot to stop his snooping.

Several customers came in and I managed to pump their gas and wash their windshields in a fog. Then Wilbur Bender drove in with his pickup, all decked out with welding gear and with a big set of deer antlers fastened to the top of the cab just over the windshield.

"Billy," he shouted as he pulled himself out of his truck. "You going out with the posse tomorrow?"

The words jerked me out of my grieving trance like a slap, and I realized that our private MOP project, or what was left of it, was about to become very public. And somehow it seemed even worse that the wild sanctity of the swamp Toby and I loved was about to be invaded by a disorderly mob.

"We're going to have us a Kraut hunt," Wilbur said. "I got my thirty-o-six sighted in and all ready to go."

That startled me, too, to think of a gang of Oxbow deer hunters roaming the swamp with rifles big enough to blow a man's head off, and with no more restraint than was in Wilbur's gleeful, "A manhunt, Billy. We ain't never had one of those before."

I thought about Otto the Kraut and how I had last seen him sitting on the log next to Margaret, smiling and nodding at something she said. It did not seem that even though he was a Kraut and was with the enemy, he should be gunned down by a wild-eyed, trigger-happy deer hunter.

"The sheriff sent Monty around to get the word out and I happened to be in the pool hall when he came in," Wilbur said. "And let me tell you, there's going to be one hell of a posse. Everyone's going."

I tried to imagine what it would be like when the Oxbow men gathered down by the river and crossed over into the swamp. None of them ever went out there, except a few in the late fall to hunt deer. Then the vegetation is all collapsed, and it is easier to get around. Now, in the summer, the swamp is a tangled jungle, and with the dry weather, it has become as tough and prickly as those barbed-wire barriers the news reels show in front of battlefield trenches. Nobody knows the trails or deer runs, and most of the men are in no condition to be running around out there with their beer bellies and flabby muscles and skin as thin as toilet paper.

"Give me a pack of Camels, Billy," Wilbur said. "Monty said there would be no smoking in the swamp. But to hell with that. I ain't going all day without a cig."

Sheriff Curtis was right to tell the men not to smoke. The swamp was beyond tinderbox dry. It was explosive, from the bottom of the dense leaf litter, up through the tangled underbrush and grass and weeds, and then up the dry bark of the pitch-soaked tamarack and pine and finally into the thick canopy of tree crowns. It could all combine in a conflagration of unimaginable intensity. Nothing would survive.

183

I looked at Wilbur as I handed him his Camels. "It's awful dry out there," I said.

"Hell, Billy, I work with sparks every day of my life and I ain't never set a fire yet."

I watched as he opened the cigarette pack and rapped it on the back of his hand to bump out cigarettes. "Never thought I'd get a crack at one of those Nazi bastards," he said.

"They're not all Nazis," I said.

"Monty said one is and one isn't. My trophy's going to be the one that is."

I looked at Wilbur and remembered how he had driven around town for weeks last fall with the big buck on his truck fender, and how Cy said it was all a stupid ego trip and a perfect example of his big antlers/big penis theory. I looked at Wilbur's greasy coveralls with the burn holes from welding sparks and the frayed cuffs and at his square hands with the scars and scabs all over them, and at his face with the bushy eyebrows and the pushed-in nose and the eyes that seemed both animal-wily and dumb. I felt a strange anger, at Wilbur and at … I didn't know what, the world in general, I guess. I wanted Wilbur to be gone, out of my life with his crude bullet mentality, and I didn't want to be nice to him just because he was an adult and a customer.

I wanted to kick his dumb ass.

"You couldn't tell a Nazi from Alley Oop," I said.

Wilber stepped back and looked at me. "Well, hell, Billy," he said. "It won't matter."

"You think they have swastikas tattooed on their foreheads?" I said.

"They both need to be shot, so what's the big deal?" Wilbur said. "I'm going for a double header."

"If either one of them gets shot, it could mean trouble for some of our prisoners," I said.

"Oh, to hell with that," Wilbur said. "None of our boys are dumb enough to end up being a prisoner of the Krauts!"

Wilbur is a sturdy guy, much bigger than I am, with lots of muscles that get used every day, so he is very strong and agile. I knew that, but there wasn't time to sort through any of it. I swung as hard as I could and my fist hit Wilbur in the eye and he stumbled backwards and fell over the long-necked water can next to the gas pumps. He lay there in the spilled water for a few seconds, then rolled over and got to his hands and knees and grabbed the side of one of the pumps to pull himself to his feet. He rubbed at the eye I had hit and looked at me with the other.

"What the hell?" he said. "Why'd you do that?

"I don't know," I said.

"You don't know?" Wilbur shouted. "Jesus Christ, you can't pop somebody like that and then say you don't know why you did it."

"Sorry," I said.

"And that doesn't get it either," Wilbur said, still shouting. "I'm gonna kick your skinny ass around the block."

I looked at him, at his thick arms and neck, and wondered what it was going to feel like when his hard hands started pounding on me. Wilbur stepped toward me, then stopped suddenly and rubbed again at his eye.

"Goddamnit, you hit my shooting eye," he said. He rubbed some more, then bent over to try to see his reflection in his pickup's side-mirror. "Damn, I gotta go get some beefsteak on this before it swells shut and puts me out of commission for tomorrow."

Wilbur climbed into his pickup then and stuck his head out the side window. "You're a little shit, Billy, and I ain't done with you," he said and then he drove off.

I felt a sense of relief, like I was coming out of one of those dreams where you're falling off a cliff and suddenly you glide out over a valley like a damned eagle. My hand hurt and I looked to see that one of my knuckles was swollen and stuck out at an odd angle. I'd probably broken it against Wilbur's forehead. It hurt good. I rubbed it and wondered when Wilbur would be back.

CHAPTER 26

The wind came up some time during the night. It brushed a
limb of the big maple against my bedroom window and that's
probably what woke me up. I lay there listening to it whispering
around the corners of the house like an ambush party: *We're waiting. Come
out if you dare.*

In my younger days, I would pull the covers up over my head to shut
out such hissing taunts. The night wind doesn't bother me that much
anymore, of course. It's just irritating, like an itch you can't scratch and
you wish it would go away. But it doesn't, and it didn't on this morning,
getting stronger and louder the longer I listened.

I raised my head up off the pillow to check for Toby on his rug by
the door and the reality of his being dead woke me up like a bucket of ice
water. It seemed only seconds until I was dressed and out of the house and
headed over to meet Lobelia. It was longer than seconds, of course, but not
by much, and if my mother had been awake, she didn't stir as I left.

Last night, when I came home from the station, there had been
something different about her. Earlier in the day, she had picked up Grandma
at the jail and given her a ride home, so she knew about the MOP plan and
how I was involved. But she didn't say much and she didn't ask questions.

Maybe some of it was because I had shown her Toby's collar and
told her how Indian John had found it. She looked at me for a long time,
then got up and walked over to where I was sitting and hugged my head
against her middle so I felt the warmth and softness of her and there was
nothing for me to do but cry like a goddamned baby.

I didn't tell her anything about Margaret because there was no point
in it. She and Mrs. Zanders would find out the truth soon enough—when
we brought Margaret home, and then maybe it would be easier to explain

why I had let them think Margaret was in Minneapolis when I had known she was out in the swamp.

Something I have learned in dealing with my mother is that a good outcome can take the complications out of a problem situation and sometimes let you off the hook for your part in it.

Daylight was just starting to come on as I walked the familiar alley to Cy's house. Gray was replacing black, and the yellow street lights were suddenly gone as if the wind had blown them out. Gusts of wind whipped at my clothes and pushed at the wooden stock of my rifle, reminding me to feel in my pocket for the bullets. They were there, and I wondered if there was really any reason for me to be taking my rifle along.

If we had to help Margaret walk out, it would just be something extra to carry. But then there was the other prisoner. We didn't know anything about him, or where he was, or if he was dangerous or armed or anything. And there's that old thing in my bones about not going into the swamp without a fishing rod or a rifle.

Lobelia was up and dressed—in her shit boots and striped overalls and blue work shirt, when I rapped on the back door.

"Come in, Billy," she said. "I'm packing lunch."

In her new get-up, she seemed taller and stronger, and I watched as she stuffed ham sandwiches into a canvas backpack and grabbed some apples out of the icebox. She moved like a dancer, with no wasted motion, as if every step had been planned out and rehearsed. The cuffs of her new shirt were turned back and I saw the row of little round scars on her arm. She must have noticed me looking because she glanced down and said, "Think of them as war wounds, Billy."

I tried to imagine what she would be like when a needle poked into her arm and the drug took hold. Did she get groggy and slow or pumped up so she bounced around like a ping-pong ball? I liked her the way she was, so steady and calm, and it was uncomfortable to think of something making her different. When I stopped by last night to tell her that Cy was in jail, she just nodded and said, "Well, we thought that might happen."

Then she had paused and said, "We're lucky they didn't lock you up, too."

"They wanted to, but the sheriff wouldn't allow it."

"And I assume he let your grandma go home?"

I nodded, and then I had told her about Indian John's finding Toby. Lobelia sat down and listened with her head cocked to the side, and then she suddenly smacked her hand down on the table and shouted, "Son of a bitch!"

A startled cat went streaking out the door and another clawed its way up Cy's bookshelves. Lobelia shouted, "son of a bitch", again, and then she looked at me and said, "I'm not going to tell you you'll get over it, Billy, because you won't, not really. Toby will be a part of you as long as you live."

That was exactly the right thing to say and it kept me from going over the edge so we could talk over our plan, which was pretty simple. We would go out there early and get Margaret out before the posse found her, and we'd bring Otto along if we could.

So, on this wind-blown morning, we were about to try to do just that. I was anxious to get started and as I reached for the backpack, a cat appeared in a side door with a tiny kitten dangling from its mouth. Lobelia stared at it, then whooped and laughed. "I'll be damned! Poor Little Thing is moving out. She can't stand a clean place."

The cat looked at us and walked toward the outside door. "Let the little whore go," Lobelia said. "There's room for only one of us in this house," and she jerked the door open.

Poor Little Thing stalked out with the kitten swinging back and forth from her jaw like an odd little purse. "I'll leave a window open so she can get the rest of her brood," Lobelia said, "and you'll have to help me convince Cyrus that it was her decision to leave and not mine."

We were ready then and I shrugged into the backpack and picked up my rifle. Lobelia flipped a canteen strap over her shoulder and we walked out the backdoor, past Cy's garden of weeds and into the alley.

"That is a mean blow," Lobelia said when we crossed a street, where the wind got a clear shot at us. Now in the daylight, the wind seemed to have even more of an aggravating edge. It wouldn't make the swamp any more hospitable, that's for sure. It might handicap the mosquitoes some, but in all other ways, it would just add to the misery: dust and debris blowing in your eyes, tall weeds and grass bending to trip you up, and the surf-like waves of brush and reeds making so much noise you couldn't hear anything else.

I had been out there on days like that. I remembered I always felt relief when Toby and I would cross back over the river and leave all the wild bluster and chaos behind. Once on a windy day in the swamp, it had occurred to me that the wind is probably why people first crawled into caves, and that had made me feel smart, like I could figure out anything.

But I didn't feel smart as Lobelia and I leaned into the wind sweeping down the alley. I thought about what it would be like later as the wind whipped at the posse when it gathered around Sheriff Curtis down at the park. There was no way for me to know what would go on and I felt a jolt of anxiety. Sheriff Curtis had asked me to join him because I knew the swamp better than anyone else and I had agreed. I put down a little build-up of guilt as Lobelia and I reached the river. Maybe if we hurried, we'd be back before the posse headed out and I could make good on my promise to the sheriff.

The wind grabbed and pushed at us as Lobelia and I walked to where my boat was tied. I paused long enough to fish cartridges out of my pocket and push them into the rifle clip. Lobelia watched as I snapped the clip into place and pumped a cartridge into the firing chamber.

"I hope we won't be using that thing," she said.

I nodded and climbed into the rowing seat. Lobelia settled onto the wide back seat and I pushed us off.

"Not muddy like the rivers back home," Lobelia said as she trailed her fingers in the clear water. She watched me row and smiled. "Just like my daddy. He had a little old boat, until some white boys chopped it up for campfire wood."

I pushed us out into the river and felt the current twist the boat like a big invisible hand from deep down below. I pulled hard on first one oar and then the other to avoid the huge boulders that bulge up out of the slithering water like worn tombstones. On top of one of the boulders there is a perfectly round hole that lumberjacks must have drilled to somehow help break up a log jam, and every time I see it, I think about the geezers' tales of roaming lumberjack ghosts.

In all our days in the swamp, Toby and I never really saw one. That stuff is all nonsense, I knew that. But there had been a time or two when I saw something drifting through the shadowy top of a tall pine or scurrying off the trail and I couldn't put a comfortable label on whatever it was.

And there had been times when Toby would bark for no reason, and when I looked at him, he would put his head down like he was embarrassed. Thinking about him now made me grip the oars tighter, and one of them banged against a boulder. The noise startled a great blue heron. It pumped into the air so close we could see its snaky eyes and dagger bill and its big feet trailing behind like extra equipment. Lobelia watched the bird as it slowly gained enough height to catch the wind and swing out of sight over the trees.

"Beautiful," she said. "I've got the feet but not the wings," and her laughter sailed off on the wind like the heron.

Once across the river, we pulled the boat up on the sandbar and headed down the trail. I could tell immediately that Lobelia had told the truth when she said she knew her way around a swamp. She stepped over windfalls as effortlessly as a doe and her long feet seemed to give her great stability. She not only kept up with me, but bumped into me if I hesitated over my next step. I looked back at her once and she grinned and said, "Under other circumstances, Billy, this would be the most fun I've had in years."

I thought how incredible it was that she seemed to enjoy the swamp, a woman from a big city actually fitting in to the wildness that was so special to me—and to Toby! It was hard to believe, until I remembered where she had come from. We stopped to catch our breath once, and Lobelia tilted her head back and said, "Oh, Lord, I've been too long away from my roots." I wasn't sure what she meant so I didn't say anything, and I guess she didn't expect me to anyway. She looked up at a nervous blackbird fluttering just over her head, and she smiled and said, "I know, I know, it's your place, Mrs. Blackbird. We can take a hint."

The wind seemed to get stronger as we went on. It bent the trees into graceful arcs and whipped the tall grass into frenzied dances and it was like the whole world was caught up in a wild sea of motion. We weren't that far from my camp when out of the loud swishing of the wind, I heard a noise that stopped me dead. It didn't fit into the hot bluster of the wind or into anything I could identify with the swamp. I wondered if it had been made by a human, but it wasn't a cry or a laugh, or even a shout. In its mystery, it sent a shiver up my sweaty spine.

I held up my hand and we stood still and listened. There was another faint noise, a different one. Then there was nothing but the wind. I looked at Lobelia and shrugged. We listened again but there was nothing. I moved closer to Lobelia so I wouldn't have to shout.

"I'm going to sneak in for a closer look," I said. I handed her the rifle and shrugged out of the backpack.

"Be careful, Billy," Lobelia said as I dropped to my hands and knees and crawled slowly down the trail. I glanced back at her once and saw the furrows in her brow and the easy way she held the rifle. Somehow it comforted me. Then as I turned away and crawled around a bend in the trail, I heard the sound again and I knew instantly it was coming from Margaret. It was like the sound she had made in church that Sunday when Reverend Thorston said Uncle Jeff's name, only it was different too, more mournful and breathless.

I stopped and felt a sudden helplessness, so complete it paralyzed me, and I knew I had just done something incredibly stupid. Then, it all got so much worse. Behind me, almost over me it seemed, the voice of Deputy Blasser came out of the loud, hissing wind: "Well, I'll be goddamned. It's Billy Forrest!"

There will be times in your life, I suppose, when circumstances are suddenly so hopeless and threatening that you just want to say, "Oh, to hell with it, I'm done!" You can't do that, of course, but the feeling is there, which is what I felt with Blasser standing over me. It didn't last long because the next second, he kicked my rear end and sent me sprawling face first into the grass and dirt on the trail. It was a hard kick and I felt it all the way up to my shoulders, like a big hammer had tried to drive me into the ground.

I landed with my head twisted off to the side and I didn't have to move it to see Blasser. He looked as big as a giant, and as details came into focus, I saw the revolver in his hand, and his face with its narrow pig eyes and downturned grin. His cheeks were scratched, and the wind had pushed his hair down over his forehead, so he looked like he had been in a fight.

"That'll do for starters, you little son-of-a-bitch," Blasser said. "You've been needing your ass kicked for a long time."

I looked at him and felt a desperate rage.

"Get on your feet, Billy boy," he said. "You're just in time for the big show."

I didn't move and Blasser nudged me with his foot.

"You need another kick in the ass?" he said.

I pushed against the bogs of matted grass to get back on my hands and knees and slowly stood up, swaying in the wind like the brush and weeds all around.

"Don't even think about it," Blasser said, and I knew he had tuned in to my quick glance to see if there was any chance of diving off the trail and making a run for it.

"I'd just as soon shoot your ass as kick it, so don't tempt me." He gestured with the revolver. "Get on down the trail. We're going to a party."

I turned and walked in the direction of the camp, feeling the hard pokes of Blasser's revolver in my back and thinking that there was no doubt he would actually shoot me.

"The sheriff sent me out early to do a little scouting," Blasser said. "And guess what I found."

We rounded the last clump of alder brush and then I saw Margaret. She was lying back against a log, her chin down on her chest and her arms hanging at her sides. Strands of her tangled hair whipped in the wind and there were bruises on her face. The sick feeling in my guts got worse and I stopped and stared at her. Margaret lifted her head and stared back. Then her mouth opened and she screamed my name and lunged toward me. A rope around her waist anchored her to the log and she collapsed back onto the ground. "Billy. Oh, Billy," she said through choking sobs, tossing her head and straining against the rope.

"How touching," Blasser said. "She's so glad to see your skinny ass."

I raised a hand toward Margaret, and Blasser whacked at it with his revolver.

"None of that," Blasser said. "All you do is watch."

So many things jammed into my brain, but then they were all gone, except a total, awful hopelessness. Off to the side, behind a half-rotted windfall, I saw Otto. He was lying on his side and I thought he was dead, but then he moved slightly and I saw that his hands and feet were bound together with rope, and a rag had been stuffed into his mouth and tied around the back of his head. I couldn't tell if his eyes were open, but I could see dried blood around one of his ears.

"Your Nazi pal wouldn't shut up so I shut him up," Blasser said.

I looked back at Margaret and saw the rips in her clothing and the bruises on her face and arms. Her eyes were wide and staring, and she kept repeating my name in a coarse whisper.

"Billy's here to cheer you on," Blasser said, and his cackling laugh was sucked up by the wind.

Margaret turned her head and spit at him.

"Nothing like a woman with spirit," Blasser said. "Damn near had to knock her out to get her ready. I'm calling it foreplay, Billy. What do you think?"

I knew I had to keep control, but I must have made some involuntary move because the next thing I knew, I was flat on the ground and my head felt as if it had exploded. Through waves of dizziness and strange flashing images, I heard Blasser, "I told you, goddamnit. Next time I won't just hit you with this thing, I'll jam it in your mouth and pull the trigger."

The hurt from Blasser's kick was nothing compared to the pain in my head. It was worse if I moved, even the slightest, and I tried to lie as still as possible.

"Time to get on with things here," Blasser said.

I blinked to try to clear my vision, but it didn't help much. Through the blurring swirl, I saw Blasser take a pair of handcuffs off his service belt and click one of the cuffs around my wrist. Then he dragged me by the arm over next to Margaret. The movement made my head hurt so badly, it knocked the air out of my lungs and I gasped in pain. Blasser grabbed Margaret's arm and snapped the other cuff on her wrist and stepped back.

"Billy! Oh, God, Billy!" Margaret screamed. She tried to lift her arm but the handcuffs stopped her. She glanced down and reached out toward me with her other arm. Blasser was standing between us and he bent over and slapped Margaret's face.

"Don't reach for that little shit, Sweetheart," he said. "Reach for me." And he grabbed Margaret's hand and pulled it against his groin. Margaret made a choking sound and jerked her hand back and swung it at Blasser's head. He was far out of her reach and she tried to pull herself up and swung wildly at him again.

Blasser laughed and there was muffled grunting from Otto. Blasser glanced at him and laughed again. "Oh, yeah, you're going to be watching, too," he said. "I like that."

Blasser stood near Margaret's feet and reached for his belt buckle. I felt a terrible panic building in my aching head.

"Got to break her of laying up with Nazis," Blasser said as he unbuckled his service belt and put it on the log behind him.

"Ready, Sweetheart?" he said, zipping his fly down and stepping toward Margaret. She screamed and lunged away from him, but Blasser stuck out his foot and pinned her to the ground. I looked up at him and knew in that second that I was going to die; I would try to stop the horror that was coming even if it meant a revolver exploding in my mouth. I was immediately comfortable with that, strangely so, as if my whole life had led up to this point and it was going to end in a blaze of futility.

Blasser grinned as he fumbled at his open fly. He glanced at me and our eyes met for an instant. "Watch close, Billy," he said, "You might learn ... "

His speech was suddenly cut off in mid-sentence, and then his body jerked slightly and stiffened in a slow, twisting spasm. I had been watching his face, waiting to time my desperate leap, and at the exact instant he stopped talking, a little red mark, like a sudden pimple, appeared in the middle of his forehead. His eyes closed and then opened again, very wide, like they were trying to take in something that wasn't there. His body suddenly stretched tall and rigid, and a tiny trickle of blood ran from his forehead and down the side of his nose. Then, like a big tree toppling in the wind, he fell slowly backwards until he disappeared and all I could see were the soles of his boots. They jerked a couple of times and then were still.

CHAPTER TWENTY-SEVEN

It is impossible to know just what goes on in somebody else's head at any given moment. That's mostly a good thing, and it sets off endless speculation. But trying to guess what must have gone through Margaret's mind when the brutal assault on her stopped and her cruel attacker suddenly disappeared—that is speculation of the wildest kind, like wondering what the condemned might be thinking as the firing squad loads up. If she was capable of even the most ragged thought in the horror that enveloped her, maybe Margaret was thinking about Uncle Jeff and how he had disappeared from her life and made it not worth living and so now it was ending.

Margaret had no way of knowing that a totally unexpected outside force had forever changed everything: that a small whirling piece of lead had smacked into Blasser's forehead and bored through his brain like a high-speed, metallic worm, destroying enough critical brain tissue to kill him almost instantly and finally puncturing through the back of his skull and tumbling off into the swamp.

I know from reading the shooting columns in *Field and Stream* that the muzzle velocity of a .22 caliber long-rifle bullet is 1,100 feet per second and like it says on the cartridge box, it is dangerous for up to a mile. And I know from watching the butchering out at Grandpa 's farm that a .22 bullet will kill a pig just like that!

I thought about some of these things later, much later, because for a long time after the bullet zapped through Blasser's head, I couldn't think about anything. It was like the wind had swept away my ability to process sights and sounds. And along with that, it had whisked away my last ounce of energy. I couldn't move, might not ever move again, in fact.

Measuring the passage of time under such circumstances is impossible. I have no idea how long I lay there, handcuffed to Margaret, listening to the wind pick up her moaning and whip it away. Seconds? Minutes? It seemed like it could have been an hour. Whatever it was, nothing seemed to change. And that's probably what slowly brought me around—the fact that, except in the gusting of the wind, nothing was changing. There was no Blasser coming to stand over us, no kicks or whacks to the head, no more menacing threats to Margaret.

For a few seconds, I considered the possibility that I might have died and that was the reason the ugliness had gone away. But then my head throbbed with needle-like pain and it didn't seem like I should feel pain if I were dead.

I raised myself up and stretched my neck out far enough to see Blasser's boots, the toes sticking up and obscuring what was beyond them. Margaret was very still next to me. Her eyes were closed, but then she blinked them open, as if she were just waking up. She turned her head and looked at me for a long time, her expression as flat as a bird's. Neither of us moved and then Margaret's eyes suddenly widened.

Her head jerked back and she opened her mouth and screamed with such intensity it was like an expression of terror from deep down in the swamp itself. I turned my head and saw the reason: standing almost in the same spot where Blasser had last stood was Lobelia. The sun put a black sheen on her face and ringed it with a yellow halo and her floppy hat moved in the wind like wings coming out of her ears. In her striped overalls, she seemed to be eight feet tall. She carried my rifle in a way that pointed over us, then she bent toward Margaret and Margaret screamed again, even louder this time.

I don't know if Margaret had ever in her life seen a Negro woman. Probably not, except maybe in the movies. And there's no way to know what Blasser's brutality had done to her already addled brain. If you think about all of that, it's almost natural for Margaret to have reacted as she did. Here she is hanging onto her sanity by her fingernails and just when it seems there might be a let-up in the horror, she opens her eyes and there is this tall, very black creature in striped overalls and a wild, flopping hat bending toward her with a rifle.

This instantly became obvious to Lobelia and she quickly stepped back behind the alder thicket where she was out of sight. I still hadn't moved, except to raise my head up enough to lean it against the log. I pulled myself up farther and looked over Blasser's boots to see him flat on his back beside the trail. Only a dead man could sprawl in such an awkward way, and the big circle of wetness around his crotch meant that his private muscles had relaxed one final time. I glanced at Margaret. She seemed to have passed out. For a second, I was startled at her stillness, and then I saw she was breathing and her eyelids were flickering again.

Then Lobelia shouted, "Billy, you okay?"

I didn't honestly know. Except for an ugly headache and a bruised backside, I seemed to be fine.

"I think so," I said loud enough for Lobelia to hear over the noise of the wind.

"You've got to fix it so that poor woman will let me help her," Lobelia yelled back.

And that's what I did. Slowly and as gently as I could, I worked with Margaret as she blinked awake and stared at me with glazed eyes and began to mutter my name. I didn't know how much was getting through, but I talked to her steadily, repeating over and over that Blasser was gone and wouldn't be back, and that she was safe and wouldn't be harmed anymore. I stroked her forehead as I talked, brushing her tangled hair back and rubbing the back of her neck. The touching seemed to help, and slowly the dullness in her eyes faded until she was looking at me as if she really saw me. I told her about Cy's Negro wife and how she was a good and kind woman who was here to help, and as before, I had no idea how much, if any of it, was getting through to Margaret.

So, that was the way the nightmare began to slowly turn around. While I worked at bringing Margaret back into the real world, she suddenly looked over my shoulder in the direction of Otto. "Jeff," she said.

That seemed to work like a password to break us out of our tight, little, personal focus, and over the next half hour or so, we dealt with things that had to be unique in home-front war history. It started with the keys to the handcuffs. They hung from Blasser's service belt, which was on the log where he had left it. Reaching it meant stretching out to hook the belt with my toes, then dragging it within reach. I tried to put as little pressure on Margaret's arm as possible and finally, after a fumbling struggle to find the right key, I was able to unlock the cuffs and we were free of each other.

Otto was in a twisting frenzy when I went to him and used my jack-knife to cut the rope from his feet and hands, and then pulled the gag from his mouth. He gushed with whimpering gratitude and tears ran down his cheeks as I fished the key out of my back pocket and unlocked Toby's chain from around his neck. There was a big bump on the side of Otto's head where blood had dried around his ear, and his hands were cut and bruised. At some point, I noticed that his POW uniform had been replaced by some of the clothes Margaret had apparently brought in her suitcase. I recognized an old shirt of Uncle Jeff's and a pair of his slacks.

Once he was free, Otto scrambled on his hands and knees over to Margaret. She put her arms around him, and he looked at me over his shoulder. "It's been horrible for her," he said.

I turned away and watched as Lobelia eased into view, moving slowly out from behind the alder thicket and standing where Margaret could look at her from a distance. They stared at each other for a long time, like cautious deer eye-balling a field from opposite hillsides. Lobelia talked to me in a low voice, saying comforting things that were obviously intended for Margaret. Then, Lobelia was on her knees in front of Margaret and Otto, and she opened the knapsack and offered sandwiches and the canteen. They both drank from it, Otto first and then he held it for Margaret. She gulped and choked and gulped some more.

Minutes went by as the wind hissed, and a faint sense of relief seemed to seep down over us like strange pollen. I looked at Lobelia and saw her glance toward Blasser's sprawled body. I watched as she walked over and picked up Blasser's revolver from the log where he had put it. She looked at it briefly, then stepped over to where Blasser sprawled. She bent and placed the muzzle of the revolver over the small pimple mark on Blasser's forehead. She hesitated for just a second, tilting her head to look at the angle of the revolver's barrel, and then pulled the trigger. Even muffled by the wind, the gunshot was loud, and Margaret gave a startled little scream.

Lobelia reached down to Blasser's hands. She grasped the fingers of his right hand and worked them around the revolver handle and stuffed his index finger into the trigger guard. Then she stood and looked down at what she had done. She nodded and turned toward me.

"The son-of-a-bitch killed himself, Billy," she said. "Imagine that!"

CHAPTER TWENTY-EIGHT

If we were going to get ourselves and Margaret out of the swamp, we would need Otto's help. Margaret wouldn't let go of him and would only move if he kept his arm around her and helped her stand.

"She thinks I'm her Jeff," Otto said. "Has from the start."

Margaret grasped Otto like a clinging baby and she stared wide-eyed at Lobelia and me, occasionally muttering my name and then staring again at Lobelia.

"The poor girl desperately needs help," Lobelia said.

"Her mind was not right before he got here," Otto said. "And then it got so much worse."

"We can't wait for that damned posse," Lobelia said.

"If we go slowly, I can help her walk," Otto said.

Lobelia looked at him and then at Margaret. "She seems so weak."

"I can take her other arm," I said.

Lobelia glanced my way and nodded, "Let's try it." She took a step or two down the trail and I moved over next to Margaret and lifted her arm over my shoulders. She was as limp as something dead and she barely moved her feet as we turned to follow Lobelia. We had only taken a few steps when Lobelia stopped suddenly. She held her hand up and tilted her head back like an animal testing the wind.

"What is it?" I said.

Lobelia didn't answer. Then she didn't have to: the smell of burning grass and brush suddenly filled my nostrils as unmistakable as skunk stink, and much more ominous.

"You smell it?" Lobelia said.

I nodded and glanced at Margaret and Otto huddled just behind Lobelia. A thousand thoughts suddenly swarmed like bees. None of them made any sense. I once heard the geezers tell of a forest fire catching some of their lumberjack friends in dry cutover, and I remembered how they told of hearing the screams. And then the geezers had gone quiet, until one finally said he had helped build a dozen coffins out of fresh-sawn white pine.

Lobelia stared at me and sniffed the air again. "It's getting stronger," she said.

I looked up to see a thin wisp of gray smoke slither through the top-most branches of a pine. Dread took hold like something I had never felt before, worse even than when Blasser had been standing over me. That had all moved so fast there had been only seconds to consider its horror. This was different. There was time for things to sink in. I looked at the tall trees and thick vegetation all around us, all of it so dry it would explode like gunpowder at the slightest spark.

The trail from the river crossing to the camp cuts off an oxbow of the river, which means it's a long way from the river at some points. The sink holes had dried up this summer and there would be no protection from fire anywhere along the trail. There was no way to tell where the fire was or what direction it was traveling. It was like doors slamming in my face as I tried to think of a way out. Maybe if we hurried along the trail, we could make it back to the crossing. But we couldn't hurry, not with Margaret barely able to move. The confusing threats galloping through my head left me weak.

Then, the sound of the wind changed. The gusts were still there, huffing and puffing at everything, but over it now there was a low humming. The humming grew to a distant roar, like a hundred freight trains barreling toward us through the swamp. In the midst of it was the faint sound of rifle shots, and what sounded like shouting. Then, those sounds were gone and there was just the roaring, louder by the second. There was more smoke then, blending into the highest leaves and pine boughs, and swooping down in sooty, gray streaks to brush at the tree trunks. It was like someone reached into our lungs with dirty hands to make us choke and cough. And it had all only taken seconds.

"The river," I shouted. "It's our only chance!"

I jumped over a log, pulling Margaret along, and waited while Otto got lined up on her other side. We stumbled through the tall grass and thick brush to the back eddy closest to the camp. I glanced back once to see

Lobelia behind us. Otto and I fell as we waded into the thick mud on the edge of the river. Margaret fell with us, and there was a sloshing struggle before we finally got to our feet and waded farther out into the river.

The air was suddenly thick with smoke, and Margaret was crying and gasping for breath. Big trees, some of them dead and dry, arched out over us and I knew our only hope was to get to a spot downstream where rapids dumped into a wide pool. We were stumbling and falling and I felt the fast water grab at my lower legs and suck me under the first plunge of the rapids. I lost my hold on Margaret and tried to keep from crashing into the boulders as the swirling current carried me like a helpless bug. It lasted only seconds, but it took me to the edge of drowning as I kicked and flailed against the water and the rocks, holding my breath against the pressure of the water and feeling it in my nostrils like cold worms.

Then I was in the pool and the river was suddenly gentle and caressing. It tumbled me over the sandy bottom and in a final desperate lunge, I got to my feet in waist-deep water, spitting and gasping for air. There was no sign of Margaret or Otto, but I saw Lobelia as she was swept out of the rapids and into the pool. She staggered to her feet and stood swaying in the current.

The steady roar of the rapids was drowned in the surging howl of the fire that surrounded us in hot, smothering sheets. I stumbled over next to Lobelia and grabbed her hand and pulled us under water just as a powerful gust of wind toppled a blazing treetop into the pool. Lobelia lost her footing and I grabbed her striped overall suspenders and hung on until she got control of her legs and feet. For what seemed an eternity, we did the same thing over and over, ducking into the cold water and holding our breath while blazing trees toppled all around, some narrowly missing us, or a wall of flame and smoke seared across the surface of the pool like a giant blowtorch.

Once, when we came up for air, Lobelia shouted, "Where…?" But that was as far as she got before we had to go under again. There was so much dry fuel it seemed the fire would never burn out. It hovered over us like a vicious predator that wasn't leaving until it got us. I began to doubt we could outlast it—that we could keep ducking into the water long enough to survive the smoke and heat and burning trees that kept crashing down.

Then, there came a few seconds when Lobelia and I stood looking at each other.

"Where's Margaret?" she shouted.

"I don't know," I shouted back, and we had to pull ourselves under again to avoid a wall of smoke and flame.

But those times of relief slowly got longer, and during one pause, I told Lobelia I last saw Margaret and Otto in the rapids and maybe they got swept through this pool and into another one just downstream.

"It's even wider than this one," I said, "If they made it there, they will be okay."

"Oh, God, I hope so," Lobelia said.

CHAPTER TWENTY-NINE

The immediate aftermath of the fire was ugly and unbelievable—a blizzard of black snow whipping over a hell worse than anything Reverend Thorston could ever have imagined. The swamp seemed part of a lifeless planet hurtling through dark, stormy space, and from where Lobelia and I stood waist-deep in the ash and debris-cluttered pool, we could see dozens of fires burning: old stumps, clusters of fallen trees, and ancient logs that would suddenly flare up as if in anger. Wisps of gray and black smoke twisted up everywhere and were knocked flat by the wind. The only sound was the hissing of that wind and the occasional snap of exploding embers.

It was a long time before we moved: the cold water that had saved us was like a security blanket and I guess our instinct was to stay with it. Even after the galloping flames had long passed, there were still waves of heat and clouds of smoke on the wind. It was a great relief to duck beneath the surface and come back up blinking and shaking our heads to clear the water from our eyes.

Neither of us said anything. I had an odd feeling that talking might change everything and the fire might come back, which was crazy because there was nothing left for another fire to burn. Lobelia apparently didn't feel like talking either. What was there to say? We were alive and that was it. It crossed my mind to thank God, but that seemed pretty dumb, like saying thanks for getting knocked on your ass.

Lobelia looked at me, then around at the blackened remains of the swamp. She reached out and put a hand on my arm. "You saved us, Billy."

I looked at her, at this tall Negro woman in the dirty, wet bib overalls, her face streaked with soot blacker than her skin and her tight red curls thick with gray ash. A wave of something came over me that I didn't expect or understand. It was like my brain tilted so some of the juvenile trash sloshed out and made room for something different. I didn't know what it was, maybe a newfound kinship for somebody or something, like what I'd felt for Toby, but stronger and more complicated.

People are forever singing and talking about love, and it's one of Cy's favorite lecture subjects. He says most of the time, love is just the sexual "hots" dressed up with flowers and poetry. There certainly wasn't any of that going on between Lobelia and me, so if what I felt for her was love, it was a different kind.

We stood for a long time, waist-deep in the cold water while the wind hurled clouds of ash and smoke in ugly swirls around us; and floating logs and limbs, charred black and smoldering, bumped against us and twisted off with the current. Something moved on the river bank and I watched a raccoon struggle over a log. Most of its fur had been burned off, and it looked grotesque and pitiful and I felt an odd comfort when it toppled off the log and splashed into the river.

Then my mind was suddenly flooded with thoughts of Margaret. What had happened to her and to Otto? I knew of the fast water downstream and the wide pool below it, and I wanted to believe they had made it there and were waiting—as we were—to climb out of the river and struggle across the blackened, miserable swamp back to Oxbow. I wanted to believe it so much that it couldn't be otherwise.

"They'll be okay," I said, and though we hadn't spoken of Margaret or Otto since that first brief mention, Lobelia knew what I was saying, and she nodded. We had to find them. That meant stumbling our way out of the river and crawling up the bank, falling and slipping and reaching out to each other for support. It was torturous going, every foot a risky, filthy step across burning brush and steaming bogs. But we finally made it and stood on the burned, boulder-strewn bank of the lower pool. It was wider and longer than the one Lobelia and I had survived in. It had more back water, and an expanse of burned cattails stuck up out of it like singed quills.

I ached to see them—Margaret clinging to Otto while he supported her with his arm, and both of them lifting their faces to breathe in life. They would be next to one of the boulders or standing in the center of the calm water waiting to join Lobelia and me for the trip back to town. They would be there somewhere amid the dirty, swirling smoke.

But there was no sign of them. Nothing.

We stood for a long time as the wind swabbed our faces with smoke and ash and filled our eyes with tears until we could not see and had to turn away.

"They might be farther down the river by now," I said.

"He's strong," Lobelia said. "He will take care of her."

We looked at each other through stinging, watery eyes and Lobelia reached out to touch my arm.

Our struggle out of the swamp was painful and, in the end, depended on reserves of energy I'm sure neither one of us knew we had. Simply climbing out of the river and struggling down to the next pool had been an ordeal. The grass and weeds and shrubs that normally offered convenient handholds and support were gone and in their place was a blackened tangle of soot-covered debris that most often crumbled at the touch. All the familiar trail markings were gone and I felt as if we were stumbling through a filthy, cluttered graveyard. I didn't recognize anything until we came past what was left of the logging camp. The last of the old building and the corner where Toby and I had made our camp had fallen down and was buried beneath a crush of huge trees that had toppled and were still flaming. Somewhere under the smoldering mess was Blasser's body. I stopped and Lobelia stepped up beside me.

"It's the camp," I said.

A gust of wind made the flames flare, and I thought of my rifle buried somewhere in the burning logs and limbs.

"It all looks so different," Lobelia said.

"Blasser's in there somewhere," I said.

"Good place for him."

"They'll never find him."

"So nobody will ever know he killed himself."

I nodded and looked at her.

"Well, we had it covered," she said, "but it's better this way."

Then we stood in the stench and swirl of the filthy wind, looking at each other as if we were outlaws silently agreeing to a pact of secrecy. After a few minutes, we turned away and headed down what I hoped was the trail. There was little left to mark it and all I could do was try to keep us headed in what I thought was the general direction of Oxbow.

"I wonder how the posse made out," Lobelia said once when we stopped to catch our breath. I wondered, too. I remembered the faint shouting and shooting we had heard just before the fire hit us. It hadn't been a good sign. The fire had been so fast and ferocious, there would have been no escaping it unless the men got to the river, and as spread out as they likely had been, it was horrible to think of what might have happened.

The fire had consumed most of the vegetation and turned the swamp into a wide open, black desert so it was possible to skirt what was still burning and stumble about with a weird freedom. The wind still filled the air with thick soot and bits of ash and it was hard to keep our eyes clear enough to see where we were going. We saw the first dead deer then, its hair gone and its burned carcass sprawled next to a stump. Then there were other dead creatures: a family of raccoons huddled beneath a smoldering stump, a squirrel that clutched a branch while its hairless tail twitched in the wind, and a rabbit oddly hanging in the crotch of a tree ten feet off the ground, as if it had tried to climb up out of the fire.

We passed more dead deer, their half-burned bodies bizarre lumps on the blacked earth. Each time, it had been a relief to see the carcass wasn't human, and as we saw more and more of them, we stayed far enough away so we could only tell it was something big and dead. But then as we skirted a smoldering windfall, the blackened body of a man suddenly appeared directly in front of us. We stopped and stared. The man was on his back with one arm raised as if he were giving a salute with his mangled, blackened fist. Most of his clothing had been burned away and his hair was gone and there was a metallic glint in his opened mouth. His stomach protruded like a big, ugly balloon, and it was hard to think the ugly mass had been a living human only hours ago.

"Oh, God," Lobelia said.

It was as if the dead man commanded us to stand there staring at him forever. It was probably only seconds, but it seemed like much longer. I finally turned and pulled Lobelia away.

"Do you know him?" she said.

I shook my head and we moved on. There was nothing about the blackened corpse that I could identify, and I wanted to think it was someone I didn't know, maybe one of the soldiers from the prison camp.

It got tougher and tougher to keep going. I felt as if I had energy for only one more step, and then just one more. Lobelia fell several times, and once when I went to help her, she said, "I don't know how much more I can take, Billy."

I told her it wasn't much farther, but I didn't know if that was true. Some of the time, I thought I knew exactly where we were and other times I felt completely lost. The blackened tangle seemed to get thicker, then it abruptly opened slightly, and there was the river behind a willow thicket. We had come out at the exact spot where I had pulled my boat up onto the sand. The boat was gone, and I remember thinking it had probably been appropriated by the posse.

Then, in the soot-covered mud, I saw a footprint, a small, footprint that made my heart miss a beat. I bent to look more closely. It seemed to be a distinct print of one of Margaret's shoes, the ones I had looked at so many times to keep from staring at her swinging legs as she sat on the station pop cooler. There were other scuffed prints in the mud, one more partial one that seemed to have that tread pattern I knew so well. I grabbed Lobelia's hand and pointed. "Look!" I said.

Lobelia looked down and stared at the scuffed mud. Finally, she looked back up at me and said, "What?"

"Margaret's," I said. "Margaret's footprints!"

Lobelia looked back down at the mud and so did I. And what I had seen so plainly before was suddenly not there. Now I saw only a jumble of deer tracks and there was no shoe tread pattern to them whatsoever. I stared down at the mud for a long time, but nothing changed: the deer tracks stayed as solid as if they were in concrete. Lobelia and I looked at each other then, and I shook my head and turned away.

"We don't know, Billy," Lobelia said.

She was right, of course, but mistaking a jumble of deer tracks for Margaret's footprints was pretty bad and a new wave of hopelessness swept over me like a cloud of the foul smoke that had been swirling around us for hours. We moved out from behind the thick willow then and stumbled into the water and waded across the river. It is wide and shallow at the crossing, but I could still feel its power as we stumbled over the gravel bottom. We were just upstream from the park, and people on shore saw us and rushed down to help as we crawled up the river bank.

"Oh, my God, he's burned black," I heard somebody say, and another voice said, "It's Cyrus Butler's nigger wife."

More people crowded around, reaching out to give us support and shouting questions: "Did you see ...?" "Where is ...?" "Could they be alive ...?"

Doc Smith was in front of us then. He swabbed at my face with an alcohol-soaked cloth and snipped some hair from around the bump on my head.

"Billy," he said, "You hurting anywhere?"

I was hurting everywhere, but I shook my head no, and Doc turned to Lobelia.

"I'm okay," she said.

Doc looked at her and handed her a clean cloth. "Let me know if I can help, Mrs. Butler," he said. Then he was gone and I saw him bend over a man stretched out on top of a picnic table.

From somewhere close by, I heard a woman crying, and suddenly my mother was there. She loomed over me, and the sound she made was halfway between a scream and a squeal. I felt her arms around me and that was it.

CHAPTER THIRTY

It must have been almost hibernation, a sleep so deep you don't even wake up to eat or go to the bathroom. Once, in the depths of it, I heard Toby barking, but mostly I drifted in a silent, dreamless void. Coming out of it was like being pulled backwards through a knothole. My body ached, my skin was tender and sore, and it hurt to move so much as a little finger. My chest felt as if it were full of ashes, so it even hurt to breathe.

I wasn't sure how long I'd been out, and I had no memory of getting from the river to my bed. I was staring up at the leaf shadows on the ceiling trying to fill in time blanks when my mother suddenly appeared in the door. She looked at me and stepped over to the side of the bed and put her hand on my forehead. "How are you doing, Billy?" she said.

I didn't know how I was doing but I knew what she wanted to hear. "I'm okay," I said.

Then with no warning whatsoever, she dropped on me and put her arms around me and squeezed so hard it almost knocked the wind out of me. Over the top of her head, I could see raindrops on the leaves of the maple outside the window, and beyond that, the gray sky looked soft and sad. Crushed as I was between the bed and my mother and hurting all over, I started to feel a little better.

Later, as my mother fixed scrambled eggs and bacon, she talked as if she had a lot of news stored up that I needed to hear. She started by saying that Dorothy Zanders hadn't heard from Margaret. It took me a minute to realize what this meant. Margaret was apparently not safely home as I might have assumed if I had thought about it. Where was she? My mother and Mrs. Zanders knew nothing about Margaret being out in the swamp. They still thought that in her confused grieving, she had packed her suitcase and run off to Minneapolis.

209

I was suddenly jolted by the realization that I had to tell them what had really happened. I almost opened my mouth to get on with it, but something held me back. If I started with Margaret, there would be no stopping and I would have to lay it all out, going way back to Cy telling me I had some growing up to do, and then how we had talked Grandma into signing the letter to Mrs. Roosevelt, and everything that happened after that. I remembered how Cy had not mentioned anything about Margaret's being out in the swamp when we had gone to the sheriff's office.

Of course, that had been back when we thought we could rescue her before anyone knew she was out there. It was a different situation now, but since I wasn't sure what had happened to Margaret, it didn't seem like a bad thing to let my mother and Mrs. Zanders think she was in Minneapolis, at least until we knew different.

My mother said Cliff Huston had called and said I shouldn't worry about coming to work until I felt like it, and Lobelia had called to ask how I was, and Cy was out of jail, and my dad had called three times from Kansas to make sure I was okay. She said Dooby Lemke's funeral was tomorrow afternoon, which stopped me cold. Dooby was dead! Good old Dooby, who was everybody's friend and knew most of their secrets. My head dropped like my neck had broken.

"Who else?" I said.

My mother looked at me, "Well, there's Deputy Blasser and Indian John." She stopped and picked up a copy of the *News-Banner* and handed it to me. "It's all in here."

Indian John, too! My hands were shaking as I unfolded the newspaper. I didn't want to read it, but I knew I had to. Deputy Blasser's name was in the headline. It said he and three others, along with two escaped prisoners, were "presumed dead." Fifteen people were in the hospital with burns and many more were recovering at home. Sheriff Curtis said that Blasser had been sent out as an advance member of the search party and had apparently been trapped by the fire.

I stopped reading and shut my eyes and saw Lobelia holding the revolver to Blasser's forehead over the bullet hole that was already there. I knew I would be living with that image for a long time, like a brain trash banner.

The news story went on to tell how a farmer named Floyd Hubert and Indian John and Dooby died: Mr. Hubert from a mysterious explosion and Indian John and Dooby when they were apparently overrun by flames as they tried to guide people to the safety of the river. It was hard to read, and I let the newspaper drop in a crumpled heap on my lap. I tried to think of how I might somehow be partly responsible for people dying, especially the ones like Indian John and Dooby, who had been part of my life. If it hadn't been for our MOP Exchange plan, none of it would have happened.

I stared out the window at the splattering rain, and then finally forced myself to pick up the newspaper and straighten it out enough to read the rest of the article. There was a paragraph about how some people had survived the fire by ducking under water in the river as the fire passed overhead. It mentioned my name and Lobelia's, and identified her as the only woman member of the search posse, which of course wasn't exactly accurate because she hadn't been with the posse, and it said that Wilbur Bender had been among the last to make it back to Oxbow. Toward the end of the article, I looked for Margaret's name but then I remembered that nobody but Lobelia and Cy and I knew she had been out there. And apparently Lobelia had not mentioned anything about her.

Reading about the fire brought it back like it had happened minutes ago. I thought about Dooby and Indian John and what it must have been like when the choking smoke and heat had filled their lungs and shut them down. I could feel it in my own lungs and in my eyes that stung and filled with tears. My mother touched my arm as I put the newspaper down.

"Sheriff Curtis has been calling," she said. "He's anxious to hear from you."

I tried to remember all the things she had said before, but there was no way. My head was too filled with old smoke and flames. Only the part about Sheriff Curtis stuck. Then all the awful things that had happened came crashing over me like a big wave of dirty water and the thought of telling the sheriff about it seemed totally impossible.

I needed to talk to Cy and Lobelia. Where did the awful details stop and start? What about Margaret, what did we say about her, about Blasser, about the burned body we had seen? All these questions made me more anxious to get on with whatever had to be done, but when I finally got myself together and walked through the soft rain over to Cy's house, both he and Lobelia were gone. I peeked through the back door into the clean kitchen and there weren't even any cats to be seen. I thought about going back home and climbing into bed, but while the prospect was inviting, I knew that eventually I would have to come up with my account of what had happened, even without consulting with Cy and Lobelia. It was going to be a challenge and I hoped it would be only for Sheriff Curtis. But that didn't seem likely from what I saw as I got within sight of the courthouse: two jeeps and an Army staff car and two other cars were parked beside the sheriff's car, and there seemed to be an unusual bustle of activity.

I hesitated at the bottom of the steps, then climbed them and stepped through the door into Monty's glass-eyed menagerie. Monty looked up over his glasses and shouted in the direction of Sheriff Curtis's office, "Billy's here." He turned back to me, "They've been waiting for you," he said.

Sheriff Curtis came out of his office and stopped and looked at me. "Glad to see you're up and about, Billy. You had us worried there for a while."

Behind him, through the office door, I could see people sitting around his big wooden table. One of them had on a uniform and another wore a white shirt and tie. I only got glimpses of the others.

Then Cy stepped out of the office and stood in front of me. "Billy," he said. "You're a sight for sore eyes." He stuck out his hand and grinned as we shook hands. "My lovely wife says you saved her life," he said. "I'm just damned sorry I couldn't have been out there to see it."

Cy was somehow different than I had ever seen him: straighter and somehow taller and with a healthier complexion, almost like he was wearing makeup to hide his age. Somebody moved in front of me just then and I looked up to see a tall, thin man with protruding front teeth. He wore a fancy straw hat tipped back to show thick, black hair, and his eyes turned down to give him a hound-dog look. "You the kid who was out there?" he said.

Before I could even think about answering, Sheriff Curtis grabbed the man's shoulder and spun him around. "Damn you, Poster, I told you to stay away from people in this office," Sheriff Curtis said.

"I've got a job to do, Sheriff," the man with the front teeth said, and he turned back to me. "You see any bodies?"

Cy nudged me. "Ignore the son-of-a-bitch. He's got a Chicago press card and thinks he's hot shit."

"At least the kid's brain isn't pickled like yours," the tall man said, and he turned his long face back in my direction, "Your chance to be a hero, kid."

"We're pretty picky about who we talk to," Cy said. "We draw the line at assholes."

Sheriff Curtis stepped forward then and looked at the man with the teeth. He pointed at the door, "Get your ass out of here, Poster, or I'll arrest you for interfering with the law."

"It's a public building," the tall man said, but he eased toward the door as Sheriff Curtis glared at him.

Monty looked up as the man passed his desk. "Goddamned reporters been calling here from all over hell," he said, and waved a handful of papers in Sheriff Curtis's direction. "They all want to talk to you."

"Tell them to stick it," Sheriff Curtis said and turned to me. "Come on in, Billy."

I followed him in through the door and stopped at the sight of all the people around the big table. Lobelia was in a chair near the door, and when she saw me, she got up quickly and walked over and threw her arms around me. "Billy," she shouted, "I've been worrying about your skinny little ass. You okay?"

Over her shoulder, I saw some of the others in the room staring at us. There were two Army officers—a captain and two soldiers with Military Police bands around their arms, and a fat man in a suit. Lobelia gave me a final squeeze and stepped back and stared into my eyes. "We wanted to wait for you, but they woke us up and hauled us down here early this morning."

"Yeah," Cy said, "I'm suing for sleep deprivation."

"Just trying to keep you tuned into jail hours," Sheriff Curtis said.

"Can we please get on with it here?" the MP captain said like he was giving an order. He was tall, with a long neck and pale, blue eyes that looked worn and faded, like they'd been rolling around in the bottom of a bucket. "We've got reports to file."

"Well, no shit," Cy said. "We've got people dead and in agony because you didn't do your job and you are worrying about goddamn reports!"

"Can it, Cy," Sheriff Curtis said.

"Oh, to hell with it," Cy said. "The longer this war goes on, the dumber the military gets."

"That kind of talk could get you in big trouble," the MP captain said and scowled at Cy.

"Treason, I suppose," Cy said, "Plotting against the government in wartime. Damn serious."

"Cyrus," Lobelia said, "it may be time to listen up here."

"That's why we're here," Sheriff Curtis said, "to listen. We need to know what the hell went on out there."

"I want to hear the kid first," the MP captain said and he looked at me in a way that made my insides twist like a hog-nosed snake doing its dying act. I knew that no matter what I said, I was going to get us deeper into the mess we were already in. I felt the eyes of everyone turn my way, and I wanted to be back in bed with the covers over my head. I looked at Lobelia, and when she smiled and nodded, the knot in my guts loosened just a trifle.

"Billy," Sheriff Curtis said, "We expected you to join the posse down at the river and take us to the prisoner, so why don't you just start there and tell us why that didn't happen."

"I can help with that," Lobelia said suddenly.

"We don't need any help from a damn…a damn … ," the captain said.

"A nigger," Lobelia said. "You don't need any help from a damned nigger, a damned nigger bitch, is that it, Captain?"

"Go get 'em, Lobelia," Cy said.

"Hold on! Hold on!" Sheriff Curtis said in a raised voice.

It was like the room had been full of hot air and the sheriff's loud voice suddenly cooled it off.

"We're going to listen to Mrs. Butler and Billy and I don't want another word out of anyone," Sheriff Curtis said.

It got quiet and I felt their eyes again. I had no idea what I was going to say. There was so much. Where did I start and where did I stop? What about Margaret? If I mentioned that she was involved, it would change everything and it wouldn't just be Cy and Lobelia and me knowing about her. And what had to come out about Blasser?

"Billy," Sheriff Curtis said. "Go ahead."

CHAPTER THIRTY-ONE

I was shaking inside and just as I opened my mouth to stammer something—I had no idea what— there was suddenly loud knocking on the door and Monty stepped into the room. "These guys insist they have to talk to you right now," he said, looking at Sheriff Curtis. Behind Monty stood Flat-top and Baldy, the two FBI agents who had talked to me at the station. Raindrops glistened on their black raincoats, and they took off their hats and shook water from them.

"Come on in," Sheriff Curtis said. "Join the party."

"We need to talk in private," Flat-top said.

"Oh, to hell with that," Sheriff Curtis said. "I'm tired of private talks and whispers and rumors and the whole goddamned secret thing. Everyone here is in this up to their eyebrows. Let's get it all out."

Baldy and Flat-top looked at each other and then around the room. Baldy shook his head and said, "It's your call, Sheriff."

The two of them shrugged out of their raincoats and sat down at the table. Flat-top looked at me for a second or two, long enough for his expression to remind me I was no longer one of them, and then he turned to face the sheriff.

"What have you got?" Sheriff Curtis said.

"We've got your deputy," Flat-top said.

"Blasser?" Sheriff Cutis asked. "What do you mean, you've got him?"

"Did you know he's been working for the Nazis?" Baldy said.

"I knew he hung around with some of that Bund gang," Sheriff Curtis said. "I talked to him about it and he said he was doing it so we could keep an eye on the Bund. That seemed like a good idea to me."

"He and that whole Almira bunch have been taking orders from a cell of Nazi sympathizers on the East Coast," Flat-top said. "They've got big plans to blow up your power dam and the pea factory."

It was very quiet in the room, and Lobelia and I looked at each other.

"That's the dumbest goddamned thing I've ever heard," Sheriff Curtis said.

Baldy nodded and said, "Some of these crazy Nazi worshippers are getting desperate.

"But a little old power plant and a pea factory out here in the middle of nowhere, it makes no sense," Sheriff Curtis said.

'They don't know how to give up," Flat-top said.

"And Blasser? I can't believe it," Sheriff Curtis said.

"So, where is he?" Flat-top said.

"He's been missing since the fire," Sheriff Curtis said. "We presume he's dead."

"We need to find him," Baldy said.

"Yeah, well, welcome to the swamp," Sheriff Curtis said. "Nobody's going out into that mess to look for anything,"

"He might not be out there," Flat-top said. "If he got to the river, the fire might have missed him. The prisoners might not be out there either. They could have gone down the river and made it over to the highway."

"There is a lot of traffic on that road and they could be in Minneapolis or Chicago by now," Baldy said. "It's a main truck route."

It was quiet again, and Sheriff Curtis said, "I haven't been able to verify it yet, but at least one of the prisoners is apparently out in the swamp."

"What do you mean?" Baldy said.

"There's pool hall gossip that Wilbur Bender cut three fingers off a prisoner's body."

"What the hell...?" Flat-top said, and there was mumbling and gasping from some of the others.

"Yeah, well, you have to know Bender, I guess," Sheriff Curtis said. "He flashed a jar of alcohol to his pals up at the pool hall and claimed it held the fingers of a POW he shot just as the fire was starting.

Lobelia glanced my way again.

"My pool hall informant tells me that Bender said he would have taken the guy's gold teeth, but he had no way to get them out."

"That could be the Nazi," the MP captain said. "He had gold teeth."

"I had Bender in here for a couple of hours and he denies the whole thing," Sheriff Curtis said. "But it wouldn't surprise me if that jar doesn't end up on the pool hall back bar with some of Bender's deer heads. He's big on displaying trophies."

"Jesus," Flat-top mumbled.

It was quiet in the room again. Sheriff Curtis shook his head and muttered, "Blasser. I should have fired the bastard years ago, but his daddy is county board chairman."

"Blasser's big in Nazi circles," Baldy said. "His code name is Duffy."

"How the hell could he buy into all that bullshit?" Sheriff Curtis wondered aloud.

"All of Germany bought it, why not your deputy?" Flat-top said.

Sheriff Curtis cursed and turned toward me. "You FBI guys might as well sit in on this," he said. "Billy and Mrs. Butler were about to tell us what they saw."

There was a lot of chair scraping and shuffling and finally everyone was seated around the table looking at me. My heart was in my mouth and I wasn't sure I could talk. Lobelia suddenly spoke.

"Sheriff Curtis, and gentlemen," she said, "I would ask that you let me talk first because I think I have a better perspective than Billy. He was too busy saving our lives to really see what was going on."

As long as Lobelia was talking, I knew that I didn't have to and I felt a great sense of relief.

"I want to hear the kid first," the MP captain said.

Sheriff Curtis looked at him, then at me and Lobelia. "Well, Captain," he said, "this happens to be my meeting."

"She'll make up some wild-assed story," the captain said. "You can't believe anything a damned…"

"Anything a damned nigger says," Lobelia said. "Is that what you were trying to say, Captain?"

The captain glared at Lobelia and she smiled at him and said, "We coloreds have our storytellers, Captain, just like you have yours. But I'm not one of them, and I would very much appreciate it if you would shut your goddamned mouth and listen to what I have to say."

Lobelia's voice went up in volume toward the end of her talking and the smile went off her face and she banged her fist down on the table right in front of the MP captain so hard it rattled Sheriff Curtis's coffee cup down on the other end. Everyone jumped about a foot, except the captain; he jumped about two feet. He leaped to his feet and shouted, "I will not be treated with disrespect by a goddamned nigger!"

Then it got quiet, except that Cy was trying to keep down the sound of his laughing but he wasn't having much luck. Everyone was looking at the captain. His face was red and his jaw stuck out as he bent toward Lobelia. "You'd better remember me, nigger," he said. "Captain Lester Cowley, U.S. Army Military Police. I ain't done with you."

"Mrs. Butler is one of our residents and not under your jurisdiction, Captain," Sheriff Curtis said. "Don't be threatening her."

"The way things are going around here, this whole stinking community could end up under military control," the captain said.

"Don't be threatening my community either," Sheriff Curtis said, and turned to Lobelia. "I think you have made your point, Mrs. Butler," he said. "If you are ready, we would like to hear what you have to say."

"Thank you, Sheriff," Lobelia said. "I appreciate that."

"Sheriff," the captain said, "I am ordering you to have the kid talk first."

Sheriff Curtis twisted in his chair so he was facing the captain. He dropped his chin so he was looking over his glasses and he didn't move for what seemed like a long time. Finally, he cleared his throat and said, "Captain, you are military police. What's going on here isn't military. As the lady said a minute ago, shut your goddamned mouth and listen."

Sheriff Curtis leaned back and nodded at Lobelia. She smiled and started talking. She said we went out to the swamp early so we could get the prisoner back to town before the posse got involved. And she said we thought we had plenty of time and felt we owed it to the prisoner to keep him from possible harm, but when we got out to where he had been chained up, he was gone.

"He somehow got the chain unlocked from around his neck," she said, "and there was no sign of him."

I watched her as she talked. Her hands were folded in front of her and she looked from one man to the next all the way around the table. They were direct looks, not defiant, but like her eyes were saying 'we're dealing with the truth here, thank you.' Cy and I were the only ones who knew otherwise and as Lobelia talked, I knew I would never again be so happy listening to someone tell lies. She was so good at it that as I listened, her account of things seemed to turn into the way I remembered it. I had a feeling that was going to be very good for me.

When Lobelia went on, she said we were about to head back to Oxbow when the fire started and blocked our way and we heard shots and shouting. She told how we went into the river and survived by ducking under the water and staying there until the fire passed and then made our way back to town. I guess you could say I listened to the whole thing in awe: it was an amazing performance the way she pulled everything out of our experience about Margaret and Blasser as slick as thumbing the guts out of a trout.

"If it hadn't been for Billy, we wouldn't have made it," she said and nodded in my direction. She said we saw lots of dead deer and other critters on the way out, but she didn't mention the dead man with the upraised arm and the mangled hand.

When she paused, the men were all staring at her and at me. Lobelia looked at me and smiled. "You're a hell of a guy, Billy," she said.

I smiled back and nodded, and had a strange urge to go over and give her a big hug. The men around the table were quiet.

"There's more to it than that," the MP captain said.

The rest of the men looked at him. "She's lying," the captain said. "I can tell you sure as I'm sitting here. I'm from Mississippi and I've been dealing with coloreds all my life and you can't believe a damned thing a ..."

"You can't believe a damned thing a nigger says," Lobelia said. "You said that before, Captain."

"They turned that prisoner loose, that's what they did," the captain said as he got to his feet again. "He was their friend and they let him go so he wouldn't get shot by one of your trigger-happy deer hunters, Sheriff."

The captain was talking loudly and waving his arms and he pointed at Lobelia and said, "I told you we should have had the kid talk first."

"Sit down," Sheriff Curtis said.

"I will not be disrespected by a goddamned, lying nigger," the captain shouted. "She's making fools out of us. Can't you see that?"

"I asked you to sit down, Captain," Sheriff Curtis said.

The captain looked at him and at Lobelia. "This isn't the end of this," he said.

Lobelia stared at him as he sat down and there was something in her eyes, some little flinch, that didn't make sense. Sheriff Curtis turned to me. "Billy, do you have anything to add to Mrs. Butler's account of things?"

"No, sir," I said. "That's the way it happened."

It was very quiet. Then Sheriff Curtis said, "Neither of you saw anything of Blasser?"

"Maybe he was in on some of that shooting we heard, but we didn't see him," Lobelia said.

"He once told me he knew all about your camp out there, Billy," Sheriff Curtis said. "I would have thought that's where he might have gone."

"Maybe he's the one who let the prisoner go," I said and was immediately shocked at my blurting out something I hadn't given the slightest thought to.

"Damn, Sheriff," the captain said, "now you got the kid dreaming stuff up to go along with the nigger lies."

Lobelia looked at me and I wasn't sure if she blinked or winked. My heart pounded at the thought that I might have opened my mouth when I should have kept it shut.

"You have totally screwed up this interrogation, Sheriff," the captain said. "Now, we'll never know what went on out there."

Sheriff Curtis looked around at all of us. "You may be right, Captain," he said. "We may never know it all. I think I might be okay with that."

CHAPTER THIRTY-TWO

Everybody was at Dooby's funeral. He had been Oxbow's milkman forever and everyone knew him, and liked him, except maybe a few who let their milk bills get so high Dooby cut them off. Byron Becker was one. He works at the McCormick tractor shop so he has money, but he just quit paying Dooby. He said milk was mostly water and Dooby was charging too much for it.

The Becker house is out on the edge of town and is full of kids, so of course they had to have milk. Mr. Becker ended up renting a cow from Mr. Rockford. That didn't last long because none of the Beckers wanted to milk the cow and so she developed udder trouble. Mr. Rockford took the cow back and tried to get Cy to sue Mr. Becker for damages but Cy wouldn't take the case because Mr. Rockford already owed him money. Cy and Dooby talked about it one morning at the station. Cy called it the "caked-cow-bag case" and said he would liked to have tried it because he would have made an official exhibit of the cow and demanded that Judge Travis feel her lumpy teats.

Some of this was going through my head as I sat next to my mother and tried not to look at Dooby's coffin. They didn't open the lid because I guess Dooby got burned pretty badly, so everyone was sitting there in the church trying not to think about what he must look like in there.

Reverend Thorston prayed for Dooby so long you had to wonder if maybe he knew that extra effort was needed on Dooby's behalf. There are always rumors about everybody in Oxbow, but the only one I ever heard about Dooby was that it took him a really long time to deliver milk to Mrs. Klingerhaus, the widow down on the end of Third Street. But Dooby wasn't married, so what if he was stopping to be with Mrs. Klingerhaus, if that's what he was doing. There's no sin there, no adultery, at least. And if there was fornicating, as the Bible calls it, well it's hard to see where that was such a terrible thing considering how popular it seems to be and how much people think and talk about it. This wasn't the time for me or anyone else to be thinking about such things in regard to Dooby, except for Reverend Thorston, of course, it being his job to sort through such stuff for the living and the dead.

It was odd to see Cy in church, but there he was. He had bent over and whispered in my ear as he walked past where we were sitting, "I came for the cookies and milk." I knew immediately he was referring to communion. He had once ranted about how it was barbaric to simulate cannibalism and drinking human blood in a religious ceremony, and how absurd it was that it had been embraced by most of organized religion. He said instead of wine and wafers, the churches should serve cookies and milk and that would symbolize nothing more threatening than a bedtime snack that would encourage Sunday afternoon napping. That had been another time when I knew he was headed for Hell.

Cy sat with Lobelia in the third pew and seemed to be listening to Reverend Thorston like everyone else. It must have been a shock for Reverend Thorston to see Cy come walking down the aisle with Lobelia. Maybe like seeing the Devil and his girlfriend coming into your church. Lobelia was wearing a slinky black dress and a black hat with a wide brim and she had on makeup that made her face look like it was something from up on a high shelf at an expensive store. She was getting a lot of looks, some of which turned into stares. She had smiled at me and touched my shoulder as she and Cy passed by.

A couple of the Johnson girls sat a few rows back. I could see Tulip Johnson looking down at a hymnal and I remembered the last time she had walked past the station. She had given me a look that said I was a jerk for staring at her, but she could handle it. As I thought about it, it seemed that she and some of her sisters had been walking past the station more than usual lately, but that could be my imagination.

Then I started thinking about their little white asses flashing in the night down at the river, and that was certainly not the kind of thinking you should do at a funeral, either. So, I tried to get things back on track and think about Dooby and how I was going to miss him. But I would no sooner get focused on Dooby and there would be a little white ass bobbing into view for a second or two. I tried looking up at the stained-glass window where the purple Jesus is praying next to a big rock, which has always helped me control things before. But this time it didn't work, and I felt stirrings that just seemed to be doing their own thing and there wasn't anything I could do about it.

Then, everyone stood up to sing *Amazing Grace*, and everything changed, and I do mean everything. It started slow, with all the usual voices—the squeaky ones, the out-of-tune ones, and the ones in the wrong octave so they give out in the high and low places—all of these gradually falling into the kind of jangled harmony you might hear early on a summer morning when all the different birds first tune up. This more or less settled in toward the end of the first verse and *"Was blind, but now I see,"* sounded like the usual ragged church singing.

But as the second verse started, *"T'was Grace that taught my heart to fear,"* something different seemed to poke up through the jumbled sound, something soft and mournful but with a certain authority to it that made you want to hear more. And I think that's what happened: people gradually stopped their own singing, so they could listen to that voice that was starting to fill the church with the kind of sound it had never known. When the third verse, *"Through many dangers, toils and snares,"* came up there was only that one voice singing. It was Lobelia's and it was something to hear!

If there are songs written with one person in mind, *Amazing Grace* had to have been written for Lobelia. It has never been sung the way she did it, and it didn't take any musical sense to know that; you just had to be there and listen to the way she took the melody and the words and wove them together like she was fixing a flat tire and frosting a cake and holding your hand all at the same time. She would come at a note from the side and slide under it and give it a little kick and then pick it up and hold it like it was her own precious baby. You could feel in your bones that here was someone doing up a song in a way that made you want to reach in and get your heart out and hand it to her.

Everyone was staring at her with their mouths open, even Reverend Thorston up behind the pulpit, and Florence Walker, who was supposed to be playing the pipe organ but had stopped and was staring along with everybody else. I looked over at Lobelia and she didn't seem to be paying any attention to anyone or anything except her singing. Her eyes were closed and her body was moving with …well, with Amazing Grace, that's the only way you could describe it.

I looked around and people were starting to move with her, just making little swaying moves with their heads and then with their shoulders. My mother gave me a quick look. Her eyes were big and I could tell she was impressed. I glanced up at Reverend Thorston and he seemed to be swaying a little too, but his eyes were on Lobelia like she was Eve coming at him with the apple. I think it's safe to say that he was more or less hypnotized by Lobelia's singing like everyone else, but he didn't dare really go all out with it and this put him on the edge of panic. At least, that's the way it looked to me.

When Lobelia got into that last verse, with its *"Amazing Grace, how sweet the sound,"* the crowd was swaying like there was a strong wind, and some people had reached out and were holding hands with the people next to them, and there was smiling and somewhere in the back, I heard laughter.

Then it was over, and somebody started clapping and a few others joined in until half the mourners were applauding, and a few were even cheering. They stopped only when they realized Reverend Thorston was scowling down at them. The rest of the funeral was quiet and subdued, but the people were different; they weren't all down and droopy like you might expect them to be on such an occasion. I wouldn't say they were skipping around with good cheer, but they had definitely been uplifted. And it wasn't from Reverend Thorston's preaching or praying; it was from Lobelia's singing.

Finally, it was over and everyone started shuffling out of the church behind Reverend Thorston and the pallbearers. I eased away from my mother and over toward Cy and Lobelia as the crowd slowly oozed out the door and down the front steps. I was just behind Lobelia when the buck-toothed Chicago reporter stepped in front of her and started asking questions. I couldn't hear what he was saying but it was something about her being a big time pro and didn't she once sing with Dizzy Gillespie and did she know Charlie Parker?

Then Cy reached over and jerked the reporter's necktie so hard his hat fell off. "Get the hell away from her," Cy said and he said it loud enough for everyone to hear, including Reverend Thorston, who was standing nearby waiting for Dooby to get loaded into Wagonback's old hearse. Reverend Thorston glanced up at Cy and Lobelia and then went back to tending to Dooby. He watched as they slid the coffin into the hearse, then shut his Bible and climbed into a car with some of the pallbearers.

Cy saw me and smiled. "Dooby would have liked that," he said.

I didn't know if he was talking about the whole ceremony or just Lobelia's song but it didn't matter. I nodded and looked at Lobelia. She was just turning toward me when a soldier stepped in front of her. He had on a dress uniform, which you didn't see much with the POW guards except occasionally on weekends. He was tall and slim and had a pointed nose and when he took off his hat you could see that he had long, skinny fingers. There were several ribbons across his chest and the three stripes on his arms meant he was a sergeant. He stared at Lobelia and she looked back at him, and they stayed that way for what seemed like a long time.

"Chester?" Lobelia said.

"Yeah, Red Honey, it's me," the soldier said, and a big grin cut across his face. Lobelia made a loud whooping noise so everyone turned to look at her. Then she reached out and grabbed the soldier and folded him up in her long arms. They stood that way—with their arms around each other for a long time, swaying back and forth and laughing. Then, Lobelia stepped back and said, "I can't believe it!"

"Ain't it great?" the soldier said.

"Cyrus," Lobelia said, "This child sergeant here was my pal at the Alvin way back when I first got there."

Cy and the soldier looked at each other and shook hands. "Was he into music or stripping?" Cy said.

Lobelia laughed and patted the soldier on the head. "Chester Thompson plays about the meanest piano this side of Art Tatum," she said. "We used to do numbers together."

"I can't tell you how I've missed that," the soldier said.

Lobelia looked at him and said, "Well, hell, Chester, we've got an old piano and you just come on over and we'll pick up where we left off."

"Oh, my God," the soldier said, "I learned so much from you, and then the damned draft ended it all."

"It hasn't ended," Lobelia said.

CHAPTER THIRTY-THREE

Nobody could ever have predicted what the meeting between Lobelia and Chester would lead to. Just when it looked like people were moving on from the fire and things might be headed back toward a boring old Oxbow routine, all of a sudden there was this new situation, wonderful at first, but at the end turning ugly beyond imagination.

Maybe it was just more of the war coming to Oxbow, and if that is true, maybe I should do a little rethinking. I remember how great I thought it was going to be when we heard the Nazis were coming to town; if I couldn't go to war, the war was coming to me. There is obviously no substitute for being right up there on the front where bullets are flying and artillery is thumping in like giant fists pounding the ground and people are getting blown apart and dying. But some of what's been happening around here has been violent enough to take the edge off my feelings of being left out of the real war.

The bad stuff hasn't all been war-related, of course. The fire, that was an act of God, I guess, though I have never been able to figure out just what isn't an act of God. Apparently, there is no doubt about such things as fires and storms; He is definitely in charge there. War? I don't know. There's all that high-level praying asking God to whack the enemy and to be on your side, so He must be in charge of war, too.

It's confusing. And it's confusing as to how far the war gets into things around here. It's safe to say that the fire out in the swamp was different because of the war: there wouldn't have been so many people killed and burned if it hadn't been for the POWs and the Army guards being here in Oxbow. And this latest thing wouldn't have happened at all if they hadn't been here. When I think about it that way, I feel guilt creeping in for the way I prayed to get into the war and was so excited when it came to Oxbow in the form of POWs. I cannot think that I had a hand in what happened with the MPs, that it might be partly due to God answering my prayers. That would be too much. And then if I think of it as an act of God without any prayer input from me, I have to wonder what kind of a God we are dealing with.

There has been no word about Uncle Jeff; he is still missing. How long can you be missing or "gone"? Forever? So now in an odd way, Uncle Jeff and Margaret are in the same place, both missing. It's been almost two weeks since the fire and there has been no sign of Margaret or Otto, or their bodies. I haven't really been expecting anything. It has been raining almost every day and the swamp is a big, black, muddy quagmire with the river running bank full of swirling, coffee-colored water. Nobody goes near any of it. It must be about a one-hundred-percent sure thing that Margaret and Otto drowned and their bodies got carried miles down the river, maybe all the way to the Mississippi.

That's happened before. They never found Barbara Wallace, and the geezers always talked about lumberjacks falling between the floating logs and never coming up. So, there's a history there, of the river helping dispose of the dead. But I can't think of Margaret as dead. She's gone, that's all. I could never think of Toby as dead either, until Indian John found his body and brought me his collar and then I had no choice but to change him from gone to dead. Unless there's some proof like that with Margaret, she's going to stay "gone" in my book.

As far as Mrs. Zanders and my mother and everyone else are concerned—except for Lobelia and Cy and me of course—Margaret is missing in Minneapolis and not in the river. Mrs. Zanders is so sure of it that she told my mother that Margaret had tried to call her. She said the telephone rang late at night and there was no one on the line, but Mrs. Zanders said she just knew it was Margaret because she heard breathing that sounded like Margaret's. That seems like a good way to leave things, for now, maybe forever. I wish I could be more firmly in the innocent missing-in-Minneapolis camp, which is a better image to think about, and there is more hope there. I try.

Even though it is totally absurd, I have this dumb little fantasy where when the fire came and we all went into the river and got separated, the current swept Margaret and Otto downstream where they survived the flames in one of the pools and then they floated on downstream until they came to my boat which they used to drift on out of the burned swamp, past Oxbow and over to the state highway, where they got a ride with a trucker into Minneapolis and that is where they are, holed up in some charity shelter, Otto wearing Uncle Jeff's clothes and Margaret smiling at him and calling him "Jeff."

Then I think about Margaret's footprints in the mud, the ones that turned into deer tracks and how they have since slowly turned back into the familiar imprint of Margaret's shoes. And I think about Mrs. Zanders' telephone call and how every time the phone rings now, it is different. When I answer it at the station, I want to hear Margaret singing, *"Oh, where have you been, Billy Boy, Billy Boy. Oh, where have you been, charming Billy?"* It doesn't happen, of course, but who is to say it couldn't?

Never for a moment do I think of Margaret and Otto's lifeless bodies doing a slow, watery tumble down toward New Orleans. If there is even the slightest hint that thoughts are headed there, I shake up the brain trash until something else pops up. There are so many holes in my survival fantasy that I don't even try to plug them. I just go with it whenever Margaret comes to mind, which is often. And it would be even more often if it weren't for Lobelia and all the things that have been happening with her and Cy and the Army.

Shortly after Dooby's funeral, Lobelia and Cy started having jam sessions at their house with Chester, the piano-playing soldier, and some of his friends, who were also musicians. Soldiers would start dropping in about the time it got dark and you would hear music drifting out of the windows—the tinkle of Cy's piano, which Chester had tuned up; the wail of horns or reeds, and finally the voice of Lobelia doing her magical thing with all kinds of songs. People from around town started dropping in to listen, especially after that Sunday when Lobelia sang with the Lutheran church choir.

"It was like when I was a little girl," she said later, "all those good, God-fearing folks worrying about their souls and wanting somebody to sing to them."

I was there that Sunday because, as usual, I hadn't been fast enough to dodge my mother's Sunday morning church draft. When she told me Lobelia was going to be singing, I didn't put up my usual resistance. My mother said Florence Walker, the church organist, went over to Cy's house and asked Lobelia if she would come and sing with the choir because they were short on members due to the fire. Mrs. Walker apparently did that without consulting Reverend Thorston, according to church gossip. The word was that so many people who'd been at Dooby's funeral wanted to hear Lobelia again that they more or less forced Mrs. Walker to go make the request.

Cy didn't come with her, and so Lobelia sat up there with the choir looking like musical royalty. Before the service, as people were filing in to the church, a crowd had gathered around Lobelia. People were smiling at her and making comments about how they appreciated her singing, and she was smiling back and shaking hands and patting people on the arm or the back. I happened to glance up at Reverend Thorston about then. He was sitting in a chair up in front waiting to give his sermon and he looked like he couldn't quite figure it all out. And there were some things that might have been puzzling to anyone if you got to chewing on them, like how in the world did all these white people come to admire and respect this red-haired Negro woman when most of them had never so much as seen a colored person?

Oxbow doesn't have any rules for how to treat colored, except for Indian John, of course. And in his case, it had been to respect and take care of him and never mind that he didn't have white skin, though that fact makes it easier to be nice to him because he is, after all, an Indian. So what the people seemed to be doing in regard to Lobelia was going with things that made sense to them, and skin color wasn't really one of them, except that she was, after all, a Negro.

The whole thing seemed pretty simple to me—Lobelia has a way of singing that gets inside people and they don't have to be jazz or blues fans or know anything about music for that to happen. I don't remember much of what Reverend Thorston said that Sunday—I think it had to do with the King of Babylon roasting men in a fire for lying and being with their neighbors' wives, which I supposed was Reverend Thorston's idea of a timely message. But I sure remember Lobelia's singing. She did a few songs with the choir and you could tell she was holding herself back. She got going a little with *Onward, Christian Soldiers*, especially that verse that says, *"We are not divided, all one body we. One in hope and doctrine, one in charity,"* and then took charge toward the end and she was doing a solo with the last verse.

If you heard it you would never forget it: *"Onward, Christian soldiers, marching as to war, with the cross of Jesus going on before. Christ the royal Master, leads against the foe; Forward into battle see His banners go."* As ready as I've always been to go to war, by the time Lobelia got through singing that song, I was ready to jump up and run out of the church and follow the Almighty into the bloodiest war in all of history.

But Lobelia's rendition of *Onward, Christian Soldiers* was nothing to what she did with *The Old Rugged Cross*. The minute Mrs. Walker hit the organ keys and the old, familiar refrain started coming out of the pipes, Lobelia grabbed onto it like a cat pouncing on a mouse, not a hungry cat, but one that just wanted to exercise its ultimate authority in the name of personal satisfaction and any incidental public entertainment. Everyone knows and loves the song and so the choir was romping away with it even before you started to hear Lobelia.

My mother and I were singing along and I wasn't even doing those joke lyrics she always scowls at me about: *"On a hill far away stood an old Chevrolet. Its tires were all tattered and torn."* Out of respect for what I knew was coming from Lobelia, I was singing the real words: *"On a hill far away stood an old rugged cross, the emblem of suffering and shame."*

Then, the same thing happened that had happened at Dooby's funeral; people started swaying a little, and then more and all the rest of us stopped singing and Lobelia took control. Everyone in the church just seemed to come together in a great swaying dance that looked like something you might see in a movie about missionaries saving souls at an African village, except everyone in the church was white, of course.

At some point, somebody shouted, "Halleluiah!" And somebody else said, "Praise the Lord," and Lobelia was so into it that it was almost like she was giving birth. When there were just four lines left, she stopped writhing with her efforts and opened her eyes and looked out at the people. "Everybody sing," she shouted, and the roof almost blew off the old church as everyone clasped hands and swayed and sang at the top of their lungs: *"So I'll cherish the old rugged cross, Till my trophies at last I lay down, I will cling to the old rugged cross, and exchange it someday for a crown."*

Reverend Thorston was looking up like he thought the roof might actually fall in. His lips were moving as if he was singing along with everyone else, but I think he must have been praying because his lips kept moving as *The Old Rugged Cross* came to a thunderous end and people clapped and laughed and some even hugged each other. I think maybe the truth was that his old Lutheran Church would never be the same again after Lobelia, and that worried Reverend Thorston, so he was trying to shore things up by praying.

It was on the heels of this that Cy and Lobelia started having their jam sessions, and they kept getting bigger and bigger and attracting more and more people until some nights there would be standing room only in Cy's house. I went over and listened as often as I could and it was like nothing I had ever experienced. Different soldiers from all over the country played their instruments like they'd never enjoyed themselves so much before in their lives, and Lobelia was joking with them and making musical suggestions, and then singing with them so they would shut their eyes like they were in some kind of a rapture.

Cy always sat in a corner chair with his head back and a grin on his face. Sometimes he would get Poor Little Thing out of her new nest box on the back porch and hold her on his lap. Everyone in town was talking about the jam sessions and a lot of people were dropping in and staying around to listen. It added something to Oxbow that it had never had before, music and fun on a regular basis. Some of the soldiers even started calling Cy's house "The Cotton Club" after one of the New York jazz places, I guess. It was a party every night.

CHAPTER THIRTY-FOUR

It happened at one of the jam sessions that had gone on late, way past the time I should have been home, but my mother had been easing up on that kind of thing, so I wasn't really worried. It was a typical crowd, a dozen or so soldiers and maybe that many Oxbow residents, all men except for Bobbie Holt, who works at the library and sometimes plays her clarinet all by herself down at the park. I had found a place to sit in a corner of the living room and was listening to the music and thinking how nice it was, especially when Lobelia sang, when suddenly there was a loud crashing and thumping out on the front porch.

Everyone looked at each other and the musicians hesitated a second, but they kept playing. Lobelia looked toward the door just as a very tall soldier in a Military Police uniform came charging through it and stopped in the middle of the room. He was wearing a white helmet and carried a long, shiny, wooden club. He swiveled his head and looked around like he was trying to see everything at once. He had sergeant stripes on his sleeves and wore a black leather belt with a holstered 45 strapped to it. Two other MPs came stomping in behind him, and then three others appeared from the direction of the back door. They all wore white MP helmets and carried shiny clubs and had pistols.

"This is a raid," the MP sergeant shouted. "Don't anybody move."

The musicians stopped playing and stared at the MPs like they couldn't believe their eyes. Lobelia was off to the side, scowling and shaking her head slowly back and forth. Cy jumped up out of his chair and took a couple of steps toward the MP sergeant and shouted, "Now just a goddamn minute here, you have no …."

But that was as far as he got before one of the other MPs stepped in front of him and shoved at him with his wooden club. "Stand fast, sir," the MP said.

"Stand fast, my ass," Cy shouted. "This is my goddamned house and ...."

The MP shoved him again, and then the big, tall sergeant MP spoke. "This here's an official military operation, sir. We would appreciate your cooperation."

"Official operation! What the hell are you talking about?" Cy shouted.

"Army regulations permit us to enter civilian housing to stop immoral military behavior," the MP sergeant said.

"Music is not immoral, you asshole!" Cy shouted.

"Prostitution is," the MP sergeant said. "We're here to shut you down."

There was an odd little moment of silence before Cy seemed to gather himself and then explode. "Jeeezus Christ Almighty," he shouted. "You and your shithead MPs get the hell out of my house before I ...."

I don't know what Cy was going to threaten because it didn't seem like he had a lot of options. It didn't matter because the MP sergeant nodded, and two MPs grabbed Cy from behind and wrestled him to the floor. Cy cursed and grunted and twisted frantically to try to get away, but the MPs forced his arms behind his back and snapped handcuffs onto his wrists.

The MP Sergeant looked down at Cy and then around the room. "All military personnel are officially in our custody," he said. "You are ordered to proceed out the front door and wait for transportation back to camp."

The soldiers who had been playing their instruments were still more or less frozen in the positions they had been in when the MPs came busting in. They stayed that way, staring at the MP sergeant until he opened his mouth wide and shouted so loud it seemed to crack the walls: "Move it! Now! That's an order!"

The soldiers jumped and began scrambling to case up their instruments. Some of them glanced at Lobelia, and she nodded and said, "It's okay, boys. We'll get this straightened out." But the way she said it didn't have any zip behind it, and I had the feeling she might not believe it herself.

Then the MP sergeant looked at her and said, "We have orders to take you into custody, Ma'am."

From where he was down on the floor, Cy apparently heard what the sergeant said and he bellowed like a bull. "Goddamn you miserable bastards," he shouted. "You will take my wife out of this house over my dead body!"

As he shouted, he twisted and tried to get up and the MP sergeant nodded at the two MPs holding him. One of them raised his club and whopped Cy on the head so hard his skull must have cracked, for sure. It knocked him out cold, and Lobelia let out a wail and made a lunge to get over to him, but a couple of the MPs grabbed her and slammed her up against the wall. She cursed and struggled, but the MPs held her tight and when the sergeant nodded at them, they dragged her out of the room and out of sight and apparently out of the house, because she was cursing and screaming all the way and when I last heard her, it sounded like it came from out in the front yard.

All the soldiers filed out of the house, carrying their instruments and looking sideways at the MPs. The sergeant looked around the room at the Oxbow people who had been there listening to the music and who had sat stunned and quiet through the whole MP thing. He glanced my way briefly and I looked back at him and tried to get my head around what had just happened. One moment it had all been cool and exciting and fun and the next minute, it was all a pile of shit.

Cy groaned and the sergeant looked down at him. "If he's still out, take the cuffs off," he said. Then he turned to the people in the room. "You all can go on home," he said. "The captain says we won't need statements from any of you, so just go on about your business."

The sergeant looked around again. "Okay, men, let's take our little prize back to the captain. I think he will be pleased."

He turned and walked out the door and the other MPs followed. The whole thing had only taken a few minutes. The Oxbow people looked around at each other, their eyes wide and unbelieving. Doc Clauson had been sitting over by the wall, and he jumped to his feet and rushed over to where Cy was sprawled on the floor. He put his hand behind Cy's neck and lifted his head. Cy groaned, a long groan like he was being forced to leave some place he didn't want to leave.

"Jeez, they whacked him hard enough to kill a horse," Doc said.

I was down on my knees next to Doc, and I bent over Cy and saw his eyelids flicker. "He's coming around," I said.

"That's good," Doc said. "I thought they might have killed him."

Cy groaned again and blinked his eyes open. They didn't seem to be really focused and he shut them.

"Easy, Cy," Doc said. "You're gonna be okay."

Cy opened his eyes and looked at Doc. He blinked and stared for a minute or so. "Goddamn, the vet's here. Have I turned into a goat?"

"You're one hard-headed SOB," Doc said. "You took a hell of a blow."

Cy looked at him. "I don't remember a goddamn thing."

"Just as well," Doc said.

"What the hell happened?"

"You got whacked. Your memory will likely come back but you've got to take it easy."

"I have no choice. I can't move a damned muscle," Cy groaned.

We helped Cy over to his couch and he eased down onto it and seemed to pass out.

"You'd better stay with him, Billy," Doc said. "He'll sleep this off, but if there's any change, call Doc Smith."

I sat next to Cy's couch, listening to his uneven breathing and watching him twitch and then relax like he was dead; and what had just happened played over and over in my head like some dumb scene from a movie. But it wasn't the crooks or bad guys who had gone down, it was the good guys—happy, soldier musicians and Lobelia, and the people watching and listening, like me and Doc, and Cy, of course. He got it the worst, although there was no telling what had happened to Lobelia.

From her screams and shouts out there in the yard and the street, the MPs must have been jerking her around pretty bad. I remembered the look in her eyes when the first MP came busting in. There had been that flash of anger and it had suddenly drained and been replaced by a kind of strange emptiness I had never seen before, not even in the eyes of cornered critters. They always seem to save a little glint of hope like they're going to make a dash for it. There was none of that in Lobelia's eyes.

CHAPTER THIRTY-FIVE

Planter found her. He was walking past the POW camp on his way to the cemetery to dig a grave for Gary Winthrop, who had finally died from his swamp burns, when he saw her in the ditch. He said later he thought it was just a big bundle of rags, but then he looked again and saw movement. He poked with his shovel and heard a groan, bent over, and saw it was Lobelia.

Planter said he knew who it was immediately because he had heard her sing in church and had even gone over to Cy's house one evening to listen to her. For someone who works around the dead as much as he does, Planter is a pretty lively old guy. I heard later that he told Sheriff Curtis that when he first saw Lobelia's condition, he just wanted to go grab somebody and beat them with his shovel.

I don't know who that would have been because there was no way to know for sure who had done anything to her, at least at that point. And even to this day, there are no real names to put the blame on. War does that, I guess—shuffles people around so much that it is easy to get away with being a total asshole, or worse. Of course, if you gave it the least little bit of thought you had to immediately remember the MP captain telling Lobelia at the sheriff's office that he wasn't done with her. He was from Mississippi and from the way he talked, it was pretty easy to figure out that down there the Civil War had not done a lot to even things up between the whites and the coloreds.

The day Lobelia and I went shopping and she had talked about separate entrances, she said Colored people down south either live like scared rabbits or they ended up in some white man's stew pot. Then she had looked at me and said, "You live in a state of beautiful ignorance, Billy. You don't know how lucky you are."

I didn't understand it at the time, but I knew it wasn't an insult.

Then if you keep poking through the weirdness leading up to the assault on Lobelia, you remember that when the MPs dragged Lobelia kicking and screaming out of Cy's house, one of them said the captain would be pleased at the "little prize" they were bringing him. So, for my money, the MP captain was behind the horror. And in an odd way, I think Lobelia saw it coming, or at least the possibility of it: there were a couple of times when there had been some little flicker in her eyes, like when the MPs came busting in to Cy's house that night, or when the MP captain stood over her in the sheriff's office and told her to remember his name. It was as if her eyes were light bulbs that went dull just long enough to let you know of a lurking darkness.

Planter said when he saw there was nothing he could do for Lobelia, he hurried to the sheriff's office and told Monty, and Monty called the Wagonback ambulance. Sheriff Curtis picked up Doc Smith at his office and they went out to where Lobelia was. I heard Doc Smith tell Monty about it later, and I am going to do my best to forget all the details. She was still alive and had a strong pulse, Doc said, but there was bleeding around her throat from puncture wounds and air was leaking out, and there were other injuries, bad ones. They took Lobelia up to Doc's office where he has some rooms with cots, and he got her bleeding stopped and shot her with enough pain medicine to put her out.

Then they called Cy. It was the morning after the MPs had raided his house and taken Lobelia. I had spent the night sitting next to Cy's couch where he had alternately snored quietly or groaned and thrashed about like he was trying to climb out of something. It had been a long night. I don't think I slept much, and I felt groggy and out of it when Cy finally started to come around toward morning. He sat on the edge of the couch staring at me and shook his head. That was probably not a good thing to do because he groaned and put his hands up over his ears. I brought him a glass of water and he downed it in a couple of glugs and held the glass out for more. He felt the bump on his head, which stuck up so much you could see it through his hair.

"How'd that happen, Billy?" he said.

"The MPs," I said.

He looked at me and scowled. "MPs?"

I nodded. "They were here last night. Don't you remember any of it?"

Cy looked around the room like he was seeing it for the first time.

"Little pieces are coming back. Where's Lobelia?"

Before I could say anything, the phone rang. Cy pointed at me and I answered it. It was Sheriff Curtis. He said Lobelia was at Doc Smith's office and Cy should get over there as soon as possible. I hung up and told Cy, and he stared off into space for a second like he hadn't heard me. Then he suddenly jumped to his feet. "Let's go!" he shouted.

Cy seemed to have made a miraculous recovery from the whop on his head because he walked so fast I could barely keep up with him.

"I'm starting to remember some of it, Billy," he said as we trotted across First Street. "The bastards took her, didn't they?"

It's only a couple of blocks from Cy's house to the big white corner building where Doc has his office, and we made it in seconds. Cy took the stairs two at a time and we came busting into Doc's outer office just as he came out of one of the side rooms. "How is she, Doc?" Cy said as he stumbled to a stop.

All it took was a glance at Doc's face to know maybe you didn't want to hear the answer to Cy's question. Doc looked at Cy and reached out to put a hand on his shoulder. "She's hurt bad, Cy. We've got to get her to a hospital."

"Well, what the hell," Cy said. "Let me see her."

"She's out cold. There was a lot of pain and I medicated her pretty good."

"What happened?" Cy said.

"I don't know, but if I had to guess I'd say she was assaulted by somebody using a bayonet or a nightstick or maybe both, top and bottom."

"Jesus Christ!" Cy said.

"It's bad," Doc said. "There is massive internal damage."

"Oh, goddamn it," Cy said, and dropped his chin down on his chest.

"The human body has an incredible capacity for healing," Doc said. "But there are limits."

"What are you saying, Doc?" Cy said.

"She needs surgery to repair eating and breathing tubes, and her larynx and vocal cords look to be mangled beyond repair, and there's no telling how severe it is in other places."

Cy groaned and swore.

"We can't know anything for sure at this point," Doc said, "but right now, she needs help just to keep living."

Cy stood in a half crouch with his arms out and his head jutting forward. He looked like a cornered animal desperate for a way out. He stayed that way, unmoving and staring, until Doc said, "The Wagonbacks are gassing up the ambulance and they'll be here shortly."

Finally, Cy blinked and straightened up. "Where, what …?"

"St. Barnabas Hospital in Minneapolis," Doc said. "I've got a friend who is a thoracic surgeon there. I'll try to keep her stabilized on the way in."

It was quiet then, and it seemed like a strange natural thing, so much awful information had come down in the last few minutes that it needed time to soak in. Doc stepped over and opened the door to the side room and turned back to Cy. "You can see her, but I don't know if she'll wake up or know you if she does. She's pretty doped up."

Doc led the way into the room. Lobelia lay covered with a sheet pulled up under her chin. Her bruised black face and tangled red hair stuck up out of the stark whiteness of the pillow and the bedding like a grotesque Halloween getup that made you suddenly sick and weak. I couldn't look at her, but I couldn't not look at her either. Cy swore and groaned and dropped to his knees next to the cot. He cradled Lobelia's face in his hands and stared at her.

"Careful, don't move her," Doc said.

Cy jerked his head back and shut his eyes. "Oh, Jesus Christ, Doc," he wailed. "What are we going to do?"

I don't know if it was a shudder or a sob that made Cy's body clench up the way it did, but as he turned back to Lobelia, it was as if he'd been hit by a rifle bullet. Doc reached a hand out toward him. Cy tilted his head back over Lobelia just as she opened her eyes. She might as well have left them shut because she obviously wasn't seeing anything. Cy stared at her and groaned. Lobelia's eyelids drooped, and then her eyes closed again.

"It's going to be okay, baby," Cy said, and he put his head down on Lobelia's chest and began to sob, jerky sobs that filled the room like the sound of retching. From the edge of the cot, Lobelia's hand eased out from under the bedding. She slowly lifted it to stroke the back of Cy's neck.

CHAPTER THIRTY-SIX

It was another damp, gray morning that just seemed to set the mood for what's been going on. Since the word about Lobelia got around you just feel how people seem to be sinking lower into the dumps. A morning of bright, cheery sunshine would be an insult. It is hard to believe how many people seemed to have such strong feelings for Lobelia, considering how she was such a newcomer and so different from all the rest of us.

I was mulling over some of this as I sat at the station counter and watched an occasional car or truck go past. The radio was on, and I half listened to a newscast about FDR naming Harry Truman as his running mate, and some German officers screwing up a scheme to kill Hitler. Jeez, how could that happen? Nothing goes according to plan in a war, I guess, especially killing, even if you are trying to kill somebody as important as Hitler.

What's been happening in Oxbow is that people are getting tired of having the POWs around. The novelty wore off a long time ago, and the pea crop is pretty much harvested and there's still a lot of fighting and killing going on in Germany, so the news is full of casualties, which doesn't do anything to warm up feelings toward enemy prisoners.

Then Oxbow got another Gold Star when Teddy Mossruder was killed by a sniper. Artillery and bombing are war things that you hear about and don't really feel, but that sniper business is different. It's the kind of thing that you can understand and that could happen anywhere, right here in Oxbow, or out in the swamp. It's like turning a deer hunt upside down: so you're walking along a trail minding your own business and whammo, a high-powered rifle bullet—like the kind that comes out of a deer rifle at about three thousand feet per second, blows you apart and you're dead. Around Oxbow, you could feel the bullet that hit Teddy. The

Army only said that Teddy was killed in action, but then one of his buddies wrote to Mrs. Mossruder and said Teddy was walking through a village that was supposed to be safe when a sniper got him from a window in a church steeple.

Teddy had worked at the stockyard before he got drafted. The story about him in the *Oxbow News-Banner* said he liked to fish for bluegill and hunt rabbits. And it said he was engaged to Delores Whitmore, the chubby little blonde who clerked at the dime store. It didn't say anything about deer hunting, of course.

With this kind of thing going on, people were just getting weary of the war in general and of the things that remind them of it, like the POWs, and even the soldiers at the POW camp. Then when the Lobelia thing happened, that part of it got worse. People blamed the soldiers. And they didn't bother to distinguish between MPs and the rest of them. That was a mistake, because when the big fight between Sheriff Curtis and the Army finally died down, it was revealed that the MPs at the camp were a separate unit of red necks from down south who bragged about belonging to the Klu Klux Klan and considered themselves so elite that basic military rules did not apply to them. The rest of the soldiers hated their guts.

Right after Lobelia was found, Sheriff Curtis went down to the POW camp and demanded to talk to the MPs and Captain Cowley, specifically. The guards wouldn't even let him inside the camp. But Sheriff Curtis wouldn't leave until finally the camp commander, Major Jesse Court, came out to the gate and talked to him. The Major told Sheriff Curtis that civilian law enforcement had no authority within a military area and he said if the sheriff persisted, he would have no choice but to take him into federal custody. He also said none of the soldiers had anything to do with what happened to Lobelia.

Sheriff Curtis tried to get District Attorney Quincy Elgers to help, but the DA told him there was nothing he could do. Cy always complained about DA Elgers. "He wouldn't make a pimple on a good DA's ass," Cy liked to say. Cy's opinion was obviously shaped over the years by the many times Elgers brought charges against him, usually for something Cy did when he was drunk.

Then Sheriff Curtis called the State Attorney General and when he got the brush-off there, he tried the Governor's office, where someone told him it was a local matter. Sheriff Curtis talked about all of this one morning when he stopped to have coffee with my mother. He said it made him sick that nobody was being made to answer for the terrible attack on Lobelia. My mother asked him about getting a local petition going and sending it to J. Edgar Hoover.

Sheriff Curtis laughed. "Truth is, nobody seems to really give a damn," he said. "So a colored woman got assaulted. Who cares?"

In the end, not a thing happened except that Major Court restricted the soldiers to the camp and so the only time you saw any of them was when they were escorting prisoners. The people in town seem to be comfortable with that. They are war-weary and the only soldiers they want to see are their own family members or neighbors coming back from the fighting.

I was thinking about that when Mr. Rockford drove up to the pumps. There was someone in the passenger seat of his old pickup and when I went out to do the windows, I saw that it was the tall reporter with the beaver teeth who had been at the sheriff's office.

"Give her the works, Billy," Mr. Rockford said, as he heaved himself out of the pickup and walked toward the station, his big gut sticking out and his thumbs hooked in the suspenders of his bib overalls. "I've got to have clean windows for my client."

The reporter scowled at me as I wiped at the bugs on the windshield.

"I'm working for the *Chicago Bulletin*," Mr. Rockford said. "Reporter's assistant and driver. What do you think of that, Billy?"

I looked at Mr. Rockford, then back at his passenger. The reporter showed his beaver teeth and nodded. "Hurry it up, kid," he said, "I'm on a deadline."

I didn't like the tone of his voice, and I didn't like being called "kid."

"You ready to tell me about your big fire adventure?" the reporter said.

I stared at him and shook my head.

"Make you a big hero around here; boy outruns fire and saves colored woman, real headline stuff."

I kept rubbing at the dead bugs as the reporter stuck his head out the window. "You and that nigger whore see any dead bodies?" he said.

There was no planning in what happened next, not even a second of thought. I wadded up the dirty, wet, windshield rag with all the bugs on it and wiped it down over the reporter's long face, starting up by his hairline and going down over his eyes and long nose and ending up at his chin, which I gave an extra little swipe.

"Jesus Christ!" the reporter shouted as he wiped at his smeared face and spit out bits of insects. "What the hell are you doing?"

Mr. Rockford turned from where he stood by the station door. "What happened, Billy?" he said.

"I'll tell you what happened," the reporter yelled. "This goddamn kid attacked me. I'm going to beat the shit out of him."

"Billy," Mr. Rockford said, "what's going on?"

"Never mind, Rockford," the reporter yelled. "We'll come back after I file my story. I'm on a deadline. Get me down to the telegraph office right now!"

Mr. Rockford stood staring at me, and the reporter shouted, "Come on, Rockford, move your ass!"

Mr. Rockford climbed slowly into his pickup, looking back over his shoulder and scowling. As he drove off, the reporter stuck his head out the window and shouted, "I'll be back, you little bastard."

I went into the station and sat on the counter stool and tried to figure out if I felt better or worse for having swabbed the reporter with the bug rag. I guess I felt better, and thought about what I would do when the reporter came back and started after me, run circles around the grease pit, and hope he falls in maybe. I remembered when I hit Wilbur Bender in the eye after he made that insulting remark about GIs being prisoners, and he had said he was coming back to kick the shit out of me. He hasn't so far but I suppose it is never too late. Now I've got two guys to look out for.

I watched kids playing war in the yard across the street, aiming their wooden guns at each other and grabbing at their chests and falling backwards. I remembered doing that and thought how important it is to stay dead just the right amount of time; too short and you get yelled at for not being fair; too long and you risk the war moving on to the next backyard without you. For a moment, I wished I could be one of the kids, just pretending to kill and die. But it was a brief moment. Then I came to my senses and remembered that what I really wanted—what I had always wanted—was to be old enough to fight in the real war with Uncle Jeff and the others. Then this strange image flashed as brief as lightning: Uncle Jeff clutching at his chest and falling, then staying dead for just the right amount of time.

CHAPTER THIRTY SEVEN

They are gone now, all of them—the soldiers, the FBI, the reporters, the whole kit and caboodle. Nobody's sorry. Oh, maybe Mr. Rockford because he was getting paid good money to haul away the Army's garbage, which he fed to his pigs. And one of the older Johnson girls who got engaged to a corporal from Iowa, so she's probably sorry to see him leave. Her sister Tulip told me about the engagement when she came into the station for a Coke.

That was the second time Tulip had stopped in. The first time it was just to ask what time it was, but that second time when she said she wanted a Coke, I said I would have one, too, and suggested we play long-bottle to see who paid. Every Coke bottle is stamped on the bottom with the city it comes from and it turned out her bottle was from Rochester, Minnesota and mine was from Peoria, Illinois, so I had to pay, though I don't remember if we ever said long bottle or short bottle paid before we fished them out of the cooler. I do remember that Tulip seemed intrigued by the bottle game and she giggled when I ended up paying.

Eventually, I suppose, Oxbow will sink back into its boring old routine, but it doesn't seem to be happening very fast. It would have been different if it hadn't been for what happened to Lobelia. Except for that, the POWs would have shipped out and the soldiers would have packed up and left, and everyone in Oxbow would be juggling their own little set of memories about the summer the Kraut prisoners were here. And probably most of those memories would have been more pleasant than hostile, which would make it hard to consider them part of a bloody war.

It isn't a problem to hate somebody who's shooting at you or at somebody you love, but how do you feel about an enemy sitting peacefully at your supper table passing you the mashed potatoes and maybe making eyes at your daughter? That is complicated, but people could have sorted through it and come up with their own way of dealing with it, probably a lot of them recognizing that good young men try to kill each other because demented old men convince them it's a heroic thing to do. I think I heard Cy say something like that a long time ago, way back before the prisoners even got here, maybe one day when he was lecturing me about how dumb I was to want to get into the thick of it. I guess I still felt that way, but it wasn't something I thought about every minute like before.

What makes it even more complicated around here is the way people got to feeling about our own soldiers at the POW camp. I learned more detail about this one afternoon when I went up to the sheriff's office and the jail to visit Cy. Yeah, he's back in his usual cell, and that's another thing to feel bad about—that Cy fell off the wagon like a keg of whiskey rolling over the tailgate.

Nobody was surprised about it, of course. Something had to give, the way he was when he came back from Minneapolis, like a crazy man, walking the streets at night, cursing and shouting so you could hear him for blocks, then going into his house and playing scratchy old jazz records that sounded like Lobelia with the volume turned up so high the house seemed to shake. I had gone over to see him a couple of times, but he was like a zombie, a drunken zombie. He just more of less stared at me and didn't say anything, even when I asked him questions. It was like he had no more personality than a fish.

When I asked him how Lobelia was doing and if she was coming back to Oxbow, he just looked at me like I wasn't there. I knew from Doc having told me at the station that Lobelia had made it to the Minneapolis hospital okay, and doctors were waiting for her to get strong enough so they could start doing surgery on her throat and try to fix the damage to her other insides. Doc said Cy had ridden in the ambulance with him and stayed with Lobelia until after she had been examined and admitted. "We weren't sure she was going to make it," Doc said. "There was so much internal bleeding."

Doc rode the Wagonback ambulance back to Oxbow but Cy had stayed at the hospital with Lobelia. A few days later, a Minneapolis taxi cab dropped him off in front of his house in Oxbow. That must have cost him a bundle, but I guess he didn't want to ride the train. A lot of people saw the taxi and commented on it because it might have been the first genuine, big-city taxi ever seen in Oxbow. Doc said Cy came home because the hospital stopped him from visiting Lobelia.

"They barred him after he made threats," Doc said. "He told my surgeon friend that unless they could fix her up completely, including her voice, he was going to jump out a hospital window and take Lobelia with him because that was what she wanted."

Doc said he didn't know how Cy could tell what Lobelia wanted because she couldn't talk and might never talk again. So Cy came back in that crazy condition that obviously couldn't last. People started saying that something had to be done about him yelling and bawling up and down the streets and blaring out that loud jazz music half the night. Then he got totally drunk and did that thing out in the cemetery that landed him in jail.

Planter came out one morning to mow the grass around the graves and he said Cy was staggering around with a big jar of peanut butter and a roll of toilet paper smearing up all the veterans' gravestones, so they looked like somebody had crapped all over them. Planter told Sheriff Curtis that Cy must have been out there half the night because most of the cemetery was a mess with even a couple of old veteran's markers from the Spanish-American War smeared up.

Word got around fast and people didn't believe it at first. A lot of them went out to the cemetery to see it for themselves. By the time I went out later in the day, many of the grave markers had been wiped clean, by family members probably. But there were still enough of them with ragged strips of brown-stained toilet paper blowing in the breeze so the cemetery looked like the site of a bombed outhouse.

Of all the things Cy has done to make people mad, this caper might have been the worst. It was just so grotesque and insulting. People were still feeling sorry about what had happened to Lobelia, but even with that, they figured Cy had gone too far. They seemed particularly upset about the peanut butter and toilet paper on the fresh graves from the war that was still going on. Planter said he cleaned some of those markers himself so the families wouldn't have to see them so messed up. Some people suggested that Cy must be a Nazi sympathizer and others called him a traitor and a war criminal. Most were just disgusted with him for dishonoring the dead, and I heard someone say he should be run out of town.

Cy sat on the edge of the jail cell cot and stared past me. He looked terrible, as if he were literally falling apart, his skin gray and his eyes glassy. I didn't know what to say so I just stood in front of him and waited. Finally, he shook his head and said, "She will probably live, Billy, "but she doesn't want to."

I wanted to ask how he knew that, but it somehow seemed like a rude question, and then Cy answered it anyway. "You can see it in her eyes," he said.

It was quiet again, and Cy put his head back and took a deep breath. "I'm going to take care of her, Billy." He said. Then, he nodded at some legal-looking papers lying on the cell bunk and said, "I'm fixing my will so she'll have the best care money can buy."

He looked at me and his face was the saddest thing I have ever seen. Without thinking about it, I stepped over and leaned down to put an arm around his shoulders. He didn't move from where he sat on the cot and I felt like I was trying to hug a stump.

They kept Cy in jail for a few more days. Then they let him out, and of all the mistakes that have been made around here lately, that was probably the biggest.

CHAPTER THIRTY EIGHT

The day started with the usual routine stuff, people going to their jobs and to the stores and puttering around their yards. Since the rains started coming the day after the fire, lawns have been greening up and will have to be mowed soon. I suppose that means I'll be back pushing the stupid mower around Deggerton's lilac bushes. But I wasn't letting that bother me this morning.

I saw Tulip Johnson walk past earlier carrying a couple of books and I figured she was going to the library, so I was wondering when she would come past on her way home. I think she had sneaked a peek to see if I was working the station, but I can't be sure. Maybe if I'm out hosing off the drive or something I'll have a chance to talk to her.

I kept thinking how she had made me feel better yesterday by saying she was sorry about Lobelia, and maybe I could tell her more about how I felt, maybe even talk about Toby. I opened the station this morning, so Cliff was due to take over at two o'clock and I would have the afternoon off. Who knows what that might bring if Tulip should happen to have some time?

Then I saw Chief Edwins drive past. He was going over the speed limit, which he rarely does, and he didn't have his siren or red light on, which made it all the more unusual. He always looks over at the station and waves, but he sure didn't this time. He sat hunched over the steering wheel and stared straight out the windshield. A couple of other cars came along behind him headed down the same street, and Eddie Clinton from the *News-Banner* drove past going in the same direction. Something was obviously going on and I wondered what it was. Then Vernon Pickert came skidding across the drive on his rusty old bicycle.

"Billy," he shouted. "You heard?"

"Heard what?" I said, wondering how many times I'd played this game with Vernon.

"It's Cy," Vernon shouted. "He's up on the water tower."

I did not want to believe it.

"He's up there drunker than a skunk," Vernon said. "I'm going for a camera."

I watched Vernon pump off down the street and felt my stomach start a slow roll. I thought about how the water tower stuck up so much higher than anything in town and I tried to imagine Cy way up there on the catwalk that circles the bottom of the tank. There's a ladder on one of the tower legs that he must have climbed.

Once, several years ago, some high school kids had climbed up there during the night and painted their class year on the tank. A week or so later, a trap door had been put on the bottom of the ladder to keep that from happening again. Cy must have gotten around that somehow. I tried to think of why he would do such a thing. But he's done so many crazy things over the years that had no "why" behind them there's no point in trying to figure this one out. I remembered how he had talked to me when we were planning the MOP Exchange, about how he wanted to shake peoples' cages, but I couldn't fit that into him being up on the water tower.

I had been hoping he would stop at the station after he came back from Minneapolis, but he hadn't, and when I had gone to see him it was like visiting a rock. So, I had no more idea what was going through his head than anyone else in town. All anyone knew was that he was acting goofy with all his bellowing and ranting and loud music and drinking. Everyone just figured it was because of what happened to Lobelia. It's probably safe to say that, except for when he was in jail, he's been boozed up to the point of stumbling over things with both his feet and his brain.

Considering that, it's hard to figure how he managed to climb up the water tower ladder. Once, a long time ago, he tried to climb up there, but he only got a few feet off the ground before his whiskey bottle dropped out of his pocket and smashed and he came back down. He had been in jail for a few days after that, and I remember him commenting afterwards that among the many good things whiskey did for him was help overcome his fear of heights. "Stone sober, I panic on a tall bar stool," he said, "but a few nips and I can climb like a damned monkey."

He'd been having more than a few nips lately, that's for sure.

When Cliff showed up to take over the station, he said he had driven past the water tower, and Cy was sitting up there dangling his feet over the side of the catwalk, looking down at the crowd. "Chief Edwins is yelling up at him to come down," Cliff said, "but Cy isn't paying any attention."

Cliff knew, of course, that Cy hung around the station a lot when I was working and that he was a good friend, if you can call it that. And I guess you can. Friends don't have to be the same age, or like the same things or even be the same color; Lobelia's certainly a friend. Cliff looked at me, "Maybe Cy would listen to you."

I shrugged.

"It might be worth a try. Maybe you can get him to climb down."

"He doesn't listen to anything or anyone, especially when he's drinking," I said.

"Well, he can't stay up there forever. He's got to climb down or fall down, and it's a hell of a drop."

It is a hell of a drop, maybe seventy or eighty feet, and there's nothing to land on but hard concrete. I tried not to think about that as I walked toward the woolen mill and the water tower. A thousand things were going through my mind, none of them making any sense: Uncle Jeff, Toby, Margaret, Tulip Johnson, Dooby, the fire, the river, Windigo Swamp, the war. It was a jumble of people and things I had no control over, and it grew, like an explosion in slow motion; Lobelia, and Cy, always Cy. What the hell is he up to now?

The tower loomed into view from three or four blocks away, sticking up over the roofs of the houses and the trees like some odd-shaped thing out of a fairy tale. As I got closer, I could see a little black speck up there that had to be Cy. He looked like a bug clinging to the side of a big can balanced on top of a tall, flimsy step-ladder. The closer I got, the taller the tower seemed to get. A crowd of people stood in a semicircle around its base, back far enough so they could look up at it and still be safe from anything—like Cy—who might fall off it. I recognized almost everyone there, and a few people glanced my way as I walked up.

Vernon Pickert came running over. He was carrying a black box camera, and he waved it and said, "Nothing has happened yet, Billy, but when it does, I'm ready."

Vernon's face was red and sweaty and he grinned so his yellow teeth showed. "Maybe sell a picture to the Minneapolis paper," he said.

I looked up and tried to see Cy. All that was really visible was his lower legs and his feet hanging over the edge of the catwalk. You couldn't see his face, just the top of his head, sticking up over the edge of the railing. He was wearing his bowler, and I wondered for a second how he had managed to climb up the metal ladder without losing his hat. More people began to show up, driving in and parking their cars or walking in from different streets. I was surprised to see my mother and Mrs. Zanders standing off to the side amid a cluster of women from the church. More kids ran around as the crowd grew, and they shouted and pointed up at Cy.

There was a subdued buzz of conversation, and then Chief Edwins blew his whistle and it got quiet. The chief leaned back so his big belly stuck out as he tilted his head to look up. "Cyrus," he shouted. "Can you hear me?"

Everyone looked up and listened but there was no response from Cy.

"Cy," Chief Edwins shouted. "You need to talk to us."

There was nothing from Cy, not even any change in the way his dangling legs swung back and forth as regular as pendulums. People started talking to each other again, mumbling and clucking their tongues, and shaking their heads. I heard somebody say, "He's been up there three hours."

"He ought to be sober enough to come down by now," somebody else said.

"He's probably got a bottle," another voice said.

Sheriff Curtis drove up then and walked over to stand next to Chief Edwins. They stood with their heads tilted back looking up at Cy, and I edged over close enough to hear what they were saying.

"It's no damned use," Chief Edwins said, "I've been yelling at him for hours."

"He clams up sometimes when he's drunk," Sheriff Curtis said.

"What the hell do we do?" Chief Edwins said.

"Damned if I know," Sheriff Curtis said. "There's no way to climb up there and get him."

Suddenly from back in the crowd, a man's voice shouted, "Jump, you traitor bastard!"

There was a little nervous laughter, and Sheriff Curtis looked out at the people and shouted, "There'll be no more of that."

There is no doubt but what Cy's cemetery antics had offended most Oxbow residents, but it's hard to tell how deep the hostility ran, pretty deep with some people apparently, if they wanted Cy to jump off the water tower. But that could be just one loudmouth. I think most people feel sympathy for Cy for what happened to Lobelia. And over the years, of course, they've come to accept him for the town character that he is. Now, as they stared up at him on his ridiculous perch, they knew he was in trouble and they seemed concerned.

I looked around and tried to figure out just what the thinking might be toward Cy. There were some furrowed brows and some head-shaking, but there were a few fleeting smiles too, so there was no way to come up with a consensus that made any sense. For some reason, I remembered how Mrs. Deggerton had manipulated me into praying with her when she asked God to send Cy to hell. Was she getting her damned prayer answered? And since I'd been kneeling down with her, was it partly my prayer?

As I peered up at Cy, I felt my insides do another slow roll and I started remembering things: the Bund meeting at Almira when he had stood up and shouted that thing about Lindbergh that practically guaranteed he would get beat up, insulting the veterans and telling them they should wear dunce caps, getting kicked out of the town hall meeting for shouting that the Army officer was lying about the prisoners, and the countless times he had sat on the pop cooler at the station and said outrageous things that tilted my brain until things seemed to spill out. Then I remembered his talk about my needing to grow up and his rattling cages, and then how he had put his arm briefly around my shoulders when I agreed to join him in setting up MOP.

Suddenly, I realized that Cy had been like a godfather in an odd sense. Maybe some—Mrs. Deggerton for one—would say a "goddamned" father. In the wartime absence of my real father, Cy had happened along and filled the void with fascinating, exciting things that my bloodline never could have provided, things that turned the humdrum and the dull into excitement and entertainment, and trouble. I looked up at him again and remembered when he said that he drank whiskey to keep from getting tapeworms and it occurred to me that he would sure be safe from them for a while.

CHAPTER THIRTY-NINE

As Sheriff Curtis looked around at the crowd, he must have spotted me. "Billy," he shouted, waving his arm, "Come on over here."

My guts jumped, and a funny feeling zipped through me, like I'd touched a sparkplug wire. Sheriff Curtis and Chief Edwins eyeballed me as I walked up to them. The funny feeling was still there, and I wondered if they might ask me to climb the tower and talk to Cy. I hoped not because I'm worse with heights than Cy ever could be. I get nervous standing on a stool to replace a light bulb.

Sheriff Curtis reached out and put a hand on my shoulder. "Billy," he said, "you're a good pal of Cy's. You think he might talk to you?"

I doubted it. He hasn't said a thing to me since he came back from Minneapolis. I shrugged and Chief Edwins said, "He won't give us the time of day."

"Why don't you give it a shot, Billy?" Sheriff Curtis said. "We don't want you climbing the tower or anything like that. Just yell up there at him and see if anything happens."

"Wait 'til I get it a little quieter," Chief Edwins said, and he fished his whistle out and blew it loud enough to be heard a mile away. The crowd got quiet and Chief Edwins and Sheriff Curtis looked at me. Sheriff Curtis nodded. "Okay."

It had all come on so sudden and I didn't know how to feel, nervous and embarrassed certainly, but there seemed to be more. It was like being asked out of the blue to sing a solo in church or call bats out of a cave or some crazy thing like that. I glanced around at the people, and looked up toward Cy. "Do it," Sheriff Curtis said.

I cupped my hands around my mouth and shouted, "Cy, it's me, Billy."

It sounded to me like I shouted loud enough to be heard all the way to Almira. Echoes seemed to bounce off every house in Oxbow. As they died down, Cy's feet stopped swinging back and forth and after about a minute, his head poked over the edge of the catwalk. Even so far away, you could see that his face was puffy and red, and his eyes seemed to be sunken back in his head so they were like little black holes. He stared down at us and didn't say anything.

"Tell him he's got to come down," Chief Edwins said.

I looked at him and then at Sheriff Curtis. He shook his head and scowled. "Not yet," he said. "Let's see if we can get him talking before we give him any orders."

I looked at the sheriff and waited. "Ask him if he needs anything," Sheriff Curtis said.

I cupped my hands again and shouted, "Cy, you need anything?"

There was a pause, and Cy's crazy laughter came echoing down like the cackle of a loon. It was followed by his scratchy voice: "Whiskey, Billy. I'm getting low on whiskey."

"Tell him he can have whiskey if he comes down," Sheriff Curtis said.

"You have to come down and get it," I shouted up at Cy.

Cy's jagged laughter drifted down again. "I'll be down," he shouted.

"Ask him when?" Sheriff Curtis said.

"When?" I shouted.

There was a long pause, and Sheriff Curtis nudged me.

"Cy, when are you coming down?"

There was his laughter again and his shout came down behind it. "Drunk or sober, I can't handle climbing that goddamned ladder."

"What the hell does that mean?" Chief Edwins said.

"He's probably afraid to climb down," Sheriff Curtis said. "Ask him what he means."

"What are you saying, Cy?" I shouted.

"I can't climb, Billy, afraid of heights. I've got to jump."

Sheriff Curtis swore, and there were gasps from some of the people behind us.

"Tell him we'll get him something to land on," Sheriff Curtis said.

"What the hell would that be?" Chief Edwins said.

"I don't know," Sheriff Curtis said. "A stack of pea vines, a load of hay, any damned thing to keep him from landing on concrete."

Sheriff Curtis turned and looked around at the people like he was looking for somebody special. "Clarence," he shouted as he motioned to a man on the edge of the crowd. Clarence Morkenson, a farmer from east of town who stops at the station once in a while for chewing tobacco, walked up to where we stood.

"Clarence, you got any loose hay around?" Sheriff Curtis said.

It took a minute or so for Mr. Morkenson to understand what Sheriff Curtis was talking about. When he finally did, he scratched his head and said he had cut ten acres of clover and timothy yesterday and was planning to pick it up tomorrow.

"How long would it take you to get a load of it up here?" Sheriff Curtis said.

Mr. Morkenson hesitated and glanced up at Cy. "Maybe an hour or so," he said.

"Good," Sheriff Curtis said. "Get on it." He turned to me. "Tell Cy to hold tight; we've got a plan."

I didn't know quite what to say but I finally went with: "Cy, they're bringing hay for you to land on."

The only response was a long session of Cy's goofy laughter. His face disappeared from the edge of the catwalk and his legs started doing their pendulum thing again. It was getting late in the afternoon, but instead of people going on about their business—heading home to make supper and finish up chores and things like that—nobody left the area around the water tower. In fact, more cars pulled up and more people came walking in from town until the crowd was so big it spilled out into the street and slowly got nosier and nosier. At some point, somebody set off a firecracker—it could have been Vernon Pickert—but anyway, it made everybody jump like they'd been goosed.

I looked up to see Cy peeking over the edge of the catwalk. It looked like he might have been smiling. Then, he stood up and started waving his arms like he was directing an orchestra. People quieted down and stared up at him. Finally, it got quiet enough to hear his scratchy voice. He was singing, or trying to sing at least. It was very strange, his grating voice coming down out of the sky as strange as his loon laugh. But you could make out the words, just barely: *"Onward, Christian soldiers, marching as to war...."*

Everyone looked up at Cy, and then around at each other. Cy kept singing: *"With the cross of Jesus going on before..."*

Then he poked his head out far enough so you could see it and he waved his arms and shouted, "Everybody!"

From somewhere on the edge of the crowd, over near where my mother and Mrs. Zanders had been with the church women, some soft voices took up the song. That was all it took for it to sweep across the crowd until everyone was singing: *"Christ the royal Master, leads against the foe; Forward into battle see His banners go!"*

Some of the church women must know every verse there is to *Onward, Christian Soldiers*, because the song seemed to go on forever. Between each verse you could hear Cy laughing, and once he whooped and it sounded like he shouted, "Yes, Jesus!" It was hard to tell just how drunk he was because I've heard him whoop and shout like that even when he's been almost sober.

To say that the singing there at the water tower was different is an understatement. I think everyone felt that something odd was happening and everything was pretty much on automatic. There was no way to know what was coming next, but whatever it was, nobody wanted to leave and risk missing it.

Sheriff Curtis and Chief Edwins looked around and shook their heads. They didn't join in the singing. Everyone was waiting for Mr. Morkenson to show up with the hay. When he finally did, the singing stopped and a cheer went up. The hay was heaped up on a big wagon that Mr. Morkenson pulled behind his Farmall tractor. He and several other men climbed up with pitchforks and unloaded it into a tall stack just under the water tower. You could smell the freshness of the hay and see that it was soft and pliable. Sheriff Curtis stuck his hand into the side of the stack, then stepped back and looked up at it. It stuck up three or four feet over his head, and he turned to Chief Edwins.

"That should do it," he said.

"If he lands on it," Chief Edwins said.

"No reason why he shouldn't," Sheriff Curtis said. "It's right under him."

Cy was back sitting on the edge of the catwalk, swinging his legs again. Occasionally, he had peeked over to look at the men as they unloaded the hay, but mostly, all you could see was his feet and lower legs.

"Hey, Cy," somebody shouted, "you know how to fly?"

There were a few snickers and somebody else shouted, "You got the wings of an angel, Cy?"

Cy's legs just kept swinging and he didn't look down. Sheriff Curtis looked up at Cy and scowled. Then he turned to me. "Cy seems to communicate with you the best, Billy. Tell him it's all ready down here."

I looked up at Cy's swinging legs and cupped my hands and shouted, "Cy, you can jump now."

Cy's legs stopped and his face showed over the rim of the catwalk. He peered down at the hay stack, and then gazed out over the crowd. Then it was hard to tell what he was doing but it looked like he struggled a little and got to his feet and moved to the opening in the catwalk railing. The crowd had gone quiet, except for an occasional yelp from a kid, and I heard a woman's voice say, "If they don't get on with this, I'm going to have a burned-up casserole."

Then in the quiet, Cy's scratchy voice came down: "One more song," he shouted. *"Amazing grace, how sweet the sound..."* He was waving his arms and teetering on the edge of the catwalk, and he shouted: "Everybody sing."

And they did, tentatively at first, with the church ladies leading the way, but then stronger as more people joined in: *"That saved a wretch like me. I once was lost but now am found, was blind, but now I see."*

Sheriff Curtis looked around impatiently and then turned to me. "Cy's a damned showman. He'll have us here all night. Tell him to jump."

I looked up at Cy standing so precariously high over the stack of hay. It looked like an impossible situation, like the set-up for some ridiculous stunt, but like Chief Edwins said earlier, Cy would be okay if he landed right.

"Tell him to jump," Sheriff Curtis said with an impatient nod.

I would have to shout really loud to be heard over the singing, so I cupped my hands and shouted, "Now, Cy! Jump now!"

Cy leaned out over the catwalk, and the singing faded. Then, he suddenly stepped off the edge and began to plummet down toward the hay. There was a scream then as his falling body was snapped to a sudden halt and his legs kicked briefly as he dangled from a rope half-way between the stack of hay and the catwalk. His bowler hat sailed down to land on the hay, and he swayed back and forth on the end of the rope with his head bent at an angle that could only mean his neck was broken.

CHAPTER FORTY

Where do you go after you shout for your friend and mentor—somebody who has been part of your life beyond measure—to jump to his death and he does it? There is no place, no place dark enough or deep enough to take you in. An upstairs bedroom with the shades pulled is not good enough, but it was all I had. So I went there—though I don't remember doing so. I stayed there, taking an occasional nibble out of the food my mother left on the nightstand, and resenting the times when I could not force sleep to blot out all remembering. And, I don't know if it actually happened or if my battered brain made it up when it was sorting through the horrible trash, but there was a point where Reverend Thorston stood beside my bed and said he had come to pray with me and I told him to get the hell away from me. I don't know if I would have done that. I just don't know.

And I don't know how long it went on. You don't put a stopwatch, or even a calendar, on the disintegration of your life, when your very being becomes so rotten you cannot bear it and you want some kind of total transformation that takes your cells and makes something else out of them, anything, a tree, a lump of dirt, a dog, no, not a dog, they carry too much baggage.

But nothing could go on forever, and this morning in the bathroom mirror, I got an accidental glance of somebody, of me. It made my stomach turn, but not as much as it had turned yesterday. You can't go any farther down when you are at rock bottom, and so I forced myself to clean up and dress and head downstairs. There was nothing exhilarating or exciting about it. It was more like crawling out from under something.

I was grateful that my mother was not home. Something told me I would need her in the days to come, but not just yet. I know she had been trying not to hover and I appreciated that. I made some toast and poured cereal into a bowl, and then I saw the *News-Bulletin* lying on the table. The headline caught my eye like a flashing red light: "LOCAL ATTORNEY DIES IN WATER TOWER INCIDENT."

I did not want to read it, but I had to. I don't know why, maybe because I thought there might be something in it to blunt the cruel reality of my own version of things. But the first paragraph was a punch to the guts and I pushed the cereal bowl away and felt my insides twist: "Cyrus M. Butler, well-known Oxbow attorney, died in a plunge from the city water tower Friday afternoon before the horrified eyes of a hundred or more witnesses."

It all came crashing back and I tried to shut my eyes tight enough to erase the horror they had recorded so vividly. It didn't work, and I opened them and made myself read more of the story, about Sheriff Curtis saying it was a suicide since Cy had tied a rope around his neck and fastened it to the tower before he jumped, and the rescue attempt with the hay had been in place, and nobody knew about the rope. The story went on to tell of the hymn singing, even how Cy had "made his tragic jump" as the crowd was singing the line from *Amazing Grace, "was blind but now I see."*

It wasn't just my eyes that had been so painfully efficient in detailing the horror, it was my ears, too. I could hear the singing—and how it had turned to screams as if it were all happening again just outside the kitchen door. If you can't erase the awful things you have seen, there is certainly no way to wipe out what you have heard. Lobelia said it that day when she stopped on the street to listen to the sparrows. I remember the words: "Sights and smells bring things back, but sound does it better."

The newspaper story said Cy had no heirs and "in keeping with the terms of a family trust, the sizable Butler estate has gone to set up the 'Lobelia Cardinalis Recovery Unit' at St. Barnabas Hospital in Minneapolis as specified by Cyrus prior to his death."

It came back then—Cy saying so long ago how he was going to be "a goddamned rich dead man," and joking that he might direct the Butler money to the Woman's Christian Temperance Union. I thought about that for a long time, and then remembered Cy's crazy talk about putting some "entertainment value" into his dying and coming back as a dog so I could talk to him. Damn him! He hadn't thought it through. He could have left me out of it so I wouldn't be sitting here wanting to die, too.

The newspaper story quoted Reverend Thorston saying that since Cy jumped off the tower just as people were singing *"was blind but now I see"* that was "a clear indication that Mr. Butler had accepted the Lord before he took his life."

Who would think that in a story about something so horrible there could ever be anything to make you feel that you might smile again... someday. But there it was. That last paragraph would have made Cy do more than smile—he would have slapped his leg and whooped; and then he would have said something of course, maybe something about Reverend Thorston making a "spiritual leap" or "taking a cue from the draft board."

Maybe someday I will at least be able to smile about that, maybe when, or if, I come out of shock. And that is obviously what I'm suffering: shock. Nobody knows what shock is, Doc said, and when we had talked about Margaret being in shock, he said I should take her trout fishing. Totally dumb! But if they don't know what shock is, it figures that they wouldn't know how to treat it. Trout fishing may be as good as anything. I guess, when it comes right down to it I don't really know if I'm in shock, but from that unspeakable time of the explosive, ceaseless screaming and the crowd's stampeding panic to get away from the horrific sight, then standing frozen and unbelieving beneath my friend as he died so horribly—at my command—since that unimaginable horror I have been pretty much unable to function, like I broke a lot of bones that weren't there, as Doc might have put it.

I sat at the kitchen table for a long time and tried not to think about anything, but it was no good and I thought about everything. It didn't get me anywhere, even when I thought about Margaret and how I didn't know for sure about her. Maybe the fire and the river didn't get her and Otto and they somehow escaped and they will live on in a secret life somewhere with new identities and the remains of a war-torn love. It could happen. There is no limit on the weird things war can do. I know that, but I know about the odds and there is no joy there

When I finally stood up, I had a strange, overwhelming urge to shake myself violently like Toby always did to lighten up a load of water in his fur. The urge turned into a shudder that didn't lighten up anything. I put the newspaper back where I had found it and then I called Cliff and said I would be in for the afternoon shift.

Then I took my trout rod and borrowed a boat from Pete Andrews down at the power dam and rowed across the river. It was running at flood stage and so were the trout streams, so fishing wasn't going to be any good. I didn't care. I wandered the blackened, soggy swamp like a lost animal, skirting around ragged heaps of burned trees and stumbling over roots buried in the muck. The fire had changed everything and all the familiar old land marks were gone. I sloshed through it for miles and wasn't sure where I was most of the time, but it didn't matter. Then, more by chance than any intent, I walked past where my old camp had been. Somewhere deep down in the depths of the burned, tangled heap are the remains of Deputy Blasser, the fingers of his right hand wrapped around his revolver as Lobelia had arranged them—smart, wonderful Lobelia with that voice that cradled your soul better than any god ever could. Also, down in there is what's left of my rifle.

A quick glance at all of it was enough. There had been so many great times there when Toby and I had spent hours resting from our swamp-roaming, sharing hotdogs, and talking; Toby had been such a good listener. So, seeing the old camp the way it was now only added one more thing to feel bad about. Also, it was where I had last seen Margaret, sitting on the log with Otto, calling him Jeff and stroking his arm. I didn't need reminders of that. And then there were the skeletons of the great pine. That things so strong and massive and majestic could be stripped of life along with everything else meant there were no limits. With their millions of green, hissing needles, they had whispered to Toby and me in a way that allowed us to put a special claim on summer afternoons. Now in their black, prickly nakedness, they stood like bizarre grave markers for good times, for a life style, for generations, for dreams—even dumb ones like mine.

The swamp was ugly, like Hell with the fires gone out, Reverend Thorston might say. But I needed ugly. I needed to look at things that were so ugly they would fill my head with repulsive images that I never wanted to see again. That was the game, I guess, to hang out with ugly and hope that there might be a chance for the ugliest image ever to dim somewhat in the face of competition. It will never get the job done completely. What I'm dealing with is the ultimate, horrific, brain trash. It has no purpose whatsoever and never will have. But the image does not fade: the rope-twisted smile, one arm lifting in a final spasm, and then dangling lifeless.

I was wading through ankle-deep muck near one of the spring holes when I tripped over a submerged tree root and stumbled to my knees. The black muck oozed up over my lower legs and I struggled to get to my feet. There was nothing to grab onto and I lost my balance and fell, plunging my hands deep down into the mud. My face was close to the muck and the smell of it came up strong and earthy. I stopped struggling then and stayed motionless on my hands and knees, mired in a misery so powerful I could not breathe.

Slowly, as if I were pulling it out of sticky tar, I lifted one hand and smeared some of the filthy muck across my face. It felt gritty and damp and good. Then with both hands, I wiped the dirty mixture all over my face and neck and everywhere I could reach until I was totally covered with the stickiness and stench of it. I grabbed up more of it and put it on top of what was already there until my arms lost their form and I sank deeper into it so I was sprawled face down, almost buried in it, and I felt its soft, lumpy texture like cold groping hands.

Then, there was Margaret, between me and the muck, under me like the night in her bed and I felt her arch against me and heard her gasp, "Oh, Jeff." I didn't move for a long time, lying like a spent frog in the black mire, sinking, very slowly sinking. The mud and slime and water felt good, like better clothes than I had ever worn. I settled deeper into it until I could feel the sucking and pulling and swallowing of it, like a birth in reverse, an agonized straining to return to a place of mindless darkness. And in the cocoon of that, in a dark private place, a slow immersion in the primeval soup of the swamp seemed as natural and fitting as the decay of dead deer or the rotting of fallen leaves.

I don't know how long it went on, a long time, that's for sure, long enough so when I tried to move, there was nothing I could do. It was like being encased in concrete that became more unyielding by the second, and the seconds piled on like flies. The sinking pushed the level of muck and water up the side of my face and into my nose and mouth and I tasted the cold filth of the swamp.

And then out of the blue—or maybe the black—something kicked in, some core survival signal powerful enough to overcome any pretense of surrender, like a supreme mother shouting "NO!"

Suddenly I was fighting like I had never fought before, straining mightily against the hardening mud until I could move one hand and then the other and then my legs. Chunks and globs of the muck began to drip and drop off as I struggled to free myself and staggered to my feet, rubbing at my eyes and spitting out bits of watery grit.

It wasn't something to think about. It was just something that happened, something that needed to happen maybe. I can't say for sure that it made me feel better, but it did something, maybe made me somehow better able to handle brain trash. I headed back toward the river and the boat, noticing for the first time that tiny sprouts of green were poking up through the muck—slim, delicate blades of grass and tiny, unfolding leaves on stubby new twigs. Then I heard a raven, its gargling call coming across the black landscape like a friendly belch.

At the river, I thought about ducking under the water to rinse off the mud and muck, but I didn't. I rowed across and walked home, leaving a trail of dirt and mud on the sidewalk. If anyone saw me, I didn't see them. I used the garden hose to rinse off in the backyard and went in and took a bath in water so hot it left me feeling as weak and vulnerable as a baby. My mother was not home and I don't know how she knew I was going to work—maybe Cliff had called her—but she had left a lunch sack on the kitchen table and I grabbed it up and headed for the station.

Cliff was obviously happy to see me, and he asked if I was sure I felt up to working. I told him I was, and he finally left and said I could close up early if I felt like it. It was a slow afternoon with just an occasional gas customer and I tried not to think about anything. The time in the swamp had helped, and I remembered the smell of the muck when my nose had been down in it. That was a good thing to think about—how it had been like inhaling a mixture of living and dying that I could never hope to figure out.

As I got out my lunch sack, a radio news guy said there was very heavy fighting around St. Lo and Caen, and then somebody was singing about bluebirds over the white cliffs of Dover. I sat outside on the chair by the door, and as I was about to bite into the baloney sandwich, something caught my eye back by the hedge. It was the motley mutt from Pickert's junkyard that has been tipping over the station garbage can. It was sitting on its haunches watching me, and I opened my mouth to yell at it. Then, I changed my mind and broke the sandwich in two and tossed half of it toward the dog. It jumped backwards slightly and then stopped and walked slowly out to sniff the offering. Then, with one sudden gulp, the sandwich was gone and the scruffy mutt went back to its place by the hedge and sat down to lick its chops and watch me.

Thank You Note

When you have lived as long as I have and you finally complete a project that has been part of your life forever, the list of people you should thank is endless. I could start with my real Aunt Margaret and go through family and friends and co-workers, and in the end I would likely leave out an embarrassing multitude.

So I want to thank everybody, especially my daughter Pat and four sons Larry, Scott, Rick and Mike. They know better than the many others who have been on life's great stage with me that, while it might have had its miscues and fumbles, it has been a wonderful show.

Thanks to you who now read these words. I hope you continue reading on and get to know Margaret and Cy and Billy. I hope you find them interesting and I hope you find their story as important to history as I did. I am thrilled that you are here sharing it with me.

Thanks again, everybody!

Young Billy working at the garage

About the Author

Bill Stokes was a newspaper columnist/feature writer for 35 years, the last ten with *The Chicago Tribune*. His personalized writing style was appreciated by readers and won him numerous awards, including the Scripps-Howard Ernie Pyle Award when he was with the *Milwaukee Journal*, and another from the Wildlife Federation that ended with martinis with Ansel Adams at a local cocktail venue.

From riding the *Delta Queen* for three days with Jimmy and Rosalynn Carter to swapping fish stories with Liz Taylor and chatting with Ed Gein, Bill's career spanned the declining glory years of newspapering. It was, in his words, "a helluva ride."

Bill has authored half a dozen books, some of which were compilations of his newspaper work. One such book—*Hi-ho Silver Anyway*, was awarded "Best Nonfiction by a Wisconsin Writer," and another, *Trout Friends and other Riff Raff*, was recently awarded first place in an audio book competition.

Bill's writing has always reflected a deep appreciation for the natural world—human and otherwise. That is apparent in *Margaret's War* as Billy, Cy, and Margaret grapple with the oozing cultural demands of what it takes to be a boy, a man, or a woman--especially a woman.

Bill's house is on a hill overlooking the village of Mazomanie and the Wisconsin River valley. He lives there with a small black Schnauzer named Boo who can play the piano, and assists Bill in watching the weather and the seasons as they—in Bill's words—hurtle by much too fast.

CPSIA information can be obtained
at www.ICGtesting.com
Printed in the USA
FFHW020936271218
49996018-54708FF